Praise for the previous novels of David J. Walker

For *Applaud the Holy Ghost* (St. Martin's, 1998)

"Walker has given us a real gem here. The plotting is well worked out, Foley is interestingly complex, and the secondary characters enrich the book like well-chosen herbs in a thick broth."
—*Washington Times*

♦

For *No Show of Remorse* (St. Martin's, 2002)

"Walker is at the top of his form here, weaving his puzzle skillfully into a jolting tale of loyalty and betrayal."
—*Kirkus Reviews* (starred review)

♦

For *All the Dead Fathers* (St. Martin's, 2005)

"A timely mystery with a plot focused on controversial contemporary events...Walker writes with a sure hand and a fine eye for character and plot. His story is both thought-provoking and entertaining."
—*Chicago Sun-Times*

♦

For *The Towman's Daughters* (Severn House, 2011)

"A night on the town lands the Wild Onion, Ltd. partners in the middle of another case with oh-so-many moving parts... Another fine outing for Kirsten and Dugan, who set the standard for plotting, pace and hard-boiled humor."
—*Kirkus Reviews* (starred review)

Also by David J. Walker

WILD ONION, LTD. SERIES

The Towman's Daughters

Too Many Clients

All the Dead Fathers

The End of Emerald Woods

A Beer at a Bawdy House

A Ticket to Die For

♦

MAL FOLEY SERIES

No Show of Remorse

Applaud the Holy Ghost

Half the Truth

Fixed in His Folly

♦

STAND-ALONE THRILLER

Saving Paulo

COMPANY ORDERS

DAVID J. WALKER

Allium Press of Chicago
Forest Park, Illinois
www.alliumpress.com

This is a work of fiction. Descriptions and portrayals of real people, events, organizations, or establishments are intended to provide background for the story and are used fictitiously. Other characters and situations are drawn from the author's imagination and are not intended to be real.

Book and cover design by E. C. Victorson
Front cover images:
"Cobblestone Alley, Chicago" by Christian Legan
"Apache Helicopters at Sunset" by aquatic creature/Shutterstock

ISBN 978-0-9831938-5-2

Publisher's Cataloging-In-Publication Data
(Prepared by The Donohue Group, Inc.)

Walker, David J., 1939-
Company orders / David J. Walker.

p. ; cm.

ISBN: 978-0-9831938-5-2 (trade paperback)

1. Catholic Church--Clergy--Fiction. 2. United States. Central Intelligence Agency--Fiction. 3. Priests--Illinois--Chicago--Fiction. 4. Guardian and ward--Fiction. 5. Chicago (Ill.)--Fiction. 6. Guyana--Fiction. 7. Detective and mystery stories. I. Title.

PS3573.A4253313 C66 2012
813/.54 2012941434

To Rich Prendergast
who helped get me off one path and onto another

Traveler, there is no path;
the path is made by walking.

Antonio Machado, *Campos de Castilla*
(translation, David J. Walker)

ACKNOWLEDGMENTS

This is a work of fiction, and all of the organizations and characters mentioned herein—whether governmental, ecclesiastical, or commercial—are imaginary or used fictitiously. Even so, I am glad that they all showed up and seemed pretty real to me.

In addition, I am grateful to very many actual persons, including: Emily Victorson, the indefatigable body and artistic soul of Allium Press, for her belief in Paul Clark and his struggle to become what he thought he'd never be; Bernadette Page, M.D., and David Moore, M.D., for their help with medical issues; Diane Piron-Gelman, for her careful and valuable editing advice; and everyone in the Red Herrings writers group, especially Libby Fischer Hellmann, Michael Allen Dymmoch, and Jerry Silber, for their generous—if occasionally painful—critique work.

COMPANY ORDERS

ONE

Mid-July. Only four in the morning and already eighty-eight degrees Fahrenheit, humidity maybe ninety. The man they called Otoe—he was one-quarter Native American—cut the lights on the ancient Ford Bronco and turned where the sign said *Avenida del Convento.*

"'Avenue,' my ass," he said, easing the stolen, mud-caked Bronco forward through near-total darkness. The A/C was out and his clothes—5.11 tactical pants and loose-fitting sport shirt—were soaked through. "More like a goddamn alley. We meet some vehicle coming the other way, Tree, we're screwed."

"I figure the door to be twenty yards up," his buddy said, "on the right." He was tall and lean and hard—thus the name 'Tree' he'd picked up in the SEALs—with skin the color of black coffee. "And there won't *be* any vehicles. It's all taken care of. A pre-paid package."

"I know. I'm just saying..."

"Just flappin' your lips, like usual, 'fore the fun starts."

"Shouldn't *be* any fun," Otoe said. "Not if it's 'all taken care of.'" He leaned forward, peering through the windshield. "Jesus, gimme some light here."

Tree slipped the night ops torch from a low pocket in his cargo pants and held it out the window, throwing a thin beam of light ahead of them along the wall that lined the street on their right. "There!" he said.

They parked and walked to the door of what everyone still called "the Convent," though no nun had stepped inside for over a hundred years. They were each packing maybe fifteen pounds of weaponry and gear, but they were large men and their clothing hid it well. Tree knocked, using a pre-arranged pattern, and the wood plank door was pulled open by a short, skinny, dark-skinned man in a blue uniform. They stepped inside.

The uniform was too big for the little man, and the old .357 Magnum on his hip seemed oversized, too. He looked up at the two *gringos* towering over him and said nothing, just handed Tree a ring with two keys on it and pointed to their left.

"Pasaporte," Otoe said, and the guard gave it to him. He glanced at it, then showed it to Tree. *"Gracias*, little *amigo*," Otoe said, and he and Tree turned and headed down the hallway.

The floor was unvarnished wood and the walls concrete, painted a faded green and blotched with dark stains here and there on both sides, mostly around head level. Blood. Or brains, maybe. The only light came from one low-watt bulb behind a wire screen in the twelve-foot ceiling. Enough to see the big dark cockroaches that darted around on the walls and the floor.

About fifteen feet down, the corridor ended at a locked, windowless door. Tree looked at the lock, then the keys. He tried the smaller of the two keys. It worked.

"Genius," Otoe said, and then squashed a two-inch-long centipede against the wall with his palm and wiped the gooey remains off on his pants.

Tree pulled open the door and they stepped through. The stench was overpowering—sweat, urine, feces; vomit, too, and dead animal, maybe a rat. The wall on their left, the one running along the street, continued on, with two small windows up near the ceiling. On the right, though, the walkway was lined with iron bars. Behind the bars the space opened up into a single concrete-floored cell, maybe twenty-by-twenty, with cots bolted to the walls and a stainless steel toilet smack in the middle of the floor. A pit toilet—no plumbing in this cell.

Again the only light came from a dim, bare bulb in the ceiling above the walkway, and the closely set bars kept much of the cell in shadows. There was enough light, though, to see lots more roaches, and to see maybe fifteen men crammed in there, all in dirty white pants and shirts. Most were lying down, about half on the cots and half on the shiny, damp floor. Heads turned and dark eyes stared at the intruders, but no one said anything.

"Jesus!" Otoe murmured. "You can *taste* shit in here, like it's floatin' in the air. *This* where they keep the guy?"

"This here's a holding tank. I understand he's usually deeper inside." Tree held up the larger of the keys. "Let's get to it," he said, and unlocked the barred gate and pulled it open.

Both men stepped into the wide opening to the cell.

"Hey! Listen up!" Otoe yelled. *"Atienda, atienda!"*

Some of the prisoners sat up, and a few even got to their feet. Many growled protests in Spanish. No one, however, moved any closer to Tree and Otoe, because Otoe, crouched in a shooter's stance, was sweeping the area in front of them with a .45 caliber semiautomatic, a Heckler & Koch MK23, looking all the more threatening with a suppressor attached.

"We want the American!" he yelled. *"El Americano!"*

Several heads turned toward the right rear corner of the cell. When whoever was back there in the shadows didn't move, Tree took the torch from his pocket, widened the beam, and shone it on two men. One sat on his rear, his head slumped between his knees, his long greasy hair hanging down. The other, a much larger man, crouched beside him. The larger man was Mexican, with thick black hair slicked back from his forehead. He had his hand on the smaller man's shoulder, and wore on his face the ugly scowl of a professional prisoner—made even more threatening because his left eye was just a slit looking out from a lump of swollen, purple-and-red-mottled skin.

"So whatcha think, Tree? See anyone else in this sty that looks like our man?"

"Nope."

"You!" Otoe called. "Sitting in the corner. Look up!"

The head started to rise, but the larger man quickly pushed it back down. "You don't do nothing with this one, *gringo*," he said. "This one, he is under my protection."

"Really?" Otoe fired just one shot, the suppressor keeping the pop to about that of a .22 caliber pistol, and splinters of stone flew out of the wall near the big Mexican's head. "That change your mind, *amigo*?"

The Mexican stared back, showing no fear, but then smiled and took his hand off the other's head.

The sitting man looked up, and wiped his hair out of his eyes. His pale, thin face showed no sign of a beard. He was very young. Upper teens, maybe.

"That's him," Otoe said.

"C'mon up here, son," Tree drawled. "We're goin' for a walk."

"No, I…I can't." The boy's voice was thin and weak, and he was obviously terrified. "When I come back he'll…he'll be mad." He nodded sideways, toward the man beside him.

"Well, then, y'all *both* come up here. We'll all go for a walk together."

"Good idea," Otoe said. "You come up here too, *amigo*."

The man made no move to comply and Otoe fired again, almost as though without meaning to. More chips flew out from the wall beside the Mexican, but closer this time. He stood up. He was about the same height as the two Americans, but stockier than either of them. Fat, actually.

No one else moved, but the young American stood up and then he and the Mexican came slowly forward. When Otoe finally raised his hand to stop them they were maybe a yard away. The young man in front of Otoe, the Mexican in front of Tree.

"Who is this gentleman, son?" Tree asked. "He really your protector?"

The boy was trembling. "He…that's what he said."

"Well, now…that ain't what I asked, is it? What's he done…to *protect* you?"

"He…I guess…he kept the other men away from me. I mean… earlier tonight."

"You know him before you were put in this here cell tonight?"

"No. He was already here. They all were. Most of them are being transferred here from some other prison, I think."

"But the two of you got to be friends?"

"No." That came out louder. "No, he's not my friend. He…he…" his voice trailed off.

"This dude ain't really been protecting you, has he, son?" Tree's voice was very gentle.

"No, he…I fought…tried to stop him, but he…" The young man was shaking so hard now that even his head was moving.

The Mexican leaned forward then, as though to do or say something, but a slight wave of Otoe's HK stopped him cold.

"Tell me, son. You tell ol' Tree what this sumbitch done to you."

"He…he raped me."

"Well, damn," Tree said. "That ain't the kinda thing a 'protector' does, is it? A 'protector' should—"

"We got business here," Otoe interrupted. "What's done is done." He stepped to his left and gestured with his head, and the young man went past him and stood just outside the cell.

The Mexican shrugged and gave a sly grin. "You two, you are professionals, yes? You understand, I think." He pointed to his swollen eye. "This *muchacho*, he is a fighter. I *like* that. You know how it is."

"Yeah, we know," Otoe said. "These things happen."

"They *do* happen," Tree agreed, and he suddenly shot his left hand up high in the air over his head.

The Mexican couldn't help but look up, which is when the knife in Tree's right hand—how it got there, who could say?—slashed through the air…from right to left…across the man's throat.

Just one cut, and then Tree leaned in and wiped the blade—one side serrated, the other razor sharp—on the man's own shirt, and folded the knife and put it away again.

Otoe and Tree backed out of the cell as the dying man dropped slowly to his knees, his mouth wide open, clutching his throat as though he could hold the blood inside.

Tree locked the cell closed behind them. "You see, son?" he said, taking the young American by the arm and guiding him away. "*That's* the kinda thing a 'protector' does."

TWO

On the morning he knew he would have to lie once again to his friend, Father Paul Clark said the six-thirty mass. It was Monday and weekday masses, even at Holy Name Cathedral, were rather perfunctory events, so by five after seven he was back in the sacristy, removing his vestments. Hank Manion had been the altar server, and Paul barely had the alb slipped up over his head and off when Hank grabbed it out of his hands.

"Thanks," Paul said, resisting the urge to snatch the alb back. "But you don't have to—"

"Hey, it's the least I can do, Father." Hank held the long white robe by the shoulders and gave it a shake to get the sleeves straightened out, then hung it with great care—no, with reverence—in the alb closet. "By the way, that woman you told me about…from your parish…did she ever get a lawyer?"

"Oh…well…I misspoke. She wasn't from the parish." Paul slipped on a black windbreaker. "But she asked for help, and I…I told her about your recommendations and, actually, I never saw her again." He knelt to re-tie his shoe…and to hide his anxiety.

"People are funny, aren't they?" Hank was at the little sink now, rinsing out the wine cruet. "Anyway, I'll finish up here, Father. You go say your prayers."

"Um…right." Paul grabbed his gym bag from the top of the vestment case, and left the sacristy.

Out in the body of the church he knelt down at the end of the second pew on the far left. Priests were supposed to be men of prayer, and no one could say he didn't try, these days more than ever. In fact, every day before mass he spent thirty minutes trying, minutes that produced no more peace or consolation—or anything close—than the ten or fifteen he usually spent after mass. Like today. Kneeling in the usual spot. Getting the usual result. A sense of God's presence was hard to come by, given the million other things churning through his mind.

Leading today's post-mass parade of distractions was the devout, if sometimes irritating, Hank Manion. Certainly no "altar boy," Hank was fifty-something and had been serving mass at the cathedral—whenever he was in town—since before Paul came on the scene. He was an international trade consultant, the head of his own firm, and he lived in a huge condo near the top of the Hancock building. That was *one* of his homes, anyway. Paul had been to cocktail parties there a few times, and loved the panoramic view of the lakefront, and the quiet, elegant ambience.

There were things about Hank, though, that annoyed Paul. One was his old-fashioned, condescending respect for priests. *It's the least I can do, Father.* Another was the unconscious arrogance with which he ordered people around. *You go say your prayers.* Still, the guy was both hugely successful and obviously devoted to the church. And most importantly, he was the only one who'd actually *done* something, a few months ago, when Paul had been flailing around, reaching out for help.

Paul preferred not to talk about that now. Not with Hank. Not with anyone.

†

He closed his eyes and gave it his best shot, but even after he got Hank Manion offstage, his so-called "prayers" consisted of his mind wandering like a puppy from one distraction to another—mostly from this worry, to that guilt, to this fear. By the time ten minutes had passed he was deep into the really heavy stuff...and was glad it was time to go.

He took his gym bag and walked down the long side aisle to the rear of the cathedral, toward the vestibule and the main doors that opened onto State Street. On the way he passed maybe twenty people kneeling or sitting in different pews. Most saw him coming and nodded and smiled as he passed. None of them knew him personally, but he was a priest, right? So he was someone they were sure they knew a lot about.

They were right, of course, about him being a priest. Not in a parish any longer, but at the archdiocesan headquarters, formerly called the "Chancery Office," now the "Office of Pastoral Care." That sounded more people-friendly. Although he often insisted he was "just a guy with a desk job," in fact he was Vice-Chancellor of the archdiocese, a rising star in whom the cardinal expressed great confidence. On his way to being a bishop himself one day. Something he'd never dreamed of when he was ordained a priest…but something he'd eventually come to desire, to work for. But now? Now he wasn't as sure about anything as he used to be.

There were so many things these people *didn't* know about him as they nodded and smiled. They didn't know he lacked what they assumed all priests had: a sense of peace that came from a God he felt close to. They didn't know that, although he'd never intended to separate himself from God, his world had taken a sudden turn that left him with the sense that God was far away. They didn't know that he had a past that had recently re-appeared…carrying with it issues he'd never even dreamed of, but now had to be dealt with. And all that was only the beginning of what the people in the pews didn't know about Father Paul Clark.

†

He passed through the vestibule and out the tall cathedral doors into a cold, dismal, September morning, with a misty rain that seemed to just hang in the air, rather than fall to the ground. He walked over to Jimmy Grogan, the burnt-out police officer who kept watch over the cathedral entrance. Most people avoided Grogan. Talking to him was a downer. But Paul always tried. "Hey, you're looking good, Jimmy. How you doing?"

"Still above ground, Father. But that's about it. I hate rotten days like this. First this damn rain. Then I get that creep, the Monk, moochin' around. Botherin' people when they're comin' to church. Wish the sonova...sorry...wish he'd finish drinking himself to death. If you run into him, don't you give him a dime. That's just encouragin' the bum, and—"

"Got it," Paul said, and hurried down the wet stone steps.

Dodging back and forth among moving cars, ignoring the angry honking of horns, he made it across State Street to the parking lot. Time was short. On Mondays at eight o'clock he met his friend and fellow priest, Larry Landrew, at the University of Illinois campus, just west of the Loop.

When he got to his car, a ten-year-old Toyota Corolla, the man most people called "the Monk" was there, sliding a dirty towel around on the hood, rubbing the light rain in circles into the dust on the maroon finish. He was a greasy, smelly man, with a perpetual scared-rabbit look on his face, a face usually half-hidden in the shadow of the filthy hooded sweatshirt he wore, summer and winter.

Whether the Monk drank or not, he was always asking for "a little change for a sandwich." Instead, Paul usually gave him one of the McDonald's gift coupons he tried always to have with him. Maybe he *was* "just encouragin' the bum," not doing him any real good. Still, he never liked to pass the poor guy by, not given how secure and comfortable his own life was. Or...used to be.

Today, though, the Monk claimed he was washing the car—and he may have thought he actually *was*—so Paul gave him all the singles he had, four of them. "Good job," he said.

The Monk's jaw dropped open. He walked away counting the bills, and Paul felt a fleeting sense of accomplishment.

†

He got in the Corolla, started the engine, switched on the lights and the wipers, and headed out of the lot. For several years he'd been saving for a new car, but that wasn't to be—not for the foreseeable future—and he was glad he'd kept this one in good shape.

He was barely out on the street when his cell phone rang. He had to keep his eyes on the traffic, and by the time he'd managed to fumble the phone out of the gym bag on the seat beside him it had stopped ringing, apparently switching to voice mail mode.

He dropped the phone back into the bag, and it rang again. This time he grabbed it right away. "Hello?"

"It's me," she said. "Why didn't you answer? It sounds like you're in the car."

"I am." A Chicago city ordinance forbade talking on a handheld phone while driving, but he didn't dare raise that issue…not with Ann Swanson.

"So," she said, "did your friend agree to keep his mouth shut a little longer?"

"Look, it's barely seven-thirty. I'm on my way to see him right now."

"To play racquetball, right? U of I?"

"Ah…yes." It was handball, actually, not racquetball, that he and Larry played. A minor error on Ann's part, for sure, but something to hold onto. Even a small lapse in her knowledge kept alive the idea that she was human, that she didn't know *everything*. "We get the court for an hour."

"Enjoy yourself," she said. "And get me a few more days."

"How much—" A horn blared and he slammed on the brakes. His tires slid on the wet pavement, and he barely avoided rear-ending a taxi that came out of nowhere. "How much longer?" he tried again. "You told me you'd be out by today and have a cover story in place, so I could explain away what he saw."

"I need a few more days. 'Til Thursday. Shutting down an operation like this is…complicated. You haven't admitted anything, right?"

"No. I told him that as the cardinal's liaison with the clinic I'd know what was going on down there, and that he must be mistaken. I'm sure he believes me. I asked for time to look into it, and he agreed to wait until today, as a favor to me, before he goes public. I'll try, but I don't know that I can get three more days. To him it's a matter of principle."

"Yeah, right," Ann Swanson said. "Principle. That's great. People like him—and their damn 'principles'—they're the real enemy," she said. "If he's so convinced the government's involved in something, then why isn't he convinced it's for the good of his country? What ever happened to the 'principle' of patriotism?"

"I don't...like I told you, Larry's...anyway, I'll keep denying everything. I just need you to get out of there." Talking to this woman made him nervous. "I'm doing the best I—"

"Just get me to Thursday. Period. For *your* sake."

"For *my* sake? I lose either way. Once you're out of there I lose what you've been—"

"You'll get by. You might even be surprised. Hold up your end and... well...who knows how far up you might go? But if this gets out before I'm ready, it'll knock you right off that golden ladder."

"Ladder? I'm not sure I under—"

"Spare me," she said. "I know your ambitions, and I'm sure you *do* understand. So, my dear Father Clark, lie to your friend. But *not* to me." She hung up.

Paul dropped the phone in his gym bag and exhaled deeply. He'd counted on Ann and her people being gone by today, and their creating a good cover story for what Larry claimed he'd seen.

Then Paul could have gotten back to his other problems. Money, for one thing. Because, whatever Ann Swanson thought, he couldn't see how he'd possibly "get by" without what he'd been getting from her...not with Robert in the picture.

One thing at a time, though. Right now he had to convince Larry to hold off again...until Thursday.

THREE

Lie to your friend. That's what Ann Swanson wanted. And that, sadly, is what Paul would do.

And because Larry was late for the handball game, Paul had extra time to sit on a couch in the lobby of the UIC field house and beat himself up about it. Not that Larry Landrew was a really close friend. Paul didn't feel really close to anyone—except for Robert, and that was new...and something altogether different.

Paul and Larry met in the seminary. Unlike long generations of priests before them, neither of them had grown up sheltered in seminaries from high school on. They were both college grads when they answered the call to the priesthood, and Paul had even done a stint in the army. They shared a common interest in sports—handball and basketball, mostly. Although they were different in so many ways, they respected each other as tough competitors, and came to like each other.

Over the years Paul had come to hold Larry in high regard. Larry was a radical thinker, always willing to take strong public stances. As a priest he'd written so often to the newspapers that the *Sun-Times* finally gave him a bi-weekly column, which was widely read and very often controversial. He wasn't afraid to criticize both church and political leaders about war, injustice, and racism. Most importantly to Paul, though, Larry was one of those few who walked the talk. He was the pastor of St. Manfred's, a parish in one of the city's poorest, most crime-ridden neighborhoods. He was there by choice. And he didn't just work there, he thrived. Who wouldn't admire a guy like that?

These days, although both were Chicago priests, they lived in different worlds, and their relationship revolved entirely around their weekly handball games. Their use of the university's courts was thanks to Hank Manion, who had friends on the UIC board of directors and had arranged a pass to the gym facilities for Paul. It was like membership in a private club, more proof that a priest could live well on his paltry salary—with a little help from wealthy patrons. He and Larry played every Monday. Last week, though, Larry had been away on vacation and Paul was left with an hour on the Stairmaster and the stationary bike. A good workout, but he did that three or four times a week, anyway. And, like time spent praying, solo exercise left too much opportunity to think—which meant to worry.

Then Larry got back Wednesday and called him—in itself unusual because they almost never talked except when they played handball. Larry said he'd spent a week volunteering at Fair Hope Clinic. *Bad news.* Fair Hope was a medical clinic sponsored by the archdiocese in northwestern Guyana, near the border with Venezuela. A place Paul would have done anything to keep Larry away from if he'd known.

Larry started talking about something he'd seen there, but Paul had cut him off, saying he was in the middle of something important and would get back to him. He knew what Larry must have seen, so he put off calling back, which led to an urgent voice mail message from Larry.

Paul finally called him back, and Larry told of his insomnia, and his late-night walks around Fair Hope. And the trucks he'd seen entering past midnight and pulling up to this old barn near the far edge of the property, which had been abandoned for years, but was now being used by some mining company.

It got Larry curious...and suspicious, and as a result Larry had seen and heard way too much, including men unloading boxes he claimed held weapons. Paul pled shocked surprise and ignorance, and promised to look into it, which led to more messages from Larry, and—

"Hey! Wake up!" It was Larry, coming through the lobby door. "Car wouldn't start." He was already headed for the stairway.

"You need a new car," Paul said, as they trotted together down the stairs to the locker room. "Haven't you had trouble with it before?"

"Constantly. Maybe I should get a Toyota, like yours."

"Maybe you should take *care* of it, whatever you get."

"Yeah, well, there *is* that." Larry took the last five steps in one jump, then looked back up at Paul and grinned. He was a dark-haired, wiry guy, long on energy, if sometimes short on common sense. "Maybe I should be more like you."

God forbid.

†

"I just got a new battery, too." They were in the locker room, changing into shorts and t-shirts. "I told that to the guy who came to tow it to the shop and he said maybe it's the alternator...or generator or whatever. That sound right to you?"

"What? Oh...I don't know." Paul's mind was on getting more time for Ann, and he didn't even know what Larry was asking. Something about the car. "I guess so."

"Anyway, I took the bus and I thought I gave myself plenty of time."

"Don't worry about it." Paul knew he should bring up the Fair Hope issue and get it over with, but...

"Those CTA bus schedules are a joke." Larry lifted a foot onto the bench to lace up his Nike knockoff. "But no one cares, not when it's mostly poor people riding."

"Why didn't you call me?" Paul already had his eye protector and gloves on, and was bouncing a handball up and down on the floor at a furious pace. "I'd have picked you up."

"No need for that. That's why God invented buses." Larry switched to his other foot and then, without looking up, said, "So...you check out what's going on at Fair Hope? You said if I held off a couple days you'd look into it."

"Actually...no, not yet. Just haven't had time. But you gotta be wrong about what you saw. I mean, it's a while since I've been down there, but I'd know about it, wouldn't I?"

"You ask the cardinal?" Larry was slipping his gloves on. "He must know about it. Or…maybe he doesn't. That's why they call these agencies 'secret.' Nobody knows what they're up to. Or where. I mean… Guyana? Most people never even *heard* of it, have no idea where it is. Me, though, I *do* know. And I know this government of ours runs on oil." Larry was on a roll now. "And if the oil folks think it's a good idea to sneak weapons through Guyana into Venezuela, to help take down a democratically elected government, it'll be done. And they're *not* gonna hold a press conference about it."

"I agree. That is…I'm not sure I totally agree, but I see your point. I got your messages, but I got tied up in meetings all day Friday and Saturday. I want to get to the bottom of this as much as you do, but with my schedule, and everyone else's, talking to the cardinal, or anyone down at Fair Hope, is impossible on Sundays." A sharp pain, like a cramp, passed through Paul's stomach. Lying was making him sick. "I'll get to it this week, and get back to you by…let's say Friday? Honestly, I just didn't have the chance over the weekend." *Honestly.* "On top of everything else there's this…this MacKenzie thing."

"Uh-uh." Larry's eyes narrowed. "Don't get me started on MacKenzie…and the others. I'm so sick of those damn creeps. Just when you think you can walk down the street in your collar again and not get spat at, some idiot fondles another kid. I'd like to strangle—"

"I know, but this allegation's from twenty-three years ago. And *you* know Mac. Maybe he didn't mean to—"

"Yeah, right. And maybe the buses run on time." Larry headed for the hallway to the handball courts. "Let's go."

"I'm with you," Paul said, trotting behind him. The smells of sweat and dust and floor wax were familiar, even comforting, while the muffled shouts from behind closed doors and the *thwack-thwack-thwack* of balls hitting walls and racquets—most people played racquetball—had his blood flowing. "I reserved Court C."

The court was empty so they went inside and Larry slammed the door shut. "Look," he said, "I saw what's going on down there and it's gotta be the CIA, and they're using Fair Hope, and the public's entitled to know. I've got a column pretty much ready to send to the paper."

"I understand, but you caught me off guard with this. Just give me till Friday afternoon to get back to you. Please? As a friend?"

"I don't know...but...well, I waited this long, and I guess I can give you till...not Friday. With the *Sun-Times* that means another whole week. But till Thursday." He must have seen the relief on Paul's face, because he added, "Not 'cause I really think you can show me I'm wrong, but 'cause you didn't know about it. It's not fair to get you caught up in the middle of something you're not ready for." He bounced a handball up and down a couple of times. "Especially after I beat your ass off today at handball."

†

Forty-five minutes later Paul and Larry left the field house and stepped out into a cold, light rain. The wind had picked up, and it was very dark for nine in the morning. Paul shivered under his thin jacket. They'd both just pulled on street clothes over sweaty shorts and tees. That's what they always did, and then each would drive to his own rectory and shower there.

"C'mon," Paul said. "I'll drive you home."

"What, are you nuts? It'll take you an hour or more to get out there and back. I'll get the bus."

Just then there was a loud crash of thunder, and rain started pouring down, instantly soaking Larry's hooded sweatshirt. The two of them ran to the car, got in and slammed the doors. Just as Paul started the engine his cell phone rang. He reached into the back seat and dug it out of his gym bag. "Hello?"

"Did he agree?" It was Ann Swanson.

"Um..." Paul looked at his watch. "It's only ten after nine. I'll call you when I get to the office."

"Wait," she said. "Just...you mean someone's with you now?"

"Right. Good. Talk to you later." He turned off the phone and put it back in the bag.

While Paul pulled out into traffic, Larry fooled with the radio until he found some jazz. "Man," he said, "do I hate cell phones."

Paul didn't respond. His mind was racing. He could easily have told Ann Swanson *yes* before he signed off. But he'd been nervous, preoccupied with his growing realization that, whatever she did, his own problem wasn't going away.

Yes, he'd lied again and gotten Larry to agree to do nothing until Thursday. But just talking to Larry face-to-face made Paul realize he'd been dreaming to think that Ann pulling her people out of Fair Hope would be enough to keep the guy quiet permanently. Even if the cover story Ann cooked up might explain away what Larry would say he'd seen, the cardinal would know something had been going on, something Paul hadn't told him about.

So, thanks to Larry's willingness to help a friend, both Ann and the church might come out all right, but that wouldn't save Paul. His reputation as someone whose judgment could be trusted, his shot at becoming a bishop—all that would be wiped out. Along with maybe his priesthood.

And he really couldn't blame it on Larry. His own choices were what had brought him to this point.

FOUR

Although it hardly seemed possible, the fact was that, until just a couple of months earlier—the week of the Fourth of July—Paul had never even heard of the woman who was now giving him orders…orders he couldn't possibly ignore.

The Fourth itself had been a Thursday, and two days before that, on Tuesday afternoon, he'd been visiting his mother's grave. He'd seen no one else in the cemetery, and was lost in thought, when a woman stepped up beside him. "My name is Ann Swanson," she said. "I know about your problem. And I can help."

He'd been startled, and would have sent her on her way, except that it became clear at once that she not only knew his name and who he was, but also knew about Robert—much more about Robert, in fact, than Paul himself knew. She claimed to be with "an agency of the federal government," but refused to be more specific. She did nearly all the talking, and when the conversation was over she said, "Take a few days to think about it. I'll get back to you on Saturday."

†

On Friday, the day after the Fourth, the Office of Pastoral Care was closed, and Paul had done nothing *but* "think about it." The weather was oppressively hot and humid, and he was spending his day off in the cool comfort of his study. Not relaxing, though. Obsessing. Unable to focus on anything but the proposal the woman had made.

How did he know she could do what she said she could? In fact, how could he even be certain she worked for some unnamed "agency of the federal government"? And *what* agency? Given the nature of her proposal the obvious assumption was the CIA, but was there any possible way to verify that?

He took his coffee and went to the window. Looking down, he saw a cluster of workers around the rear of a phone company truck parked across the street. Some people didn't have the luxury of a day off, no matter the weather. And then the truck, and its phone company logo, gave him an idea.

He retrieved a Chicago phone directory from the rear of his bottom desk drawer. It was ten years old, but it was the only directory he was aware of in the rectory, and worth a try. He looked under "Federal Government" and was pleased—and more than a little surprised—to actually find a listing for "Central Intelligence Agency." What didn't surprise him, though, was the address given. One of his duties for the archdiocese—that of being point man in the sexual abuse crisis—had made him only too familiar with the justice system, and he knew the building at that address. It was the Dirksen Federal Building, a high-rise structure in the southern end of the Loop, and it housed the federal courthouse for the northern district of Illinois, as well as a number of other federal agencies. But the CIA?

He picked up the phone—the rectory landline—and tapped out the number. The voice that answered was female and automated. "The number you are calling is no longer in service. No further information is available." He hung up.

He walked to the window again and stared out, this time seeing nothing.

Who *was* this "Ann Swanson" who knew so much about him, knew things he himself hadn't known until recently? How did she gain such knowledge? He went back and sat down, then stood up again. He reached for his coffee and discovered the mug was empty. He went down to the kitchen for a refill and was headed back up the stairs when he heard the phone ring. Not the rectory phone. His cell. He'd left it on his desk.

He ran the rest of the way and made it to the phone. "Hello?"

"I'm calling to remind you of something." It was Ann Swanson herself. "That conversation we had...and the fact that we *had* a conversation... that's between the two of us. We agreed on that."

"We did," he said. "And I've told no one."

"Because if we can't trust each other, then there's no use going forward." Her voice was pleasant enough, but he sensed an underlying impatience and aggression.

"I understand, but...okay...I'm concerned. I don't really know who you are, or who sent you. How do I know you can do what you say you can?"

"I explained all that. Even if you say 'yes' to my proposal, you'll have no obligation at all, unless and until I carry out my part of the bargain first. I *will* do that. And when I do, it'll be because I trust you to do *your* part after that. Right?"

"Yes."

"Then really, you don't have to trust me to carry out my part. You just wait until I do. That's clear enough, isn't it?"

"Yes."

"Good. I'll call tomorrow, on this line, for your decision." She hung up.

He set the cell phone down on his desk and stared at it. It was a phone she'd given him, to be used for all their communications because she knew it was "clean." Whether or not he used the phone for his own affairs was up to him, but he was to keep it turned on and with him always. She might need to contact him. Of course he couldn't call her. He had no number for her. When she called him the cell phone display just said "Unknown caller" and she'd set it up somehow so that the phone didn't retain her number and he couldn't return her calls.

Why would she have called, though, at this particular time? Did she actually *know* that he'd just called a number listed for the CIA, but "no longer in service"? Setting aside the question of *how* she could know that, if she *did* know, then she must be with some powerful federal agency, very likely the CIA. That, although it frightened him, was a great relief.

Because he was facing a very serious problem, and he had nowhere else to turn.

FIVE

During the remainder of the drive Paul and Larry hardly spoke at all, other than Larry reminding him which streets to take, since Paul hadn't been to St. Manfred's in a couple of years.

Paul never drove into the west side at all, unless he had to. The poverty and lack of hope were too depressing. Worse yet, the people—especially the tough-looking young men slouching around the corners—frightened him. He always made sure to hit the lock button if he had to stop at a light. Whenever Larry spoke of the suburban white kids who drove to a corner near his church to buy drugs, all Paul thought of was that those kids—as foolish and self-destructive as they were—had way more courage than he did.

As they got close to St. Manfred's, he recalled that the church and the rectory were on one side of the street, the school on the other. The street itself, Manfred Court, was just a half-block long. Eighty years ago, when the archdiocese had way more clout—and could get away with using it—the short street had been created to accommodate the buildings for a new parish. At the corner Paul started to turn, but Larry said, "No. Go straight and take the alley. There's no street parking here, so I always go in through the back yard."

By now there was frequent thunder, and a fierce rain pounded on the roof of the car. It had gotten pretty dark, too; so dark that the street lights had been triggered on. Paul turned in at the alley and they drove past the rounded rear wall of the church—looming up on their left like a ship in the storm—and came to the "back yard," which was nothing but a vacant space covered over with concrete. The ancient pavement, uneven and cracked, was losing its battle with weeds. What little was left of a chain link fence around the area was rusty and sagging, with many of the metal poles bent over to the ground.

"Home sweet home," Larry said, pointing toward the rear of an L-shaped stone building, two stories tall. "Drive right through here."

Paul steered the Corolla through a missing section of fence and they splashed across the potholed concrete. At Larry's direction, he pulled into a small courtyard, a "U" formed by the wings of the rectory and the wall of the church, and stopped. His headlights shone through the rain onto a set of slightly leaning wooden steps which led up to the back door.

"My God," Paul said, "don't you get depressed living here?"

"What?" Larry seemed surprised. "Oh...well, the rectory itself is okay inside. A little neglected and musty-smelling, but it's solid. The upstairs plumbing is mostly shot and, except for me and a few mice and roaches, the place is empty. I'd like to fix it up and use it as a shelter for the homeless, or for recovering addicts, but the archdiocese says it's too expensive to bring up to code. They'd rather tear it down, so I keep on living in it...in the old housekeeper's room and the kitchen... to keep that from happening."

"I'm telling you," Paul said, "I could never live in a place like—"

"Hey, things are going great here. There's lots of meeting space in the church basement. We have a food pantry and a soup kitchen, and a thrift shop where people can buy clothes and stuff cheap. The school's getting better and we have programs for all ages." Larry was digging into his pocket and finally came up with a single key. "Anyway, I'll give you the grand tour someday. But for now? Get back to me by Thursday, okay?"

"I'll call."

"Good." Larry opened the car door a little. "I mean, I can't promise—"

"Out, mothafucka!" Larry's door flew open, yanked from outside. "Get out the fuckin' car!" A male voice, deep and harsh. From Larry's side of the car.

It was too startling for Paul to process. And apparently for Larry, too, because Larry didn't move.

"I *said*...out the fuckin' car, man."

The rain pounded down on the roof and Larry still didn't move. He seemed frozen in place.

Paul leaned down to see past him. The man was out there. Of course. But through the pouring rain Paul couldn't see anyone. Or maybe...yes. Dark pants legs, a long black coat like a raincoat.

"All's I want's your money, bitch," the man said. "I know you ain't deaf, so—"

"Okay." Larry's voice was thin and trembling. Not at all like Larry's voice. Not at all like Larry. "Okay, please, we have money. You can take it all." He twisted his body around to get out, at the same time raising his hands and holding them palms forward, up near his shoulders.

Paul knew that meant Larry saw what Paul couldn't see. A gun.

Larry was out of the car now, standing, facing the man.

"And *you*, mothafucka." The man spoke a little louder.

"Me?" Paul managed, his own voice weaker than Larry's.

"Who you think, pussy? Stay where you at." Then he said, "Gimme your wallet." Obviously talking to Larry again.

Paul watched Larry take his wallet from his rear pocket. The man must have taken it, although Larry blocked Paul's view.

"Shit! Ain't nothin' in here, man."

"I know," Larry said. "I just remembered, I didn't—"

"You fuckin' with me. You say, '*Pleeeease*,'" imitating Larry's thin, frightened voice, "'you can take our money.' But then you ain't *got* no money. You fuckin' with me. I don't like no one fuckin' with me."

"I'm sorry," Larry said. "I didn't mean—"

An explosion then. A gunshot. Paul heard it over the thunder and the pounding rain and the car's idling engine, and knew just what it was. But still not as loud as he thought a gunshot would be. And then two more shots, close together. Larry crumpled to the pavement.

Paul squeezed his eyes shut. He knew he should be running away by now, but he couldn't move. He couldn't yell for help. He forced his eyes to open and stared across through the car. "Larry?" he said. "Larry?"

His friend didn't move.

Suddenly, right behind him, the driver's door was yanked open and a hand grabbed his collar and pulled him out into the rain. He was thrown hard against the car and then somehow he ended up lying flat on his face, his nose pressed into the concrete.

"Don't move." The same voice. "You hear me?"

"Yes. Please…don't hurt me." He mumbled it into the concrete. He couldn't breathe and couldn't stand the pressure on his nose. He twisted his head to the side.

The man kicked him in the ribs, a kick so hard that it lifted him up onto his side. "Fool, *you* fuckin' with me, too."

"No, please." He rolled over onto his belly again. "I just needed to…" But what good were explanations?

He lay perfectly still and felt a hand at one back pocket, then the other. Felt his wallet being taken out. He *did* have money, he thought. Maybe a hundred dollars. Maybe more. He wasn't sure. But so what? Larry was probably dead. The man was crazy. Paul would be dead, too.

He suddenly thought of Robert, and panicked. He couldn't die, not now. Robert needed him. He struggled and made it up to his knees.

And then came the blow to the back of his head.

SIX

Paul came half-awake with a vague sense of someone moving his arms and legs, tugging at him. Then he felt fingers pressing hard on a spot on the side of his neck. It hurt, but the pain faded away. Everything faded away.

Then he was coming awake again, belly down on concrete, rain pelting his back, his left cheek resting in a cold puddle and gritty water leaking into his mouth. He couldn't remember where he was. Or why. He was too sleepy to want to wake up; but cold, too, chilled down into his bones. His arms were bent at the elbows, his palms open on the pavement, as though to say "I surrender" to the earth.

So cold, and *so* sleepy. He might have dozed off again, or maybe not, but it gradually came to him that a mugger, a truly disturbed man—maybe drug-crazed—had hit him from behind, and then squeezed a pressure point or something in his neck. A dull ache throbbed in his head, from the back of his skull, up and over the top, and down to his forehead.

Don't move. Don't even open your eyes. Maybe he'll think you're dead. Maybe he'll go away.

The rain kept coming, and he heard it striking sheet metal. The roof of a car close beside him. His car. The Toyota Corolla. This rain didn't come in drops, but in pellets that drove right through his skin to his bones, and he finally understood why it felt that way, and why he was so cold. He had no clothes on.

His mind was clearing, but so slowly, and he had to fight the urge to sleep.

Was the mugger still there, standing over him? Probably not. He couldn't hear anyone. And anyway, with his face turned toward the car no one would know if he opened his eyes. So he did. He saw his right hand and his bare forearm, and beyond them—looking under the car—he saw a bundle of wet clothes on the ground on the passenger side. Not his clothes, though. No, that motionless bundle of clothes… that was Larry. Dead.

Suddenly, through the pounding rain, he heard a car drive up, way back in the alley. The car stopped. Maybe it was the *police*. He wanted to stand up, say something, call for help. But he was too scared, and he squeezed his eyes shut again and didn't move. Then he heard something else. Was it a car door closing? He wasn't sure.

The car drove away.

He lay there with his eyes closed. *So* cold, and *so* sleepy. But still alive. The mugger…the *killer*…had taken his wallet and hit him in the head, and now he must be gone. Maybe the car took him, or maybe he was gone before the car stopped. Or maybe he was just lying low, letting the car drive away.

The rain pounded down and seconds passed, and even though he was certain the killer must be gone by now, that didn't seem to matter much. Right now his head hurt and all he wanted was to lie there on that cold wet pavement and go back to sleep. For just a few minutes.

Instead, he gathered all the willpower he could, and managed to get up to his hands and knees. Whether the man was gone or not, and no matter how tired he was and how much his head ached, he knew he mustn't go to sleep. He'd read or heard somewhere that people with head injuries should stay awake. He got himself into a sitting position, scraping his naked buttocks on the rough pavement. The mugger had taken his clothes. Everything. Leaving him nothing but cold, bare skin… and a terrible sense of exposure, of vulnerability.

Sitting naked in a cold puddle in the rain, he reached up and put his hand to the back of his head. His hair felt sticky…or was it just wet? He looked down, then, and in the dim light he couldn't tell whether the puddle was just dirty water, or a mixture of water and blood. He felt his head again, and rubbed slightly. It was painfully tender, but he looked at his hand. No blood.

He struggled to his feet, using the car for support, and looked around. His clothes weren't in sight. He looked through the car window into the back seat. His gym bag was still there. His phone should be in the bag, if the mugger hadn't found it and taken it.

He pulled on the door handle. It was locked.

He tried the driver's door, but that was locked, too. He leaned and peered through the car window and saw that the door on the passenger side—the one Larry had been dragged out of—was closed. Also, he was sure he'd left the motor running, but now it wasn't. And the headlights weren't on, either. He looked in again through the window and saw that the keys were gone.

He checked his watch, but his watch was gone, too.

Why am I just standing here? Larry might not be dead at all. He might still be hanging on.

Keeping one hand on the car, he moved around to Larry's side, stepping gingerly on bare feet. He didn't really want to get that close to Larry, or to *touch* him. If he was alive Paul couldn't help him, and if he was dead...

When he got there, he had no need to look too closely. Larry lay on his back, fully clothed, with his head at an impossible angle. There was a gaping hole in his throat, and an empty socket where his right eye should have been. His left eye was wide open, but rolled up so that only the white part showed. He wasn't bleeding now, and his skin had been washed clean by the rain, but dark blood stained the front of his hooded sweatshirt. His left arm was stretched out with his hand closed into a fist, and the watch was gone from his wrist. From the smell, he knew that Larry's bowels had emptied.

The need to get help fast had vanished, and somehow it had taken away with it Paul's fear of touching Larry. He knelt down on his bare knees on the concrete and leaned over and slid his left hand under Larry's head and lifted it slightly. He couldn't anoint Larry because he had no oils.

Even so—and because who knows how long it takes a person to really die?—he could give absolution. As he cradled Larry's head in his left hand, with his right thumb he drew a small cross on Larry's forehead. "Be at peace, Larry," he said. "I absolve you of all your sins, in the name of…" He spoke the words aloud, lifting his hand and tracing a larger cross in the air above Larry's face. And, as was the case for him in so many contexts these days, he relied more on hope than on faith that his ceremonial gestures and words meant something, and worked God's forgiveness.

He wanted that to be true, because even if Larry hadn't been a *close* friend, he'd been the nearest thing to it Paul had. He lowered his friend's head back onto the pavement, gently, as though it mattered that Larry not be hurt any more.

SEVEN

His head still pounding, Paul stood in the rain near the trunk of the Corolla. The storm seemed to be easing a little. From where he was, hemmed in by walls on three sides, he had only a narrow view across the alley, toward the back of a run-down apartment building. He walked out closer to the alley, noticing for the first time the smell of wet ashes hanging in the air. There must have been a fire in the building. It was obviously vacant, its windows all dark, and some boarded up.

More apartment buildings flanked both sides of the vacant one, a few showing dim lights here and there. But his bare feet were so tender that every step made him want to scream. Could he possibly get to those buildings, through broken glass and rubble, past the garages and fences that lined the alley? And if he did, what then? Climb up the porch steps naked and bang on doors?

If the mugger had taken his clothes to delay his getting help, he'd succeeded.

He went back to the car and looked in again at his gym bag. Besides the phone, there might be an extra pair of shorts in there. . .and his gym shoes, too. He tried hitting the window sharply several times with his elbow, but it didn't give, and he was afraid if he hit it with all his strength it might break and sever an artery or something in his arm. So he ventured away from the car again and looked around for a brick, or a chunk of concrete, or a piece of pipe.

What he found were a million small stones, a broken bottle, and three crushed beer cans.

There was nothing to do but forget his nakedness and his bare feet and run around to the street and then, if he saw no one to ask for help, march into the parish school and get someone in the office to call the police. Right, and there'd be kids all around, and everyone would scream and call him a pervert.

Then he remembered the key. Larry had dug a key out of his pocket and had it in his left hand while he was opening the car door.

He went back to the body and knelt beside it. He stared at Larry's closed left fist and wondered if he could pry it open. He knew, of course, that you weren't supposed to disturb a dead body before the police came. But he'd already touched Larry's body once, and there'd certainly be a phone in the rectory.

Larry's hand opened easily. The key was in it.

†

The screen door was aluminum, with the screen intact except for one L-shaped rip, which someone—probably Larry—had repaired with duct tape, on the inside only. He pulled the screen door open and inserted the key in the lock of the solid-looking door behind it. It was a dead bolt lock and it turned smoothly. Paul removed the key, pushed the door open, and stepped into a short hallway lined with cleaning supplies: mops, brooms, a vacuum cleaner, a couple of pails. He walked through into the kitchen.

He switched on a bright ceiling light and, except for the laptop sitting on a table in the middle of the room, felt as if he'd been transported back to the 1950s, complete with linoleum flooring, wooden cabinets painted light green, and a shallow sink with exposed pipes beneath it. There was a microwave, though, sitting on the counter beside a coffeemaker. He could smell bleach, or maybe Lysol, and there wasn't a crumb of food in sight. No dirty dishes lying around, either. Despite the cleanliness, however, there was an unopened three-pack of mouse traps sitting on top of the microwave, and a cockroach crawling around in the sink. Larry'd been fighting a losing battle.

Paul looked around for a phone. On the wall beside the doorway to the back hall, above the light switch, was a small wooden plaque with a picture of Saint Christopher and four brass cup hooks, on one of which hung a ring of three keys. He realized he still had Larry's single key in his hand, and he hung it on another of the hooks.

There was no phone.

To his left was a closed door, a swinging door, and he pushed through and stepped into what was once a formal dining room. Now it was storage space, with at least a dozen large cardboard cartons piled on top of each other, the words *Sweetheart Cup Company* printed on them. One carton lay open on its side on the old dining room table, and it was half-full of paper cups in plastic-wrapped stacks. There must have been a ten-year supply of cups in the room, scrounged up by Larry from somewhere, and this—one more sign of something Larry had given his time to—suddenly brought tears to Paul's eyes.

Yesterday the guy was patching screens, battling mice, mooching supplies for the soup kitchen. Today...he's dead.

Paul hurried back into the kitchen and from there went through another door, into the room where Larry lived...or used to live. He had called it the housekeeper's room. There was a low, mirrored dresser—a woman's dresser—and a sofa which was unfolded into a bed and neatly covered with a bedspread. A pair of slippers sat on the floor, and on a bedside stand...finally...a telephone.

He went over and sat on the bed and picked up the receiver...and then set it down again. His whole body was shaking. He was naked, and terribly cold.

He slipped his feet into Larry's slippers and stood up and walked to the closet. Larry was shorter and thinner than he, but he found a pair of sweat pants and a sweatshirt with "Dallas Cowboys" on the front. He put them on and they were too snug, but felt soft and warm. He went back and sat down again and dialed 911.

When the woman answered, Paul discovered he couldn't talk. Not at first. He was crying. The woman was very patient with him, telling him to relax and to speak very slowly.

"St. Manfred's, behind the rectory," he finally said. "There was a man with a gun. Father Landrew is dead. And I'm hurt. Manfred Court. I don't know the exact address."

"That's all right, sir," she said. "Officers are on their way."

The woman seemed to want to keep him on the phone, but he hated sitting on Larry's bed, so he hung up and went back into the kitchen and sat by the table. Another chair sat facing him. That half of the table was empty, and must have been where Larry ate. This half was his desk, with the laptop—its power cord stretching up in the air to a socket in the ceiling fixture—and some spiral-bound notebooks and ballpoint pens, along with a foot-high stack of newspapers. There was no printer in sight, and no phone line running from the computer. Wireless? Larry? Not likely.

Paul remembered Larry telling him last summer that someone had given him his first computer. He'd already started writing on it, he said, but he didn't want Internet service. All the rectories in the archdiocese were supposed to be connected to the Internet, but Larry couldn't be bothered. He said the *Sun-Times* wanted his columns emailed, too, but he snail-mailed his. They didn't like it, but—

The laptop. The notebooks.

Larry had said his column for the *Sun-Times* about Fair Hope was almost completed. So, what Larry had seen at the clinic must be on the laptop, and the notebooks might have his notes. Now it would all fall into the hands of someone else—Larry's relatives, or the police. In fact, Paul could hear sirens wailing now. The police would be here any minute. Did he dare take Larry's computer and notes, temporarily, to see what they contained? Even if, technically, that wasn't stealing, was it illegal? They'd been locked inside the rectory, so they certainly weren't evidence in his murder, which had happened outside.

He stood up and went to the back door and looked out through the screen. It was still dark, but not raining now. He felt dizzy, and decided he wasn't thinking straight. He couldn't get Larry's computer and notes out of here without being seen. They were too bulky to sneak out under his clothes, and he couldn't hide them in his car because it was locked. The police would see what he was taking, and want an explanation.

Still, the risk of exposure—and the resulting harm to the church, and to himself—was too great. Maybe he could hide the things right there in the rectory… and figure out later what to do. He couldn't just do nothing, and hope for the best.

He heard police cars roaring up, turning into the alley. He closed the back door and locked it, and went into the kitchen, his mind whirling. He grabbed the computer and the notebooks—there were three of them—and stood there, hearing doors slamming. Men yelling. There wasn't time to look around the house for a hiding place.

He yanked open a cabinet door. The cabinet was almost empty, just a few cups and glasses, and a stack of plates. A higher shelf looked totally empty and he stood on his tiptoes and slid the books and the laptop onto that shelf and pushed them back against the wall, out of sight. The police were pounding on the back door.

He closed the cabinet door and stood for a few seconds, breathing hard and listening to the police banging on the door, calling for whoever was in there to come out. They were obviously unwilling to break in unless they had to. They might run head-on into a killer with a gun.

"I'm coming," he yelled back. "I'm coming!"

He got as far as the back hall doorway and felt dizzy again—more than ever—light-headed and nauseated. He put a hand on the wall by the light switch to regain his balance…and found himself staring right at the little key rack. Acting on impulse, he took Larry's key off the hook he'd hung it on. One of the three keys on the other ring looked exactly like it, and he stuffed the single key into the pocket of the sweat pants.

There was more banging on the door, so loud now that it hurt his head and made him feel sick. He stumbled through the hall and unlocked the door and pulled it open.

"Please," he called out, "I'm not feeling well."

EIGHT

She sat in a small conference room down the hall from Jessie's room, drinking tea and killing time with Carl, the physical therapist. Like all the hospital personnel, Carl knew her as Christine Conrad. She found it helpful, both to herself and to her own people, to keep the various names she used for different purposes quite dissimilar in sound. "Christine Conrad" and "Ann Swanson," the two she was using most just now, were easy for anyone to keep straight.

She and Carl were waiting for Dr. Salvo, the orthopedic surgeon who was to operate, for the second time, on Jessie's ankle. Over the last couple of months, she'd gotten used to conferences like this, and to the fact that whichever doctors were involved were invariably late.

It had been a freakish bicycle accident, with no one to blame but Jessie herself. The same free spirit that made Jessie a cutting-edge artist, willing to take chances, made her reckless with her own body. She'd fallen fifteen feet to a rocky ledge off the side of the Blue Ridge Parkway, and given the number of bones she'd broken—thirteen fractures, including her pelvis and her left shoulder, hip, and ankle—the fact that she had no brain damage or spinal injury was remarkable. Still, she'd suffered a collapsed lung, a bruised heart, and significant facial lacerations.

At least she was able to talk now, whenever the meds didn't make her too drowsy.

"...one tough lady, that Jessie of yours," Carl was saying. He was a black man, probably gay, and he really seemed to care about Jessie. "I understand today's surgery might be put off. We'll see what the orthopod says."

"Right." She put down her lukewarm tea. Her cell phone was vibrating. "I have to take this call."

She stood up and went out the door, lifting the phone to her ear. "It's about time," she said. "Tell me— *Damn*!" She flattened herself against the wall as a fierce-looking, bearded young man sped past in a wheelchair. No warning. No apology. Still, it wouldn't do to yell at a guy—likely a veteran of Iraq or Afghanistan—getting used to life without legs. "Okay," she said into the phone. "Go ahead."

"I guess you're out of the loop," the man said.

"What are you talking about?"

"That fucking egomaniac you signed on with? You better talk to him about strategy. We're gonna have some pieces to pick up."

"Dammit, Otoe, tell me what—shit, hold on again." A man in green scrubs had stepped off the elevator and was headed into the conference room. The orthopedic surgeon, Dr. Salvo. He'd kept *her* waiting, but she knew *he* wouldn't wait. "I'll get back to you. Matter of minutes."

She hurried into the room. The doctor was already seated at the table, dumping a packet of sweetener into his coffee. "Sorry I'm late," he said, and the apology seemed genuine. He opened a folder that lay in front of him, and looked down at the page.

"Will you be operating today?" she asked.

"Jessie's making good progress." They always used her first name. "It's just this pulmonary infection that she picked…or…that's developed." She'd noticed no one liked to be explicit about patients picking up bugs hanging around in the hospital air. "…and difficulty breathing," the doctor was saying. "I can't finish rebuilding the ankle until the infection's cleared up. Hopefully tomorrow. In the meantime, her physical therapy will continue." Dr. Salvo turned to Carl, who nodded in agreement.

Her mind wandered while Carl and the surgeon discussed the therapy. She had to call Otoe back right away, and find out what was going on. If she had to go to Chicago it was a two-hour flight. She'd save an hour with the time change, but then lose it again on the way back, and she had to be here in the morning. She couldn't stand being seven hundred miles away when Jessie was under the knife.

At the same time, she couldn't let things in Chicago get out of control. She'd signed agreements—dozens of them, it seemed—taking responsibility for all of Jessie's medical bills. Because there was no insurance coverage most of the surgeons offered discounts and payment plans. But their fees were still huge, and the plastic surgeon wouldn't even look at the chart without pre-payment. Also, she had to arrange for a place for Jessie after her discharge, and for continuing therapy, and for round-the-clock attention until she was really on her feet.

It all had to be paid for, and to get the money she'd do whatever had to be done, even if that meant getting involved with "that fucking egomaniac" Otoe was right to complain about. Because, except for Jessie, what did she have to live for?

NINE

Much of what happened after the police came was a blur. Paul's thinking was clear enough, but there were so many squad cars, so many officers talking and shouting all at once, so much confusion. Fire department paramedics took him aside and had him walk a few steps while they watched him. They had him lie down on a wheeled cart, then slid him into the back of an ambulance, and closed the door. He was suddenly in a different world: quiet, bright, clean, and smelling of bleach. A paramedic—his name tag said *O'Brien*—had him sit up again and checked him over, taking his blood pressure, shining a tiny light into his eyes and his ears, and asking a few simple questions.

"We'll be leaving for the hospital in a few minutes," O'Brien said. "First, though, one of the detectives wants to talk to you."

The paramedic left, and a heavy-set black man climbed into the ambulance and sat beside Paul, who lay back down again. "Detective Maddox," the man said. "Chicago Police Department. Tell me what happened."

Paul recited what he could remember, especially how Larry told the robber he could have his money, but there *was* no money in his wallet and the man—who sounded like a black man, though Paul never actually saw him—went berserk and shot Larry. He told Maddox how the man hit him on the head and when he woke up his clothes were gone, how he took the key from Larry's hand and went into the rectory, and how he hung the key on the key rack. He explained how cold he'd been, how he'd put on Larry's slippers, pants, and sweatshirt, and called 911. He even mentioned how nice the woman was on the phone. He tried to be as accurate as possible—except he said nothing about Larry's laptop and spiral notebooks.

Detective Maddox wrote things in a small black book, and when Paul stopped talking he looked back over what he'd written. Then he said, "These were on one of the key hooks." He held up a ring with three keys on it.

"Right," Paul said.

"But there was no single key, and you just said you took 'a *key*' from the vic...from your friend's hand."

"Oh...right," Paul said. "I mean...I'm sorry. Maybe I'm still a little confused. There were three keys, of course, but I just used one." He reached up and touched the key that he thought was a match to the one in his pocket. "I think this is the one to the back door."

"Uh-huh," Maddox said. "So...we'll be wanting to talk to you again, but right now they want to get you to the hospital so a doctor can check you out."

"Is that...do you think that's really necessary?"

Maddox shrugged. "A blow to the head...they have to check you out."

"What about my car? Will someone bring me back here to get it?"

"We'll be keeping your car for a time. There's blood...that is...it's part of a crime scene. You'll need a ride home from the hospital. Can you call someone?" When Paul nodded, Maddox took a business card from his pocket. "Call me tomorrow. Maybe I'll know when you can pick it up."

The detective left and the paramedic returned. He closed the rear doors and stayed with Paul, while his partner got into the front seat. The ambulance started to move forward, but there was a yell from outside, and it stopped. The rear doors opened again and Maddox leaned inside. He had Paul's gym bag. "We got into your car," he explained. "I see no reason to keep this."

Paul sat up and took the bag. "Thanks."

"Anything missing?" the detective asked.

Paul looked inside. "Everything's here, I think. My gym shoes, my cell phone and—"

"An officer found your wallet in the alley, too." Maddox held the wallet up. "Money's gone, but he left your credit cards." He dropped the wallet on the cart beside Paul's legs and backed out of the ambulance.

"Detective?"

"Yeah?"

"My wallet." Paul pointed at it. "Might there be fingerprints on it?"

The man stared at him for a second and then said, "The tech took a look at it. Nothing. We *do* know what we're doing, believe me."

"Sorry. It's just that...well, the man killed Larry for no reason, and I—"

"'*No* reason?' Try cocaine or heroin, or a bottle of wine." He shook his head. "A couple o' white guys...y'know...driving into this neighborhood? You look like money to some folks. You were taking a chance."

"But Larry...Father Landrew...he *lives* here. He's lived here for years."

"I'm just saying," Maddox said, "you gotta *think*. Use your head. Maybe if you'd worn your priest collar..." He closed the ambulance doors.

To Paul that sounded like the detective thought that what happened was his own fault...his and Larry's.

†

"So," Paul asked, "are we in that big a hurry?" The ambulance had just careened around another corner, engine roaring, siren screaming.

"That's Potocki, Father. He loves to drive like a life depends on it. But you're gonna be fine."

"What hospital are we going to?"

"The County, Father, that's the closest trauma center." He paused, then said, "I got a cousin who's a priest, y'know? Or at least he used to be. Married a young widow in the parish, and got three kids now. I suppose you don't approve of that, though."

"Well, not for me to judge. I bet he's a good parent."

"Yeah, he is...I guess. When he's not drinking, y'know, and when— Oh, here we are." The ambulance had turned and headed up an incline. When it stopped on level pavement again he said, "End o' the line. Everybody out."

Paul would have walked, but the paramedics insisted he lie on the cart while they took him into what O'Brien called "the County." Paul knew that meant Cook County Hospital, which had been taking care of poor people at that location since right after the Civil War. In about 2001, a new, state-of-the-art facility had been opened on the site, and the Cook County Board renamed the place the "John H. Stroger Hospital," in honor of—no surprise—the president of the Cook County Board. The man had since died and, because he'd managed to remain unindicted to the end, his name stayed. The paramedics, though, as they wheeled Paul in on the cart, agreed that for them the place was still "the County."

They pushed through doors marked *EMERGENCY ONLY* and, after O'Brien huddled momentarily with a small Asian woman in a lab coat, they bypassed the crowded waiting room and took him straight into an examination area.

"Don't I have to wait?" Paul asked, as they wheeled him into a curtained-off space. "Or sign in or something?"

"That's taken care of," O'Brien said. "They got our report and all your info. Plus, the nurse in charge? Me and her been knowin' each other for years. She's from the Philippines, and she's more Catholic than the pope. I told her you're a priest, and here we are." He gave Paul a conspiratorial wink. "Still works sometimes, right Father? Even these days."

"I guess so. But really, I'm not hurt so bad. Maybe someone who's worse off should—"

"Look," O'Brien said, "it's a done deal. I put the word in." He nodded solemnly, and Paul could tell he was feeling like a man who knew how to get things done. "They'll treat you right."

As opposed, Paul wondered, to how they'd treat some *ordinary* person?

†

They left him alone in a room as big as his own bedroom, lying on an examining table. Two of the walls were curtains pulled closed. Along a third ran a long empty countertop and above that were cabinets.

He sat up. The place was bright and modern-looking, and smelled of cleaning materials and alcohol. On the wall behind the head of the examining table, there was a large panel with about a dozen receptacles for plugging in various medical gadgets. He moved his head from side to side, stretching his neck. His headache wasn't quite so bad, but the pain in his side, where the man had kicked him, was worse than ever. He wondered if he had any broken ribs, and lifted his sweatshirt—Larry's sweatshirt. There was an ugly, dark purple bruise on his side.

He unzipped his gym bag to get out his cell phone, then decided he didn't feel up to talking to anyone. He noticed he had two messages. Both had the caller's number blocked, and he was sure they were from Ann Swanson. He had no number for her and couldn't have called her back even if he'd wanted to, which he didn't.

He sat and waited. His toes felt cramped and he realized he still had Larry's slippers on. He took them off and put them in his bag, and dug out his gym shoes and some sweat socks—not a clean pair, but his own—and put them on. He had a sweatshirt of his own in the bag, too, and a baseball cap. It would be cold out, and maybe still raining, so he could wear the cap and the two sweatshirts when he left.

He waited some more. Time passed slowly and he wished he had his watch. He could hear activity all around him: patients being wheeled past, doctors and nurses conferring in hushed tones, even occasional cries of pain. At the same time, it was surprisingly still inside his little enclosed area. He noticed a folder lying on a small wheeled table beside him and he picked it up, to give his mind something to do besides think about Larry...and the laptop hidden in the cabinet in his kitchen.

The folder was a brochure touting the hospital's new emergency room, and he was on page two when a young Hispanic man came in. His name tag said *Ruiz*, and he wore a white lab coat. His job was apparently to sign Paul up as a patient. Paul was happy he'd gotten his wallet back, because that's where his insurance information was.

Ruiz asked questions and wrote the answers down on a form on a clipboard, and then looked up and said, "A doctor will be with you pretty soon, but tell me how you feel now."

"My head aches, but no more than…you know…just an ordinary bad headache. And my side hurts, too. A lot." He lifted the sweatshirt to show the bruise.

"Uh-huh." Ruiz seemed surprisingly unimpressed. "What sort of pain? Does it come and go?" He was writing again on the sheet on his clipboard.

"It's a sharp pain, like broken ribs. And pretty much all the time, although it's worse when I breathe."

"Uh-huh. So…have you tried *not* breathing?" The man looked up from his clipboard, smiling at his own joke. "Your memory seems good. And your thinking? You don't feel confused?"

"I don't think so." Paul held up the brochure. "For example, it says here you serve a hundred-and-sixty thousand people in your emergency room a year, and I was able to calculate that as over four hundred patients a day. Sounds like an exaggeration."

"Really?" the man said. "Sounds low to me. But I'll put that down. Dr. Hasanali can check your math."

†

Dr. Hasanali was a woman with a beautiful smile and what sounded like an Indian accent. He was surprised when she announced that she was a Catholic, born in Goa. She seemed proud to be treating a priest, but she didn't waste time chatting. After going through much the same examination the paramedic had performed, she said he might have suffered a mild concussion. When she checked his scalp, though, she found no laceration or bruise, and wasn't even able to tell where he'd been struck without his indicating where the tenderness was.

He mentioned the pressure he'd felt on his neck before losing consciousness the second time. "I was in the army a couple of years before I went into the seminary," he said, "and I met a couple of Special Forces guys who claimed they could render a person unconscious that way—a jiu jitsu technique."

"This is perhaps true," she said. "But, if that happened to you, there is no sign of any damage. Do not exert yourself the rest of the day, and do not drive. And call your own doctor if you experience any dizziness, or if the headache increases."

She checked his ribs and, despite the pain, she didn't think he had any fractures. "We could take X-rays if you wish, but even so…there is nothing to be done for your ribs beyond rest and pain meds."

He declined the X-rays. He felt okay—as long as he didn't breathe.

TEN

She had talked to Otoe again after Dr. Salvo left. When she found out what had happened, she knew at once what needed to be done, and told him to do it. "Take Tree with you. Get inside as soon as it's clear." She told him the sorts of things to look for, and what to do if they found them.

She had lunch with Jessie in her room and, while Jessie was at physical therapy, she got another call from Otoe. "Mission accomplished," he said, meaning they'd found the obvious items and taken care of them. Still, someone would have to go back for a much more thorough search after dark, when there'd be less chance of interruption.

She still had to deal with Father Clark, convince him she knew nothing of the killing of his friend and fellow priest, but she decided to do Jessie's nails first, more to settle her own nerves than anything else. She hadn't finished the first hand when her cell vibrated. She was expecting the call, and she knew it wasn't Tree or Otoe. "Yes?"

"Is this connection secure?" he asked.

"Would I answer if it wasn't?" *What an asshole.*

"Have you heard about—"

"Of course I heard. Jesus, why wasn't I consulted on this?"

"Odd, isn't it?" he said. "What I expect from you are results. What I get is attitude. You weren't 'consulted,' because you're not in charge. I am."

"Uh-huh," she said. "And you think this morning was a good idea? How do you know what notes or records the guy left around for the cops to find?"

"It was a mugging. The police won't be thinking about notes and records." He paused. "And you'll see that no one else stumbles across anything."

"I'm already on it. But that stuff could be almost anywhere. Plus, how do you know he hadn't told other people what he saw?"

"Because you assured me that he hadn't."

"I said there's no *indication* he'd told anyone but Father Clark. And Jesus, I *need* Clark. So for God's sake, don't—"

"I'm not a fool. You still have him. And you better be sure he keeps quiet."

"Don't worry about that." Although *she* worried. "Look...sir," she added, "everyone knows you're not a fool." He *was* an asshole, though, and he'd let his inflated opinion of himself get him into a hugely expensive deal that could go bad in a heartbeat. Still, she had to back off a little. "I'll clean things up here, okay?" She tucked the phone between her ear and her shoulder, and started on Jessie's left hand. "You know I can handle problems, sir." He liked being called *sir.*

"What I know is that, when *this* problem came up, your proposal was to abort the mission and start over. I don't operate that way. As you can see now."

"Right. And that was your decision to make." A reckless, stupid decision by a man too worried about losing his deal to use good judgment. But she didn't say that. For Jessie's sake. Jessie, who wasn't even able yet to comprehend what her expenses were running. "I'll take care of things, sir. Relax."

"No," he said. "I will not relax. Losers relax."

"Yes, sir."

"Drop the ball on this and you'll never get another assignment anywhere, from anybody. Do you *get* it?"

"Yes," she said. "I get it. Good-bye, sir."

He was a bully, and he thought he scared her. Which was bullshit. She'd long ago stopped letting bullies—male or female—intimidate her. Her brother Walter had done her that favor.

†

Walter, two years older than she, had always picked on her. But when she entered adolescence, things took a frightening new turn. Foul remarks, lewd stares. He'd let his tongue hang out and grab his crotch. He'd even "accidentally" brush up against her. A bully. And a pig.

Turning to her spineless mother was useless. "Oh, Walter, stop teasing," her mother would say, and then walk away. And her father? He drove a truck and was seldom home. And was mean and usually drunk when he was.

She woke up every single morning scared of what Walter might say, or do. Until that hot summer Friday night—she was about to be a sophomore in high school, and he a senior—when everything changed.

She was home alone, her mother at the emergency room with little Billy and one of his scary asthma attacks. Walter was at the park playing basketball—which meant chugging beer after beer—and wouldn't be home for hours. She was in bed, reading, when suddenly—it wasn't even ten o'clock—she heard the front door slam. Walter was home, and she hadn't locked her bedroom door yet.

She was getting out of bed when her door flew open. It was Walter, sweaty and wild-looking, and she knew he'd been drinking, plus messing around with God knows what kind of drugs. "Go...away," she managed to say. But Walter stood there...between her and the door.

"Uh-uh." He pulled his t-shirt off and stepped out of his shorts, and she saw his pale skin where the sun never hit. "It's time you'n' me had some fun." He had on a jock strap and yanked it to the side and exposed himself. "I know you been wantin' to."

He spread his legs and cupped his scrotum with one hand, stroking himself with the other, making himself hard. She tried to scream, but had to swallow down the sour puke that rose in her throat.

He took his hands from his crotch and spread them out. "Can't take your eyes off it, right?" he said, swiveling his hips, waving it from side to side.

He lunged and grabbed at her. She leaned back, and he caught her gown and tore it open. He put his hands on her shoulders and tried to push her backwards onto the bed. And right then—when he actually *touched* her—that's when everything changed.

The vomit surged up again. She didn't fight it and it burst out of her mouth, splattering onto Walter's naked chest. "Shit!" he said, and when he looked down she charged into him and drove him backwards. She had his confusion, and her own panic, on her side. But more than that, she had hatred—furious, white-hot, pent-up hatred. She kept pushing him backwards toward the door, and he tripped on the little threshold board, fell on his back, and smacked his head on the wooden floor outside the room. She slammed the door and locked it, gasping for breath.

"Bitch!" Walter yelled. "Goddamn bitch!" But she heard him go away, down the hall toward the bathroom.

She lay awake all night, hearing her mother come home with Billy, and alternating between feeling very afraid...and feeling very proud of herself.

The next morning, Saturday, while her mother was downstairs washing clothes, she got a long, very sharp knife from the kitchen drawer. Walter was still asleep, his bedroom door closed and locked. He didn't know that she had a key.

The mess in his room—and the stink of stale beer and sweat—sickened her. She tiptoed among piles of dirty clothes across to his bed. Asleep on his back with his mouth open, he looked stupid and weak, and she wanted to spit in his face. Instead, she touched the point of the knife against the side of his throat. No reaction. She pressed harder and drew the point across his skin toward his ear.

He stirred then.

"Walter," she whispered, clamping her left hand hard over his throat and pressing down.

His eyes bulged open and she drew the knifepoint a little farther, pressing deep enough to break the skin this time, and then held the blade up in front of his face. There was blood on it. "Touch me again," she said, "and you better not ever go to sleep, *ever*. Because I will kill you. But first I will cut off that skinny little thing of yours and shove it down your throat." She said it just as she'd rehearsed it, and she meant every word.

A year later, Walter joined the army and she never said good-bye.

†

So…yes, she *did* "get it." She got it that she was tied up with a self-important asshole who'd overextended himself and stood to lose, not just this deal, but everything. She got it that he'd gone into panic mode and acted stupidly. But she also got it that he really *was* in a position to threaten her career and her future…and so Jessie's future as well…and that right now she needed him.

She took Jessie's hand in hers and gently stroked the pale skin. When the nurse came in and said it was time to leave, she leaned over and kissed Jessie's forehead and left the room.

ELEVEN

Paul left the ER with a prescription for some pain medication. By now his side hurt far worse than his head, but Dr. Hasanali had suggested he not take the pain killers that day, so as not to mask any possible change in his headache. "Rest and quiet, Father," she'd said, "that is the important thing for you today. No work. No stress."

Right, no stress.

On Mondays he usually got to the Pastoral Care Office at about ten o'clock. That meant he was long overdue. He considered calling in to explain his absence, but didn't. Certainly by now the cardinal would've already learned what had happened—either from the police or from someone at St. Manfred's. There might even be someone on their way to pick him up. He hoped not. He wasn't up to explaining over and over what had happened.

It was colder outside than before, and raining again. Paul was glad he had on the baseball cap—with the band loosened a notch so it wouldn't squeeze his aching head—and both his and Larry's sweatshirts. As he headed for the first in a line of waiting taxis he noticed a man in a camel hair coat get out of a black limo and walk toward the entrance to the ER. Although Paul couldn't see his face, the man seemed familiar somehow. His clothes and shoes looked way too expensive for "the County," and just as Paul decided he must be a doctor, the man turned his head. It was Hank Manion.

Paul looked away quickly, certain Hank hadn't seen him. He

hurried on to the first cab in the row, and got in. He really didn't feel like talking to anyone.

It really wasn't so surprising that Hank would volunteer to pick him up. When Hank wasn't out of town—which he often was—he not only served mass at the cathedral, but could often be seen around the Pastoral Care Office. He was something of an unofficial adviser to the cardinal on financial matters, and the two would often go to lunch or dinner at one of the private clubs Hank belonged to. He didn't neglect the others in the office either, occasionally having lunches delivered for the entire staff. He especially liked to hang around with the few priests on the staff, often treating them to Cubs or Bears or Bulls games, always in VIP boxes. The man could be irritatingly overbearing, but he had lots of money and was free with it. Clearly, he was generous with his time, too—like showing up here today—and Paul felt guilty for avoiding him.

He gave the cabbie the address of the rectory at St. Hildegard's parish. He lived there with Jake Kincannon, an eighty-seven-year-old retired priest with bad hearing and a small, yappy dog named Max. Both priests were officially "in residence" there; neither was the pastor. In fact, St. Hildegard's—with a big beautiful church, but few members these days—had no resident pastor. A priest who lived at a neighboring parish served as pastor of both places, meaning the headaches were all his.

It was a great arrangement for Paul because the drive from St. Hildegard's to the cathedral was just ten minutes in good traffic. His living quarters were plain, but comfortable enough, and he enjoyed the isolation and privacy, sometimes going days without seeing Jake. As an only child, whose father died when he was a toddler, Paul had grown up used to solitude...and sometimes wondered these days whether he'd grown *too* comfortable with it.

He sat back as the cab drove through the rain. He was exhausted, and might have fallen asleep if his side didn't hurt so much. Still, he closed his eyes and imagined how good a hot shower, or maybe even a bath, would feel. He might even take the doctor's advice and lie down for a while. And some fresh, clean clothes would—

The cab lurched to a stop and he was startled to see they were already in front of the rectory. He dug out his wallet to pay the fare… and then realized what he had to do.

"This isn't where I want to go," he called to the driver. "I changed my mind."

†

Because he'd already stopped the meter, the driver insisted Paul pay up that amount before he'd take him anywhere else. His English wasn't very good, but he made it clear he thought he'd picked up an oddball, and then got positively surly when Paul said he had no cash, and paid him with a credit card.

Paul could have gone in and showered and changed and been back on the street again in another cab, assuming he could find one, in half an hour. But he felt very tired and was afraid he wouldn't resist the impulse to lie down. He couldn't afford to do that.

They left St. Hildegard's and had gone just two blocks when Paul saw an ATM sign and had the driver stop while he got some cash. Back in the cab he gave the driver two twenties and they were on their way again. Cash in advance seemed best because he needed this guy on his side. It was always hard to get a cab in the rain, and probably impossible in *any* weather where they were going. And he'd need a ride back home.

When they got to Manfred Court there were no police cars parked on the street and Paul had the driver go down the alley to the rear of the rectory. Again, no police cars. No Toyota Corolla, either. Also no yellow police tape like you see on TV, and no CSI people crawling around in the rain with tweezers and plastic envelopes.

The cabbie refused to drive through the broken-down fence and pull close to the rectory, or even to wait in the alley. "If I wait," he said, "I wait in front. Is not good neighborhood."

"Okay." Paul gave him another twenty. "Wait for me out on the street. I'll only be a minute."

He got out and watched the cab drive away. He kept watching as it got to the end of the alley and turned right, when it should have turned left to go back to Manfred Court. He shook his head, feeling naïve for giving the guy the third twenty.

†

With gym bag in hand, Paul went up the back porch steps and pulled open the screen door, noticing again the repair Larry had made. He unlocked the inner door and repocketed the key he'd taken. *Stolen*, actually.

Is there a better word for my taking that key? Or for what I'm going to do now?

He went inside and down the short hallway into the kitchen. The set of three keys was gone from the hook beneath Saint Christopher, but if anything else had been removed or disturbed, it wasn't obvious. Looking around the neat, clean room he felt again the same sad awareness of sudden death. Just hours ago Larry had washed up after breakfast and carefully put everything away. Now he wasn't coming back, and things he'd thought worthy of attention—a hole in the screen, a mouse in the cupboard—were no longer important at all. Not to Larry. Not to anyone.

He was nervous and, at first, couldn't recall which cabinet he'd used. But the second one he tried was the one. And—*thank God*—the laptop and the notebooks were still there.

If he hadn't earlier removed his own gym shoes, sweatshirt, and cap—to wear them—the gym bag wouldn't have been big enough. It was still a tight squeeze, even after he remembered to take Larry's slippers out, but he managed to get the laptop and the books inside. He stood there, wondering whether he should look around any further for other Fair Hope notes Larry might have made. His inclination was to get out of there, in a hurry.

But it occurred to him that maybe he shouldn't take the notebooks and the laptop at all. He could look at them right here, right now, and see whether he found any references to Fair Hope Clinic. Then he wouldn't be stealing them, just looking at them. He decided the notebooks, at least, should be easy, and he took them back out of the bag.

There were three of them. Spiral bound, eight-and-a-half-by-eleven, one hundred pages each. Different colors, but otherwise identical. Two were filled from cover to cover, one side of the page only, with Larry's handwriting. The third was the same, but with three blank pages at the end. Paul was relieved to find that the books weren't a journal. He'd have felt even guiltier if he'd had to poke around in someone's confidential ramblings.

But no, what he found were jottings about things Larry saw, heard, or read about on a given day, nothing really personal. Sometimes there would be a little "S-T" in a circle in the margin, which probably meant Larry thought the item might be useful in a *Sun-Times* column. Other times there'd be an "H" in a circle, maybe indicating possible use in a Sunday homily.

The entries were all dated. Sometimes there were several days' worth on one page, and sometimes a day's notes took more than a page. Some days didn't appear at all. The most recent book started with May 26th of that year and ended with September 9th—a few days *before* Larry went to Guyana—and then the three blank pages.

So...no need to take the notebooks. He put them back with the stack of newspapers on the table. What about the laptop? Maybe easy; maybe not. He was already in a sweat. Should he take the time? Would there—

A noise at the back door stopped the mental whirlwind...stopped his heartbeat, too. Someone was coming inside.

TWELVE

"My God! Who are *you*?" The woman switched on the kitchen light. She was thirty-something, African-American, with light brown skin. She was obviously as startled as he was. "What are you *doing* here?"

She was attractive, but looked somehow frantic, as though she'd just missed a train she'd been running for. Water dripped from her wet, curly hair and from her shiny pink raincoat. From her right shoulder hung a large black handbag—actually a briefcase, he decided, or a computer case.

"My name is Paul Clark," he said. "*Father* Paul Clark. I was—"

"Clark? Father Clark? You're the one who was here when...when..."

She didn't finish, but stepped forward and pulled a chair out from the table—the chair Paul had stood on to unplug Larry's laptop cord from the ceiling fixture earlier that morning. She put her briefcase, which had the words *ST. MANFRED'S SCHOOL* printed on it, beside the stack of newspapers—and notebooks—on the table and sat down. She was crying.

Paul wanted more than anything to get out of there. But he couldn't just run away; he was trapped. He sat down across the table from her and put the gym bag on the floor beside him. Then he realized he was still holding the slippers, and he set them on the table.

"Those are Larry's," the woman said, wiping her eyes with a tissue she'd taken from her raincoat pocket.

"Yes," he replied, surprised she would know that, and surprised she said *Larry*, and not *Father Landrew*. "I was just...just going to put them back. That man who...the man with the gun...he took my shoes. I came inside and called the police, and I saw Larry's slippers, and I wore them to the hospital." He couldn't stop talking. "I was just returning them when—"

"Please," she said, with a sad smile, "I'm not *accusing* you of anything."

"Oh." He told himself to stop acting like a guilty person.

"I just said they were Larry's slippers. I know, because I bought them for him."

"I understand," he said, thinking it seemed like a rather intimate kind of gift. "So...I guess you work at the school?"

She nodded. "I'm the principal." Suddenly her eyes widened. "Oh, I'm sorry, Father. My name is Celia Jackson. Celia *Landrew* Jackson. I'm Larry's sister."

"His...sister?" He'd heard Larry had a sister, but he'd never met her. If he'd been over-talkative before, he was tongue-tied now.

"I know what you're thinking," she said. "I'm black...he's white. Actually, I'm his *half*-sister."

He felt embarrassed, and stared at the slippers sitting on the table. "I...I can't tell you how sorry I am about Larry." When she didn't answer, he looked up and saw that she was crying again. "But now," he said, "I really should be going." He grabbed the gym bag and stood up. "I took a cab back here because...to ask the police about getting my car back. But they were gone. And my car, too. So I asked the cab to wait and I came inside to...to return Larry's slippers." Another lie, but what choice did he have? "So I should go now."

"There's no cab out there," she said.

"No? Well, maybe he—"

"I'm surprised the police would leave the door unlocked." She turned and looked behind her. "There are usually keys on the hook there. Did you—"

"Oh...you mean the ring with the three keys? The police took them. A detective...Maddox."

"They didn't stay here very long," she said, apparently forgetting about the unlocked door issue. "Didn't do much of an investigation."

"I don't know about that. Maddox interviewed me and I told him everything I saw and heard."

"They didn't seem really interested. Just acted so...matter-of-fact."

"I know they searched for evidence. They found my wallet, and tried to get fingerprints from it. I mean...it was pouring rain when it happened. I don't suppose there was much more they could do. It didn't seem to me like they weren't interested."

"It did to *me*. I mean, the cops don't *like* Larry. It's those columns of his. He did a lot of his writing in the school office and he'd put stuff on CDs for me to print out. I'd see what he wrote, and tell him he should ease up a little. Then off he'd go to some community meeting and say the same things. Like how the cops are brutal, and don't do anything to stop the drug traffic—and even take a cut of the profits."

"Yes, well, Larry never backed down from—" He realized he should shut up. "I should go now." He took a step and the stabbing pain in his side took away his breath.

"You don't look so good," she said. "Your cab's gone. I'll take you home. Where do you live?"

"Near downtown...St. Hildegard's. But no, I'll call another cab." He reached for his cell phone.

"No. I'm not going back over to the school, anyway. Driving you home will give me something to do." She looked around, as though wondering where she was. "I don't know why I even came over here."

†

Paul waited at the bottom of the steps while Celia locked the back door, fumbling with her keys. He got in the passenger side of her car, a small Ford. There wasn't much headroom but at least he finally found the lever to slide the seat back.

She got behind the wheel, and again had trouble with her keys. He stared at her hands, stunned to see how badly they were shaking. After she managed to find the right key and get it in the ignition, she just sat there with her hands on the steering wheel and sobbed, tears streaming down her cheeks.

"Celia, where do you live?"

"I'll be okay in a minute," she managed. "I just—"

"Where do you live?"

"Near LaSalle and North Avenue. It's a tiny little apartment, too small for the two of us, but we—" She stopped and turned to look at him. "Oh, you mean is it out of my way to take you? It's not." She started the car, her hands still trembling.

He reached across and turned off the key. "I'll drive you to your place. It'll be easy to find a cab in that neighborhood, and I can get home from there in five minutes."

She gave in. They switched places and he put his bag—with Larry's laptop in it—on the seat behind him. He took the route she said was best at that time of day: north to Chicago Avenue, and then east. It felt good to be able to do something to help.

She cried for a while and, when that subsided, she said, "The police… they kept saying it was some neighborhood addict. But people in that neighborhood *loved* Larry. No one from around there would have hurt him." She burst into tears again.

When her crying eased again, Paul asked, "Are you going to be all right? Will your husband be home?"

"I don't…I've been divorced a long time."

"Oh, sorry. But I should take you somewhere else then. You should be with family."

"Larry…Larry *was* my family. That's it."

"Oh, well…maybe some friends. Maybe a doctor can give you something to help you relax…or sleep…or…or I guess I don't know what."

"I'll be okay. Really. I have a friend, a roommate. She'll be home from work by the time I get there."

Neither of them said anything more the rest of the way. She lived in an apartment building, maybe ten or fifteen stories high, and directed him to her space in a parking lot in the rear. He parked and grabbed his gym bag and walked her to the entrance. She thanked him, and went inside.

He walked to LaSalle Street and easily found a cab. He was glad he'd gotten Celia home safely, but on the ride to St. Hildegard's it struck him that he hadn't said much of anything to console her. Nothing about God, or faith, or prayer. Worse than that, she had no family and he hadn't even offered to help her with the funeral arrangements. What kind of priest *was* he?

But he knew the answer. He was a priest who lied—to his friend, to the police, and now to his friend's sister.

THIRTEEN

It was three-thirty when Paul finally climbed the front steps of the rectory at St. Hildegard's. He felt dizzy and faint. He hadn't eaten since the previous night. His head ached and the stabbing pain in his side made him wish he didn't have to breathe. He was carrying a corned beef sandwich and some chocolate chip cookies he'd bought at the deli around the corner...and a laptop he'd stolen from his dead friend's kitchen.

He stepped inside the door and, as always, was met by two things: the stale, musty odor of a house not much used, and the sound of Max yapping wildly from upstairs.

On the first floor only the kitchen—way in the rear—got any use these days, while hardly anyone ever set foot in the dining room or the various offices and meeting rooms in the front. The entire third floor of the building wasn't used, either, because both priests lived on the second floor, with Paul in the rear and Jake Kincannon in the front—with Max. Just what mix of breeds Max was, nobody knew, since Jake had gotten the mutt from a shelter. He weighed maybe ten or fifteen pounds, and what he lacked in size and social graces he made up for in good ears and powerful vocal cords.

Max's frantic barking when Paul came home never bothered Jake, probably because the sharp yaps were among the few things Jake could actually hear. "Good boy!" he'd yell at Max, nearly as loud as the barking, and then he'd open his door and yell down the stairs, "That *you*, Paul?"

"Yes!" Paul would scream back. "It's me!"

"Good! Catch up with ya later!" And the door would close.

Whatever catching up later they did was usually in the kitchen, where the two saw each other briefly over coffee and toast some mornings, and ate supper together a few times a week. The suppers happened if Paul brought something home, or if Jake was inspired to prepare a frozen entree, or if the woman who came in once a week to clean brought them leftovers. Even on those occasions, though—which Paul endured because Jake clearly relished them—the conversations were mostly monologues, with Jake going on at high decibel about something he'd seen on TV, usually the news or some sports event.

Jake's fading capacities might have depressed Paul, reminding him that we're all headed down the same road, except that Jake was still so active and upbeat. Heat or cold, rain or snow, he walked Max at least three times every day. He stayed up with current events, too and, despite what Paul saw as bad news pressing in from all sides, the older priest's faith and hope for the future of the world, and the church, rivaled those of a ten-year-old Cubs fan.

Jake must have been napping just then, though, or watching TV with the volume high through his earphones, because he didn't holler down, despite the barking. Paul went to the stairway and called, not very loudly, "It's me, Max," and the dog quieted at once.

Paul knew he had to eat something before he collapsed, so he went down the hall to the kitchen and made a meal of the corned beef sandwich and a pot of fresh coffee. As for the chocolate chip cookies, he left them in the center of the table. They were for Jake—his favorites.

Finally, he headed for the second floor where, like Jake, he had three rooms: a study, a small bedroom, and a bathroom. He was home, and glad to be there.

There were two messages for him on the rectory voice mail. One was from a TV reporter who wanted to interview him. The other was Hank Manion. "I'm here at the hospital to pick you up, but it looks like I missed you. Sorry. But glad to hear you're okay. If there's anything I can do, Father, anything at all...give me a call. I'm here to help. Meanwhile, you get some rest."

He took a long, hot shower. After that he didn't dare lie down for fear he might sleep until morning. Instead, he sat in his recliner, wondering what he would do if he found Larry's column on the laptop.

†

It was nearly six o'clock when he woke up to hear Jake and Max out in the hall, obviously returning from a walk. He dragged himself out of his chair and went to the desk. He phoned the Pastoral Care Office and left a message that he wouldn't be in the next day, and called the cathedral rectory to say he wouldn't be saying mass, either. Finally, he cleared a space on his desk and turned his attention to the laptop.

No password was needed to access the files and he was encouraged by how easily he found a folder labeled *Sun-Times.* He opened it and found about twenty of Larry's columns. They started with July of the previous year—about the time Larry said someone had given him the computer—and ended with one published just before Larry went to Guyana. Nothing more.

He was sure he'd read all of the columns when they'd originally appeared in the paper, the first and third Tuesdays of the month. He scrolled through and looked at a few at random. They seemed to be in their final form. No working drafts, outlines, or preparatory notes for any of them. So it must have been Larry's practice to type a column, rework it until he was satisfied with it, then print it out and mail it in—by US mail, not email.

He closed the *Sun-Times* folder and, one by one, opened the only other folders he found. One, labeled *Hom,* held about a year's worth of Sunday homilies. Another, labeled *LetEd,* held ten or fifteen letters Larry had written to various publications. The third, labeled *Fun,* had just one item, a very sketchy outline of a funeral service. That's all there was.

Paul didn't have a clue how to look for any hidden files, but Larry wouldn't have known how to do anything like that, anyway. He couldn't be bothered learning much about computers, which was why he refused to get email or Internet service.

Mystified, Paul opened the *Sun-Times* folder again, as though what he was looking for might have magically appeared in the interim. It hadn't, and he wished he could feel relieved at that. But Larry had said his Fair Hope column was "pretty much ready to send to the *Sun-Times*."

So dammit, Larry, where—

The rectory phone rang. It startled him and he grabbed it and answered right away…and wished he hadn't.

"Why aren't you taking my calls?" It was Ann Swanson.

"Oh," he said, "sorry. I've had my cell phone off."

"Why would—hang up and turn it on."

He did, and it rang at once.

"So what did he say?" Ann asked.

"You don't know what happened? It must be on the news. Larry's dead. I was there."

"What are you talking about?"

"A man with a gun, behind Larry's rectory. He wanted our money and he…he shot Larry. And he died."

"What were *you* doing there?"

"It was raining and I drove—" He stopped. "I don't feel like talking about it now. I don't feel well. Anyway, it's over. He can't say anything now, and you'll be out of Fair Hope soon. So it's over."

"How do you know he didn't tell someone else what he saw?"

"I don't know that at all. I *do* know that he said he hadn't sent his article in to the *Sun-Times* yet."

"He hadn't sent it *in*, but did he *write* it? Where is it? Did he make any notes about it?"

"I don't…I mean he just said he… Look, I don't really feel so good. The man with the gun…he kicked me, and hit me on the head, and I went to the hospital, and…and I can't talk about all this right now. I just can't."

"Okay." He was sure he heard her sigh, before she said, "Keep your phone turned on and keep it with you. I'll be in touch."

"In touch? About what? We—" But she'd already hung up.

It struck him that it hadn't taken her five seconds to recognize that

Larry's death didn't necessarily mean that the evidence of what he'd seen had died with him. Ann didn't need to see a computer sitting on Larry's kitchen table to remind her that he might have written his column already, didn't need a stack of spiral-bound books to remind her he might have left notes. And right now, wherever she was, she was considering what to do about those possibilities.

He could have told her about the notebooks, about taking the laptop. But he didn't. He was tired and confused, and he wasn't sure he wanted her to know what he'd done. He didn't like her, didn't trust her.

He stared down at the computer and was about to turn it off when he thought of something. It had a CD drive. He opened the drive... and there was no CD in it.

Even his good ideas got him nowhere.

FOURTEEN

Paul sat at his desk and tried unsuccessfully to concentrate. Larry's laptop revealed nothing. The problem crying out for attention now was what to do with it.

Instead, though, the tape in his mind kept replaying Larry's murder. *Why did this terrible thing have to happen?* The question, of course, led nowhere. Events happen, and human beings scramble around trying to make sense of them, looking for causality. *Why did Grandma have to die of lung cancer? Because she was a life-long smoker. Why didn't she quit smoking? Because she couldn't. Why couldn't she? Because…*

Push back far enough and…according to believers, anyway…you got to the "uncaused cause" of everything. *It's all God's will.* So…*Grandma died because God wanted her not to be able to stop smoking, and to get lung cancer, and to die.* Or… *Larry was murdered because God wanted him to forget he had no cash, and to enrage a crazy man, and to get shot in the face.*

Which made no sense. Or, in other words: *No one knows why.*

†

He stood up, switching off his desk lamp as he did, and was surprised at how dark the room became. Had he dozed off again? He must have. He moved to the window. The sun was down and the street lights were on. The rectory fronted a narrow, one-way street, with cars parked on both sides, but there was no moving traffic now, at nearly seven o'clock. The rain had finally stopped and a breeze ruffled the shimmering leaves that still clung to the young trees in the parkway between the sidewalk and the street.

The neighborhood had begun to burst into new life recently. Lots of money pouring in, and the excitement money carried with it. Yet, despite the muffled urban noise that floated always in the background—buses rumbling, sirens wailing, horns honking—on this short side street it was very peaceful. The only person in sight was a tall, bent man shuffling along the sidewalk, wearing a long shabby raincoat and a hunting cap with earflaps hanging down, pushing a grocery cart full of puffed-up garbage bags stuffed with his belongings.

A new one, not one of the regulars. But if the guy stuck around for a while, one of these days he'd notice the brass sign that said *RECTORY*, and ring the doorbell. If Paul was home he'd go down and the guy would ask for money, and Paul would dig out his wallet and hand him a McDonald's coupon, or some cash. He struggled to treat such men—and the rare woman—with respect, tried to talk to them a little, but nine times out of ten that was hopeless. It was food or liquor they wanted, not conversation. They'd mumble something and shuffle away, leaving Paul wondering whether he'd really done them any good.

The man passed out of sight, and Paul stood in the dark room looking down on the quiet street. He realized that his thinking for the past half hour had been a lot like his prayers, his mind flitting from one thing to another. Worse yet, he wasn't sure at all that the question that started it—*Why did this terrible thing have to happen?*—had even been primarily about Larry...how Larry's life and future were snatched away. How much of it was about himself...his own life, his own future?

While Larry lay dead on the concrete, Paul's primary concern had been that word of Ann Swanson's operation at Fair Hope might get out. When he took Larry's key, and when he went back for the laptop and the notebooks...it was to keep that from happening.

When he was ordained he'd thought all he wanted was to be an ordinary parish priest, but—and it happened surprisingly quickly—he developed bigger ambitions for his role in the church. He told himself that his desire was to serve God's people, to build God's kingdom, but even then he would occasionally wonder how much his dreams had to do with God's work, and how much with ego. And now? Now things were even more complicated. Now he had Robert's future to think about, too.

He turned away from the window and, although he longed to go to bed, he went across and sat down at his desk again. In the dark.

What to do with Larry's laptop? It contained nothing harmful, and both his weary mind and aching body told him to stuff it in a garbage bag and toss it in the dumpster in the alley. But he knew that was unwise. Sooner or later *someone* would be looking for it, and might ask him about it. The police might not be interested, but Celia would know it ought to be there...and would tell them it was missing.

He could call her—or maybe even call the police—and make up some explanation for why he had the laptop, and ask what do to with it. Then he wouldn't have to live in fear of someone later confronting him about it. But what innocent-sounding story could he concoct? Besides, Ann Swanson had already brought up the issue with him. She was almost sure to find out if he told Celia or the police he had it, so maybe he should tell Ann, and ask *her* what to do. Except he didn't really like Ann, didn't trust her, and certainly didn't like the idea of inserting himself any deeper into whatever she and her people were doing.

He could go back and forth about this decision forever, he thought, but the answer was unavoidable. The laptop had to go back to where it belonged, with no one ever knowing he'd taken it. And, as exhausted as he was, it couldn't wait until morning. Tomorrow the police might be back there. And even if they weren't, *someone* would be.

†

Renting a car at seven o'clock in the evening in the heart of the city was surprisingly easy. Using first the Internet and then the phone, Paul found a rental agency on Lake Street, near Madison. They said the sort of car he wanted, a mid-size sedan, would be ready for pickup in about an hour. He was afraid if he napped he wouldn't wake up until morning.

To fill the time he put on a pair of handball gloves and, with a clean t-shirt, did his best to wipe away any trace of fingerprints he might have left on Larry's laptop. He wasn't sure why he thought the police might look for fingerprints. But he *was* sure that methodically removing his prints made him feel like a true criminal.

Then he dressed all in black—no stretch for his wardrobe—substituting a black windbreaker for his suit coat. He wore a Roman collar, too, remembering what the police detective had said about going into the neighborhood around St. Manfred's. Also, if someone actually caught him going in Larry's back door at ten o'clock at night, his being a priest—and looking like it—would lend him an air of legitimacy.

He left the cell phone on his desk, despite Ann Swanson's directions to keep it with him. He didn't want her calling him while he was doing something he didn't want her to know about.

He was about to leave when he suddenly remembered that Jake Kincannon must be worried about him, so he called the retired priest on the intercom. That buzz was so loud that Jake couldn't miss it, and it was easier to talk to him that way because he could set his receiver to a high volume. Usually, like tonight, Paul could hear the old guy just about as well through their two closed doors as through the phone. "I didn't know you were back yet," Jake shouted. "Poor Father Landrew, God rest his soul. I saw all about it on TV. But, hey, you all right?"

"Just tired," Paul said. "But I'm pretty psyched up, so I'm going out to get some fresh air. Then maybe I can sleep."

"Hey, ya want a sleeping pill?" Jake asked. "My doc gives me free samples of everything. I got more damn pills than Walgreens."

"No, that's all right. The ER doctor gave me a prescription." Which he remembered he hadn't had filled.

"Yeah? Well, okay. Catch ya tomorrow. And hey, I gotcha in my prayers, kid."

A common thing for Jake to say, almost a throwaway line. But that night, as he trotted down the stairs with his gym bag, Paul was surprised at how comforting those words were.

†

The front door had a small window of one-way glass which Paul, out of habit, glanced through before he turned the deadbolt key. The homeless man was standing by his grocery cart, out in the middle of the street, his face turned up toward the sky, his lips mouthing words that Paul couldn't hear.

He'll see the Roman collar, and he'll be the one guy in ten who wants to talk… to tell me his life story.

Paul turned and went down the hall, through the kitchen, and out the back door. With the storm having finally passed through, it was colder outside and he almost went back for a heavier jacket. But he was nervous and wanted to get his task over with, so he went out to the alley and headed toward LaSalle Street…and a taxi.

FIFTEEN

Even though he paid cash, Paul had to present his credit card at the rental agency to get the car. Funny how a thing like a paper trail—not to mention a Roman collar—looms large in your mind when you'd rather stay unobserved. Then he had to walk around the car—a blue Dodge Avenger—and sign a paper saying there were no dents or other damage.

"You'd be surprised the way some people lie, Father," the young man explained. "I mean, like, I know *you*, bein' a priest and all, wouldn't do that, but we still gotta go through all the bullshi— I mean procedures. Sorry."

"That's okay, but can we move along? I'm in kind of a hurry."

†

Driving through the west side that morning in the rain had made him a little nervous, but at nine o'clock at night—even with the rain over and so many people out on the street—he was terrified. And that made him ashamed. His fear labeled him a coward...maybe even a racist. He had a baseball cap on again and he tugged the bill down low. He didn't know how much harder that made it for some potential carjacker to tell that he was a white guy, but it made him feel safer. A little.

He'd often heard Larry say that when there were lots of people out on the street it was safer, not more dangerous. Maybe so, but the people Paul saw were mostly teenagers, laughing and shouting raucously, and he didn't feel safe at all. He noticed, though, that even when he stopped for red lights—doors securely locked, of course—no one seemed to pay any attention to him. He recalled Larry arguing once in a column that the whole racial fear thing was mostly in people's minds. Street gangs, of course, were violent, but Larry claimed that, aside from the damage to customers who ingested the drugs they sold, they were more of a menace to rivals threatening their market share than to the ordinary person on the street.

He was surprised to find himself calming down as he drove. *Nothing to fear but fear itself.* He made wrong turns twice, but they were easily corrected. When he finally drove past Manfred Court, he noticed several cars parked along the curb, something Larry had said was illegal. One of the things Larry used to complain about was how the simplest city ordinances went unenforced in neighborhoods where people had no money, and no clout.

He turned into the alley and drove past the rounded rear wall of the church, wishing he could stop obsessing about *Larry*, for God's sake.

He came to what Larry had called his "backyard" and drove in, bouncing over the rough pavement, splashing through puddles. He stopped near the porch in the little courtyard formed by the rectory and the church, and suddenly the fear rose up again, worse than ever. He peered out through the car windows in every direction. The dim security light that lit up the area around the porch made the shadows beyond its reach look even deeper and more ominous.

The safety of being inside a parked car was illusory. It hadn't protected them from the crazy man that morning. But still...he really didn't want to get out. He sat clutching the steering wheel, the motor running. He took the envelope containing the paperwork for the car rental from the seat beside him and tucked it under the sun visor. He looked in every direction, then backed the car away from the porch steps and turned it around so it was facing toward the alley. That way, when he came back out—he knew he'd be in a near-panic to get away—he could jump in and drive off in a hurry.

Finally, he switched off the ignition.

†

He stood on the porch, shifting the gym bag from his right hand to his left, and holding the screen door open with his elbow. Despite the cool night air, he was sweating. He dug his hand into his pocket and for a brief, terrifying instant, couldn't find Larry's key amid the coins. Then he had it. He unlocked the door and went inside and locked it behind him. There was a security chain, too, so you could unlock the door and open it a little and talk to someone. But he didn't need that and the chain looked pretty flimsy, anyway. He went through the short hall and was at the doorway into the kitchen before he realized that it wasn't as dark in the kitchen as it should have been. Light was coming in through the open door to the dining room.

He stepped back into the hallway by the back door and stood there, holding his breath and trying to remember. Had he and Celia left any lights on? He didn't think so, but he couldn't be sure. Maybe—

Thudding sounds, like footsteps on a carpeted floor, came from somewhere beyond the dining room. Quick steps, or...no, it was someone coming down a flight of stairs, and certainly not taking any special care to be quiet. Paul still had time to make it out the back door. Even if whoever it was heard him and ran after him, he'd be down the steps and into the car and gone before they could see who he was.

But if he ran away, he'd have to come back again later. He wasn't sure he had the nerve for that. Besides, there were no lights on in the kitchen itself, and maybe whoever it was wouldn't come into the back of the house. Maybe they'd go out the front door. He stood there in the hallway, barely breathing, and waited.

The footsteps reached the bottom of the stairs and for a few seconds Paul couldn't hear anything. Then he did. The person was in the dining room, coming toward the kitchen. Heart pounding, Paul stepped silently to the back door and twisted the dead bolt key. It wouldn't turn. He set his gym bag on the floor and fumbled with the lock as quietly as possible. Whether it was an expensive lock, or just an old one, he didn't know, but it had a little spring-loaded button he had to hold down while he turned the key knob.

By now the footsteps were already in the kitchen, but they kept right on going, through the kitchen and apparently into Larry's bedroom. Paul finally got the door unlocked, and if whoever it was would just stay in Larry's room, even for a moment, he could get out the door without being heard. But then, as he started to pull open the door, he heard something new. This time from outside. A car's engine, and the sound of its tires, coming from the alley toward the back of the rectory.

In a panic, he pushed the door closed again. But he had to know whether he was right, or if the car had just gone down the alley, so he slowly opened the door again, just a crack, and peeked out. The car's headlights were turned off and it was coming toward him, making its way slowly over the pot-holed concrete. It stopped, nose-to-nose with his rented Dodge. The new arrival was an SUV…a silver SUV. As the driver was getting out, Paul pushed the back door closed.

He didn't get a good look at the driver, just enough to know it was a large black man. He locked the door and slid the security chain in place this time, too…whatever that was worth against someone who really wanted in. Then he went to the kitchen doorway. The light was on in Larry's room, and someone was definitely moving around in there.

He moved into the kitchen and called out, but softly, "Hello?" He heard the tremble in his voice. "Can I come in? Is anyone home?"

"My God!" the answer came. Celia appeared in the door to Larry's room, wearing the same pink raincoat she'd had on earlier. "Father Clark! How did you get—"

"Shhh!" He held up his palm to quiet her. "I…there's a man outside." By that time he was over next to her, and he grabbed her arm. "We have to get out of here."

She yanked her arm away. "What are you talking about? What man?"

"I don't know." Their heads turned together at the sound of someone pushing and pulling on the back door.

"That's a heavy door back there," she said. "And it's obviously locked. We're safe, but we should call the—"

"Listen to me." Paul grabbed her by both shoulders and squeezed tight as she tried to twist away. Then she must have seen something in his eyes, because her own expression changed...from bewilderment to fear. She stopped struggling, and he let go of her. "It's an old door, and an old lock. It might not hold for long."

"We should call the police," she said. "They can—"

"Shh." He put a finger to his lips, and grabbed her arm again and pulled her close to the entrance to the back hallway. A scratching, scraping sound, metal on metal, came from the door.

"He's picking the lock," Paul whispered. "Let's go." He pushed her ahead of him and she didn't resist.

They were through the dining room and into the hall by the stairway, when he remembered. "Wait for me in front," he said. "I have to go back."

"No. You can't go—"

"I have to. I forgot something. Is your car out there?"

"Right in front, but—"

"Hurry! Go get the car started. Wait for me."

He ran back, through the dining room and the kitchen, and then into the back hall as quietly as he could. His gym bag lay on the floor by the door.

He could hear the man working on the lock and, just as he picked the bag up, he heard a slight click. The man must have overridden or disabled the spring mechanism because in the dim light Paul saw the dead bolt key turning. He grabbed it and turned it back, and felt resistance as the man tried to turn it again from the outside...but couldn't.

It was a momentary stalemate, but Paul couldn't stay there forever. When he let go the man would get the door open immediately. The security chain might delay him, but not for long. He tightened his grip on the gym bag, took a deep breath, and let go of the lock. The door opened, but the chain held and Paul ran, deliberately scattering mops and brooms and the vacuum cleaner down onto the floor behind him.

Passing through the kitchen he could hear the man throwing his body against the door. Paul ran through the dining room and was in the hall by the stairway when he heard the loudest crash of all, which meant the chain had torn loose from the molding and the door had flown open and slammed against the wall.

But he made it out the front door and found Celia's little Ford right by the curb, with the motor running and the passenger door open. He jumped in and she pulled away as he yanked the door closed. Holding the gym bag on his lap, he twisted around to look through the rear window, and saw a man burst out the front door of the rectory, stare for a moment at the departing car, then turn and go back inside.

SIXTEEN

Celia took a left at the corner, going way too fast, then fought to regain control of the car. When they were straightened out she asked, "What's going *on* here?"

"I don't know," Paul said. "But thanks...for waiting, I mean."

"I'd have called the police while I waited, but I left my phone at home. It's in my purse. I don't even have my driver's license. Do you have a cell phone?"

He'd left his at home, too, but all he said was, "I'd rather not call the police."

"What? Are you nuts?"

He remembered Larry asking the same question that morning, with the same tone of voice. "I just...I mean...by now that man is long gone, and we'd have to go back there with the police and stick around half the night explaining everything." His mind was whirling. In fact, he wasn't sure he wanted the man caught. It might have been someone Ann Swanson sent to look for evidence of what Larry had seen at Fair Hope. "I just don't think I'm up to that."

"But that guy will take everything that's not nailed down. He—"

"He had a pretty new car. Maybe he's not a burglar." As soon as he said that, he wished he hadn't.

"What?" She glanced over at him. "Then who would he be?"

"I don't know, but like I said, he won't be sticking around there and... Hey, you're driving pretty fast. You don't want to get stopped without your driver's license."

"Oh, right." She slowed down. They were headed north, taking the same route they'd taken earlier that day. "Tell the truth, there's not much in there a burglar would *want.* Only thing Larry had worth stealing was his laptop. That's what I went back for."

"His laptop? Why?" His heart skipped a beat. "That is, are you okay? Do you want me to drive?"

"I'm terrible, but I'm okay to drive. My roommate was home and I cried, and I ate some soup, and...anyway, I'm okay. Carol—that's my roommate—she had a date and she would have called it off, but I insisted she go ahead."

"You'd be better off not being alone."

"Maybe, but...well...Carol's sweet, but she's kind of talkative and... Anyway, I didn't want to watch TV. And I couldn't read...or sleep, either, so I thought I'd go back and get the laptop. Except for his car, that's the only thing Larry owned that's worth more than a few bucks, and we could use it at school. He got a printer with the laptop, but he already gave *that* to us. So there I was, when you came in and scared me to death."

"I thought *you* were an intruder," he said, grateful that the idea of going to the police had been dropped. "Larry told me the rectory's unused except where he...except for his room. It scared me to hear someone coming down the stairs."

"Yeah, well, I was looking for the damn laptop. Which was stupid 'cause there's nothing up there but musty old furniture. I never did find the thing."

"When I heard you on the stairs I was about to run out the back door to my car, but that's when that guy drove up." He stopped, considering how much to tell her.

"Why'd you come back, anyway?" Celia asked. "I don't get it. Larry's killed and you're attacked, and you come right back to the rectory as soon as you get out of the hospital. Then you go home, and then come back again...this time after dark."

"It's hard to explain. Like you, I couldn't sleep, and...I don't know."

"Yeah, well, if I had any sense I'd drive straight to a police station. But

I guess I'm kinda like Larry, not crazy about cops. Plus, he mentioned you to me a few times."

"Really. I hope he wasn't too...negative."

"Uh-uh, he liked you." She stopped at a red light. "Larry was a really good person, but he never had any close friends. He was always a loner. Plus, he was too...well...too *busy*. Finding some mother a place to live, and food for her kids. Or trying to get a teenager back into school, or out of jail, or *something*. Day after day...it never ended." She seemed about to cry again, but stopped herself and went on. "The thing is, he was also...well...kind of bitter. Disappointed with the church. And the government. And...well...it seemed like you were one of the few people with any authority that Larry seemed to respect."

"That's...nice to hear." In fact, it was *shocking* to hear. "But maybe," he said, "it's because I don't *have* much authority."

"Maybe." The light changed and she drove ahead, probably thinking he was being humble, when he was just stating a fact. "Anyway, that's why I'm willing to cut you some slack...to trust you."

"I...I don't know what to say."

"I know from Larry...and it was in the news, too...that you've got some big-time job at the archdiocese, that you're...I don't know... *vice*-something."

"Vice-Chancellor."

"That's it. Except I don't even know what a 'vice-chancellor' *is*."

"Yes, well, even at the Pastoral Care Office it's a little vague. But I'm...sort of an assistant to the cardinal."

"Anyway, Larry trusted you. But I still wonder, why *did* you go back there?"

"I...I'd really rather not say."

"Damn." They stopped for another light and he felt her attitude changing again. "Maybe I *should* go right to the cops, let *them* ask some questions. Like where you got your key. And why you told me the police took Larry's keys and left the door unlocked."

"First, it's true that the police took Larry's keys. And I didn't say they left the door unlocked. You assumed it."

"And you didn't correct me." She turned toward him. "Look, my brother was killed today. Murdered, by some damn…" She turned away, crying again.

He could think of no words to soothe her grief, so all he said was, "The light changed, Celia."

She jumped, then stepped on the gas too hard and they lurched forward. "Damn," she said, hitting the brakes and stopping. Luckily, there was no other traffic around.

"You know," he said, "I still think you should let *me* drive."

She wiped tears from her cheek with the heel of her palm, then nodded and pulled to the curb. They switched places for the second time that day. They drove in silence for a while, until she said, "I still want to know why you went back to St. Manfred's."

Paul knew he had to offer at least a partial explanation. "Okay," he said. "To start with, Larry and I played handball this morning. You knew that, right?"

"Yeah. Larry *loves* hand—I mean he…" She didn't finish.

"I hate talking about this just now, but you asked about it and… Anyway, Larry told me about a column he was working on."

He glanced over and saw her smile a little, although it was a sad smile. "Knowing Larry," she said, "he was giving someone hell."

"I *did* get the idea it was pretty negative. He wanted my thoughts on it. He wanted me to look at it before he sent it in." Not *exactly* true, but pretty close.

"But what does that—"

"Obviously, he didn't get a chance to show me. But I could tell it was important to him, and I knew he did his writing on a laptop, so while I was at the hospital I decided to go back and look for it, and see if I could find out what he'd had to say. I thought if I waited too long, someone else might get hold of the laptop, and might—"

"Oh, my God." He looked over again, and she was staring at him. "You wanted to make sure that if Larry wrote something bad about the church, it'd never get out."

"I didn't *say* that. I said he wanted my comments about something he'd written. That was his last request, and I wanted to see what it was. Maybe I could *do* something about…about whatever it was."

"But you couldn't find the laptop earlier today, right? Because I interrupted you. And wanting to know what he said was so important that you came back again, tonight, to look for it."

"Not exactly," he said. "The thing is, I *did* find the laptop, and—"

"What? Then where is—"

"Let me finish. I found the laptop. But then you came in and…well, anyway, I took it home to look at it. It wasn't password protected, so I was able to get in and find his columns. But the only columns I found were ones that had already been in the newspaper."

"But you said he wanted you to look at something he'd already written."

"That's what he said, but…anyway, there was nothing there. The problem is, I didn't find that out until I got home. But I had a key and I knew I had to return—"

"So you lied. You *did* take Larry's keys."

"No, like I said, the police detective took the set from the kitchen. I had another key…one I got from Larry. So…tonight I was returning the laptop." He took a breath. "See why I didn't want to go through all this with the police? It's too…complicated."

"It's bizarre, is what it is. You stole Larry's property. You invaded his private—"

"It *looks* bad, I know." And he'd *felt* like a thief and a snoop, too, when he did it. "But actually, I *borrowed* the laptop, with no intention of keeping it. I was only looking for what he'd already mentioned to me. But the trouble with telling all this to the police, just to explain why I was back there tonight, is…well…"

"Yeah, well, forget it," she said. By then they were only a few blocks from her apartment. "I don't want to spend the rest of the night with a bunch of damn cops, either. In the morning, after I see what damage was done, I'll call them."

"I think that's a good idea." Although he knew the police would want to know why she—and he, too—waited so long to call.

SEVENTEEN

She was in the airport, standing in the boarding line for her flight to Chicago. It broke her heart to leave Jessie, but no way would she try to handle the fallout from the priest's killing by long distance. She'd already booked her return flight for the morning, and if she didn't make it in time for the pre-op procedures, at least she'd be there when Jessie came out of the recovery room...unless they canceled surgery again. Either way, she'd be right back in Chicago again tomorrow afternoon. She'd have to catch what sleep she could during the flights.

Meanwhile, she waited in line, longing to collapse into her seat on the plane, but at least feeling confident that she was on top of things... and then Tree called.

"I went to look around," he said, "like you told me. But I didn't get a chance."

"Jesus, what happened?"

"Turns out I wasn't the only one poking around. There was a rental car behind the place. I figured I better see who it was, but I hadda pick the lock. They heard me, and got away out the front door. In a different car, not the rental."

"Damn! Who was it? Did they see you? Did they take any—"

"Wait. Let me finish. They didn't get a good look at me. There was two of 'em. One was your guy Clark."

"What? Where the hell was Otoe?"

"I don't know, but it was the priest, no question. He jumped in the car. I didn't see the driver. I got the plate number. I don't know for *sure* if they took anything, but the priest had a gym bag and the laptop was gone, so it's likely he had it. I didn't stick around. I'm a block away now, watchin' the place."

She stepped out of line and let the people behind her move forward. "And the cops?"

"Nothin' yet."

"Okay, sit tight awhile. Use your head. If the cops come, wait till they're gone. But whatever happens, you gotta get back in there. Tonight. Remember...discs, flash drives, notes, whatever. The school, too."

"Not the whole damn school, right? Just the office?"

"Right," she said. "He did a lot of his work there."

"Won't be time now to do it alone without leaving a mess. They're gonna figure it was the same person at the school as at the priest's house."

"Maybe. Look, I'm getting on the plane. Get hold of Otoe and tell him he fucked up. Tell him about the gym bag. Gotta go." She closed the phone.

The end of the boarding line was already through the gate. She ran to catch up, hurrying down the empty boarding bridge, smelling the jet fuel, longing to be back with Jessie, to comfort her and stroke her hand.

At the same time she wondered how badly she might have misjudged Father Paul Clark, and what she might have to do about that.

EIGHTEEN

At Celia's building Paul parked in her assigned spot, then turned to her and said, "About Larry's funeral…"

"I can't even *think* about a funeral."

"I know. But the cardinal will want something special. There's a woman at the Pastoral Care Office, Phyllis Conover, who handles these things." He took one of his business cards and wrote on it. "Here's her number. I'll tell her you're calling. She'll help with everything. Funeral home, mass, burial. Everything."

Celia stared down at the card he gave her.

"Talk to Phyllis," he said. "And don't worry about the cost, okay?"

They got out of the car and he took his gym bag from the rear seat.

When they reached the back door of the building he said, "I'll have to pick up my rental car in the morning, and while I'm there I'll stop over at the school. To see how you're doing." *And to look for any CDs Larry might have left lying around.*

"Yeah, okay." She unlocked and pulled open the door, then turned and said, "Oh, what about the lap—"

"That's okay," he said, already walking away. "I'll bring it with me in the morning."

†

He walked to LaSalle Street, surprised by his sudden reluctance to give up the laptop. It wasn't a reasoned decision. He'd gone to such trouble to return it...and then he didn't feel like letting it go.

He found a cab easily. During the ride he found one more thing to worry about—his finances. A car rental and three cab fares, all in one day. That was a stretch for his meager income.

Until recently, money hadn't been an issue. He never had much, never spent much. Yet, as a priest, he'd enjoyed a level of ease and security that few people had. He thought back to his first assignment, at a posh North Shore parish called Our Lady, Mother of Wisdom. He'd been surprised at how easily he fit in at "the Wiz," as they called it. He felt comfortable—maybe *too* comfortable—being around people with money. They had a certain easy confidence. And they could be surprisingly generous to their church and their priests...as long as the Sunday sermons didn't get too "political." Larry wouldn't have lasted there two weeks.

As they got closer to St. Hildegard's he realized that he was way too keyed up to sleep. He thought it might help to walk for a while, so he had the cabbie drop him a few blocks away. He walked along the dimly lit street toward the rectory, his mind still chewing over his years at the Wiz. So many of the parishioners there had been people of influence, and it was there that his ambition to get ahead in the church took shape. His next two assignments, first at the seminary high school, and now at the Pastoral Care Office, were positions he'd lobbied for, to put himself on the road to—

"Hey, man. How you *doin'*?"

He whirled around...and found himself caught in the classic urban nightmare.

A dark, deserted street in the middle of the night. Two street punks in baggy pants sagging low on their hips, cuffs dragging on the ground. These two happened to be Hispanic. One was Paul's height, but wider and heavier, with a shaved head and a stretched-out, oversized sweatshirt. The other was a couple of inches shorter, thin, in a black warm-up jacket and a White Sox cap so big it covered the tops of his ears. He had some sort of bird—maybe a gang emblem—tattooed on one of his cheeks. The two men could have been eighteen…or thirty. And the years had been hard ones.

"Um…hi," Paul said. "Can I do something for you?" Like a store clerk, he thought, as if he didn't know what they wanted.

The two men turned their heads and grinned at each other. "Man wants to know can he *do* something for us," the tattooed one said, and they both chuckled.

The big one pointed a crooked finger at Paul. "That thing 'round your neck, that mean you a priest?"

"Yes," Paul said. "At St. Hildegard's." He turned and pointed out the church and the rectory, taking the opportunity to look for anyone else on the street, or lights in any nearby windows. But nothing. "I've been to a meeting and I'm—"

"He's a priest," the tattooed one said, nudging his partner. "So he don' mean can he do somethin' *for* us. He means can he *do* us."

"Uh-uh, man," the big one said. "A priest don' wanna fuck me and *you* up the ass. We're too old." He stepped closer, and Paul smelled the sweet, acrid smell of marijuana. "That right?"

Paul turned to run away, but before he could take even one step he felt a huge arm wrap itself around his neck. The big man was very strong, and was cutting off Paul's breath. He probably could have broken Paul's neck if he wanted to, but he loosened his grip a little. "Give up your wallet, bitch. Or I stomp your faggot ass into the concrete."

Paul still held the gym bag with one hand, but with the other he pulled out his wallet. He thought if one of them had a gun he'd have shown it already, but so what? It was too late now to try to resist…even if there weren't two of them. His hand shook uncontrollably as he gave the wallet to the tattooed guy, and he knew they could tell he was terrified.

The man looked into the wallet, shook his head in obvious disappointment, but still slid the wallet into his jacket pocket. Then he ran his hands over Paul's body. "No cell?" he asked.

"No, I—"

"Shut up, fag head. What's in the bag?"

"Nothing. Just...you know...gym shorts and and socks and stuff."

"Give it to me."

"I told you. It's just—" The arm tightened around his neck again, and he gagged and dropped the bag.

The tattooed man grabbed the bag and lifted it. "A little heavy for 'gym shorts and socks and stuff.'" He shook his head. "Let's get outta here, man. These lyin' church people fuckin' make me sick."

The arm around Paul's neck dropped away, and as he stood gasping for breath he suddenly felt hands slide under his armpits from behind. He was lifted off his feet and whirled around through the air like a child. He was spun around twice, maybe three times, his legs stretched out by centrifugal force. And then, when the man let go, Paul flew a few feet, and landed square on his rear end on the concrete, jarring every bone in his buttocks and up into his spine.

He squeezed his eyes shut, but that did nothing to ease the pain he felt all over his body, so he opened them. The sidewalk was empty and it took a second to get his bearings and realize he was facing the wrong way. He struggled to his feet, feeling as though his muscles were tearing loose from his ribs. Supporting himself with his hand against the brick wall of the building beside him, he turned around.

There were the men. Walking. They may have run at first, but now they weren't even bothering. Still, they were half a block away already. With his wallet and his gym bag...and with the laptop he'd have left with Celia, if he'd been thinking straight.

NINETEEN

Paul didn't have the cell phone and, even if he could have called 911, those two would be long gone by the time the police arrived. He wanted to sink back down to the sidewalk and let them go their way. But Celia knew he had Larry's laptop. If he showed up tomorrow without it, she—and maybe the police—would think he'd destroyed it for some reason. He had to get it back. He wasn't helpless. He forced himself to run.

His breath came in short, hard gasps, each inhalation like a knife stabbing into his bruised side, each step on the concrete sending a new shock of pain into his tail bone and up through his spine. He was in decent shape, though, and his legs were still strong. He'd been a long distance runner in college, and knew that few people could actually run very far... not like in those TV chases, where they went block after block, up and down fire escapes and across rooftops. Even if the two muggers heard him coming, and ran, he had a decent chance to catch them.

They were getting close to the corner and he was still thirty yards back. He could hear traffic noise two short blocks away, and even distant sirens. But on this dark street there were only the three of them. Or four, actually. The homeless man was still down at the corner, shrinking back from the two men, hunched over his grocery cart, safeguarding his belongings.

Paul tried to run silently, but one of the men finally heard him and glanced back. They both stopped walking and turned around. They were clearly surprised to see that he kept on coming, and seemed unsure whether to run away or stand and wait.

He slowed to a walk, but kept moving toward them. "I need that gym bag," he said.

It may have been the tremble in his voice, or the fact that they were two against one, but they glanced at each other and reached their decision. They came at him.

Or they *would* have.

The homeless man was suddenly there—as though he'd magically materialized—right behind the two. He was taller than he'd seemed, and held his right arm high up in the air. He swung the arm down very hard, at an angle, and the side of his fist slammed into the heavyset man's neck where it met his shoulder, and the man sagged to his knees. The tattooed guy turned, but the homeless man grabbed his wrist and swung it up and behind him in a way that might have torn the arm from its socket.

But then he slowly, even gently, brought the man's arm forward and down again, and stood beside him, still holding onto his wrist. "Okay, *mi amigo*," he said, in a surprisingly friendly tone of voice, "now you can hand the *padre* here his bag."

"Yeah? And *you* can kiss my fuckin'—" His arm flew up and over his head again and was yanked down hard and fast, behind his back this time, and Paul could tell from the sickening crunch that either the arm was dislocated or the shoulder broken.

"The bag, *amigo*," the homeless man said, letting go of the wrist. "The bag."

Tears ran from the tattooed man's eyes as he reached down with his good arm and picked up the gym bag he'd dropped, and handed it to Paul.

"And now his wallet, too."

The man pulled the wallet from his pocket and gave it to Paul. Then, clutching his left arm to his side with his right hand, he turned away, maybe so they wouldn't see him crying.

Paul slid the wallet into his pocket and backed slowly away. "Thank you," he said to the homeless man. "Were you—"

"Go home. And forget any of this happened." He turned to the heavyset one, who was just getting to his feet, his head tilted to one side as though trying to touch his ear to his shoulder. "And you, *cabrón*, take your little friend away. It's all over here."

"I understand," the big man said. "All over...'cept the part where you go to the priest's place and you suck each other's dicks."

The homeless man stared at him, shaking his head in disappointment. "My, oh my," he said, and reached behind his back and came out with what looked like part of an antenna broken off a car.

"Wait!" Paul said, but the antenna whipped through the air and slashed across the man's face and left a dark line of blood, then came back from the other side and opened a new gash on that side. The man cried out, dropped down to his knees again, bowed his head and covered it with his hands. But the lashes kept landing... shredding the skin on his hands and the back of his neck.

"Stop!" Paul yelled. "Please, you're hurting him."

The man stopped. He turned and looked at Paul. He still wore the cap with the long bill and the flaps hanging down over his ears. "This gentleman," he said, "needs to learn to do what he's told. And not to talk so much." He paused and watched the bleeding man get to his feet and stagger away. "And," he said to Paul, "so do you. I told you to go home...and to forget all this."

Paul turned and left, and didn't look back.

He was shivering, and his back and side hurt as he climbed the stairs to his room. He felt sick to his stomach. What sort of fifth dimension had he crossed into? There was no way he could explain what was going on, and no one to explain it to, even if he could. He felt very helpless, and very alone.

TWENTY

Max may have barked when Paul went inside and up the stairs, but Paul never heard him. He was too drained, too confused, too *afraid.* It was only when he opened the door to his room that he heard his cell phone ringing. It was on the desk where he'd left it. He rarely got a call after ten p.m., and then it was always Ann Swanson.

He didn't want to talk to Ann, or to anyone else, but his caller ID wasn't blocked, so it wasn't Ann. "Ames Beaumont" was calling. He didn't recognize the name, or even the area code, but he was afraid he knew who the caller must be. "Hello?"

"It's me."

"Yes, I thought it might be. Where are you, Robert?"

"I'm right here."

"Where is *here*? Where's Area Code 419?"

"What? Oh...I don't know. I'm using somebody's cell phone. I guess that's his number."

"Is something wrong?" It was way too late for Robert to call, and he wasn't supposed to have access to a cell phone. Still, Paul couldn't help feeling happy to hear his voice. "How's everything going?"

"I can't stay here anymore, man." So it seemed that at least he hadn't run off.

"You *have* to, Robert. You know that."

"I can't. I mean...these people, they're too...anyway, I can't stay here."

"Who is Ames Beaumont?"

"No one. I mean, he's one of the other prisoners."

"You're not 'prisoners,' Robert. You're students."

"We're just *like* prisoners. And if I *have* to stay here, what's the diff—"

"Robert, you've *been* a prisoner, and you know how much worse that was." Young people had such short memories. "And you have to stay hidden…at least for a while…so you don't end up right back where you were."

"I don't know about that. I been asking around, looking on the Internet, and I don't think they can come and get me now that I'm back here in the US. Plus, you're the one got me out, so the government won't let—"

"'Asking *around*?' You're not telling anyone what happened, are you?"

"No, no, no," Robert said. "I'm just asking, like, theoretically."

"Look, I told you to never even hint at what happened. And I'm telling you now that it *is* possible. You *could* be taken back down there and locked up again. We have to let some time pass." There'd been no sign anyone was looking for Robert, but fear was the only motive Paul could think of to persuade him to stay in the boarding school Paul had found for him. "You have to be careful for now."

"Yeah, but this place sucks."

"It's only temporary." He needed Robert out of sight until he could figure out how to deal with this whole new part of his life. He knew that by now he should have told Robert he was his father, but he hadn't figured out how to do that. For one thing, he'd been looking for some sign that Robert had anything but negative feelings and opinions about him. "I'm serious, Robert, don't believe what you hear from friends, or what you read on some Internet site."

"Yeah…well…it's like being in jail here again, man. 'Do *this*. Do *that*. Don't be *late*.' I mean, I can't even have my own fucking computer, and that's like my favorite thing. That's what I *do*, man, mess with—"

"Robert?"

"What?"

"Calm down, would you please? What is it you're upset about?"

"What *is* it? Every…fucking…thing. That's what."

"Tell me." Paul ignored the language. "What is it…exactly…right now?"

"It's that creep Fredericks. He told me yesterday I could go into town in the van today, and then he wouldn't let me. It's not fair. He says one thing and does another."

"Did Mr. Fredericks say why he changed his mind?"

"I don't know. I mean. . .yeah. He said I had to go to detention instead."

"And why the detention?"

"He said 'cause I slept in this morning. But that sucks. I mean, he didn't give me a warning. They should give you a warning and then if you do something they can do what they said in the warning, y'know? But he didn't, and—"

"The rulebook says you get up at five-thirty, right?"

"Yeah, but—"

"And it says the second time you don't get up, you get detention after class, right? So this must have been your second time, right?"

"Yeah. . .well. . .it's the second time I got caught. But still, they should, you know, tell you what they're gonna do." His tone said he knew he was wrong, but he wasn't about to give up. "I mean, first he says I can go into town and then he makes me go to detention. Says I have to wait till Wednesday to go into town. That sucks."

"That's just the day after tomorrow."

"Yeah, I know," Robert said. "And it sucks."

Paul thought he heard thunder over the phone. "Is it raining there?"

"Yeah. All afternoon. It still is. That sucks, too."

"So. . .there you go. Wednesday will be a better day to go into town, anyway."

"Yeah, but that's not the point. They should—"

"The point is, they want you to obey the rules." One of which was: *No cell phones*. But that was broken already, so he asked, "What else is going on? How are classes?"

"Classes?" Like he'd forgotten about them. "They're okay, I guess."

"That's it? Just 'okay'? Are some of them easier and some tougher? Do you like some more than others?" He knew he was pushing too hard, but he needed some sign he'd done the right thing. "C'mon, tell me *something*."

"All right, I'll tell you something." Robert paused, then said, "The classes are boring and the kids are mostly stupid and the teachers are all idiots."

"You have to give it a chance, Robert. You haven't even been there a month." He took a deep breath. "Look, I'm only trying to—"

"I can't *stay* here. I mean, I'm glad my gramma remembered about you and...you know...that you used to be a friend of her and my mom and you got all those connections and stuff so you could get me out of that place. But that doesn't mean I have to...well...anyway, I can't stay here. I wanna go home. To Minneapolis."

"Robert, listen to me. Your grandmother was all the family you had. And with her gone you can't..." He gave up. They'd been through this before. "Look, we had an agreement. Now promise me you'll—"

"I can't *stay* here," Robert said again, and then he was gone.

TWENTY-ONE

After Robert hung up on him, Paul lay back in his recliner, aching and exhausted, replaying over and over the scene of one man savagely whipping another with a car antenna, with Robert's plaintive cry—"I can't *stay* here!"—as a soundtrack.

It was staggering to consider how quickly his life, a life once so carefully planned out and organized, was unraveling.

†

It had been mid-June—such a short time ago—with a warm, bright sun pouring through his office window. Paul's secretary buzzed and told him there was a woman on the phone who seemed anxious to speak to him, but wouldn't give her name.

"Put her through," he said. He'd taken a dozen calls that day already, and there'd be a dozen more to come.

The woman sounded elderly and said her name was Joanne Smith. She insisted on coming to see him, and wouldn't say what it was about. "It has to be in the evening," she said. "Please. I don't have a lotta time."

There was something almost desperate about her that was troubling. He decided she'd heard that he was the one at the archdiocese who dealt with sex abuse cases and she probably had an accusation to make. For an evening meeting they could use an office in the rectory at St. Hildegard's.

When she arrived the following evening in a taxi, he was watching for her. She was not only elderly, as he'd guessed, but also obviously unwell, and he hurried out the rectory front door and down the steps to assist her. She looked vaguely familiar, although he was sure he hadn't met her before. She was very thin and her eyes were sunken in a face that was too pale, under too much makeup. The scarf wrapped around her head announced, rather than hid, the fact that she'd lost her hair. She struggled with a large cloth bag hanging from her shoulder, and he took it and carried it in for her.

He helped her to a chair in one of the rectory offices, feeling the bones in her arm as he did, and put the bag down on the floor beside her. "That cab ride must have been a struggle for you," he said, as he sat behind the desk. "Are you sure you're okay?"

"Cab ride was easy. I took the bus from Minneapolis."

"Minneapolis?" *Just a coincidence. It had to be.*

"Yeah, and I'm not okay. I got breast cancer." She waved a thin hand at him. "But I'm not here about me, okay?" Her voice was weak, but she was obviously determined to get to the reason for her visit. "It's about Robert, my grandson. I don't see how he's gonna make it."

"Is he...ill?"

"He's in jail. In Mexico. A place I can't even pronounce the name of."

"I'm sorry," Paul said, "but I don't know what I can do to help. Maybe if—"

"He's seventeen years old, almost eighteen." She acted as if she hadn't heard him. "He went down there with some other boys. I told him not to, but he did, and he got arrested."

"I still don't see why you came here."

"They say he had marijuana with him. I don't know. He's not a bad boy. Those other kids he went to Mexico with were older. They must've put the blame on *him.* Anyways, they won't let him out on bail, so he sits there. He don't even know when he's gonna get a trial. I raised him. I'm the only relative anyone knows about, and even if I had the strength, I don't have the money to go clear down there and get him a lawyer and all."

"I understand the problem," he said, when she finally paused for breath, "but honestly, I don't know what I can do."

She stared at him, her sunken eyes unblinking. "Me and Marty... God rest his soul...we hardly even knew you. And now I guess you're gonna hate us. Or me, anyway. But you're the only chance Robert's got."

"You and *Marty*? Who's...wait...oh my God!" He knew now why she looked familiar.

"Susan said you didn't know," the woman said, again as though she weren't listening to him at all. "By the time *she* found out, you were off God knows where in the army. I know we should've tried to look for you somehow. But things just got ahead of us. There was all kinds of complications all through the pregnancy and when Robert was born things went really wrong and...and anyway Susan died. Just like that. Our only child...gone. And after that, me and Marty, we couldn't stand the idea of losing Robert, too." She reached down and started pulling papers from the cloth bag. "I know we were wrong. Telling Robert we had no idea who his father was. We figured you'd take him and we'd never see him again. And you can go ahead and hate me if you want. But still, you gotta help Robert. You gotta help your son."

His first instinct was to insist she was mistaken, but she brushed his objections aside. She had everything organized and sorted out, and she showed him the papers she'd brought, along with some photos. Her name wasn't "Joanne Smith," of course, but Abigail Johnson. Susan Johnson's mother. She laid out all the facts, and in the end he was shaking and barely able to speak, but everything fit and he knew she was right.

And when he told her he'd do everything in his power to help Robert, he heard his own words as though someone else was saying them.

Ten minutes later he was helping Abigail Johnson into a cab he'd called, and she was gone.

†

It had been a brief, bitter chapter in his life, but Paul had gotten over it surprisingly quickly and had honestly never thought about it again in almost twenty years.

By the time he had gone off to attend the University of St. Thomas, in Minneapolis, he'd already decided he was going to enter the priesthood. But then, as a sophomore he'd met Susan Johnson, and it seemed his life was taking a surprising, wonderful turn. He'd never even dated seriously before that, and he thought they loved each other. But whether love or not, the relationship ended in confusion and bitter disappointment... and with no hint of a pregnancy. He was badly shaken by the breakup, and he left school—which he knew his widowed mother couldn't afford, anyway—and joined the army. Later came the seminary, then ordination, then a promising ecclesiastical career.

And now, suddenly, he had a son, sitting in jail in Mexico.

He didn't sleep all night, and in the morning he took the documents and photos Abigail Johnson had given him downtown to his bank and put them in a safe deposit box. Then he contacted the US consulate in Mexico. They knew about Robert and said he was one of several hundred unlucky US citizens incarcerated in Mexico on any given day. He was stunned to learn that the US government would do nothing for Robert beyond giving Paul a list of six Mexican lawyers, one of whom he might hire. And these were lawyers for whose "professional ability or integrity" the US government would "accept no responsibility."

At a loss, he reached out to some of the wealthy and influential men he had come to know during his days at "the Wiz." He told each of them that he was asking on behalf of a parish member—the first and perhaps least offensive of an apparently endless string of lies he would tell over the coming months. When none of them offered any real help—or even seemed very interested—he finally decided to try Hank Manion. By then he was desperate and, even though he gave Hank the same reason for his interest in helping the boy, Hank seemed to understand at once how important it was to Paul. "I have business connections in Mexico," Hank said. "I'll inquire about the lawyers on your list."

Less than twenty-four hours later Hank got back to him. His contacts had whittled the list down to two attorneys in Mexico City whom they considered capable and honest, and Paul said he'd pass the word on to the person who'd asked for help. Instead, he took some vacation time and went to Mexico and talked to both lawyers. Again, he didn't tell them he was Robert's father, but said he was a friend of the boy's grandmother and guardian, who was too ill to travel.

Both seemed competent, and both did some preliminary talking to the authorities. Both were guardedly optimistic, but one seemed to Paul—who, in his role for the archdiocese in the sex abuse crisis, often dealt with lawyers—to be more aggressive and articulate. "Based on the apparent circumstances," the lawyer said, "there is some hope—by no means certainty, *señor*, but hope—that we might persuade a judge that this young defendant was duped by professionals, and deserves at least leniency." He paused, then added, "However, there is no chance of release on bail in such a case as this. And I cannot promise what is called in your country a 'speedy trial.' It may be a year, *señor*. Possibly longer."

Paul paid him a retainer and hired him, wondering how in the world he would ever pay the entire fee.

The lawyer arranged a visit with Robert. Paul was allowed to accompany him, but only after he finally explained that he was actually Robert's father, although he'd only just discovered that, and that the boy didn't know it.

It was a two-hour drive from the city to the ancient, squalid jail, a place filled with clanging and banging, and the shouts and taunts of too many hopeless, violent men. Paul spent the entire car ride obsessing over what he would say to Robert. However, as soon as the boy was brought into the interview room—a small, shabby room that smelled faintly of urine and vomit—it was clear he'd been told only that a lawyer was there to see him, and nothing at all about Paul. A guard, who gave no sign that he spoke a word of English, stayed in the room. The meeting was very brief, a formality to get a few basic facts and to have Robert sign a contract for representation.

Paul introduced himself to Robert simply as a friend of the family from before Robert was born, there on behalf of his grandmother.

"Yeah? Well, just tell her it's all bullshit and not to worry. I can handle it here."

Paul had no answer to that, and couldn't trust himself to say another word. He could only stare at this stranger who was his son, and wonder whether the boy saw the resemblance in their faces that nearly brought tears to Paul's eyes.

Robert was a very young-looking seventeen-year-old. His prison uniform, bleached colorless, hung on him like clothes drying on a line. He was unshaven, and his greasy brown hair hung to his shoulders. He was clearly wasting away in that putrid, filthy facility. Afterward, Paul complained bitterly to the lawyer, who, while sympathetic, said there was nothing to be done. "I will try to have him transferred to a facility in the city, but prisons are not happy places, *señor*, not in Mexico...and not in your own country, I think, if you were ever to look."

Paul returned to Chicago with his heart torn open by feelings unlike anything he'd ever experienced. As a priest, he had always loved people and cared about their problems. But it was one thing to love "people," and quite another to stare into the eyes of one terrified, hopeless seventeen-year-old, and to have no answers at all. It was one thing to be called "Father," and quite another to *feel* the ache in his heart for this emaciated, greasy-haired, straggly-bearded boy—with his thin, sad pretense of bravado. He had left his son in that stinking corner of hell, and he was terrified that the boy would die there, whether from disease or violence. He might not even outlive his grandmother.

But that wasn't to be.

†

The first thing Paul did when he got home was call Abigail Johnson. But he was too late. She'd already died.

And it wasn't long afterwards, on that Tuesday afternoon, the second of July, that Ann Swanson had approached him at the cemetery. "I know about your problem. And I can help." By then Paul's fear had turned to absolute conviction: Robert would not survive in that place. That Friday he tried unsuccessfully to call the CIA. On Saturday, he said yes to her proposal.

He gave her and her people the clandestine use of an abandoned building at Fair Hope Clinic. He had no authority to make such a decision, and he knew it meant entering a world of lies and deceit. He was willing to pay that price, though, because he couldn't get that starving, hopeless boy—whom he so quickly and easily thought of now as *his* boy—out of his mind.

Several days later, Robert was taken from his cell and flown out of Mexico. How this was managed was not explained. Ann Swanson delivered Robert and his passport to Paul and said the boy would be wise to avoid Mexico for the foreseeable future. Clearly, Robert's freedom was *not* the result of the sort of dry, diplomatic maneuvering Paul had imagined, and Robert was obviously too terrified to talk about his deliverance.

Paul had immediately notified the resident custodian at Fair Hope, a man named Bogdan Adjar, that contractors would be there to renovate a long-abandoned barn at one end of the property, for use by a company engaged in mineral exploration—gold, primarily, one of Guyana's chief resources. From that point on he left it to Ann's people to handle things at the Guyana end. Bogdan and the clinic's medical people obviously suspected nothing.

Within weeks an "anonymous donor" began making regular monthly gifts to the archdiocese, earmarked specifically "to carry on the work of Fair Hope Clinic," which for several years had been under-funded and in imminent danger of being shut down. These gifts, of course, came to the attention of the cardinal, who described the recruitment of the benefactor as "another of Father Clark's quiet successes."

Paul, of course, told no one about Robert, or his release, or the woman from—as he was now quite certain—the CIA. He negotiated with her for money to help with Robert's support and education. Beyond that, though, they had seldom communicated, and he'd been glad of that. She made him very uncomfortable. Which is to say, more truthfully, that she frightened him.

Now, though, he was hearing from her all too often, and he was more afraid than ever.

TWENTY-TWO

Still on his back on the recliner in his study, Paul struggled to fit the man with the car antenna into the picture. He'd dealt harshly—no, *viciously*—with the two muggers, sending them off empty-handed, but clearly not out of good will toward Paul. Was he really a homeless person? Was it luck that he'd hung around nearby for such a long time? Neither seemed likely. Nor did it seem the hand of God. More likely the hand of Ann Swanson. But why?

Even wide awake, making sense of all this wouldn't have been easy. In Paul's present state—physical *and* mental—it was impossible. He knew he should get up and go to bed, but his body ached too much in all its joints and muscles for him to want to move.

At about four a.m. he jerked awake with a start. Max was barking frantically. The dog settled down again right away, but it was unheard of for him to bark at all in the dead of night. Paul hauled himself out of the chair and went over and opened the door into the hall, but heard nothing but silence. He closed the door, went into his bedroom, and managed to set the alarm before he fell across the bed and went back to sleep.

†

He was up, and showered and shaved, by eight o'clock. This time, disregarding the advice of the detective about wearing a Roman collar, he put on black khakis and a thin black windbreaker over a long-sleeved white shirt. Grabbing the gym bag with Larry's laptop, he went down to the kitchen. His head didn't ache, but the stabbing pain in his side was still with him…and made trotting down the stairs an adventure.

Enjoying the smell of fresh coffee brewing, he set a bowl, a spoon, a box of raisin bran, and a loaf of whole wheat bread on the kitchen table. He knew Jake would already be at the church. Jake said the eight o'clock mass every day for a faithful group of ten or fifteen people, most of them as old, or older, than he was. He always went out the back door and took Max with him. The dog would make a pit stop on the way from the rectory to the church and then sleep in the sacristy during mass. After that Jake and Max would take their morning walk, and then Jake would come into the kitchen where he'd find the breakfast Paul laid out for him. Always the same routine; always the same menu.

For himself, Paul mixed powdered chocolate breakfast drink with some coffee in a plastic travel mug and snapped on the top. That was usually it for breakfast, although sometimes he'd grab a doughnut somewhere. His own routine wasn't quite as calcified as Jake's, but this morning it did feel odd to be starting a day without heading for the cathedral to say mass.

He considered taking Jake's old Buick to St. Manfred's. Jake, who probably hadn't even *seen* the car for over a year, refused to give up hope that one of these days his doctor would give him the go-ahead to drive again. Meanwhile, the Buick sat in the garage and Paul kept Jake happy by getting the keys from Jake's so-called "hiding place" under the floor mat and taking the car out for a drive every couple of weeks so he could, as Jake said, "blow the carbon out of it." He could take the car now and Jake would never know. Still, it didn't seem right to do so without asking.

He left the kitchen, gym bag in one hand and coffee in the other, hoping he could find a cab in a hurry. As he started down the long hall he was surprised to see something on the floor by the front door. When he got closer he stopped and stared down. It was an envelope, unsealed and lying face down on the mat. It must have been put through the mail slot sometime during the night, which might have been what made Max bark.

He set his bag on the floor and stooped to pick up the envelope, forgetting about the mug in his other hand. It tilted, dribbling chocolate coffee out through the hole in the cover, some onto the envelope and some onto the carpet. When he stood up he set the mug on the table by the door, flapped the envelope back and forth to dry it, and checked inside. It was the paper work for the car rental.

His hands trembled as he slid the papers back into the envelope, trying to make sense of them being here. He'd left them in the car, and the car at St. Manfred's. Why would someone—and it had to be the man in the SUV—bring the papers here?

He stuck the envelope in his shirt pocket and unlocked the front door. He looked up and down the street. It was a beautiful, bright day and he saw at once that the envelope wasn't the only thing that had been delivered that morning. A blue Dodge Avenger was there, too. . .parked right beside the fire hydrant.

He'd lost all interest in drinking the rest of his breakfast and left the mug on the table. He took the gym bag and went out, locking the door behind him, and walked to the Avenger. There was a parking ticket fixed to the windshield. He reached out to pick it off, then thought better of it. The papers through the mail slot must have been meant to alert him to look for the car. On the other hand, there had to be more than one blue Dodge Avenger in the world, so. . .

He tried the driver's door and it was unlocked, so he dug the ignition key out of his pocket and got behind the wheel. The key fit. He sat there a moment. Maybe whoever brought it here—operating it without the key—*wanted* him to drive it. So maybe that's exactly what he shouldn't do.

He pulled the key from the ignition and stuffed the envelope with the rental papers back where he'd put them before, under the sun visor. He left the car there—with the ticket on the windshield—and went to look for a cab.

†

The cab driver looked perfectly normal, but drove like a madman, the whole time speaking into his cell phone in a language Paul thought was Slavic. But at least the ride was a quick one, and when they arrived at Manfred Court there were three cars parked directly in front of the ancient, two-story building that housed the school. Two were blue and white squad cars, and the other was a green four-door sedan that Paul assumed was a detective's car.

A thin, gray-haired police officer in uniform stood just outside the school doors, looking more bored than vigilant. When Paul said he had an appointment to see the school principal, the man simply shrugged and nodded him toward the entrance. Paul pulled open one of the two heavy doors and went in. He climbed up a half-dozen well-worn marble stairs and at the top found himself looking down a wide, high-ceilinged hallway. It smelled of floor wax, was brightly lit, and flanked with windowed doors, all of them closed. It led to the rear of the building, where another stairway led upwards. The floor he stood on was oak, he thought, and spotless. The walls, too, were clean, but could have used a fresh layer of paint—and something brighter than two shades of gray.

It was a little after nine o'clock and he could hear distant voices, women's voices, apparently coming from behind classroom doors. The first door on the right, a few yards down, had a sign sticking out above it that said *OFFICE*. He was about to start that way when the door at the foot of the stairs behind him opened. He looked down to see a woman pushing in two small, giggling, dark-skinned girls in plaid skirts and blue sweaters. "You hurry up now and explain why you're late," the woman said, and the door closed behind them.

The girls, maybe six and eight years old, made it up two steps before they saw Paul looking down at them, and immediately put solemn looks on their faces. They reached the top and marched past, the shorter girl's head twisted back to look at him the whole time, while the other pulled her along to the office door. Before they reached it, though, a woman came out, saw the two tardy students, and led them away with her down the hall.

Paul went into the office…and saw at once why there were police cars outside.

A counter separated the reception area from the business side of the room. Beyond the counter there were desks for staff people, metal file cabinets, tables and shelving—all of it crammed into too small an area. Overcrowding, though, wasn't the main problem just then.

It looked as though anything that had once been sitting on top of a desk, or a table, or any other flat surface in the area, had been swept off and now lay scattered and broken on the floor. Desk and cabinet drawers stood open. Books and papers were thrown everywhere. Chairs lay on their sides; vases and framed snapshots were in pieces; pictures and posters were torn from the walls and strewn around.

Amid the chaos Paul counted seven people. Three of them—Celia and two men in sport coats—stood conversing in what must have been Celia's private office, a glass-walled cubicle at the far end of the room. Paul recognized one of the men as Maddox, the detective who'd interviewed him right after Larry was killed. They didn't appear to have seen him.

Of the other four persons, one was an older black woman who sat on a chair against the wall, staring around wide-eyed, as though in a daze. The others were uniformed police officers, two men and a woman. The male officers were white and had cameras, and were busy photographing the condition of the room and the debris scattered around. The female officer was black, and was on her way over to Paul.

"Something I can help you with, sir?"

"I'm Father Paul Clark. Ms. Jackson's expect—"

The officer raised her hand to stop him, then turned. "Hey Maddox!" she called. "That priest you're looking for? He's here."

TWENTY-THREE

So...uh...Father, let's see." Maddox was flipping pages in his notebook. "You got Ms. Jackson not to call the police, and then you went—"

"I didn't *get*— I mean, we *agreed* not to call. She said she didn't feel up to another session with the police at that time of night, and I didn't either, especially since she said there was nothing in the rectory worth stealing."

"Uh-huh. So anyway, after you left her place," Maddox went on, "you went straight home, right?"

"Yes. I took a cab to St. Hildegard's."

"And you didn't see or talk to anyone before you got there?"

"Just the cab driver, like I said."

Maddox and his partner, a pale, round-faced man named Kriswell whom Paul hadn't noticed the previous morning, were interviewing Paul in Celia's glass-walled cubicle. From the direction of their questioning, he had to assume Celia had already told them about finding him twice at the rectory, and about Larry wanting him to see a column he'd written, so he told them about both his return trips to Larry's rectory. He said he found the laptop and the three spiral-bound books "in the kitchen," omitting that he'd hidden them there.

The uniformed officers were gone and the detectives were asking some of the same questions over again, and generally going into everything in greater detail than he'd expected. It was getting warm and stuffy in the little room. Through the glass wall he could see Celia and two other women trying to put things back together in the main office.

"You must have been pretty worried about what your friend had written," Maddox said, "to go all the way back to his rectory right away after you left the hospital."

"I didn't say I was 'worried.' I said Father Landrew wanted me to see what he'd written."

"And then, when you left Ms. Jackson last night at her apartment you took that thing with you." Maddox nodded toward the laptop sitting on the desk.

"Yes."

"Why?" Maddox looked puzzled. "I mean, it belonged to Ms. Jackson's brother, and you made a special trip all the way out here last night to return it. Why not just...*give* it to her?"

"I don't know. I guess I thought I'd save her the trouble of carrying it. I knew I'd be coming here in the morning. It just seemed easier." He was rambling, he knew. Fumbling for a reason that would satisfy them. "And well...maybe I thought I'd check one more time, and see if I could find the column Larry told me about."

"*Maybe* you thought that?" This came from Kriswell.

"Or maybe I *didn't* think that. I don't know. I was exhausted. I just wanted to go home."

"And you told her you'd bring it back here to the school office this morning."

"Yes, I planned to come pick up the rental car, anyway."

"And to do that, would you have had to come to the *office*?" Maddox asked. "Or was there some *other* reason to come here?"

Paul felt uneasy. Until now he hadn't mentioned anything about CDs, but Celia might have. "Yes," he said, "I thought I'd see if Larry left any CDs that might have his columns on them. Or maybe memory sticks or something."

"You were still really anxious to see what he had to say, right?"

"I don't know that I'd say 'anxious.' It's what Larry wanted. It was the last thing he asked me to do. It was..." He let it go.

"Go on," Maddox said, staring at him. "I mean, did you want to add anything?"

"No."

"Okay. So…when you got to St. Hildegard's, you went to bed, and this morning you came straight here, right?"

"Yes." Celia couldn't have told them about the muggers and the homeless guy, and he wasn't about to, either. He couldn't forget the savage whipping the man had given one of the muggers, followed by the warning to Paul: *Forget all this.*

"So…can you think of anything you haven't told us?"

"I've told you—" His cell phone rang. "I need to answer that."

"It's a free country." Maddox shrugged. "Go ahead."

"Hello?"

"Put aside whatever you're doing." It was Ann Swanson. "We need—"

"Not now," Paul said. "I'm with some police detectives."

"We need to talk," she said, as if she hadn't heard him.

"I said I can't talk now. Call me—"

"Listen to me. Listen carefully. You're not to say anything about… about our arrangement. Nothing at all…not one word…about me, or my people. Nothing that will even *hint* at me. For your sake. You got it?"

"I have to go now." He ended the call. "Sorry," he said to the detectives.

"We know you're a busy man, Father." Kriswell nodded, as though in agreement with himself. "We appreciate your taking the time to talk to us."

"Anyway, back to last night." Maddox stood up and looked through the glass toward Celia and the others. "The silver SUV, you don't know what *kind* of SUV it was, or what the license number was, and you can't describe the driver, right?"

"Just what I told you, that's all."

"Right. Big man, African-American." The detective turned back to him. "That's it?"

"Yes. I didn't get much of a look at him and… I don't know, but it almost sounds like you don't *believe* me."

"Why *wouldn't* we believe you?" Kriswell shrugged. "I mean…you're a priest, and you're telling the truth, right?"

Paul looked at his watch. "How much longer will we be?"

Kriswell looked at Maddox, who said, "Hard to say. Not too long." He glanced at his notebook, then said, "Back to this SUV driver, though. When he broke into the priest's house you were scared. Did he threaten you?"

"He didn't *say* anything threatening. But he banged on the door, and picked the lock and broke the security chain, and chased me."

"And then he didn't take anything from the priest's house."

"I didn't know that, but Ms. Jackson said there was nothing in there worth stealing. That's why we decided not to call the police right away."

"Then, the same night, someone..." Maddox paused, as though trying to figure things out in his mind. "I guess it could have been the same man...breaks into the school here and tears it apart. Like he's looking for something."

"I don't...I mean don't you think this was just kids? Vandalism?"

"Maybe. But on the same night? A coincidence like that seems a little...well... *strange*, doesn't it?"

"I don't know." Feeling beads of sweat running down his back, he stood up to take off his jacket. "You don't mind, do you?"

"Of course not," Maddox said. He pointed at Paul's chest. "You spilled something."

"I did?" Paul looked down. There were two light brown smears just above the pocket of the white shirt. The chocolate-laced coffee he'd spilled on the car rental envelope obviously hadn't been dry when he'd shoved it in his pocket.

"I s'pose it'll wash out," Maddox said, as Paul sat back down. "Anyway, just a few more... Oh, hold on." He leaned back and stuck his hand in his jacket pocket and took out his cell phone. "Maddox here." He listened awhile, no expression at all on his face. "Okay, I got it. Thanks." He put the phone away and looked at Paul. "You came here in a cab this morning?"

"Yes."

"Your rental car...Ms. Jackson said it should be behind the priest's house. But it's not there, so we put out a lookout for it. Because of a parking ticket, and then a tow requisition, the computer kicked out its location pretty quick."

"I know where it is," Paul said. "In front of St. Hildegard's, where I live."

"And," Kriswell said, leaning in toward Paul, "you weren't going to mention that to us?"

"Yes, I was. I mean, you started asking questions, and I haven't had a chance."

"You sure you didn't come back again, Father?" Maddox asked. "A third time? To pick up the car?"

"No! I don't know *how* the car got back to St. Hildegard's. I saw it there and realized it must have been stolen, so I didn't think I should drive it."

"Stolen?" Maddox tilted his head quizzically. "Someone stole it and drove it right to where you live and left it there?"

"I don't know, Detective. I know I didn't drive it, whatever you think, and—" He was babbling again, and stopped. "When can I have my own car back?"

"We'll need it awhile longer," Maddox said. "And the auto theft guys will wanna check over the Avenger, for prints and whatever." He stood up. "Excuse us."

Maddox and Kriswell left the room. Paul watched through the glass as the detectives stood for a minute, discussing something. Maddox seemed to be in charge. He did most of the talking, while Kriswell nodded in agreement. Finally, Kriswell came back into the cubicle and, without a word to Paul, picked up the laptop and left again. Meanwhile, Maddox had gone over to Celia and was talking to her. Maddox finished with Celia and rejoined Paul. "OK," he said, "I guess that'll be all for now."

"Really? I thought you said you had a few more questions."

"Yeah, well, there are always 'a few more questions,' right? But nothing just now." He turned to leave, then said, "Oh." He turned back. "Maybe just this, to cover all the bases. You don't have any idea who threw all this stuff around in here, do you?"

"No. How *would* I?"

"Or *why*?"

"No," Paul said, and then, when Maddox seemed finished, he added, "Can I ask *you* a question?"

"Sure. Ask away."

"It's about Larry. I mean...are you getting anywhere? Are you going to be able to catch the man who killed him?"

"Father Landrew?" Maddox sounded surprised, as though Larry's murder were the last thing on his mind. "We're doing everything we can, Father. Doing everything we can."

The words, perhaps, were reassuring, but the tone seemed to carry a vague threat.

TWENTY-FOUR

When Maddox left, Paul called the Pastoral Care Office and talked to Phyllis Conover about Larry's funeral arrangements. Phyllis said she could do it all herself—would prefer to, in fact—but Paul made her promise to involve Celia on everything. Then he went into the main office, where Celia and the two other women, joined now by a school custodian, were working to straighten up the chaos in the office.

"Celia," Paul said, "I think you should go home."

She looked up from where she was crouched, brushing broken glass from the floor into a dustpan. "I'm not leaving it like this for our students to see."

"You'll have to meet with Phyllis Conover about the funeral. I'll drive you home in your car."

Celia stood up. "I'm staying." She was speaking through tears now. "Larry told me he didn't care what kind of funeral he had."

The older of the two women put her arm around Celia's shoulders and pulled her close to her side. "Miz Jackson honey, I know Father Landrew wouldn't say nothin' like that."

Celia didn't pull away, but she didn't look at the woman, either. She was staring at the floor. "But he *did*. He said by then he'd be in God's hands, and people could do whatever they wanted." She wiped tears from her cheek. "Anyway, now there's just me. And I don't care, either. The cardinal and Phyllis Whoever can—"

"Hold on, Celia." Paul's tone was louder and more harsh than he'd intended, but at least it got her to look at him. "It's not *about* what Larry wanted...or about what *you* want, either. Larry...well...Larry was an important guy. Larry *stood* for something. He made lots of people uncomfortable, including me sometimes. But they listened to him. *They're* the ones that need a funeral. They need to hear again just who he was, and what he stood for. They—" His cell phone beeped and he pulled it from his belt. "Hello?"

"I hope you're finished with the cops," Ann said. "Because I want—"

"Call back in ten minutes. I'll be free."

"You—"

He closed the phone and took Celia by the arm and led her into her office. He knew she was on the verge of collapse, but when he had Phyllis Conover on the line he gave Celia the phone. "Phyllis can't do it all by herself," he said.

†

He left Celia on the phone and went out through the office and into the hall, where he ran into about thirty children, filing toward the front entrance. They looked like sixth- or seventh-graders: dark-skinned, the girls in plaid skirts and the boys in navy blue pants, all wearing jackets or sweaters over white blouses or shirts. They walked in silence, solemnly, two-by-two, and he followed them down the steps and out the double doors. Their teacher—a tall, thin black woman who was easily sixty years old, and wearing a plain blue dress and a short veil that proclaimed her a nun—followed close behind.

Outside, the kids marched across the street and into the church, but Paul stayed by the school doors and waited for Ann to call back. She'd be angry because he'd hung up on her. He told himself he mustn't let her intimidate him.

Yesterday's storm had been pushed on by a high-pressure front moving in from the northwest, and the sky was a deep, bright blue, with wispy white clouds. The temperature had taken a surprising drop, though, and while he was sheltered from the chill wind, the shadow thrown by the tall church across the street kept the sun from warming him.

The pain in his side was no better than it had been yesterday, and he felt as fatigued and stressed as Celia looked. He was cold, too, and shivering. It didn't help to know that even an overcoat couldn't have held off the chill he was feeling.

TWENTY-FIVE

Paul stood in the cold on an empty street in the heart of the sort of neighborhood that he, and just about everyone else, liked to pretend didn't exist. He could hear distant traffic sounds, and the far-off screech of an El train rounding a curve in the tracks. The faint, sad odor of burned buildings hung in the air, and if God hadn't become so distant and unknowable recently, he'd have prayed. But he could no longer bring himself to ask for anything. If he *could* have, he'd have prayed for insight, for courage, but most of all for Robert. He'd have prayed for Robert, who was desperately alone and unhappy, and who had convinced himself that getting away from Bridgebriar School would change everything.

He watched as the children marched back out of the church and followed their teacher across to his side of the street again. They didn't come to the school, though. Instead, they filed through an opening in a tall chain-link fence that ran along the sidewalk, and went into a concrete-covered playground next door to the school.

As they did, Paul's phone rang. He answered what he hoped was the last call from Ann Swanson he'd ever get.

"We have to meet," Ann said.

"Meet?"

"M-e-e-t," she spelled. "Today."

"But where? And when? Are you—"

"Today's a good day for you to visit your mother. Four o'clock."

He folded his phone closed. The children were out of sight now, but he could hear their shouting, hear the bouncing of a basketball. And meanwhile, as the kids played, their principal—who should have been grieving the loss of her brother—struggled to put her vandalized office back together. He thought he knew why that was so important to her. Her school was one slim beacon of hope to these kids and their families. She wouldn't let them see it in ruins.

So much depended on hope. Just a couple of months—and a lifetime—ago he had tried to bring hope to Robert, the two of them sitting at a scarred table in a remote Mexican jail, breathing in air that reeked of human pain and hopelessness. Paul had been speechless, as the lawyer's routine questions and Robert's soulless answers were punctuated by incessant outbursts of unintelligible cursing and taunting from caged men nearby. But hope could not survive there, and Paul came home, soon to enter a world where deceit was the hope held out to him.

He'd grabbed onto that hope and it grabbed him back, and had slowly been sucking the life out of him, reminding him every waking moment that his career and his priesthood were over if his deceit were uncovered. In the beginning he'd told himself that the help he gave Ann served a vital national interest: the flow of information from Venezuela, which—at least if one believed the government and the media—was hostile to the United States. But in his heart he knew how likely it was that Larry was right, that the flow through Fair Hope Clinic moved in both directions, and carried things more tangible than mere information. Things like money...and weapons of death and destruction.

He also knew, though, knew deep in his heart, that he'd have done the same thing, made the same agreement with Ann, whether she'd told him she worked for the CIA or for UNICEF, for Exxon or for Doctors Without Borders.

To save that lonely, terrified teenager—a boy he'd never known existed, a boy who still didn't know he had a father in Chicago—what would Father Paul Clark *not* have done? What wouldn't he do now?

TWENTY-SIX

Paul went back into the school and up the steps, and stopped when he saw Celia at the door to the office talking to her three helpers. She had her pink raincoat on.

When she turned and saw him, she said, "Oh…you're still here?" She hitched the strap of her laptop bag higher on her shoulder and joined him at the top of the stairs. "I s'pose you're waiting for me to give you another ride home."

"If it's a problem, I can call a cab." He reached for the phone at his belt.

"No…don't. I'm sorry. I'm being rude, I know." She shook her head. "I'm on my way to meet with Phyllis Conover, and I'll drop you off. I haven't been myself."

"You're entitled," he said. "But I'll accept the ride. I'll even let you drive the whole way this time." As they went down the steps and out the door, he said, "Phyllis will be a big help with the arrangements, believe me."

"I guess so." She brushed tears from her cheek. "She said they always ask priests to give them copies of their wills, so she'll look for Larry's. That's a joke, since he had nothing to leave to anyone. Except his car, I guess."

"And his laptop," Paul said, "which the police took."

"Yeah, I know. They said they needed it, but they wouldn't say why. I still don't trust them. Anyway, everything seems beyond my control."

"I'm not surprised. And then this morning you go in and find all that...that destruction." He was trying to steer the conversation to what might have been found in the school office, and felt ashamed for doing it.

They headed down the sidewalk in the direction of the playground, where the air was filled with the shouts of children playing and basketballs thudding on concrete. "It could have been worse," she said. "Some of the computers and printers are still working. And there was none of that spray painting. No graffiti...or obscenities."

"That's good. How about theft, though?" This was the issue that had kept him waiting for her. "Were there a lot of things taken?"

"Not much. Some milk money, and a few dollars from another desk drawer."

"What about things like...papers...records...that kind of thing?"

"You *saw* how the file drawers were emptied out, papers thrown everywhere. But it looks like everything's still there." They'd reached the playground, where the boys who weren't playing basketball were standing around watching, while most of the girls were gathered together by the tall black nun. When the girls saw Celia they waved, and she waved back. "I mean, there could be *some* records missing, I guess, but we won't know until we go looking for something."

"What about backup disks, or...you know...memory sticks or something?"

"There were CDs scattered around like everything else, and—" She stopped walking and turned to look at him, an angry frown taking over her face. "You're still thinking about Larry's column, aren't you? Damn! That's *all* you—"

"I think someone wants to talk to you," he said, pointing past her.

"God *damn* it." She whirled around.

The nun was standing right behind her. "Excuse me, Ms. Jackson, but the children want you to know they're praying for you." She smiled gently. "And so am I."

"Oh," Celia said. "Thank you, Sister." The nun walked back to the children and Celia turned to Paul. "Why is that column so *important*?"

"Because it seemed important to *Larry*, so…I'd like to see what he was talking about. Let's go back and look."

"I don't really—" She stopped, and then said, "You know what? Larry didn't have a clue about memory sticks or flash drives or the like. If there's a column, it's on a CD. And if the CD you're looking for exists, it's not in the school."

"How do you know? You said—"

"Because there was no CD of Larry's among the ones we picked up."

"So," he said, trying not to look as disappointed as he was, "if there *was* one, it's gone."

"Well…" She looked down at the sidewalk, and then up at him again. "Okay, I thought of something…just a few minutes ago. It actually came to me when I was picking all those CDs up off the floor."

"*What* came to you?"

"Sunday afternoon I was in the school, working on some teacher evaluations. I do that when I get behind." She looked past Paul and waved her hand.

He turned and saw the children filing out through the opening in the fence and back toward the school, with the nun standing by like a sentinel. He turned back to Celia. "So you were in the school Sunday afternoon. And…?"

"And as I was leaving, Larry came out of the rectory. He said he had something he wanted to print out. I decided to go back to the office with him. He's got keys, of course, and he could do it, but… well…if the printer jams or something, he's hopeless. He can't…I mean, he *couldn't*…" She pulled a handkerchief from her coat pocket and blew her nose. "Sorry."

"That's okay," he said. "Take your time." But he wished she'd hurry up. She took a deep breath.

"So we started inside…when he got a phone call. Larry *hated* cell phones, but he…well…anyway, it was some mother saying how the cops had beat up her son, and Larry told me he had to go to the police station. He gave me a CD. 'We can print this out tomorrow,' he said. And off he went. That was Larry. He never—"

"And you didn't think about this when we were talking last night?"

"I never gave it a thought. Not till this morning. What, you think I'm *lying*?"

"No, no," Paul said. "Sorry. So…the CD. Where is it?"

"It meant nothing to me at the time, but I stuck it right in here." She slapped her hand on the computer case hanging by her hip. "And you know what? For now, anyway…until I figure out what I want to do…that's right where it's gonna *stay*."

TWENTY-SEVEN

Neither of them said anything during the ride to St. Hildegard's. Finally, as he was getting out of the car, Paul said, "Say hello to Phyllis for me." Then, as if it were an afterthought, he added, "Oh...and Celia? Let me know what you decide about that CD."

"Good-bye," she said, and drove away.

He went up to his rooms, intending to get some rest before his meeting with Ann Swanson. But first he checked the messages on the rectory voice mail...and was shocked to find out that he was invited to lunch at the cardinal's residence at one o'clock.

He called back and accepted. The other messages were all from news media types and he deleted them without bothering to respond. That was ironic because, as the one usually chosen to explain "the cardinal's position" on this or that controversial issue, he always called the media back...and promptly. He'd enjoyed dealing with them...until now.

He showered for the second time that day, and put on a black suit and Roman collar. It was still sunny and cold out, but not cold enough for a topcoat, so he grabbed his raincoat and went out to find a cab.

†

"Invited" to lunch with the cardinal, of course, meant "ordered to appear." And the cardinal's "residence" meant his "mansion," no matter how hard the PR consultants pushed the plainer sounding word. What else but "mansion" would people call a huge, three-story, red brick

Victorian—with, famously, nineteen chimneys—built in 1885 at what was now, and must have been then, the most prestigious location in the city?

Paul had been there maybe ten times before, always in the evening for small dinners or meetings, and always in the company of others—mostly priests. Now he was alone, though, and as his cab drew near the mansion along North Avenue he was struck by the beauty of the setting, despite the circumstances. At the north end of North State Parkway, and just a stone's throw in from Lake Shore Drive and the beach, the mansion had as its front yard Lincoln Park, a beautiful expanse of grass and trees stretching northward for miles along the lakeshore.

The cab stopped near the main entrance and he got out. The sun shone brightly on smooth green lawns and well-trimmed shrubbery, and made the brick exteriors of both the mansion itself and its coach house—where a few nuns on the cardinal's staff lived—glow as though recently scrubbed. He went up the steps under the elegant portico and rang the bell.

He didn't look forward to it, but he knew what he had to do. The hope that Ann Swanson and her people would soon be gone from Fair Hope for good had evaporated with her phone call that morning. If the CIA were really leaving, why a meeting this afternoon? He couldn't live with this terrible deception any longer. He would tell the cardinal everything, and lift the shroud of secrecy and lies he'd draped over himself. He'd have to ride out whatever storms came, but just now he felt relieved to have made up his mind. At least he'd have it over with.

Just as he rang the bell a second time, a priest—Father Tom Jason—opened the door. With a flourish, Tom bowed low from the waist. "*Velcome to my castle*," he said in a deep, melodramatic Count Dracula voice. Tom, a natural comic who was always on stage, served as both manager of the mansion and the cardinal's driver. Everyone agreed that it was only Tom's mechanical expertise, and his ability to negotiate and to search out bargains, that kept the ancient mansion in reasonable repair. He overdid the humor stuff, but Paul thought that was mostly to entertain himself in an otherwise pretty grim job.

Tom hung Paul's coat in a closet and ushered him to an uncomfortable easy chair in a small parlor. When he was gone, Paul stood up and paced nervously around. His own mood surely had a lot to do with it, but as beautiful as the mansion was on the outside, on that day he found the interior merely dark and pretentious. It smelled of candle wax and furniture polish, and was gloomy to the point of being oppressive. The parlor's two tiny windows let in very little light, and the walnut woodwork and furniture, the wall coverings and draperies—heavy on the deep reds and maroons—all spoke more of grandeur and solemnity than of welcome and comfort.

On previous mansion visits he'd been in the chapel and the dining room, both on the first floor, and he knew there were guest rooms on that floor, too, and probably Tom Jason's rooms. He'd never been up to the second and third floors, the cardinal's private quarters, and while he should have been rehearsing what he wanted to say, he found himself wondering how all that space could be used by one person. Maybe the third floor was just an attic, filled with—

"Ah, Paul, thank you for coming." The voice startled him, even though the cardinal spoke softly, as always.

Paul spun around, trying not to wince when the rib pain hit him. "Oh... Your Eminence."

Richard Cardinal Nesbitt, Archbishop of Chicago, was a tall, husky, ruddy-faced man in his sixties, with thick, curly white hair. As usual, he wore a crisply pressed black suit and Roman collar, with one strand of a thin gold chain draped diagonally across his chest. "I'm so glad you could make it," he said, stretching his hand out. "This must be a difficult time for you."

"Yes, very difficult." Paul shook the outstretched hand, aware that the man consistently waved aside attempts to kiss his ring, the traditional way of greeting a cardinal. "Still," Paul added, "I'm grateful for the chance to speak with you."

The cardinal's eyes narrowed slightly, as though he was suspicious of what Paul might say, but the look passed quickly. "Come this way," he said, and turned and left the room. He wasn't one to waste time.

Following him, Paul wondered how this man got along so well with Hank Manion, since they were both so accustomed to telling others what to do. The cardinal was a complex person, though, and Paul had long ago given up trying to understand him. He kept everyone at a distance and, in that regard at least, Paul recognized something of himself in the older man.

The cardinal continued down the hallway, past the entrance to the formal dining room, and into a room Paul had never seen before. "We'll be more comfortable in here."

It was a small room, a breakfast nook, with windows that looked out onto the lawn and actually let in some sunlight. The table, covered with a white cloth, was set for just two. Paul was glad of that. He wouldn't have to discuss the events of the last day and a half in a group setting, fielding questions from all sides. Also, he had the perfect opportunity now to tell the cardinal everything, despite Ann Swanson's warning not to. His heart already felt lighter.

They sat down and the cardinal rang a tiny hand bell and, at that gentle sound, they were joined at once by two elderly nuns in full white habits—*among the last of a dying breed*, Paul thought—who brought in iced tea and shallow bowls of what looked and smelled like shellfish bisque. Right behind the nuns came Tom Jason, who said, "Your Eminence," and handed a cordless phone to the cardinal.

Tom withdrew at once and the cardinal said, "Go ahead, Paul," gesturing toward Paul's bowl. "Don't let it get cold."

The two of them sipped their soup from fine silver spoons, while the cardinal talked on the phone about a speech he was to give in a few days on the clergy sex abuse crisis. The person on the other end of the line—probably a lawyer, or a PR consultant—was apparently vetting the speech...or maybe had written it.

The bisque was delicious and the nuns returned to clear away the bowls and replace them with plates of sandwiches. Paul was just biting into a tuna salad on thin whole wheat bread—also quite good—when the cardinal finished his conversation and set the phone down. "Sorry about that," he said, and picked up his own sandwich. "So, how are you holding up?"

"Pretty well, Your Eminence."

"Good. I suggest you take some time off. Away from the Pastoral Care Office."

"Thank you, Your Eminence, but I already have lots of catching up to do, and—"

"Excuse me, Paul."

"Yes?"

"You're taking some time off." The voice may have been soft, but the decision was not up for discussion.

"I understand, Your Eminence." Although he didn't. "What about my mass schedule at the cathedral?"

The cardinal took a sip of his iced tea. "For the time being, you will say mass only at St. Hildegard's…and in private. No congregation."

"But why? That is…" Paul's stomach was churning. "I take it there's something wrong."

"Wrong? One of my priests has been murdered, and another one says he was attacked and beaten by the same assailant."

"I know, but I—"

"I've received certain information," the cardinal said. "But you will never let on that you heard this from me. Do you agree?"

"Of course I agree, but is it about…about Fair Hope Clinic?"

That cardinal stared at him. "Why do you say that?"

"Because there's something I need to tell *you*, too. Several months ago I…well… I was approached by someone from the government, the CIA, seeking—"

"Please." The cardinal held a hand up, palm toward Paul. "My time is limited."

"But I'm—"

"If you *do* say you heard from me what I am about to tell you," the cardinal went on, as though there'd been no mention of Fair Hope, or the CIA, "I will have no choice but to deny it. So…do I have your agreement?"

"I already *told* you…*yes*." Paul was getting tired of this game and couldn't keep the edge out of his voice. "Just tell me what you're talking about."

"I intend to, Father." The cardinal was clearly surprised, and obviously not pleased, by Paul's tone of voice. But he also seemed to back off a little.

"I've been informed that the police are seeking the issuance of certain search warrants. Also, subpoenas for records…or court orders…I'm not totally familiar with the legal jargon."

"Warrants to search what? Subpoenas for what records?"

"Some from the Archdiocese. Some— Well, I'll stop there. As for you, I won't presume to tell you what to do. I would suggest, however, that you…contact someone. Brian Joplin, perhaps."

"But that's ridiculous." Brian Joplin was a lawyer the Archdiocese referred priests to…priests facing sexual abuse charges. "Are you saying someone's accusing me of sex abuse?"

"I'm not saying that at all." Just then the cardinal's phone rang and he picked it up. "Yes?"

"Wait." Paul leaned across the table. "What *is* it? What do the police want?"

"One moment, please," the cardinal said to his caller. He pressed a button on the phone, then said to Paul. "I need to take this in private." He stood up. "What the police *want*," he said, "is to identify the person who murdered Father Landrew. And they appear to be focusing, Father, on *you*."

TWENTY-EIGHT

Paul sat alone in the cardinal's breakfast nook, staring down at the tuna salad sandwich he'd taken just two bites of. Tom Jason came in with another sandwich on a plate. He pointed at Paul's lunch. "They make damn good sandwiches here," he said, "and if I were you I'd stick around and finish mine. The nuns won't bother you. And take this one, too." He set down the extra sandwich, then picked up the cardinal's plate and glass. "You can bet the big guy's not gonna skip *his* lunch."

"I take it he's finished with me, right?" Paul asked.

"I'd say so. I'm to drive him back downtown in…" he looked at his watch, "… eight minutes." He turned to go, then turned back. "I'm not kidding. Eat. It's rule number three in the Celibate's Handbook: 'Grab any decent meal that shows up, especially a free one.'"

After Tom left the room Paul took his advice and ate both of the sandwiches. And he accepted more iced tea when one of the nuns brought it in. His pulse was racing, and he didn't feel like eating, but it was the only meal he'd had so far that day. He did, though, turn down the chocolate cake one of the nuns offered, while the other cleared the table. "It's low-fat, Father," she said.

"No thank you, Sister. But…I *would* like some coffee if you have it. Regular, please, not decaf."

While she went for the coffee he got up and went down the hall to the closet by the front door and got his phone from his raincoat pocket. By the time he got back to the breakfast nook the nun was coming in from the kitchen, carrying a tray with a carafe of coffee, a cup and saucer made of delicate china, and cream and sugar. She poured his coffee and left.

He drank a cup and quickly poured himself another. That anyone should suspect him of murder was absurd. But in his dealings with priests accused in the sex abuse scandal he'd learned enough about the criminal justice system to know he shouldn't waste a minute. He had Brian Joplin's phone number programmed into his phone, and he made the call.

"Brian Joplin here."

"Yes, Brian, it's Father Paul Clark."

"Damn, when *you* call I know it's *another* one."

"This time it's...a little different. I'm the client."

"Oh." There was a pause, and then, "Don't say anything about it on the phone. Don't talk to anybody till you talk to me. Not the police. Not the press. Not the alleged victim. Not the family. Not the cardinal. Not your best friend. Nobody. Don't admit anything. Don't deny anything. Got it? But I can't see you till tomorrow afternoon."

"It's not a sex abuse charge, and it can't wait till tomorrow."

"What *is* it, then? I mean, *don't* tell me what happened. Just tell me the charge."

"I haven't been charged with anything. I haven't even been told I'm a suspect. But the police are getting search warrants and subpoenas, and there's been a...a suggestion...that they're looking at me. In connection with Father Landrew's murder."

"You gotta be kid— Well, I got appointments all afternoon, but I guess I can fit you in at...damn...let's see...four o'clock. My office. Sharp."

"I have another appointment at four. One I can't miss."

"What can be more important than—"

"This one is. What about later? What about six o'clock?"

"You priests are gonna get me divorced. But...yes...six is okay. My office."

†

Paul sat for several long moments, staring down at his coffee, taking deep breaths, trying to lower a pulse rate he could feel rising out of control. He had come to the mansion with a plan: he would tell the cardinal everything and, whatever the effect on his reputation and career, at least he'd be moving toward a resolution. But his plan, and the hope it had promised, vanished with the cardinal's refusal even to listen, and his direction that Paul "take some time off" and say mass only "in private."

That he might actually be a suspect in Larry's murder was bizarre... and truly frightening. But that the cardinal would move so quickly to distance himself, and the church, from a priest who'd served so faithfully, for so long? That was heartbreaking. Paul had a glimmer now of the hopeless abandonment an accused sex abuser—especially an innocent one—must feel.

And in addition to that, Paul was angry.

The anger took him by surprise. But it woke him up, as well. The cardinal was acting according to his own lights, and had moved firmly and swiftly. Paul's problem, however, was his own, not the cardinal's. He didn't regret for a moment his decision to save Robert. And though the path he'd chosen may not have been the wisest, it had been his choice, and now he had to find his way through to the end.

He looked up to see one of the nuns standing over him. "Is there anything else, Father?"

"Actually, there *is*," he said.

She was back in a few minutes with more coffee, a piece of chocolate cake, and a business phone directory. He drank the coffee, ate the cake, and found a low-end car rental agency, a place called Rent-a-Wreck, near Lincoln and Belmont Avenues.

TWENTY-NINE

It was a quarter after three by the time he left the rental agency in a battered, four-year-old Dodge Caravan, on his way to visit his mother. He took Ashland north to Ridge Avenue, then Ridge to Devon and the cemetery. He parked a block away and walked down Devon to the north entrance. This was where his mother was buried, in the fifth of a plot of six grave sites purchased nearly a hundred years earlier by her German ancestors.

It was a tiny, virtually unknown cemetery, a corner of Eden tucked behind a brick wall near a noisy urban intersection. It had been the graveyard for St. Henry's parish, established at the turn of the twentieth century to serve the German immigrants who lived in the area. The church itself was a handsome brick neo-Gothic structure, complete with limestone trim, slate roof, and a tall, square clock tower. By the 1970s, with the Germans long gone, the Croatian community had taken over. Since then the church had been spruced up—although none of the four clocks in the tower worked—and had gone through two name changes. The cemetery, though, remained "St. Henry's."

The grounds were still well tended by workers from a larger cemetery nearby, but St. Henry's was just about inactive. No grave sites were still available for purchase, and few burials took place there. There was no office and no staff, and it was rare that Paul saw anyone else there at all.

He walked along the wide asphalt path, then cut across the grass to his mother's grave, near the southwest corner of the property. The traffic noise was muted by the tall brick wall along the street, but the wall here was just waist high, and topped with a chain link fence. The neighbor beyond that fence was Misericordia, a Catholic home for developmentally disabled children and adults. These days the signage said "Misericordia/Heart of Mercy," as the Sisters of Mercy who ran it were gradually changing the name from Latin to English.

He stood in the grass and looked down at his mother's grave, murmuring a Hail Mary. He thought about what Larry had told Celia... that he didn't care about his funeral because by that time he'd be with God. Paul understood that. He believed—with a faith that made no claim to clarity—that his mother was somehow in the presence of God, and not here, moldering away in the ground. Still, he always said her favorite prayer over her remains, and sometimes went so far as to *talk* to her, even though he knew there was no more—and no less—chance of her hearing him here than at Notre Dame Stadium on a Saturday afternoon in the fall.

He seldom missed his monthly visits. He suspected, without feeling guilty about it at all, that he might not have been so faithful if St. Henry's hadn't been such an oasis of tranquility in an all-too-frantic world.

Now, though, peace and tranquility had to battle with fear and confusion. And, all along, he kept his eyes open. The first time Ann Swanson had met him here he hadn't been expecting her, and she'd simply appeared, as though out of nowhere. This time he was watching.

It wasn't quite four o'clock yet, and his mind went to Celia's insistence that no one from the neighborhood around St. Manfred's would have killed Larry. She was surely being unrealistic. Some addicts would kill their own mothers for drugs. But what she said *did* fit in with what he himself had heard—at least, *thought* he'd heard—when he was lying facedown in the rain behind the rectory: a car stopping in the alley...maybe a car door closing...and the car driving away.

†

He saw Ann approach, but the direction she came from—for what he hoped would be their last meeting—took him by surprise. She came from the Misericordia side, slipping through a small gap in the south wall, near the corner, a gap he'd never noticed before.

Ann was his age or a few years younger, and only about an inch shorter than him. She was attractive, and very sure of herself. Her hair was coal black and cut short, and her dark complexion and high cheek bones looked Italian to him. He found himself wondering whether "Swanson" was even her real name…deciding it probably wasn't, and that it made no difference. She wore a light tan raincoat that was belted at the waist and came to about her knees, and calf-length leather boots. Her hands were stuck in her coat pockets, and she wasn't carrying a purse. She walked smoothly, with the erect posture and casual grace of an athlete.

Anyone watching—although he certainly saw no one—would have thought she was ignoring him. She walked on by and stopped maybe twenty yards away at a monument that was about twelve feet tall and included a wide stone base with the name *SAUER* carved on its side, then a fluted column pedestal topped with a statue of the Virgin Mary. Through the years weather had rounded the edges of the letters and blurred the features of Mary's face. Ann stood there a minute, staring up at the statue, and then came and joined him.

"Walk back with me," she said. "Act like we're interested in the monument." Her gaze was direct and her voice was strong, and she was clearly accustomed to having people like him do what she told them.

He walked with her.

He'd wandered this cemetery often enough, and he knew that the Sauer monument was unusual in that it contained no words other than the surname itself. There were two grave markers in front of the base, flat stone rectangles set flush with the ground. The one on the left said simply "Jack." The other said "Helen." No dates of birth or death, not even an "R.I.P."

"We'll wait here a minute before we talk," Ann said. "I want to be sure you weren't followed."

"What? Why do you—"

"Just *wait*. And be *quiet*!"

The contempt and aggression in her voice made him cringe, but he felt something else, too. A renewed surge of anger, similar to what he'd felt at the cardinal's mansion. Ann's intention, her strategy, was to intimidate him. She needed to keep him in his place, keep him obedient to her. He thought back to the cardinal's surprise at lunch, when Paul hadn't maintained his usual deference and had spoken up to him. Maybe he didn't always have to play by other people's rules.

He pointed down at the marker on the left. "I like to think that's Sailor Jack buried there," he said. Not exactly talking back, but not being *quiet*, either. "He's the only 'Jack' I've found here."

"What are you talking about?"

"Sailor Jack. The boy on the Cracker Jack box." He knew trivia like this would irritate her. "Cracker Jacks were invented in Chicago, for the Columbian Exposition, and legend has it the boy on the box is buried here."

"Are you losing your..." She stopped, then said, "I don't have time for this. After you talked to the police this morning, you had a meeting with Cardinal Nesbitt, right?"

"Yes." She couldn't have known that unless she was having him followed, or tapping the rectory phone, or...or *what*?

"Did you tell the police, or the cardinal, anything about the agency and Fair Hope?"

"No." *Not exactly*. "Why do you ask?"

"Because I want to know. I told you *not* to."

"Yes, you did," he said. "But I don't work for you, and...and I don't appreciate your attitude." It felt good, standing up to her, but he still had to fight to keep his voice from trembling. "We had an agreement and I kept my part. It's over now."

She stared at him. "I don't know what's come over you, but believe me, what you 'appreciate' makes no difference to me. Nothing is over. You—"

Frantic screams filled the air and they both whirled around.

A pre-teen girl came bursting in through the Devon Avenue entrance, followed by three other girls in hot pursuit. It was all in fun, though, and they laughed and giggled when they caught her. Then it started all over, with a new one running from the others, weaving around the tombstones and monuments.

"Come this way," Ann said. She turned and headed east through the grave markers toward the church.

He did as she told him. He didn't like it, but he couldn't help himself. He was in over his head...and he was more afraid of her than ever.

THIRTY

They walked to the opposite end of the cemetery, leaving the girls behind. All the grave markers in this section, right next to the church, were stones set flush with the ground. Dominating the scene was a World War I memorial, a near-life-sized statue of Jesus embracing a cross while, at the same time, comforting a soldier and a sailor.

Ann went across and sat on a stone bench with her back to the monument, and Paul joined her. From there they could look out at the whole cemetery.

"What do you mean, 'Nothing is over'?" Paul asked. "You told me you'd be out of Fair Hope by Thursday."

"That was before your friend died."

"He didn't *die*. He was murdered."

"He's dead, and there's no reason now for my people to abandon a very important station."

"You can't—" He stopped. "I guess," he said, "that whoever killed Larry did you a big favor."

"There was a benefit, yes. To me. To you, too. In fact, to the whole country. It's not pleasant to look at a death that way, of course. But... bad things happen."

"Yes, they do." It was now or never for the question that was haunting him more with each passing hour. "So Fair Hope," he said, "is a 'very important station.' Is it...is it important enough that *you* had Larry killed?"

She turned and looked straight at him, but gave no sign that she was disturbed by his question. "We were on our way out. Then your friend died. Murdered, yes, by some as yet unidentified person. But he might have had a heart attack, or been run over by a bus. The effect is the same. He's dead. We're staying."

"But you were afraid he might have left something about the CIA on his computer, or some notes, or—"

"Yes, and at the very time I mentioned that to you, you already *had* his laptop. Why didn't you tell me that?"

"I hid it first, and then went back for it because I had the same idea you did. And I didn't tell you because... well...I don't know why."

"Because you thought I had Father Landrew murdered?"

"No," he said. "I thought about that later. Anyway, it's...just a question."

"I see, 'just a question.' And if you'd found something on the laptop, what were you going to do? Delete it?"

"I don't know. I never got that far. There was nothing there, nothing about Fair Hope. I'd already looked at his notebooks at the rectory. There was nothing about it in them, either."

"And now you've given the laptop to the police." It was his turn to be surprised, and she must have seen it on his face, because she said, "It's my business to know things. Just like your business is...what? Getting people to obey the rules so they can go to heaven? I do better than you do, I think."

"I didn't *give* anything to the police. They *took* it."

"And why wouldn't they? They knew how interested you were in seeing what your friend wrote. You went to such great lengths to take the laptop, look through it, and then try to return it again—in secret. They may even wonder whether you went back and broke into the school, still looking for something."

"That's absurd." *But Maddox had seemed to be going that way.*

"They know that *someone* drove that rental car back to your place." She paused, then asked, "Did he leave any backup disks, or CDs, in the school office?"

"How would I know?" He wondered if she was deliberately trying to confuse him, and decided not to mention what Celia had said.

"Uh-huh." Ann was silent for a moment, and then said, "I'm told the police have looked at the notebooks, too. There are things about them they find interesting."

"What?" His heart was beating too fast. "What did they find?"

"For one thing, one of the notebooks—the one with the latest entries—has three pages fewer than it should have."

"Three pages?" His mind couldn't keep up with what he was hearing. "Missing?"

"Assuming it wasn't a factory error, someone removed three pages. They've taken fingerprints from the books…and from the laptop as well. Do you know whether your prints are in the national database?"

"I assume so. When I was in the army I—"

"The only prints on the laptop were a few on the outside, consistent with your handling it when you gave it to them. Otherwise, nothing, not on the keys or anywhere, not even smudges. As though you wiped it clean before you set out to return it."

"I just…that doesn't prove anything."

"But you must admit, that *would* be interesting to police detectives. And something else. Their computer experts have determined that certain material has been erased…deleted…from the laptop. And not just deleted—which doesn't really remove things, as you may know—but also overwritten with gibberish. 'Washed,' it's sometimes called, although that's a figure of speech. Nothing's really washed away. Just covered up. And in this case, they say, irretrievably."

"That wasn't done by me. I wouldn't even know *how* to do that."

"Done by *someone*. And what's most intriguing is that their experts say they can tell *when* this overwriting was done. Something to do with the software used. They say it was done within the last twenty-four to thirty-six hours."

"But that's…" He found it difficult to process what she'd said. "That's…not possible."

"You understand the problem. During that time, the only persons who had access to the laptop were Father Landrew, yourself, and the police."

"I...I guess Larry could have done it."

"Theoretically, yes. And the police could have done it, too. Neither of those alternatives, however, seems likely. But you? Because you were so anxious to get your hands on that laptop, the detectives are wondering what material you thought might be on it. They wonder if it was something damaging to *yourself*, so damaging that you might kill someone to keep it secret. And then delete the material."

"But *you* can tell them what I was looking for. Larry said he discovered evidence the CIA was using the clinic as a base. I was trying to protect a CIA mission."

She stared at him. "And just when did I say the CIA was involved?"

"You were very careful not to. But that's the only...anyway, I was trying to protect your mission."

"I never told you to tear out any pages, or delete anything. In fact, I have only your word as to what Father Landrew told you. On that basis, I can hardly agree to expose my operation to the Chicago Police Department."

"But what if the police actually try to make a case against me?"

"If they charge you, it'll be a weak case, I'm sure, with many unanswered questions. You'll get a lawyer and, at the very worst, the state would accept a guilty plea to some lesser charge."

He couldn't believe what he was hearing. "You must be crazy. If it looks like they may actually charge me, I'll *tell* them what it was I was looking for."

"Really? Will you tell them you made a secret deal, with what you suspected was the CIA, to use a church facility? I won't presume to speak for the CIA, but it's safe to say they'd deny such a claim. At any rate, will you tell the police that you've been carrying on a calculated campaign of lies and deceit? That you did it all because you had an illegitimate son who was in jail on drug charges? That you also got regular payments of money in exchange?" She shook her head. "You won't do it."

"To keep myself from going to prison for the rest of my life? I'd *have* to."

"But you won't. As I said, any murder case against you will be weak, and—"

"I won't plead guilty to any crime. I'll tell them everything, and defend myself."

"No, I'm quite sure you won't." She paused, and it was suddenly very quiet within the cemetery walls. He looked around and realized the girls were gone. "You see," she added, "there's something else you need to consider."

"What?" A heavy sense of dread was building in his chest. "What else?"

"Those two men."

"Two men?"

"Yes, the ones who appeared unexpectedly one morning in a dismal Mexican jail. They went into a cell. Violence occurred. And when the guards arrived one of the prisoners had escaped…and another had bled to death. What you need to consider is whether those two men might appear again somewhere, just as unexpectedly, and might sweep up that escaped prisoner and put him back where he'd been. This time, though, facing additional charges. Jail break…and murder."

"You can't…" His throat was so tight he could barely get the words out. "You can't do that."

"I can…but I won't." She nodded slightly toward him. "You'll see to that."

THIRTY-ONE

Brian Joplin's office was at LaSalle Street and Wacker Drive and until that day Paul had never been there. He always met Brian at the Office of Pastoral Care, a mile or so farther north, to discuss the priest sex abuse cases Brian was defending. This time, though, Paul was the client. He felt the difference. His appointment was for six, and it was already a quarter after six but Brian was at his desk, on the phone with someone else.

Paul was still in a daze, disoriented by Ann Swanson's threat—made so casually. He got up and walked over to one of the office's two large windows. The view was to the north, across Wacker Drive and the Chicago River. It was a clear, bright evening, and the lowering sun made the river sparkle. It flowed from east to west here—a direction of flow created by human engineering, to keep the river from emptying into the lake—and a few blocks to the west and beyond his view, it split into its north and south branches.

He watched an evening tour boat pass by on the river, then slip under the LaSalle Street bridge and out of sight. He imagined himself on that boat. He wished—

A tap on his shoulder startled him and he spun around. Brian was right there, backing away and holding his palms up. "Hey, take it easy, Father. I was asking if I could get you something. Coffee? Pepsi? A beer, if you like."

"No thanks. I'm fine." He didn't know if he'd be able to keep anything down. "And...let's drop the 'Father.' It's Paul."

"Wow, that's a shock." Brian returned to his desk and sat down.

"Shock?" Paul went back to his chair, too.

"It's just that you're usually…I don't know…pretty formal."

"Oh. Well, lots of things are happening now that don't 'usually' happen."

"Uh-huh." Brian twisted around toward a credenza behind him, and turned back with a yellow legal pad. He took a pen and wrote something on the first sheet, probably Paul's name. "I have your office number, of course," he said. "How else can I reach you?"

"I won't be in the office for a while. Cardinal Nesbitt thinks it better that I'm not."

"Damn. Oh, I get it. That 'suggestion' you told me about—that the cops are looking at you—must have come from the cardinal, huh?"

"I didn't say that. But anyway, don't call me there."

"Okay. How about a cell number?"

"Ah…no. I almost never use a cell phone. Just call me at St. Hildegard's." He gave him the number. "If I'm not there, there'll be voice mail. Oh, and if a Father Kincannon answers…which he hardly ever does…have him switch you to voice mail. He's not good at passing on messages."

"Fair enough." Brian picked up his legal pad and leaned back in his chair. "Okay, let's start with a few questions."

"Let's start with the fact that I didn't do it."

"Did I ask you that?"

"No, but I didn't *do* it. Where would I get a gun? Do they think I shot Father Landrew and then hit myself in the head and kicked in my ribs? It's absurd."

"Y'know what, Fath…I mean…Paul?"

"What?"

"I'm hoping to get out of this damn office before my wife and kids are asleep. So, here's the plan: first, you *listen* to my question…and then, you *answer* my question. And I guarantee you, I'm *not* gonna ask you if you're guilty. I can figure that out for myself. Okay?"

"Okay."

†

An hour later, Brian Joplin walked Paul down a dimly lit corridor, past a half-dozen empty offices and out to the suite's deserted reception area.

"Man," Brian said, "I am *really* tired." He stretched and yawned widely, as though to prove the point. "But look, I *have* to know why you went back for that laptop, what you thought you might find on it. You don't wanna tell the cops...okay. For now. But you *gotta* tell *me*. Call me tomorrow and say you've changed your mind. And— Oh, you had a coat, right?" He opened a closet door and Paul's black raincoat was the only thing hanging there.

"Thanks," Paul said, and slid his arms into the coat while Brian held it for him. "I understand the problem, but I'm not changing my mind." As he spoke he took his cell phone from his raincoat pocket. There was a message waiting. From a number he didn't want a call from.

"Caught ya," Brian said, smiling. "You said you never use a cell phone."

"I said 'almost' never."

"Oh, right. Anyway, think about—"

The phone in Paul's hand rang. A call from the same number. He looked at Brian. "I...uh...can I sit here in the waiting room a minute? Alone? I should take this."

"Sure. Call me tomorrow." Brian headed back toward his office, leaving Paul alone.

By then the phone had stopped ringing, but he called the number back. "Headmaster Grayson, please," he said to the woman who answered.

"May I ask who's calling?"

"Michael Clark." Michael was Paul's father's name and, in fact, was the first name on his own birth certificate, although he had never used it, not even on legal documents. "He's been trying to—"

"Hold on, please."

There was an agonizingly long pause, and then, "Alfred Grayson here. Thanks for calling back."

"Of course, but what is it? Is Robert all right? Is he ill?"

"Robert's health is fine, as far as I know. But sometime this afternoon he disappeared. He took one of the school vehicles with him."

THIRTY-TWO

Paul raced to St. Hildegard's and changed from his clerical clothes into his "civvies"—including an expensive tie and sport coat he'd bought just for visits to Bridgebriar. As he drove away from the rectory in the Dodge Caravan, he fought to keep his speed down close to the limit. He didn't need a ticket.

Robert had warned him he would run away. And now he'd done it. Or worse, he hadn't. Paul had never told Ann Swanson where Robert was. Had she somehow found him, and moved in on him already?

It was eight o'clock, an hour past sundown. Southbound on the Dan Ryan he almost missed his turn and had to cut across two lanes onto the ramp to the Skyway. It struck him, barreling through the darkness and climbing more than a hundred feet above the tired bungalows and abandoned steel mills of the city's southeast side, that the cell phone in his gym bag in the back seat was turned off. What if Robert tried to call? But that seemed unlikely, and at least he wouldn't have to field calls from Ann Swanson.

He left the city, surrounded by the night and feeling absolutely alone. No one knew where he was, or where he was going. No one but God. *Maybe* God. He hoped so.

And all this because he'd gone to a Mexican jail and looked into the eyes of a helpless, hopeless boy. Until then Paul hadn't had a person in the world to worry about except himself, a pampered cleric whose problems were negligible. But at that table, assaulted by the fearful screams and curses of broken men that even thick stone walls couldn't shut out, his comfortable life had been shattered. A thousand times he'd mouthed the advice that helping those in need brought one "closer to God." But when faced with a real person who desperately needed someone to care about him, he couldn't believe how suddenly, how achingly, his heart had broken open. For his own son.

And then?

Then, almost immediately, his love and care for Robert had him making secret agreements he had no authority to make, telling lies that led to more lies, all the while spending time and money he couldn't afford. Was he "closer to God"?

He had a three-hundred-fifty mile drive ahead of him.

†

"Join us in the middle of nowhere, and discover how far you can go." That was the slogan of Bridgebriar School, and the "middle of nowhere" in question lay halfway between Saginaw Bay and Lake Huron, near the north end of the "Thumb" region of Michigan. Bridgebriar was modeled after a New England prep school, but the students were all "struggling teens." For most of them, Bridgebriar was their parents' last hope.

The headmaster, Alfred Grayson, had years of experience with troubled youth, and wasn't one to panic. During their phone call he'd agreed not to call the police...yet. After all, Robert might return any minute. Besides, the truck was an old junker used in the school's auto mechanics class, and Paul promised to be there in the morning and buy another truck if necessary. Which he couldn't possibly afford to do.

At four in the morning he pulled into the visitors' lot. It had taken him nearly seven hours, and he could scarcely remember the drive.

It wouldn't help to charge in and wake everyone up before dawn. Besides, he'd nearly killed himself nodding off at the wheel a few times. So he figured out how to fold the rear seats down, and tried to get some sleep on the Caravan's rock-hard cargo bed.

†

At eight o'clock Paul set out on foot across the Bridgebriar campus. He found the dining hall and went inside. A friendly teacher spotted him as a hungry parent and invited him to have breakfast in the faculty section. Paul couldn't believe how good the pancakes and sausages were, and was grateful none of the teachers mentioned Robert's having run off with one of the school's vehicles. They probably didn't know about it yet.

At nine he was pacing nervously in a luxuriously furnished, musty-smelling reception parlor. Five minutes later Alfred Grayson showed up. He was very tall, maybe six-foot-four, and combined the gray-templed good looks of a "headmaster" with the rugged, take-charge demeanor of an NFL quarterback. "Good news," he said, grabbing Paul's hand and shaking it. "During the night Robert came back...with the truck."

"Thank God," Paul managed to say, as Grayson led the way to his office.

The two men sat down across the desk from each other. "I'm glad, too," Grayson said. "I pride myself on my judgment of young people, and I'd be surprised to find out he's a thief." The headmaster droned on about how Robert was just the sort of student Bridgebriar was designed to help, and Paul felt relief replacing the panic that had been gripping him. Then relief gave way—not surprisingly, given too little sleep and too much breakfast—to drowsiness. "...doing fine academically," Grayson was saying. "But his social adjustment ..." He held out his hand, palm down, and waggled it. "So-so."

"I understand," Paul said, "but I assure you that—"

"Ahhh, just in time." Grayson rose to his feet as his secretary came in and set a tray with coffee and two mugs on the corner of the desk. "Thank you so much, Ruth," he said, sitting down again. "Mr. Clark here looks as though he could use a little caffeine."

The woman filled one mug and gave it to Paul. "Cream? Sugar?"

"No, thanks." He took the mug in two hands. The coffee was delicious, and very strong.

She filled the headmaster's mug and added lots of cream and sugar. "Mr. Frederickson," she said, "will have Robert come to the office after his first class. He has a double at nine today, so that should be about eleven. Is that okay? Or do you—"

"That's fine, Ruth." Grayson accepted his coffee with a smile. "Thank you." When she was gone he said, "Robert's not a bad kid. After all, he *did* come back with the truck, and with at least a stab at a plausible explanation. Something about test driving some new spark plugs and getting stalled. I don't believe a word of it, of course."

"He's had a tough go of it for quite some time," Paul said.

"All of our students have had 'a tough go of it' in some way or other. But as to Robert...I assume there've been no brushes with the law besides what you told me?"

"Not to my knowledge." He hadn't told Grayson anything about Mexico. "As I told you before, Robert's mother and I weren't married. She and her parents didn't want me involved. We'd broken up and I was in the army when Robert was born. She died in childbirth and her parents—Robert's grandparents—raised Robert. They never told Robert about me, never tried to contact me. They were afraid I'd take the child and they'd have nothing. His grandmother's the one who told me all this. She also said he was picked up with marijuana on that one occasion, but that went nowhere. Later, when she was dying, she contacted me. When she died...I stepped in."

"Which I find quite admirable," Grayson said. "Not many men *would* have."

"Thanks, I...well...I have no doubt that he's my son. But we're still getting to know each other. I never married, you know, and I've concentrated—maybe too much—on building up my business. I just thought this was my chance to...to make a connection."

"And you still haven't told him you're his father?"

"No, I...apparently his grandparents told him they had no idea who his father was, and he's apparently never shown an interest in finding out. I don't know that he's ready for me to tell him it's me. Or maybe *I'm* not ready." Paul sipped at his coffee, trying to concentrate. He'd told Grayson he was in international sales—*à la* Hank Manion—but had tried to keep most things as vague, yet as close to the truth, as possible. Using what was technically his own first name; staying with Robert's real last name: Johnson. There were probably thousands of "Robert Johnsons" around the country, and he and Robert had reversed some numbers in Robert's social security number so he couldn't be traced that way. "I only hope this...this truck incident...hasn't soured you on him."

The headmaster leaned back in his chair, touching the tips of his fingers and thumbs together in front of his chest. "Robert can be a little... uncooperative...even surly, at times," he said. "But he's a teenager, after all, and this is his first major lapse at Bridgebriar." He rested his hands on his desk and leaned forward. "And you yourself have been most cooperative."

"I try." For one thing, he'd paid a full year's tuition in advance—using every cent he could get his hands on, including what he'd been saving for a new car.

"So," Grayson said, "let's give Robert another chance."

Paul sighed. "You won't regret it. When he's here, maybe together we can talk—"

"I don't think so. I find it puts a lot of pressure on a young person to have to come in here and face both me and a parent at the same time. Why don't you two talk it over? Go for a walk, or a drive. Oh, wait." He opened a desk drawer and brought out a baseball glove. Brand new, with the tags still attached. "I think it helps kids—boys especially—to have something to fidget with when they talk. Robert likes baseball, and he's pretty good. Tell him you bought this for him. He just had a birthday, you know."

Stunned and embarrassed that he'd missed that fact entirely, Paul took the glove. The leather felt soft and supple. "Thanks, but I don't—"

"It's a very good glove. We'll add the cost to your supplies bill. Talk to him. See if my 'fidgeting theory' works. Go somewhere and have lunch if you like. Tell him he's getting a second chance if he wants to stay. I'll see him when you get back."

"Thank you again. And don't worry. He won't pull something like this again." The sense of relief he felt led him easily into playing the role of the stereotypical father of a teen, making promises he couldn't back up.

"We'll both do what we can," Grayson said. "But remember, he's immature for his age, but he *is* eighteen now. We can't *make* him stay at Bridgebriar."

THIRTY-THREE

"If you wait here you'll be able to see him coming," the secretary said, leading Paul to a seat by a window in the reception area. "More coffee?"

"That'd be great. Thanks."

"And I'll get you a gift bag to put that baseball glove in, so Robert won't see what it is till you give it to him. That's nicer."

"Oh, right. Thanks."

†

At five minutes to eleven Paul saw Robert coming across the lawn, not looking much like the gaunt, haunted prisoner he'd been at their first meeting. Except for the ever-present scowl on his face, he was a good-looking kid, much better looking than Paul had ever been, actually. But the resemblance was there: the wide-set eyes, the thick black hair low on his forehead, the hint of cleft in his chin. His hair hung down to an inch from his collar, the maximum length the school allowed. He still looked young for his age, was still thin, too, even though probably twenty pounds heavier than the skeleton he'd been. He seemed quite healthy now, and actually looked taller. Five foot eleven, maybe, and apparently still growing.

Closer up, it was difficult to say how Robert was doing inwardly. He seemed to be trying hard to show no feeling at all. They said hello and shook hands in that awkward, distant way they always did, Paul forcing a smile and Robert looking somewhere past his shoulder.

They walked together toward the car, Paul carrying the bag with the glove in it. "It's that Caravan over there."

"Uh-huh." They reached the car and got in. "I thought you had a Corolla."

"I do, but it's…it's in the shop." Trying to get a conversation going, all he could come up with was, "This is a rental."

"Uh-huh." The dull, sullen look and tone would have been more irritating if Paul hadn't been trying, as he always did, to remember what the boy had been through…even *before* Mexico.

They got in the car and Paul said, "Here. I got something for you." He held out the bag and Robert took it. "Open it. It's for you."

Robert reached into the bag and took out the glove. He looked at Paul. "You brought this here? For me?"

"Actually, I had Mr. Grayson buy it." He took the gift bag and tossed it in the back seat. "I don't know much about baseball gloves and I wanted to make sure it was the right kind. But I'm paying for it."

"Yeah?" The boy turned the glove over in his hands, then slipped it on. "Uh, thanks."

"You're welcome." Paul found himself wondering whether Robert sounded like his mother. Strange, he thought, and sad, too, that he couldn't really remember the voice of the girl he'd thought he loved so desperately for a few months in college.

"…*is* it, anyway?" Robert was asking.

"What?" Paul was taken by surprise. In the few meetings they'd had so far, he couldn't recall Robert inquiring about much of anything, or saying much at all on his own. Maybe Grayson's "fidgeting theory" was true.

"I said how old *is* this car?" Robert was slipping his hand in and out of the glove.

"Three years." Paul started the engine. "Best I could get on short notice. If I'd known I was going to have to drive up here last night I'd have tried for a Mustang convertible."

"The radio work?" Robert rested the glove in his lap.

"Yes, but let's have some quiet for a while. So we can talk." He twisted around to look out the rear window as he backed out of the parking space.

Robert turned, too. "How come you got the seats folded down?"

They both turned to face forward and Paul pulled out of the parking lot. "I drove all night, and that's where I slept this morning after I got here." He turned onto the long drive toward the school entrance.

"Uh-huh," Robert said. "So...why'd you do that?"

"Well, the closest hotel is—"

"No. I mean why'd you take all night and drive here?" He was playing with the glove again.

"Because I thought you stole a truck. Which meant you were in trouble, and I was worried about you."

"Oh." There was a long pause, and finally, "Can we have the radio on now?"

"No." Paul was no better at moving the conversation along than Robert, but he was the adult, so he had to keep trying. "You know, I'm glad you came back last night."

"Yeah...well...whatever."

"Why *did* you take off with the truck, anyway?"

"I don't know. I didn't...I just felt like going away. Driving somewhere." Robert lowered his window, but the incoming air was cold and he raised it again. "You never told me why you're doing all this." He wasn't looking at Paul as he spoke. Just staring ahead through the windshield. "I mean... sending your men to get me out of jail, putting me in school. You don't even *know* me. So why?"

This was the first sudden leap into an area Paul knew should already have been addressed. But he still wasn't ready to deal with it, so all he said was, "Those weren't *my* men. I don't even know exactly what they did. You wouldn't talk about it at all."

"They told me not to." Robert reached for the radio, then pulled his hand back. "Those guys...they were...you wouldn't wanna do something if they said not to. Anyway, you *sent* 'em, right?"

"Not...exactly."

"But it was *because* of you."

"I guess so, yes."

"Y'know?" Robert said. "I already figured out what you're not telling me."

Paul's heart jumped, but then realized the boy was probably mistaken. The students' Internet access was supposed to be tightly controlled, and even if Robert somehow got the opportunity, an online search for *Michael Clark* wouldn't get him very far. "What do you mean?"

"You work for the government, right?"

"No. I'm sure I told you, I'm in sales and marketing, in Chicago. It's not very exciting."

"Uh-huh."

They were entering a town called Appleville. Hardly big enough to be a town. He pulled in and parked at a gas station/convenience store called Casey's. He didn't need gas. He needed to change the subject. "Did they tell you at school if you could graduate next June? Will you have enough credits?"

"I might, if— Why should I tell *you* stuff when you won't tell *me* stuff?"

"I already *told* you. I heard you were in trouble. I was a friend of your mother's in college. There was a group of us. We were all very close. I knew your grandmother, too." He should have just said it: *I'm your father.* But he couldn't, and he didn't know why. Why was he still waiting for the boy to show some sign of...of something?

"If you were a friend, how come I never heard of you?"

"We all drifted apart after I went into the army. I actually never knew your grandmother real well. I was surprised myself when, all these years later, she came to me out of nowhere. She was desperate, and told me your mother was dead, and you needed help. I started to say no, then I thought to myself, 'I'm not married, don't have anyone I'm taking care of.' So I just...I thought I'd see what I could do. And then, when I saw the conditions you were in...well..." He looked around for some distraction. "You want a soda or something?"

"Yeah, something, I guess."

They went into the store and bought a Michigan road map for Paul and a Mountain Dew for Robert. They went back outside and stood in the warmth of the bright sun, breathing in the odors of gasoline and motor oil. "They're not kicking you out of Bridgebriar, you know," Paul said.

"They're not, huh?" Acting like he didn't care…and maybe he didn't.

"Nope. No such luck. And they're not reporting the truck stolen, either."

"I was surprised the cops weren't there waiting when I got back." He swished the Mountain Dew around in the can. "It's because *you* came, right?"

"That helped, but Mr. Grayson likes you, thinks you have potential."

"Bullshit." Robert finished his Mountain Dew and crumpled the can in his fist. "The guy doesn't even *know* me."

Wondering if all teenagers worked that hard to be unlikeable, Paul unfolded the map. He studied it for a minute, then refolded it and started toward the Caravan. "There's a bigger town on this road, about thirty miles up. We'll get lunch there, then go back."

"Whatever," Robert said. "Hey, can I drive?"

"The rental agreement doesn't—" He stopped. "Do you know *how* to drive?"

"I took Driver's Ed."

"Uh-huh, but the question is, do you know how to *drive*?"

"I drove that pickup, didn't I? And didn't crash it."

"Well then, go ahead." He tossed Robert the keys…against his better judgment.

"We should turn the radio on."

"Okay," Paul said. "But I choose the station."

He found a public radio station playing chamber music, and was surprised when Robert didn't complain. It didn't take long to realize that the boy hadn't driven very much, and needed all his concentration just to stay on the right side of the road. Paul kept his mouth shut, but he was terrified every time a car came from the opposite direction.

†

He couldn't believe it when Robert announced, "We're almost there."

"Oh." Paul looked around. "I guess I fell asleep."

"Yeah, you did." By then they were entering the town's business district and traffic was surprisingly heavy. "Um...you wanna drive?"

"No, you go ahead. You're doing great. I'll keep an eye out for some place for lunch." He felt good about letting Robert know he trusted him to drive.

Robert finally found an easy place to park, and pulled in. Paul grabbed his cell from the gym bag and they got out and walked back to a place called Estelle's. As soon as they were seated, Paul got up again and walked to the washroom. It was just off the kitchen and smelled of urine and French fries and...what? Strawberries, from that round pink brick of deodorant in the urinal.

He washed his hands, then called to check the rectory voice mail. The first three messages were from media people. The fourth was from Brian Joplin, urging Paul to change his mind—not saying about what—and asking for a return call. The fifth was from Celia Jackson. "Call me." She left a number. "As soon as you can. Please."

She sounded worried...maybe even scared.

THIRTY-FOUR

The rectory voice mail system didn't identify dates or times of calls, but he'd just talked to Brian Joplin the previous evening, so Brian's call was definitely made that morning, and Celia's call came after Brian's. Had she opened the CD?

He deleted all the messages and then tried the number she'd left.

"Hi, there," Celia said, in a happy lilting tone he'd never heard from her. "Sorry we can't take your call. But leave a message and one of us will get back to you."

He stared down at the phone. The difference between that voice and the voice that left the message was startling. He told himself she was just upset about Larry's death. Grieving. Not scared.

And this whole thing was just a bad dream.

†

Paul ordered two grilled cheese sandwiches and coffee, and Robert a burger, fries, and a strawberry shake. They waited in silence, both of them looking restlessly around the room, until Paul said, "I was tired, but I didn't think I'd fall asleep. Good thing you were able to drive."

"Yeah, no problem." Robert lined up the knife and fork on the table in front of him. "That Caravan...you know? It handles pretty well, for a minivan." As though he were a highly experienced driver. He really *was* just a boy in so many ways.

"Maybe so," Paul said. "But also, you're a pretty good driver." That was one untruth he didn't feel guilty about at all, not when he saw how it pleased Robert.

The waitress brought their food and there was more silence as they ate. Finally Robert said, "Thanks for the glove."

Paul looked up. "Oh, you're welcome." He found himself smiling, for probably the first time all day. "Mr. Grayson said you're pretty good at baseball."

Robert might have smiled too, just a little, but covered it with a bite into his burger. He chewed and swallowed and picked up his milkshake, then set it down. "I didn't exactly tell the truth, you know."

"Oh? What about?"

"I mean, I didn't exactly take Driver's Ed."

"Really," Paul said. "Didn't they teach it in your school?"

"Yeah, but...I got dropped from the class." He spent a few seconds re-aligning his knife and fork. "One of my classes at Bridgebriar is auto mechanics, and that's how I got my hands on the pickup truck. I just wanted to get away, y'know. It was stupid."

"Why'd you come back, anyway? No money for gas?"

"That wasn't it. There was enough gas in the tank to get me to Walton, where there's a bus station. I still had a little money, and I was thinking I'd leave the pickup on the street with the keys in it—where the cops'd find it and call the school. I was gonna take the bus somewhere. I didn't even know where. Maybe get a job working on cars or something. Like I said, I didn't really plan it out."

"So...what made you change your mind?"

"Like, where was I gonna go? Plus, I got...you know...scared." He grabbed his milkshake and sucked some up through the straw.

Paul didn't know what to say to this boy who'd wanted to run away, but was afraid to. "You were scared? Of what?"

"I mean, it was stupid, you know?" Robert said. "But when I went inside to buy a ticket I looked back out and saw this man. He was looking in the window of the pickup truck. I'm thinking...is he gonna see the keys and steal the truck, and is everyone gonna think I took it? But then the guy turned and walked away."

Paul waited, and finally said, “So…what was the scary thing?”

“It was that guy… by the pickup. It’s nuts, I know, but when he turned I saw the side of his face for a second and he looked like…you know…one of the two guys that took me out of jail in Mexico. The white guy. But I didn’t get a really good look at him before he was gone. It couldn’t have been him, right?”

“Right,” Paul said. “It couldn’t have been.”

THIRTY-FIVE

When they left Estelle's, it was raining, and Paul drove. He was still exhausted, and his side hurt every time he turned the wheel, but he managed. Headmaster Grayson was waiting for them when they got back, and by a quarter after two they'd all agreed that the truck incident was a thing of the past and Paul was anxious to leave for home.

Ann Swanson knew where Robert was. He was sure of it. But still, the boy should be safe at Bridgebriar—as long as Paul followed orders.

When he got back to the car he tried the rectory voice mail again. There were four new messages:

"Brian Joplin again. Call me."

"This is Celia again. Where *are* you? Don't you have a *cell* phone?"

"Detective Maddox here. We need to talk again. Today. Call me."

"It's Hank Manion, Father. I hear you're taking some time off. If there's anything I can do, let me know. Anything at all, just call."

Hank left a number and Paul wrote it down. He was surprised to hear from Hank, and encouraged, too, though he wasn't sure why. There was nothing Hank could do. Not about Ann Swanson, who could as easily send men to Michigan as to Mexico.

He called Celia, but got only her upbeat recorded voice again.

†

Pulling away from Bridgebriar, Paul had a growing appreciation of Robert's desire to get on a bus and ride away from his life. It was still raining. He drove for an hour, then stopped for gas and coffee. He tried Celia again, and again got the answering machine.

By three in the afternoon the rain had stopped. With no traffic problems, he might make it home by nine. He was headed for I-75, speeding along on a mostly empty road through open farmland. Drowsy, but making good time. At one point he saw a farm tractor ahead. It seemed far away, and he was stunned when he had to hit the breaks to avoid rear-ending it. The tractor pulled half off the road and he went around it.

A little farther along he noticed some horses, three of them, feeding on grass behind a fence up ahead to his right. It was peaceful here. The trees and the grass, and the horses and...

His head jerked up and he came awake with a start...careening to his right, leaving the road. He fought with the steering wheel, dropped into a weed-filled ditch, bounced up out of the ditch again... and hit a tree.

He switched off the engine and sat. It was easy just then—no matter how distant God had gotten these days—to say a prayer. Not asking for anything. Just saying thank you. He looked out and saw the three horses again, right up to the fence now, just a few yards away. They looked huge this close up, and stared at him with apparent curiosity.

The air bag had activated, and other than aggravation to his bruised ribs, he wasn't hurt. He got out and waded through waist-high, rain-soaked weeds to the other side of the minivan. One of the horses snorted and shook its head, and all three turned and trotted away. There wasn't much visible damage to the minivan. The ditch had slowed him down and the blow to the tree was a glancing one that pushed in the fender around the right front wheel well, pressing it against the tire.

He got a lug wrench from the spare tire well and waded again into the wet weeds. He wedged the handle of the wrench under the caved-in fender and, using the tire as leverage, managed—not without terrible pain from his bruised ribs—to pull the fender out, away from the tire. Then he got behind the wheel and backed up...and dropped into the ditch again, hopelessly trapped.

He didn't want to call 911. He wasn't hurt, and he certainly didn't want to deal with any more police officers. He needed a tow truck, and there'd been no town for miles. He sat there, hands on the wheel, pants soaking wet, and stared out the windshield. Then he heard the tractor pull up behind him.

He got out and stood behind the Caravan, and when the tractor stopped it struck him that tractors, like horses, don't seem very big until they're right up close. This one was huge, looming over him. A man who looked to be about sixty, in a denim jacket and a baseball cap, turned off the engine and climbed down.

"Afternoon," Paul said.

In lieu of an answer the farmer lifted his cap and swept his hand back over his head as though he had hair to brush back—when all he had were a few thin strands. His long, narrow face was sunbaked and his upper forehead and scalp were pale. He reset his cap and frowned. "Goin' a little too fast, were ya?"

"I guess so. You know where the nearest tow truck is?"

"Sure. Toby's Wrecker. You can call, and then you'll sit and wait and Toby'll finally come. It'll cost you a bundle."

"That's okay, I guess, but I—"

"Lemme look." The man walked up behind the Caravan and squatted on his heels and stared a few seconds, then went to the right side and laid down on his back in the wet weeds and slid half under the car. He got up and went to the other side and did the same thing. He stood up and looked at Paul. "Not hung up on nothin'. Just that wheel in the drainage ditch. I'll have you out in five minutes." He started back to his tractor.

"Uh...great," Paul said. "But...how much?"

The farmer stopped and turned and frowned again, this time as though Paul were wasting his time. "How *much*? Well, you'd be out a hunnerd bucks to Toby."

Paul checked his billfold. "I guess I can do that."

The farmer got a huge chain from a box behind the tractor seat and attached two smaller chains to one end of it to make a sort of 'Y'. He attached the two arms of the 'Y' to two places under the rear of the Caravan, and the leg of the 'Y'—the heavier chain—to the front of the tractor. The older man moved with surprising ease, was more agile than Paul, even without his bruised ribs.

"Put 'er in neutral," the man said. "And then get out and stay outta the way."

He waited while Paul did that, and then climbed up onto the tractor seat and checked the road in both directions. The engine roared to life and the tractor backed up, and dragged the Caravan—with a few bumps and groans—out of the ditch and up onto the road. Five minutes had been about right.

"Thank you!" Paul shouted.

The farmer nodded down to him. He cut the tractor engine and climbed down and unhitched the chains. "Start 'er up and make sure everything's okay."

Paul did that, trying both *Drive* and *Reverse.* Everything seemed fine.

He shut the car off and got back out. By then the farmer had stowed the chains and was obviously about to climb back up on his tractor. "Hold on!" Paul called.

The man turned and frowned again, and Paul thought maybe it wasn't impatience in the frown, after all. More like sadness. "Car not workin'?"

"No, it's fine," Paul said. "I need to pay you."

"What?" The man waved him off. "Hell, I was just talkin', is all."

"No, really. I want to pay you."

The man shook his head. "I'm not taking your money. But...I see you got one of those fishes on the back o' your car."

Paul turned. There was a little metal fish symbol stuck to the rear of the rented Caravan. A Jesus symbol. He hadn't noticed it before. "Yes," he said, "but—"

"That means you b'lieve in God...and Jesus...and all that. Right?"

"Um...yes. Sure."

"Well then…to pay me…you can say a prayer for my daughter. Name's Becky." He looked sadder than ever. "Her wedding's this Saturday."

"Congratulations! You must be very happy." He suddenly felt like a priest. "I'll remember her when I say…when I go to mass."

"Pray for *me*, too," the man said. "And the wife. We keep thinkin' it's a bad dream. But it's not. Becky just found out from the doctor last week. She got cancer, in one of her ovaries."

THIRTY-SIX

It was just past four o'clock when Paul reached the junction with I-75 and pulled into a truck stop. By then he'd nodded off again at least twice, and climbing on the interstate to go any farther was suicidal. On the other hand, checking into a motel was silly for the few hours he intended to nap, so he went inside and bought a cheap inflatable pillow and a travel alarm. He drove to a far corner of the parking lot, crawled into the back of the Caravan, and set the alarm for five hours.

He couldn't get comfortable. The pain in his side wouldn't go away, and it was colder in the car than he thought it would be. In addition, his pants were still soaking wet...and even colder than the air. He thought of taking them off and hanging them over the front seat to dry, but was afraid some security guy would come along and see him with his pants off and arrest him. Paul could see the headline: *Priest Caught Lurking Half-Naked In Public Parking Lot.*

Tired as he was, he couldn't sleep, and he couldn't turn off his fears. Thinking he could keep Robert hidden had been foolish. Keeping quiet about the CIA's involvement at Fair Hope Clinic would keep Ann Swanson from sending the boy back to Mexico, but it also might result in Paul himself being charged with Larry's murder. And what would happen to Robert then?

Sleeplessness wasn't foreign to Paul. For years he'd spent countless wide-eyed midnight hours. He'd always taken that as part of the celibate life he'd chosen, and relied on overwork and exhaustion as sleeping aids. Now, though, things were different. Having someone he cared deeply about, a son of his own, created new, more gut-wrenching, problems.

Lying on the floor of the Caravan, shivering, he actually began to feel ready to give up. But just how did a person "give up"? Was that even possible? He thought of the farmer, who'd pulled him out of the ditch. Could there be anything worse than a diagnosis of cancer for a daughter on the eve of her wedding? Yet what could the man do? Just keep living his life, going wherever it is that farmers go on their tractors, stopping to help a stranger, asking for nothing but prayers.

Despite the cold and the bruised ribs, the fear, the guilt—and, yes, the anger—Paul finally began to drift in and out of sleep.

†

He must have turned off the alarm in his sleep, and it wasn't until nearly midnight that he was back on I-75. The moon and stars were out, though, and traffic was light. He might still get back to St. Hildegard's by six or seven a.m. He might even say mass when he got there. A "private" mass, though, with no one in attendance, lest he embarrass the cardinal, and the church.

Driving through the dark he felt his anger rise again. How easily an institution—even one proclaiming mercy and forgiveness as its lifeblood—moved to separate itself from a faithful member at the mere suspicion of scandal…and bad publicity. Still, whatever his feelings, there was nothing to do but to keep on driving.

He finally pulled into the alley behind St. Hildegard's at a quarter after seven. He unconsciously reached for the garage door opener, then remembered it was in his Corolla, of course, with the police. He parked as close up beside the garage door as he could, and hurried straight into the church through the back door.

He put on his vestments and walked out into the sanctuary. Celebrating mass without at least a few other people in attendance never seemed right to him, since the entire ceremony was designed as a public ritual, to be conducted in the presence of a community of worshippers. But on that day, he found great comfort in going through the familiar prayers and gestures, even all alone and in near-darkness. It helped focus and calm his mind, and kept it from jumping from one fear to another. He added a prayer for Becky, with ovarian cancer… and her parents…and her fiancé.

Afterwards, as he was putting his vestments away in the sacristy, Jake Kincannon walked in. He had Max with him.

"Morning, Paul," Jake said. "My Lord, you look terrible. Or, like my Aunt Lillian used to say, 'Ya look like ya been drug through a bush backward.'"

"And what about you, Jake? You look a little tired, too. You all right?"

"I'm just old. Spent all night saying my Aunt Lillian's prayer for a happy death."

"Really? Is it a consoling prayer?"

"To me it is. It goes: 'I don't know if I'm ready, Lord, but I sure as hell hope you are.'" Jake tied Max's leash to a doorknob and started putting on his vestments. "Phone's been ringing more'n usual," he said. "I let most of 'em go into voice mail."

"That's fine. I'll check the messages, let you know if any were for you."

"Shoot, no one calls *me* but my brother," Jake said, "and he's a pain in the butt." He tightened the long white alb around his waist with a rope cincture. "You going to the Chancery Office today?" Jake still used the old terminology.

"No." He knew that with Jake it wasn't just curiosity, but real concern. "I'm taking a sort of…leave of absence. I don't even know how much I'll be staying here at St. Hildegard's. But I'll be checking the voice mail. And look, whether I'm here or not, if anyone calls or asks, tell them you don't know *where* I am, okay? That is, I'm not asking you to lie or anything, but…"

"No problem." Jake slipped a satiny green chasuble over his head and settled the vestment so it drooped equally on both shoulders. "If you're not right in front of me, and I can't *see* you, I don't know where you *are*, right?"

"Right. Thanks."

Jake picked up his chalice and headed for the door to the sanctuary. On the way, he bent down and patted Max on the head and said, "Keep the faith, big guy. It'll all work out." And Paul knew Jake wasn't talking to Max.

†

When he got to his study, he checked the phone messages and deleted them all, including two more from Detective Maddox.

He knew what his next step had to be. If Celia had already given Larry's CD to the police she would have said so in her message. He had to find out if the CD said anything about the CIA at Fair Hope, and he could no longer worry about Celia's sensibilities.

He peered into the bathroom mirror. Jake was right. He looked terrible. So he showered, shaved, and dressed—again, not in clerical clothes—and then gathered up a bundle of dirty clothes and headed downstairs. The cleaning woman who came in once a week did laundry, too, but suits and shirts and pants he took to the cleaners a couple of blocks away. In the kitchen he set up Jake's breakfast, keeping an eye and an ear on the TV. He caught a brief mention of Larry's murder, but no talk of him as a suspect.

He felt he'd been overdosing on coffee these past few days, and made it only because Jake looked forward to it so much. He was getting out Jake's raisin bran when the aroma of the brewing coffee filled the room, as welcome as a long unseen friend. He was getting out a mug when the doorbell rang.

At St. Hildegard's the doorbell almost never rang. He started down the hall...and the bell rang again. Odd. People who rang rectory doorbells seldom showed that much impatience—except the panhandlers. He reached the door and looked through the little one-way-glass window. His heart sank.

It was the detectives, Maddox and Kriswell. Maddox had a folded piece of paper in his hand, a paper Paul assumed was a search warrant. Or worse, maybe they were there to arrest him. He reached out to open the door, then stopped.

Do they know I'm here? Do they have others with them?

He turned and ran back down the hall to the kitchen, grabbed the bundle of dirty clothes from the chair where he'd left it, and went out the back door. He locked the door behind him and went out into the alley, sauntering now, as though not in a hurry.

Just on my way to the cleaners, officer. Why do you ask?

But no one stopped him. He got into the minivan and drove down the alley and turned south, away from the street that fronted the rectory. He knew enough about police and about search warrants to know that, if they wanted to, they could break into the rectory, and if his ignoring their phone calls made them hostile enough, they might tear his rooms apart, whether they found what they were looking for or not.

One thing they'd almost certainly take was his computer, but they'd find nothing on it that could hurt him. Nothing about Fair Hope Clinic, nothing illegal, and certainly no pornography. Even if he'd been inclined to view pornography on the web, which he wasn't, he'd heard enough horror stories to make him set his computer's parental controls at the strictest level on the day he bought it, and leave them there. He never used email except for archdiocesan business, and for that he used his office computer.

†

As he drove he thought of calling Celia, but suddenly realized that his cell phone was in his gym bag and his gym bag was...where? In his room?

At the cleaners where he dropped off his clothes, the Korean woman behind the counter knew him well and was happy to let him use her phone. He called St. Manfred's school and was told Celia would be out for a few days. He thought she was probably at home, but if he went there would she even let him in?

He called Phyllis Conover. "About Father Landrew's funeral arrangements," he said, "is Celia handling things well?"

"Actually, she must be in denial or something. She doesn't seem much interested. I told her the funeral should be at the cathedral, and she agreed. We'll send buses out to St. Manfred's for the school kids and anyone else who wants to come. Anyway, we can't set a date until the body's released by the police department."

"And meanwhile," he said, "is there anything Celia's supposed to be doing?"

"Nothing today, really. I told her I'd go with her to Mitchell's and pick out a casket. I made an appointment for tomorrow at eleven."

"Great," he said. Mitchell's was a funeral home on the near north side, and he'd catch Celia there, if he didn't get through to her by phone before then.

"And...uh...one other thing, Father. The cardinal will say the funeral mass, if it's at all possible, and I asked Celia if there were any other priests she wanted to concelebrate with him...or to say the mass if the cardinal can't. She said a lot of people knew her brother, but he was still kind of a loner. She said *you* had more personal contact with him than anyone else."

"You mean she wants *me* to handle Larry's funeral?"

"Well, she said you had the most contact with him. So I told the cardinal you should do it and...uh...he said no. He said you were taking a leave, and wouldn't be available to say the mass...or even to concelebrate. I mean, do you *want* to do it? I could ask him again. I'm sure he—"

"No, that's fine. The cardinal knows best."

What the cardinal *knew*, he realized, was that he didn't want his vice-chancellor up at the altar. He didn't want the public connecting the Archdiocese of Chicago with a man who might soon be announced as a murder suspect.

THIRTY-SEVEN

Paul called Brian Joplin. "We have to meet," he said. "I have a question. Not exactly a legal question, but you won't be representing me, anyway."

"Oh? And why not?"

"Because I can't pay your fee, and I'm sure the archdiocese won't cover it."

"Not a problem," Brian said. "The fee will be taken care of."

"No, I just told you, the arch—"

"Not the archdiocese. Hank Manion. He called. I'm sure you know him better than I do. All I know is he's got money. He said he'll take care of it."

Paul was stunned. Hank had offered to help, but Paul hadn't even considered asking for this. "Did he...did he say *why*?"

"He thinks the idea that you murdered anyone is absurd, and he thinks the cardinal's wrong not to provide you a defense. So he'll cover my fee. He asked me not to tell anybody, but I said I *had* to tell *you*, or else I wouldn't do it. He's okay with that."

"I...I don't know what to say."

"Manion's known to be close to the cardinal, and he's concerned that if it comes out that he's helping you it could embarrass the cardinal. I told him I'd consider him your agent, and consider any conversations I had with him about your case as protected by the attorney-client privilege. It's a stretch, but..."

Paul had no interest in all that. "We have to meet," he said.

†

They decided on two o'clock at Millennium Park, a hugely expensive city project just east of the Loop, between Michigan Avenue and Lake Shore Drive, with its wildly extravagant orchestra pavilion, its eclectic sculpture and artwork, its *al fresco* dining. The whole area was Disney World clean. The trees and the grass were green, the sun was out, the air was warm, even summer-like, and the wading pool was in operation. The pool was shallow and anchored at each end by fifty-foot tall, digitally-controlled faces that periodically sprayed water on screaming children through pursed lips. It was a school day, so the kids were mostly preschoolers, and Paul and Brian sat on a bench and watched them splash around, although Paul hardly noticed they were there.

"I don't have copies of any police reports yet," Brian said. "But I know why the detectives are interested in you. Your story's the kind that makes them wonder."

"It's not a *story*. It's the truth."

"Right. Anyway, to them it's a classic situation. Two white people are alone somewhere, when suddenly an unknown black assailant appears and murders one of them, while the other isn't seriously harmed. It makes them wonder."

"What are you talking about? I was knocked out, kicked in the—"

"I know, but apparently your medical records don't show serious harm. I haven't seen *them* yet, either. Anyway, homicide cops gotta cover all the bases. They found your prints on those spiral-bound books... and something else, too."

"I know. Pages were torn out."

"How do you know that? Don't tell me you—"

"No, I...I just know it."

"All right. Then there's the rental car. If you didn't go back to St. Manfred's to search some more, who drove the car to your place? There were papers in it with stains on them they think *might* match stains on your shirt...if they could find the shirt."

"I...I took the shirt to the cleaners."

"Oh?" Brian's eyes widened. "So they can't...well...anyway, with you worried about what was on his laptop, they wonder if you and Father Landrew had been arguing. They found nothing on his answering machine. So they wonder about *your* machine."

"I don't have an answering machine. I have voice mail."

"Right. So they get a warrant and go pick up your messages."

"They can *do* that?" Paul was stunned. "I mean, is every message I ever got on voice mail stored somewhere?"

"They're digitally recorded, I guess, and kept, at least for a while." Brian took a folded piece of paper from his coat pocket. "If you're charged with a crime they'll have to turn over transcripts of any voice mail messages they have, and the recordings themselves. I'm always straight with the cops. Sometimes it helps." He handed the paper to Paul. "I saw the transcripts."

Paul unfolded the paper. It was a sheet of Brian's letterhead, with typed notes titled: `Voice Mail Transcripts`.

"These are not exactly word for word," Brian said. "But I have a damn good memory."

There were two messages, both left on the Friday before Larry died.

> Hey, it's Larry. I have to get this column sent off to the Sun-Times. Like I said, I feel bad doing this to you. But I can't let it go. There's been too much covering up. Bishops…priests…all of us, it has to stop. I can't hold off on this much longer. So call me.

> Hey, it's Larry again. It's ten o'clock Friday night. Got your message. Sorry I wasn't here. I know we go way back, and I'll hold off, I guess. But not for long. You're gonna take a tough hit on this, and if I was you I'd say the sooner the better…get it over with. I know it's easy for me to say. But it has to come out. Okay, see you Monday.

Paul gave the paper back to Brian. "I can explain this," he said, "and that'll get me to the question I want to ask you."

"Fine, go ahead."

"Okay..." Paul was short of breath. He was about to do just what Ann Swanson had warned him not to do. "Telling this," he said, "makes me nervous."

"It shouldn't." Brian shook his head. "Anything you tell me is privileged. Whatever you say, it goes nowhere. Period."

"Okay, but let's...let's make it hypothetical." He knew how foolish that was, but somehow it made it easier to get started. "Let's assume that some time ago I agreed with the...well...with a certain group, to let them use a church facility for their...business. Assume it was a secret agreement, and an agreement I had no authority to enter into."

"Who's the 'certain group'? What's 'their business'? And what 'church facility'?"

"Let me finish," Paul said. "Assume Larry Landrew happened to go to the facility and...and didn't like what he saw. Assume he told me he'd written a *Sun-Times* column about it, but then was killed before he sent the column to the paper."

"And so, after he was shot, you deleted stuff from his laptop, and tore pages from his notebooks, so nobody would see what he'd written. Is that it?"

"No! That's *not* it. I looked at them to see if they contained anything about what Larry said he'd seen. But they didn't. Not the notebooks, not the computer."

"Except no one knows that but you." Brian turned and stared hard at him. "So far, your so-called 'hypothetical' fits right into the police theory: Father Landrew threatened to reveal something bad about Father Clark, so Father Clark killed Father Landrew, and destroyed the evidence Father Landrew left behind."

"I didn't destroy anything. There was nothing there. And even if there had been, the 'something bad' wasn't anything illegal or immoral. It's that I made an agreement I had no authority to make." He paused. "If it came out, I'd look pretty imprudent...even stupid...but it wouldn't be worth my killing anyone over."

"Good, so let's tell the cops who the people were, and what they were doing."

"I can't. This...group...they warned me not to." He'd given up the hypothetical pretense. "They threatened...not me exactly, but someone close to me."

"Threatened? Who the hell *are* these people, the Mafia or something?" Brian's eyes suddenly widened. "My God! Is that it? The Outfit? Holy—"

"No, nothing like that," Paul said. "It's a government agency. It's... well...I'm sure it has to be the CIA."

"Jesus Christ!" Brian said. "I mean, excuse my irreverence, but damn, you put the church into a deal with the CIA? And Father Landrew found out about it?"

"He found out about them being...where they were. He assumed I didn't know about it. Because that's what I told him." He stared down at his feet. "I...I lied."

"Yeah, well, don't take it so hard," Brian said. "All my clients lie."

"Maybe. But until all this happened, I never—"

"Yeah, I know. *Nobody* ever. Anyway, this 'facility,' I think I know where it is. The media's making a big thing about Father Landrew spending almost the last week of his life helping out at that clinic, in... where? Guyana was it? What's the CIA doing there? What'd he see?"

"Yes, Guyana," Paul said. "My contact wouldn't say what they'd be doing. Just that it was temporary and wouldn't interfere with the clinic. It's called Fair Hope Clinic. Larry said he saw men coming and going, mostly at night. Moving machinery in and out of an old barn at one end of the property, and unloading crates of...of weapons. He knew the clinic was close to the Venezuelan border."

"Jesus!" Brian stared at him. "Why'd you...? Anyway, you gotta tell the cops. What can the CIA do about it? They're not gonna *kill* someone, for chrissake, just to—"

"I'm not so sure about that," Paul said, and immediately wished he hadn't.

"Hold *on*. They threatened to *kill* you?"

"No, it wasn't a threat to kill me, or anyone." Paul was glad Brian took that meaning, because he wasn't ready to discuss his suspicions about Larry's murder. "Look...if the threat was against me I'd take the chance that once the cat's out of the bag they won't do anything. But it's a threat against someone else. I can't take that chance."

"To do what? To who?"

"Someone whose life would be ruined, who might not even survive. It wouldn't be illegal for the CIA to follow through on the threat, and I don't think the agent, my contact, would hesitate." Paul waited as a woman pushing a baby in a stroller passed close by, and then said, "But that gets me to my question. This agent, I'm sure she has to—"

"She? The agent's a woman?"

"Yes. Why?"

"Nothing. It just took me by surprise. So what's the question?"

"It's just...this agent...if she's a government employee she has to answer to someone, right? Get someone's approval?"

"I suppose. But you're a *church* employee. You have to answer to someone, too. Whose approval did *you* get when you made this...this agreement with her?"

"No one's. That's my point. If I'd have gone to the cardinal, he'd have said no. But I didn't. I needed help and I was desperate...don't ask why... so I agreed. And this agent...well...*she* seems desperate now. Possibly she's doing things her superiors wouldn't let her do...if they knew."

"Are you suggesting you could go to someone higher up in the CIA and see if they approve of what their agent's doing?"

"I know it's a long shot. If they'd even *talk* to me, would they admit that one of their agents has gone off the tracks? But if she has, and they pull her back, then I can explain my actions to the police, and not have...this other person...destroyed."

"It's more than a long shot. It's—"

"It's all I can think of. You know lots of people. Lawyers, judges, politicians, influential people. You might know someone who could get me access to some CIA official."

"Who would know who's with the CIA? They don't wear name tags."

"But they're not all undercover agents. I mean, the CIA director's appointed by the president. Everyone knows who *he* is."

"So you want to call up the head of the CIA and—"

"I just need some supervisor I can go to and say, 'Look, here's what your agent's been doing.' I know it sounds a little crazy."

"It sounds a *lot* crazy," Brian said. He stared straight ahead. "I mean, would I know anyone who..." His voice trailed off and Paul had the impression he was actually trying to think of someone. "There *might* be someone, but..." Again he didn't finish.

"Did you think of someone?"

"I'm just thinking that...well...do you know Toby Hodges?"

"I know who he is," Paul said. Hodges was the senior US senator from Illinois. "You think he could help?"

"He's on the Senate Intelligence Committee. If he wanted to, he could probably get you in to talk to someone. But first you need someone who knows Hodges."

"Who?" Maybe there was hope, after all. "You?"

"No," Brian said. "But the cardinal does. Hodges is Catholic, and they're pretty close."

Paul's heart sank. "I can't go to the cardinal. I tried that route. I mean, not about putting me in touch with someone. But I tried to bring up the CIA, and the agreement. He cut me off. Made it clear he didn't want to hear any talk along those lines."

"Well, that's the only person I can think of." Brian looked at his watch. "Hell, I gotta get to court. Look, you can't keep hiding from the cops. You and I have to..."

Brian kept talking, but Paul wasn't listening. He'd suddenly realized it hadn't been a fruitless conversation, after all.

He had an idea.

THIRTY-EIGHT

Sure, I know Toby Hodges," Hank Manion said. "And I can get you in to see him."

"That'd be great." Paul felt a surge of hope.

"And he'll be gracious, Father, and promise to help, and shake your hand...and that's the last you'll hear from him." They were in Hank's living room, and Hank lifted his glass from the cocktail table and raised it toward Paul. "Here's to the Honorable Tobias Hodges. One of the world's great lightweights...in a Senate *full* of them." He finished off his drink and stood up. "You need a refill?"

"No, thanks. It's great stuff, but..." He lifted his glass to show that he'd barely touched his scotch. "So...he's not even worth a try?"

"Waste of time. Still...cheer up, Father. We'll think of something." Hank took Paul's glass. "I'll just freshen this up." He turned and headed out of the room. "Be back in a minute," he called, "and we'll come up with a better idea."

Paul sat slumped in his chair. *Cheer up?* Celia hadn't answered her phone all day, and his lawyer thought the police had a good case against him. *A better idea?* Not a chance, unless he told Hank about Ann Swanson, and that he'd hoped Hodges could get him access to someone at the CIA. He trusted Hank, but Hank wasn't his lawyer. Didn't that mean the police could make him reveal anything Paul said to him?

He had called Hank and told him he couldn't possibly accept his offer to pay Brian Joplin's fee. "Too late," Hank had said. "It's a done deal." Paul gave in, then said he had another favor to ask, one which didn't involve money. Hank didn't even ask what it was, simply told him he was meeting someone for dinner at nine but, if Paul could come to his condo before that, they'd talk about it.

Now it was a little after eight and Paul sat surrounded by the sort of comfort only big money can buy, in the John Hancock Building, high above Michigan Avenue's "Magnificent Mile." The lighting in the spacious room was indirect and turned down very low, and the chairs were angled to look out through a wall of glass at Lake Michigan. Out on the water an occasional breeze sent ripples shimmering in the light of a full September moon. On the street far below, not visible from here, Paul knew the scene was a bustling one, with determined shoppers elbowing past strolling tourists, taxis honking and cutting each other off. But here, eighty-five floors up, it was as calm and quiet as a monastery—a monastery with comfortable chairs, smooth single-malt scotch, and piano music floating out from hidden speakers. Erik Satie, Paul thought, and as soothing and muted as the dim lights.

Hank was divorced—his marriage canonically "annulled" by the church, actually—and he lived alone, and Paul was surprised there wasn't a servant to handle the drinks. He felt a flicker of envy. Hank must have his troubles, like anyone else, but surely money solved an awful lot of them.

"I'm back," Hank said, and Paul turned to see him set their glasses on the low table. Hank dropped into his chair and looked at his watch. "We have some time. You said if I got you to Toby Hodges, he might get you entrée to someone else. If I knew who the 'someone else' was, I might be able to come up with a better lead. Or who knows? Maybe we can just omit the middleman entirely. Want to give me the person's name?"

"I...I don't have a name." Paul picked up his glass, studied it, and sipped at his scotch. Decision time. If he didn't tell the police about the CIA and explain why he'd taken Larry's laptop, he'd face a murder charge. If he *did* tell them, Robert would be sent back to die in that Mexican hellhole. Unless Paul could stop Ann Swanson...which he couldn't do alone. He put the glass down. "Let me explain," he said.

†

Hank seemed even more stunned than Brian Joplin had been. "The CIA? A church facility? You didn't *ask*, didn't *tell* anyone?" He'd gotten to his feet as Paul spoke, and now stood, glass in hand, looking out the window, his back to Paul.

"I had a very compelling reason," Paul said, "one I'd rather not explain. I knew I was taking a chance, risking embarrassment to the church, but..." He felt like a kid explaining why he'd *had* to sneak away with the family car.

"Don't misunderstand me." Hank turned and faced him. "I'm not *blaming* you for anything. I'm just...surprised." He smiled. "It was risky, yes. But a damn gutsy thing to do. So..." He raised his glass. "Here's to you, Father. You're a brave man."

Paul couldn't believe his ears. "Thanks," was all he managed. He lifted his glass in return, and this time took more than a mere sip of the scotch. "You know, you don't have to be so formal and call me 'Father' all the time. 'Paul' would do."

"Actually, 'Paul' doesn't work for me," Hank said. "You're the priest. I'm the layman. I call you 'Father.' Period." He looked at his watch again. "So...you wanna tell me why you thought Toby Hodges might be helpful?"

They sat again and Paul leaned forward. "The police want to know what I thought I might find in Father Landrew's notebooks and laptop. But I can't tell them."

"Right. You're thinking the CIA won't like it if you 'out' one of their operations."

"Not just 'thinking.' The woman...the agent I told you about? She warned me not to. She threatened serious consequences if I did."

"'Serious consequences?' To *you*?"

"Not to me, but to...to someone close to me. I guess it was a long shot, but I heard that Hodges is a member of the Senate Intelligence Committee, and they...well..."

"They deal with the CIA." Hank downed some of his scotch. "You thought if Hodges could get you in to talk to someone who's higher up in the CIA than this woman, the person might rein her in. Am I right?"

"Exactly."

"Makes sense. But…this woman, she's out there issuing threats to *you*, a senior official of the Archdiocese of Chicago. How do you know she's really with the CIA?"

It was an issue Paul had wrestled with at length himself. "First," he said, "she approached me out of nowhere when I was struggling with a problem that, except for myself and one other person, only the government would have known about. I hadn't told anyone, and the other person hadn't, either. But Ann Swanson shows up, saying she's with the federal government. She wouldn't be more specific, but every indication was she meant the CIA. She knew all about…about my problem, and said she could take care of it."

"And you believed her?"

"I didn't have to *believe* she could do it. I just had to wait and see. But I *did* try to do some checking. I called a number I found in the phone book for the CIA here in Chicago, with an address in the Dirksen Building. It was a pretty old book, though, and I got a message that the number's not in service. But then, just a few minutes later, Ann Swanson called *me*. She was angry, said I'd agreed not to talk to anyone about our conversation. I mean…how could she possibly have known I'd just tried to call the CIA?"

"I don't know, but—"

"And, within days, the problem was taken care of. She did what she said she'd do if I promised to let her use Fair Hope Clinic. And believe me, it was something not just *anyone* could do."

"Okay, so let's assume she's with the government, it doesn't have to be the CIA. These days there must be any number of clandestine governmental entities."

"Yes, and there's the CIA, the one I know about. I have to start there."

Hank smiled. "OK, your mind's made up. You can explain it all when you talk to the CIA guy." Hank stood up. "Just now, I don't want to be late for my dinner date."

"Wait a minute." Paul stood, too. "Talk to *what* CIA guy? When?"

"The man in charge of the CIA in Chicago. Name's Wickowski. We're not big buddies or anything, but we know each other. He's an administrator, a bureaucrat, not a covert agent. I know he's got an office in the Dirksen Building because I went to a conference there once, with some other business people. So why don't you meet me in the lobby there at...say...nine-thirty tomorrow. If he's in town, I believe he'll see you. If he's not...well...let's just hope he is."

THIRTY-NINE

At a quarter after nine the next morning Paul was waiting for Hank Manion on the sidewalk outside the Dirksen Building. He'd spent a restless night at a hotel just north of the city, afraid that if he went home he'd find the police waiting for him. Now it was sunny and warm, and he struggled to calm himself as he watched a steady stream of people going into the building. Nearly all of them—men and women alike—were dressed in expensive-looking business clothes and carrying briefcases, so they were surely lawyers headed for the federal courtrooms.

At 9:35 Hank Manion rolled up in a black limo. "Sorry I'm late," he said, and the two of them hurried through the revolving doors.

Despite the impressive high-ceilinged lobby, the scene reminded Paul more of an airport than a courthouse, with people herded into single-file lines to place their briefcases on conveyor belts and then walk through the weapons scanners. Once beyond security, they were all directed past one bank of elevators, apparently not in service, to another bank where a crowd was waiting. Hank, clearly losing patience, ushered Paul to an elevator whose doors were already closing on what looked like a full load.

Hank stuck out his hand and stopped the doors. "Plenty of room," he said, his tone making it an order, not a factual description. The people in front obediently squeezed backwards against the bodies behind them, and Paul and Hank stepped inside and turned to face the closing doors. Hank snaked his hand to the right and hit a button Paul couldn't see, and the elevator—after a harsh buzz of objection—lurched upward.

The first time the car stopped only the two of them stepped out, and Paul heard a collective sigh as the others shifted around, able to breathe again. There were obviously no courtrooms on this floor, and he and Hank walked down a windowless, gray-walled corridor, passing occasional closed, unmarked doors on both sides. The light came from fluorescent fixtures in a high ceiling, and the corridor seemed to run the entire length of the building. They'd gone only about a third of the way, though, when they turned right and found themselves at another bank of elevators, and beyond them a pair of glass double-doors. Above the doors, up near the ceiling, a tiny video camera looked down at them.

The only sign on the doors was a small one that said *NO ADMITTANCE*. Beyond them, in front of a wood-paneled wall some ten feet farther back, an American flag hung from an upright pole that was topped with a bronze eagle.

"I'm sure this is the place," Hank said. "Wickowski described it to me. I called him this morning. He'll give you a few minutes."

"Thanks. I—"

"You won't need me," Hank said, "and I'm sure he'd rather speak with you alone. Good luck." He turned and headed back the way they'd come.

"Hank?" Paul called. "I can't tell you how much I—"

"May I help you, sir?"

Paul spun around to see a woman holding one of the glass doors open. "My name's Paul Clark," he said. "I'm here to see—"

"He's expecting you, Father. This way, please."

†

A round-faced, bespectacled man of medium height—not smiling, not frowning—stood up behind his desk. "Stanley Wickowski," he said, "Special Agent in Charge. And you're Father Paul Clark?"

"Yes."

Wickowski's office was large and carpeted and bright, though hardly luxurious. The furniture was all dark wood. He invited Paul to an area beyond his empty desk and close to the windows, where they sat on upholstered chairs, facing each other. Between them, a low table held a coffee carafe, a few packets of sweetener and creamer, two foam plastic cups, and two white plastic spoons.

"Coffee?" Wickowski asked. He was already pouring out a cup.

"Oh...yes, sure." Paul took the coffee. He sipped some and it tasted like hot water. "I know you're busy, so I'll get right to the point. You probably know who I am."

"What I know about you," Wickowski said, "is from news reports regarding the Father Landrew murder." He poured himself some coffee and stirred in creamer.

"And that's all?" Paul wasn't sure how to proceed. He'd been certain Wickowski would know about his arrangement with Ann Swanson.

"I know from Mr. Manion...and I should point out that our relationship is through mutual acquaintances, not agency-related...I'm told by him that you're not given to hysteria or hallucination. He also said that any suggestion that you might have killed your fellow priest is absurd. But we're not here to talk about that. Mr. Manion mentioned a possible problem between yourself and one of our special agents you say you've been in contact with."

"Actually, it's more than 'in contact with.' I agreed to provide assistance to you...your agency...on a project some—"

"And this was an agent from our Chicago office?"

"I don't know for certain, but I suppose she may have been from Washington. Her name is Ann Swanson."

"So you met her in person. Here in Chicago?"

"Yes."

"And this 'project' you referred to was where?"

"South America. Guyana, specifically. The archdiocese sponsors a medical clinic there for poor indigenous people, and—"

"Sorry to interrupt again," Wickowski said, though not sounding apologetic at all. He stood up and went to his desk and lifted the phone. "Melendez?" he said. "Would you come into my office, please?" He hung up and came and sat down again. "I'd like to have Special Agent Orlando Melendez present."

"Okay. Well, the clinic is called Fair—"

"Please, let's wait for Agent Melendez."

Paul drank some more tasteless coffee and turned and stared out the window at the side of a dingy gray office building maybe fifty yards away.

"Ah, here he is," Wickowski said.

Paul turned. Melendez was a tall, thin, fortyish-looking man, deeply tanned, with wavy black hair. He wore a crisply pressed white shirt and a blue-and-red striped tie, but no coat. He nodded at Paul, then swiveled Wickowski's desk chair around and sat facing them.

"This is Father Paul Clark," Wickowski said. "He states he's been dealing with Special Agent Ann Swanson, about a matter involving a medical clinic the Archdiocese of Chicago sponsors for the poor, in Guyana." He looked at Paul. "Go ahead, please."

"Okay. Well, as I said, she approached me and spoke of the government's need to use a facility on the property at Fair Hope Clinic, near a town called Mabaruma, not far from the Venezuelan border. She said it was in the national interest."

"And you agreed?" Wickowski asked.

"Yes. The facility's a barn that's been vacant for years. Your people made repairs and cleared away a lot of brush that had grown up around it."

"You've been down to see what's going on?"

"No, not since your people have been there. But I've spoken to clinic personnel and..." He stopped and looked at Wickowski. "Are you sure you don't already *know* all this? I mean, I'm sure in an organization as big as the CIA not everyone knows what everyone else is doing, but—"

"Let's stick to what *you* know. But first, besides Ann Swanson, did you speak with anyone else at the agency?"

Paul told them how he'd looked in the phone book and called to try to check up on Ann.

"That number hasn't been in service for years," Wickowski said.

"Yes, but the significant thing was how she called right back. She knew right away that I'd tried to call your number."

"I see," Wickowski said. "And what about Cardinal Nesbitt? Did he himself try to—"

"No. That is...he doesn't know. No one knows but me. Ann Swanson insisted on absolute secrecy." Paul looked from one man to the other.

Wickowski stared back with no expression at all, while Melendez smiled and nodded, as though to say Paul was doing just fine.

"What happened," Paul went on, "was that Father Landrew...the priest who was murdered...he went down to Fair Hope to do volunteer work and discovered your people there. He was upset that the church was cooperating with the CIA, and he was going to write a newspaper column about it. He and I went back and forth about that on the phone, and I convinced him to hold off a few days. I told him I needed time to find out what was going on."

"So," Wickowski said, "you lied to him."

"Yes. It...it seemed necessary. Ann Swanson insisted she needed time to get the CIA out of Fair Hope. She said—"

"Maybe," Melendez said, "I should—"

Wickowski lifted his hand to stop him, and nodded at Paul. "Please continue."

"Okay. She said her people would be gone by Thursday. But on Monday Larry was killed. Shot, in a robbery. You already know I was there, and I called the police." He went on to tell them how he'd looked at the notebooks, and taken the laptop.

"Without telling the police?" Wickowski asked.

"Yes, but I didn't find anything. I didn't..." He paused, thinking he should get to the point. "The police are aware that Larry and I argued about his making something public that I wanted kept secret. They don't know what the secret was, but...well... these days it could be *anything.* Priests are being accused...all too often truthfully...of sexual misconduct, stealing parish funds, whatever. Just *being* a priest these days makes some people suspect you. At any rate, it seems the police think I might have killed Larry to keep him from revealing some terrible secret about me."

"I see," Wickowski said. "And you want to tell them that the secret in question was that you were allowing the CIA to use a church building in Guyana as a base."

"I *have* to tell them. I understand it will be inconvenient to you, and it will be a huge embarrassment to the church. I myself will look...well...

irresponsible. Worse than irresponsible, to some people. But the police have to be told that the secret isn't that I'm a thief, or a pedophile. That it's not anything worth killing someone about."

"And only the extremists," Melendez said, "people on the radical left, such as Father Landrew, will think that what you're describing is wrong. Others will recognize it as a service to the country, right?"

"I suppose so," Paul answered. "The thing is, Ann Swanson warned me *not* to tell. *Threatened* me, in fact. And I'm here to ask you to call her off." He could feel the tremor in his voice, and knew they could hear it, too.

"I understand," Wickowski said, "and I can assure you that Ann Swanson has no authority from the agency to threaten you, or to forbid you to do anything."

"She doesn't?" Paul felt relief sweep through him. "So I can tell the police what Larry and I argued about? And why I took his laptop?"

"The agency can't stop you, and won't try." Wickowski spoke quite firmly. "However, I don't know that it will do you any good."

That sent Paul's head spinning. "I don't understand."

"May I explain now, sir?" Melendez asked. Wickowski nodded and Melendez leaned forward in the desk chair. "This office has been shorthanded for months," he said, "which is why I'm here. On loan, if you will. My area of concentration is Central and South America, and I'm sure that's why I was asked to listen to what you had to say."

"I…I'm not sure I understand."

"You and I need to talk." Melendez looked at his watch. "Is there somewhere you need to be right away?"

Paul just stared at him, unable to form a response.

"Because," Melendez said, "this Ann Swanson person…whoever she is…she's not with the Central Intelligence Agency."

FORTY

Melendez took Paul to a small conference room and left him there. He returned carrying a laptop like a tray, on which was balanced a coffee carafe—giving off an aroma of *real* coffee—and a Dunkin' Donuts box. He set everything down. "I managed to liberate these," he said. He opened the box and there were four doughnuts in it.

"Thanks," Paul said. "I'll just have coffee."

After that, Paul did most of the talking, while Melendez ate doughnuts and took notes on the laptop. Paul explained everything again. This was his chance to get help, and he tried hard to be accurate... with one exception. He left Robert out of the picture.

Half an hour later Melendez—surprisingly, given how thin he was—was washing down his third doughnut, and Paul had nothing more to say. The agent tapped away on his laptop for a while, then looked up. "Okay," he said. "First, the agency has at present no operational base in the area known as Region 1 in Guyana, which includes Mabaruma. Second, the agency has at present no female special agent operational in any capacity whatsoever related to either Guyana or Venezuela."

"But then...who is Ann Swanson?"

"Good question," Melendez said. "But tell me, if you thought she was CIA, and she said her mission was vital to national security, why didn't you say 'yes' right away?"

"Well...lots of people, including church people, like Father Landrew, don't approve of the CIA, and some of the things it apparently does."

"They're naive," Melendez said. "The world's not a playground. You can't run home to mommy when… Anyway, you hesitated."

"At first. But she gave me a few days, and I finally agreed."

"Uh-huh, and what moved you to do that?"

"What *moved* me?" Paul desperately tried to decide how to answer. He dared not mention Robert now, remembering Ann Swanson's description of a jailbreak, and a murder. "I thought she was a CIA agent. Isn't helping one's government a good enough reason?"

"It's a great reason," Melendez said. "It's called 'patriotism.' The reason why I'm still in this job. But I have to tell you, I get a salary, too. You were taking a big chance, involving the church, putting your career in jeopardy. That is…priests have *careers*, right? I mean, do you guys call it that?"

"It's…not often put that way, but the concept is there."

"Uh-huh. Especially for someone like *you*. I mean, you're what might be called 'on your way up.' Right?"

"I *was*," Paul said. "I'm not so sure any more."

"My point exactly. You could have predicted *some* sort of trouble. So…we both know the risk was too high for you to stick your neck out like that, without some reason besides patriotism. So tell me, what was the *other* reason?" He smiled and nodded, as though they were buddies sharing secrets.

"I…I'm not going to go into that."

"We need it to find out who Ann Swanson is. So tell me."

"No," Paul said. "I won't."

Melendez sighed. "You know," he said, "you're missing something here."

"I don't think I am."

"Look at it this way. You go to the police, and you say, 'You're right, I didn't want Father Landrew to publicize something I was doing. But what I was doing wasn't dishonest, or *wrong*. I was helping the CIA, in Guyana. So the detectives, naturally, come to us and ask, 'Was this guy helping you?' I mean, what are *we* to say?"

"You tell them I'd been misled, and that I voluntarily came to your office and explained that I thought I was working with one of your—"

"Uh-huh. Or we *could* say, 'Look, detectives, we don't know *what* this mope's talking about. We have no mission in Guyana. He gave us the same story...about a mysterious woman and all that. But he wasn't helping us *before* his friend was murdered, and furthermore...he's not helping us *now*."' Melendez leaned toward Paul. "So, you see? It's the part about 'not helping us *now*' that you're missing."

"I'm not missing anything. But...well...I'm stuck."

"And the way to get 'unstuck' is to tell me everything, including how this woman persuaded you. You may not be a radical leftist like your priest friend, but still...she appealed to more than just your love for your country."

Paul felt sweat seeping through the pores of his scalp. How far should he go? "It was...well...she offered me a deal."

"Of course she did," Melendez said. "So, tell me about the deal."

"I'll tell you what I can. She knew about...about a person I wanted to help. She said that if I'd help the CIA, the CIA would...would help that person. So I agreed. And when the CIA...I *thought* it was the CIA... did its part, I did mine. I let them use—"

"I know that part. But what did *she* do?"

"I can't tell you. You'll just have to believe me and...well..." He shook his head.

"I didn't say I didn't believe you. Who's the person she helped?"

"I can't tell you that."

"You mean you *won't*."

"Look," Paul said, "this woman threatened to put my...my friend back into the trouble she got him out of. I thought she was your agent, so I came here, hoping she had a superior officer, someone I could convince to stop her. But now..." Paul hesitated, then decided to push on. "Now, I find out she's not one of your agents, so if you aren't the ones who got him *out* of trouble, you might decide to put him back *into* trouble." He paused, as out of breath as if he'd been running. "I can't take that chance."

"Right...okay." Melendez stared at Paul for a long time, as though chewing on what he'd said. Then he looked at his watch, and abruptly stood up. "You can go now."

"Really?" Caught by surprise, Paul stood, too. "So…what's next?"

"What's next?" Melendez picked up the doughnut box. "Not for me to say." He held the box out. "Want the last one?"

Paul shook his head. "What should I *do*? What should I tell the police?"

"I don't know. If you tell them you stole that laptop to protect a CIA secret mission, we'll have to tell them there is no such mission. If you tell them you *thought* you were working with the CIA, but now you know you weren't…well…" He shrugged.

"Well *what*?"

"Well…I suppose they *might* believe you." He bit into the last doughnut as he ushered Paul out of the room and down the hall. "But even if they do," he said, "they'll wanna know all about this business you say you were working on with the mystery woman. And if you tell them, might you possibly be admitting to something illegal? I mean, I can think of a few federal statutes that might apply. Or maybe some law in Guyana." They'd reached the door to the outer corridor and Melendez held it open. "You have to be *so* careful when you talk to law enforcement. Anyway, good luck."

"But what about Ann Swanson?" Bewildered and powerless, Paul let himself be maneuvered out the door. "If she's been impersonating a CIA agent, won't the CIA—"

"I can't speak for the agency," Melendez said. "But meanwhile, you should think about being a little more…cooperative."

The glass door between them fell closed, and Paul heard the lock click into place.

FORTY-ONE

Paul pushed his way through the door of the Dirksen Building and stepped out onto the sidewalk. He stood for a moment, and couldn't remember riding the elevator down, couldn't even say what floor he'd come from. He felt strangely disoriented, pressed in by the ceaseless din of traffic on Dearborn Street and the lunch hour rush of pedestrians streaming past in both directions.

A few hours earlier he'd had things finally under control. He'd convinced himself that Ann Swanson had to be with the CIA, and that going to the CIA was the answer. She would be reined in and Robert's safety would be guaranteed. The CIA, appreciative of Paul's cooperation, would let him explain what the police saw as his suspicious behavior. Although he'd certainly be in disfavor with the cardinal, at least he wouldn't have to face a murder charge.

But he had accomplished none of that. Instead, he'd—

"Wake up, for chrissake." A heavyset woman knocked into him as she hurried past, and Paul suddenly realized he was just standing there, making it difficult for others to use the door he'd come out of. In fact, he was drawing attention to himself. That brought him to his senses and he started walking north along Dearborn. He had no idea where he was going, though, or what he'd do next.

When he reached the corner at Adams Street—which was one-way, westbound—the light was red. As he waited at the curb, a long black sedan slid up from his right along the curbside lane. Despite having the green light, the black car stopped and the driver lowered his window and leaned out. His head was shaved and he wore sunglasses. "Father Clark?"

Paul stared, feeling stupid, sure he'd never seen the man before, while horns started honking behind the stopped car. Then the rear door opened and Hank Manion got out. "Hurry up, Father," he called, waving a cell phone toward the honking cars, "before one of those idiots has a heart attack."

Paul finally realized the black car was the limo Hank had arrived in earlier that morning. He climbed in and slid across the seat and Hank, cell phone in hand, got back in and closed the door. The limo stayed put, though, because by then the light had turned red. Hank spoke on the phone—mostly "yes" and "no" and "I understand"—while Paul leaned back on the soft leather seat. The angry honking of horns hadn't let up, but could barely be heard.

The light changed again and they moved forward, and shortly after that Hank closed his phone. "Sorry about that," he said, and slipped the phone into his coat pocket.

"How did you know where I'd be?" Paul asked.

"I didn't. I just finished a meeting a few blocks from here, and I thought I'd take a chance and swing by...and there you were." Hank lifted a can of Diet Coke from a cup holder and took a swig. "So," he said, "how'd it go?"

"Not well. Not at all."

"What happened?" Hank stared at Paul. "You look as though *they* threatened you, too."

"No. They told me the CIA *has* no mission at Fair Hope. They say they don't know the woman I told them I was dealing with, but that she certainly isn't a CIA agent."

"OK...but...are they going to find out who she *is*? Or who *is* using the clinic?"

"They wouldn't tell me *what* they're going to do, if anything."

"Did you tell them about the threat she made?"

"Yes, but I couldn't say exactly who she threatened, or what she threatened to do to them."

"Why not? I thought that was the whole idea behind your going there. To explain."

"I went in there thinking the woman was one of them, and they would already know what she'd done for...for this person. Then, when they told me she wasn't a CIA agent at all, I realized that if it wasn't the CIA who got the person *out* of trouble, the CIA might decide to put him right back *in*." He shrugged. "Does that make sense?"

"To some extent," Hank said. "For example, if she did something illegal to help your friend, they might tell the authorities what she did, and they might even somehow reverse what she did."

Hank seemed to understand, and Paul had nothing to add. Meanwhile, the limo driver turned north onto Wacker Drive, a multi-lane, divided street which—though it was well beyond the El tracks that encircled the city's original "Loop"—most people considered the western edge of downtown.

"So...what will you do now?" Hank asked.

"I don't know. I can hardly think straight."

"Is there anything I can do? I mean...do you need money?"

"Money?" Paul wasn't sure what to say. "You...you're already paying my attorney's fees."

"Which, so far, are next to nothing. And may never amount to much." Hank took another drink of Diet Coke. "Look, Father, I work hard, with lots of travel and long, long hours. And it's made me very successful. But there are downsides." He shook the can a little and then drained what was left of the soda. "I have an ex-wife, and my kids are grown and...well...let's just say I was an absentee father and to this day we're not very close. So I find it satisfying when a little of my money can help someone... especially someone generous enough to give his whole life to God and to the church."

"I don't know," Paul said. "I don't *feel* very generous. Actually, I feel like a fugitive. I know the police are looking for me."

Hank frowned. "There's not a warrant out for your arrest, is there?"

"Not that I know of. But I've avoided talking to the police. And I'm not talking to my lawyer, either."

"Brian Joplin." Hank pulled out his cell phone. "Let's find out if there's a warrant. What's his number?"

"No, I don't want to put Brian on the spot with the police. I'm not talk—"

"*You* won't be talking to him. *I* will. What's the number?" Paul gave him Brian's number and Hank made the call. "Brian Joplin, please." He waited. "Patch me through, then. My name is Hank Manion and... No, *listen* to me. It *can't* wait. He'll be *very* unhappy...with *you*...if he misses this call." He waited again, longer this time, and finally said, "Brian? Hank Manion here. You heard from Father Clark?" He paused. "Uh-huh, well, I'm trying to reach him, too. But I don't want a legal problem of my own. Is there a warrant out for his arrest? I mean, is he a fugitive?" He paused for a few moments, listening, and then said, "I understand...right. Oh, hold on a second." Hank covered the phone and whispered to Paul. "He says they're seriously looking for you, but they know he's your lawyer, so if they actually arrest you they'll have to be sure he's there when they talk to you. They'd rather question you alone first. So...no arrest warrant. Not yet."

"So," Paul whispered back, "can I be *sure* they won't arrest me?"

Hank nodded, then spoke into the phone. "Listen, if I see him, what should I tell him to do?" He waited, then said, "Uh...I'm in the car and reception's bad. Can you repeat that, a little louder?" He held the phone out between himself and Paul.

"...in the middle of a murder trial." Brian's voice was loud and clear over the phone. "I can't really deal with this until Tuesday of next week... maybe Wednesday. The damn cops might decide to label him a suspect at any time, and drag him in. So he should stay out of sight."

Hank put the phone to his ear and said, "Got it. If I see him, I'll tell him." He closed the phone.

"So what do I do? Lock myself up in the rectory?"

"If you do, they sure won't have any trouble finding you." Hank replaced the empty Coke can and touched a button beside the cup holder. A section of the glass barrier between them and the driver slid aside. "Pull over and stop," Hank said, leaning toward the driver.

"Yes, sir," the driver said, "as soon as I can find—"

"I *said*...stop...the damn...car."

They pulled over to the curb and stopped.

"Get me that envelope."

The driver reached across to the passenger side and under the seat and came up with a bulky manila envelope. Hank took it and bent up the prongs of the metal clip that held down the flap. He reached inside and pulled out two white business-size envelopes. He replaced one of them and handed the other to Paul. "It's not a fortune."

Paul held the envelope. He could tell it held a wad of cash. "Hank," he said, "I can't take your money."

Ignoring Paul's objection, Hank handed the manila envelope back to the driver. As the glass panel slid back into place he said, "You heard your lawyer. They could come for you at any time. If you have any sense, you'll take a few days and go fishing. Or to a resort somewhere. Go anywhere out of town. Call it a retreat if you like." He pointed at the envelope in Paul's hand. "That should be good for the weekend. If you use cash they can't track you by your credit card."

"What? Are you serious?"

"You're terribly naïve, and you're obviously exhausted. You just said you can hardly think straight. If the police take you in, and your lawyer can't get there, they'll wear you down. You'll make admissions that could hurt you. You might even tell them the exact thing you keep saying you don't want to tell them."

"I understand, but I can't take your—"

A rapping on the glass barrier stopped him. Hank hit the button and the glass slid open again.

"Sorry, sir," the driver said, "but we're in a bus stop."

Through the windshield Paul saw a woman police officer headed toward them, waving them out of the bus stop.

"I'm on my way to O'Hare," Hank said, "headed out of the country. I don't need some traffic cop making me miss my flight, and *you* don't need her recognizing you. So take the money and go…*now*."

With no time to think it over, Paul opened the car door and got out, the envelope in his hand. He leaned down to speak to Hank, but by then the limo was already moving, and he pushed the door shut. Not wanting to look at the police officer, he just turned and walked across the wide sidewalk and into the lobby of a high-rise office building.

There was a Starbucks off the lobby and he went in and ordered a decaf and took it to a table in the corner. He felt strangely disoriented again. It was encouraging that someone was really trying to help. But at this point even Hank could do nothing but give him money, and Paul didn't know how that would help.

He sat and stared at the envelope. He opened it and found it full of hundred-dollar bills. Fifty of them.

FORTY-TWO

Calm down. Drink your decaf. Pray. And if God seems too far beyond your reach, you're still a priest. You can't control the police or the CIA, or God either, but you've been trained to control yourself...body and mind. You can sit here alone, with five thousand dollars in an envelope on the table, and you can slow down your breathing. Drink your decaf.

So he sat there and tried to slow things down. First his breath, then the whirling fears in his mind that kept circling the same dilemma—he had to defend himself. And doing so meant sending Robert back.

He lifted the cardboard cup to take a drink...and discovered it was empty. Time to go. Tucking the envelope in his shirt pocket, he stood up. But there was nowhere to go, so he went back for more coffee. Caffeinated this time. And although he didn't feel hungry, he knew he should be, so he bought a huge muffin, too, then went back and sat down again.

Only a few customers came in, and none of them stayed. It was quiet here, and he felt safe.

Oh? Safe from the police? They'd gotten access to his voice mail messages and had probably searched his rooms. They'd gotten his records from the emergency room, and had probably talked to the doctor from Goa. By now they might know about the Dodge Caravan he'd rented, and be watching for it. He'd used his credit card, so they might even know where he'd slept last night. The police weren't going away.

Safe from Ann Swanson? When he'd first started doubting the randomness of Larry's killing, he'd found it hard to believe the government would shoot down an American citizen in his own backyard. If Ann *wasn't* a CIA agent—and he was unsure now whether to believe even Melendez's denial—did that make it easier to believe she'd ordered Larry's killing? Whoever she was, whoever she worked for, she could get things done. Ann Swanson wasn't going away.

The sense of safety that kept him sitting at this tiny round table, chewing on a muffin he couldn't even taste, was an illusion.

He certainly hadn't made Robert safe. He should have let that lawyer in Mexico handle things, but his fear for the boy had clouded his judgment. Right now Robert still thought Paul held some governmental position that protected him, but he'd soon realize that wasn't true. And he'd wake up every morning, for the rest of his life, wondering whether this was the day they would come for him.

The smart thing was to go back to the CIA and tell them about Robert. Maybe they'd straighten things out with Mexico. And even if they didn't, even if they just handed him back, with a good Mexican lawyer, and Paul's support, and possibly some help Hank Manion could arrange from the US government, Robert might get this whole thing put behind him. All things considered, it was a risk worth taking.

Really? For Robert's sake? And if taking that risk just happens to help you out of your own trouble? That's not the real reason you'd do it, right? Just a side benefit?

He stood up. He wasn't sure what he would do, but he would not put his son at risk to save his own skin.

He went out into the lobby and used a pay phone. In response to Celia's recorded voice he said, "It's Fath…it's Paul Clark. This is important. You may be in danger as long as you have that CD. Go to the police and give the CD to them. Right away."

†

He took a taxi to St. Hildegard's and had the driver drop him in the alley behind the rectory, and went in the back door. It was three in the afternoon and, as usual, Max barked like crazy as Paul climbed the stairs.

And, as usual, Jake Kincannon yelled, "Good boy!" and then opened his door. "That *you*, Paul?"

"Yeah, it's me."

When he reached the second floor Jake was standing in his half-open doorway, with Max trying to squeeze past him and get out. "I don't know if you been back since then," Jake said, "but yesterday morning some cops were waitin' out front when I came back from mass. They had a search warrant. I hadda let 'em in."

"Of course you did. I understand."

"I told 'em they better not mess your things up, and they basically told me to mind my own business. Which made me mad as hell, y'know? They searched your rooms and then the whole darn rectory. Even wanted to search *my* rooms."

"Really?" Paul seldom went into Jake's suite, and when he did he had to thread his way through stacks of magazines and newspapers to get to a chair, and then clear off the chair to sit down.

"Yep. Showed me where the warrant said: 'the residence in which Father Paul Clark resides.' But I told 'em maybe you reside in the *residence*, but you sure don't live in *my* rooms, and they'd have to go back and get another warrant for that."

"What'd they say to that?"

"Nothin'. They left. I think they took some of your stuff, but I don't know what." Just then Max managed to poke his head out the door.

"Stay!" Jake said, which had no effect at all, and he had to reach down and grab Max's collar. Bent over, he looked up at Paul. "Do those idiots really think you could kill anyone?"

"Apparently they do."

"Yeah, well, that's bull crap." Jake stood up, holding Max under one arm. "Anyway, if I can be of some help, lemme know."

"Thanks, Jake."

"Yeah, well, I— Oh...almost forgot. Wait here a minute." Jake closed his door, and in a few seconds opened it again and handed Paul his gym bag. "You left this in the sacristy yesterday morning. Your cell phone's in it."

†

Paul wouldn't have needed Jake to tell him about the police search. As soon as he stepped through his door, it was obvious. They hadn't really torn the place apart, or done any real damage. But it looked like everything—not only in the study, but in the bedroom and bathroom too—had been picked up and put down again…in a different spot.

He wondered if Maddox had ever searched a priest's rooms before. Did he wonder what sort of things he'd find there? Paul knew there was no simple answer. Too many priests—even the ones who hadn't become compulsive savers in their old age, like Jake—surrounded themselves with "things." The latest electronic and media gadgets, hundreds of books, artwork…as though trying to satisfy an emptiness that couldn't be filled. Then there were some, though not very many, who lived like monks.

But in Paul's experience, most priests' living quarters were a lot like his own, comfortable, but plain…although his were maybe more austere than most. Not very large, not very luxurious, and not very much for searchers to paw through. In his study there was a sofa hardly anyone ever sat on, a reclining chair which got lots of use, a desk, and a desk chair. No souvenirs or knickknacks, just a couple of photos on his desk. One was of his father, who'd died when Paul was still an infant; the other his mother, who'd been a secretary for a law firm and raised him on her own. He had no brothers or sisters, and the few cousins he'd heard of lived in Boston and he'd never seen them. The crucifix and the framed prints on the walls were the ones that were there when he moved in. He had a six-year-old TV, and a Bose radio with a cassette deck he couldn't buy tapes for any more. As for books, most priests had lots of books. Not Paul. If he wasn't certain he'd be re-reading a book in the immediate future…he gave it away.

He worked long hours at the Pastoral Care Office, but almost never brought work home, so he had no files for the detectives to look into. The only place with any clutter was his desk, and he could tell that the papers and mail on the desktop had all been rifled through; as had, he was sure, his checkbook and the few financial records he kept in the top left drawer.

More than half of the bedroom was taken up by the treadmill he tried to use every day. The contents of his closet were all tossed across the narrow single bed, on top of the clothes taken from his dresser. The drawers themselves were in place and closed. In the bathroom, everything that had been in the medicine cabinet was in the bathtub, but nothing was broken and—as far as he could remember—nothing was missing.

About a year's worth of bank statements had been taken. And just one other thing: his computer. Not the monitor or the keyboard, but the mini-tower that should have been standing on the floor beside the desk. Any technicians who pawed through that would be pretty bored. Maybe they'd enjoy the notes for a couple of years' worth of Sunday sermons.

He pulled the cell phone from his gym bag, and checked for messages. There were none.

It struck him then that the police would probably have taken the phone if it had been there. He set it down on the desk. Until the last few days he'd hardly ever failed to obey Ann's order to keep it with him at all times. She rarely called, but said she had to be certain they spoke on a "secure" phone. He'd always assumed she'd done something to the cell that gave her that confidence.

He stared down at the phone then, and thought that if the police had confiscated it they might have been able to trace who had called him, from where, and when. They might also have found whatever it was that made it "secure." And suddenly, a question formed in his mind for the first time, one he was amazed he'd never thought of before. Besides making it more "secure," what other "features" had Ann added to that phone?

It might contain a tiny tracking device...which would explain how she always seemed to know where he'd been, or where he was going. And why not a device that would let her listen in, and record, all his phone conversations? Or one that would pick up and transmit conversations that weren't *over* the phone, but merely *near* the phone? That phone might have been reporting his movements, and even his conversations. How could he have been so stupid?

Ann had probably tracked him when he left the hospital and went back to Larry's rectory, but he hadn't talked to anyone, so she wouldn't have known he'd taken the laptop. And when he'd gone that night to take the laptop back, he hadn't taken the phone along. And he hadn't had it today when he talked to the CIA agents, or to Hank Manion.

He thought hard. What about his various conversations with Celia? Which ones might Ann and her people have overheard? Did she know Celia had a CD Larry had given her on—

The phone rang. Not the cell, but the rectory phone. He didn't answer and after three rings either the person hung up or it went into voice mail. He waited awhile, then picked up and checked for a message.

It was Brian Joplin. "Listen, Paul, call my office. I'm on trial, but they'll put you through. I just found out. You know Father Landrew's sister? Celia? She rents an apartment in a high-rise somewhere around. . .I don't know. . .North Avenue? Anyway, she fell off the balcony. Or maybe jumped. From the twelfth floor. She's. . .well. . .she's dead."

FORTY-THREE

When Paul regained his senses he didn't know how long he'd been sitting there, staring at the phone. He knew only that Celia's fall was neither an accident, nor a suicide. And that his actions had led now to the deaths of two innocent persons.

When he finally started moving, he rushed around with an urgency that bordered on frenzy. He stuffed his gym bag with clothes, including an extra pair of black pants and two long-sleeved black shirts which experience had taught him were useful where he was going. He packed a Roman collar, then took it out again. He threw in his shaving kit, and then the digital camera he'd gotten last Christmas, plus the instruction manual he could study on the way.

When he couldn't think of anything else he needed, he put on a blue shirt and a sport coat, and literally ran out of his room and down the stairs. He went out the kitchen door, across the concrete yard, and into the church. In the sacristy he took a heavy, ornate key from its hiding place and went out into the sanctuary. Since it was mid-afternoon the church was empty and the doors were locked. Sunlight poured in through stained glass windows, overpowering the soft red light from the candle that burned day and night before one of the side altars. He climbed the steps to that altar and pushed aside the veil that covered the tabernacle, a square metal safe that had sheaves of wheat and clusters of grapes carved into its bronze-plated door. Using the heavy key, he unlocked the door and pulled it open. He was in a hurry, but found himself taking the time to genuflect, reverencing the Blessed Sacrament. Then, standing again, he took the cell phone from his pocket and wrapped it in a clean linen handkerchief. He put it inside the tabernacle, far in the back, behind the gold-plated cup that held the consecrated bread.

Jake would probably never notice the phone. If he did he'd be surprised, but not shocked or scandalized, and he'd know enough to leave it there.

†

When Paul retrieved Jake's car keys from under the floor mat, his hands were shaking. He had a hard time getting the right key in the ignition, and he recalled Celia having the same problem with her car just a few days before. He finally got the key in and fired up the old Buick. Jake wouldn't even know the car was gone.

The act of driving itself served, to his surprise, to calm him down a bit. His bank was in the heart of the Loop, but traffic would be snarled there, so he drove to a parking lot west of Wacker Drive and took a cab. At the bank he signed in at the safe deposit vault, where he accessed his box and removed both of the passports he'd stored there.

Upstairs in the main bank lobby he stood in line and when he got to the teller he handed her Hank Manion's five thousand dollars, asking her to break the hundreds down into fifties and twenties. She gave him a few rubber bands to hold the bills in packets, and even gave him a new thick-papered envelope to put the money in. If she thought his requests were unusual, she didn't let on. Only when he turned to leave did it strike him that the whole transaction was probably being recorded. But would anyone ever actually look at the video? He fought to keep paranoia from creeping in.

He left the bank and ducked into a convenience store, where he bought a cell phone. The clerk activated it for him and loaded with two hundred dollars of pre-paid time. Remembering Hank's warning, he used cash.

†

He was in the Buick and back on the Skyway, when he called Brian Joplin's office. "If you give me your name and number," the secretary said, "I can—"

"I'll call again."

The Buick had no cruise control and, once more, he had to fight to keep his speed within the limit. He couldn't afford to be stopped by the police. A half hour later he tried Brian again and this time they put him through.

"She's been very depressed about her brother," Brian said, "according to news reports."

"News reports?" Paul hadn't even thought of turning on the radio.

"Yes. They say he was her only living relative. She was divorced, you know. No kids."

"I know all that. I've talked to her several times. She was upset, yes, but not suicidal. She wasn't the type to—"

"Paul, hold on. She'd been alone in her apartment, with the door locked. Nothing was disturbed or missing. She left a note."

"A note? What did it say?"

"I don't know. They're not releasing that…not yet, anyway. But they're calling it a suicide note. On her computer."

"So not handwritten?"

"No, but… Look, Paul, you're under a lot of strain. You should—"

"Good-bye, Brian."

He switched on the radio. He listened to a local news station for a while, but there wasn't any news about Celia, and the chatter drove him crazy, so he turned it off again and discovered that silence wasn't much better. He considered his options.

Or lack of options. That CIA agent Melendez, who may or may not have been lying about Ann Swanson, had warned him, in essence, not to tell his story to the police. For their part, the police were only interested in him as a suspect. And the media? They'd portray him as a madman spinning tales of secret agents, international conspiracies, and murder…all to cover his own guilt and deceit. The cardinal? His goal was to distance himself and not embarrass the church. The only one willing to help was Hank Manion, and he'd already done more than Paul had a right to ask.

But he had to act. He had tried letting matters take their course, with deadly consequences. The only thing he could think of was to go to Guyana and see for himself what was going on down there. If possible, he'd document it and come back with hard evidence to take to the police, to the CIA, even to the press if he had to. It was a plan full of unknowns and loose ends, but it beat doing nothing. Also, it would keep him away from the police for a few days, which is why Hank had given him the money.

Also…he would take Robert with him.

Was that exposing the boy to danger? Maybe, but his attempt so far to hide Robert had merely put the boy far away from him, on his own and vulnerable. He was Paul's son, and he was *already* in danger. Paul wanted him by his side.

FORTY-FOUR

She walked to the window and stared out into the night. The lights in the room behind her were turned low, and Jessie had fallen asleep…finally. She'd had the second ankle repair—hopefully the last of the major surgeries—and now they'd begun weaning her off some of her meds. She wasn't taking it well, her demeanor stuck in a narrow range from sullen silence to shrill bitchiness. She was *such* a different Jessie now from that upbeat, free-spirited artist who'd managed somehow to flip herself and her bike over the edge of a cliff. The change was completely understandable, and the psychologist was sure it was temporary, but that didn't make the downbeat version any easier to deal with. Only her love for Jessie made it possible.

Feeling suddenly too exhausted to stand, she moved to the heavy visitor's chair and turned it to face the window, then sat and gazed out absently, past the dark rolling mounds of treetops, to where endless rows of Friday night headlights merged and then diverged along the distant beltway. She found herself trying to pick out which of those curving rows of lights were headed impatiently into the city, eager for a few hours' diversion, and which were moving gratefully out, toward the quiet and comfort of—

She shook her head, throwing off her drowsiness and the mindless distractions it gave rise to. Her own real world needed all her attention.

There'd been another death, and this time she wouldn't even bother voicing her objections. Wouldn't bother pointing out how needless, not to mention dangerous to the mission, it was. Questions and complaints were useless. The only positive note now was that the mission itself was drawing to a close. Not that it wouldn't lead to more violence and death, but those would come in a cause at least arguably righteous, and not the result of mere stupidity and panic. And besides, that would be violence and death which both geography and her own training would help her keep at a distance.

But the killings of the priest and his sister? These were too close, too unnecessary. Although she hadn't willed them, hated the thought of them, they were real, and she couldn't escape them. They were a part of this mission, and so they were *her* fault, too.

Yet even her own responsibility, acknowledged and accepted, wasn't the saddest thing.

She closed her eyes, listening to the rise and fall of Jessie's breaths behind her. Sweet Jessie, away for now from the pain and the vomiting, the pushing and the pulling on her limbs, the fear and the confusion. Jessie, who knew only what she'd been told, who was too worn and beaten down, and too little in control of her faculties, to be able to see through the lie: *You don't have to worry, baby. Insurance has this all covered.*

There'd been another meeting, earlier that very day, "to discuss Jessie's continued care at our facility." And no matter how sedate and calm the discussion had been, in fact it brought another warning, another deadline for some "substantial draw-down of the balance." She had responded with another excuse, another solemn promise: *There was some sort of mix-up by the brokers, but they assure me the sale's gone through now and the money will be on its way.*

So the saddest thing about the killings of the priest and his sister? Not her own shared responsibility. No, the saddest thing was that even if she had known from the start that those deaths, cruel and unnecessary as they were, would become part of it...she'd still have done just what she did. She'd still have signed on, still have agreed to work the same angles and to tell the same lies. She'd still be leaving this room and, not so many hours from now, boarding the same flight, headed for the same transaction, one which would lead to the spilling of more blood. *Much* more blood…and, as always, some of it innocent.

She didn't have to like it. She didn't even have to like herself. She only had to face the truth. She was doing this for the money. She was doing this because there was no other way.

She was doing this for Jessie.

FORTY-FIVE

This is a special opportunity for Robert," Paul said. It was nine in the morning and he and Alfred Grayson were sipping coffee in the headmaster's office. He didn't want to take Robert without an explanation. That might stir up questions or suspicions. "It's a business trip that came up unexpectedly. Robert will get a chance to broaden his horizons. And the two of us will be able to get to know each other better. It'll only be a few days."

"You have our policy book," the tall, handsome headmaster said. "At Bridgebriar we don't allow students to be taken out of school during the term." He laced his fingers behind his head and leaned back in his chair. "The only exceptions are when a student is ill, or for a death, or some other serious family situation." Grayson already knew that Robert had no other family members.

"I'm aware of the rule," Paul said. "But this…it's a special opportunity."

"Yes, you said that." Grayson tilted his head back and stared up at the ceiling. "Robert's had his difficulties here, as you know. But his attitude has visibly improved… in just the few days since you were last here."

"I…I'm glad to hear that."

"My secretary's been having him help out here in the office a little. Copying and filing and the like."

"That's great, and I'm sure this trip will—"

"But we have rules." Grayson lowered his hands to his desktop and leaned forward. "And the rule is quite clear. If you take him out of school, he won't be able to come back."

"You...you can't mean that."

"I'm afraid I—"

The phone beeped and the secretary's voice came clearly over the intercom. "Excuse me, sir. But Robert Johnson is here. He...well...he has his backpack. He says he's all set to go."

"Oh?" Grayson's eyes widened and he looked across at Paul.

"Sorry," Paul said, getting to his feet. "But we'll talk again when I get back."

†

As they drove away from Bridgebriar, Robert didn't make any remarks about the ancient Buick, or even ask where they were going. Instead, it was, "Can I drive?"

"Not this time," Paul said. "It's over a hundred-mile trip, on expressways."

"Uh-huh." He didn't sound that disappointed.

Paul had been happily surprised that morning when Robert so quickly agreed to stuff his backpack with a few days' worth of clothes and join him on "an unexpected business trip." Clearly the boy was delighted to get out of school, but there seemed to be more to it than that. As though maybe Robert genuinely trusted him.

And why not? He'd been about to die in that Mexican jail, and I got him—

"So," Robert asked, "where we going?"

"To Detroit. The airport."

"Cool. But where we flying to?"

"I'll explain everything," Paul said. "But first, let me ask *you* something. Have you seen that man again?"

"Huh?"

"The man you saw when you were buying a bus ticket. Have you seen him again?"

"No." Robert twisted in his seat and looked at Paul. "What's *he* got to do with this?"

"It's just...he's been on my mind." He paused. "Anyway, we're going to Guyana. Know where that is?"

"Guyana? It's in South America."

"Wow," Paul said, truly surprised. "Most people have no idea where it is."

"We had this movie at school about Jonestown. You know, the massacre and...anyway, I don't know *exactly*, but it's..." He thought for a few seconds. "It's on the Atlantic Ocean, and it must be north of Brazil, and south of...what? Venezuela?"

"Right. Although it's mostly *east* of Venezuela."

"Uh-huh. So...we're going there?"

"Yes."

"Cool. Uh...why?"

"I have to visit a medical clinic there, in a pretty remote part of the country. Not far from Venezuela, actually."

"So...are you a *doctor*?"

"No, I...I do work for a charitable organization that supports the place. It's called Fair Hope Clinic and the patients are indigenous people and can't pay much. I go down there every so often to see how things are going. This trip, though, came up suddenly."

"You speak Spanish? "Robert asked. "I took a year of it in school, but I could hardly understand a word when I was in Mexico."

"Not a problem. English is Guyana's official language. Although it's pretty hard to understand people because of the accent. It's a beautiful place, if you don't mind roughing it. Not many tourists yet, and..." He babbled on about Guyana, because it was the easy thing to do.

Eventually, though, he ran out of things to say, and Robert spoke up. "You said you'd explain everything. When do we get to that part?"

"It's a long story," Paul said, "and pretty...complicated."

It was a balancing act. The boy needed to know there might be danger. But he was only eighteen, and the entire truth might be too much for him to handle all at once. On the other hand, when he *did* find out the rest of it, Paul didn't want to be accused of lying about it.

So, feeling as though he were taking that first step off the platform onto the tightrope, he said, "You already know that this all started with your grandmother contacting me, and that when I went down and saw you in that terrible jail, I knew I *had* to get you out. What I *didn't* tell you before was that...that I'm a priest. A Catholic priest."

"A priest? What the hell? You told me you—"

"I need you to save all your questions until I'm finished. Okay?"

"That's bullshit. You..." Robert's voice trailed off. "Yeah, okay." He slumped back in his seat, staring straight ahead through the windshield. "Whatever."

Paul still wasn't ready to explain yet that Robert's grandmother's appeal had been based on his being Robert's father.

"I may have misled you, Robert, but I've tried to keep *lies* to a minimum. For instance, I told you my name was Michael Clark, and that's true. The name on my birth certificate is 'Michael Paul Clark.' But my father's name was Michael, too, so my parents called me 'Paul,' and that's the name I've always used." He paused, but Robert said nothing. "I also never told you *how* I was able to get you out of jail, or who that woman was who brought you to me in Chicago. But...well...now you need to know."

He explained how a stranger named Ann Swanson had approached him and identified herself as a government agent. She knew all about Robert's arrest and offered to help—for a price. He explained how, after Ann sent the two men to get Robert out of jail, Paul had let her people—the CIA, he'd been certain, although she hadn't quite said so—secretly use some property at Fair Hope. He told of Larry Landrew's discovery of the CIA presence there, of his intention to write about what he'd seen in the *Sun-Times*, and how he'd gotten killed before that happened.

"The police know I was trying to talk Father Landrew out of revealing something—they don't know what—and they think maybe I shot him to keep him quiet about something I'd done."

"They...they think you're a killer?"

"They're not calling me a 'suspect.' But they wonder why I won't tell them what the secret is that I didn't want him to write about in the paper."

"Jesus."

"I wanted to tell them the secret wasn't about anything terrible I'd done. It was that I'd let the CIA use the clinic. But Ann Swanson threatened me. She said if I told the police...or anyone...about the CIA being at Fair Hope she'd…well…she'd have her men take you back to Mexico."

He paused, but Robert said nothing at all. He sat as though hypnotized, staring straight ahead through the windshield as they sped along the highway.

"Robert?" Paul said. "Are you…do you understand what I'm saying?"

"I didn't hurt anybody." Robert spoke in a monotone, as though Paul wasn't even there. "I was just carrying a little weed…for some guys I *thought* were my friends." Finally he turned toward Paul. "I can't go back there, you know. To that jail. I can't."

"I know. And I'm doing everything I can to make sure you don't. I went to the CIA headquarters, but they say Ann Swanson isn't even one of their agents. They say they have no operation at Fair Hope, and that if I tell my story the police will think I'm lying, or crazy. The thing is, *someone's* down there at that clinic, so I decided to go there myself and bring back proof of what's going on."

"That woman," Robert said, "must know I'm at Bridgebriar. That *was* one of those men."

"I think so. I didn't tell her you were there, but she found out somehow…and sent that man to be sure it was you. Or maybe she *wanted* you to see him…to scare you. I don't know."

"Uh-huh." Robert seemed lost in thought.

"You know, Robert, I'm sorry."

"*Sorry?* For what?"

"I made a lot of trouble. For us both. In Mexico I got the best lawyer I could find, but he wasn't sure he could get you out, and I couldn't stand that. So I made that agreement. It was a terrible decision."

"Bullshit." Robert shifted around in his seat. "If it wasn't for you I'd have died in there…or killed myself."

"Don't *say* that," Paul said. "The thing is, those men killed a prisoner, and now you could be charged with murder."

"I'm *glad* that asshole's dead. I'd have killed him myself if I could have."

"Robert, don't—"

"Why not? It's true. Anyway, you got me out. So don't be sorry."

"But I should have found a better way. And yesterday, when I decided I had to go outside the country, I couldn't stand to leave you alone at Bridgebriar. That might have been another stupid decision. So if you want, I'll take you back."

"You gotta be kidding. I'm staying with *you*."

†

On the way to Detroit they stopped at a Best Buy and bought a laptop. Paul let Robert deal with the sales clerk and with making sure the laptop was wireless ready. Then they went to a food court with Internet access.

Paul was sure there were flights to Guyana from Detroit, because his previous flights to Fair Hope had always included a stop first in Detroit, then in Miami, and sometimes in Trinidad and Tobago, from which it was a short hop to Guyana.

Robert got online to check out flight times and prices. "I bet it'll cost you," he said, "buying tickets last minute like this. What's the city we're going to?"

"Georgetown. That's the capital."

Within minutes Robert had found several flights from Detroit to Georgetown that evening, one of them shortly after seven o'clock. Round-trip tickets were just under twelve hundred dollars each. "If you give me your credit card number," Robert said, "I'll buy them."

Paul shook his head. "We can't be sure we'll be on time for that flight. Besides, I'm not using the card. We'll buy tickets at the airport."

"Yeah, if they have any left," Robert said. "But…whatever."

†

They made it in time for the flight.

Paul had prepared an explanation as to why they were buying same-day tickets and paying with cash, but the agent didn't seem interested, maybe because their return flight was a week later. His actual plan was to return home in a day or two, and he knew they'd have to pay extra to change their tickets.

Then there was the passport problem. "Robert should stay away from Mexico," Ann had said when she gave Paul the boy's passport, "but otherwise, he's as free to travel as anyone." When she said that, he'd had no reason not to believe her.

But that was *then.*

His mind bounced around the issue like a pinball. By now the Chicago police might have gotten their arrest warrant. Would they put a watch or a hold on his passport? Could they? And if Ann wasn't with the CIA, could *she*? Or if the agents had lied and she *was* with the agency, would she suspect he might try leaving the country? *He* hadn't been considering it, so why should *she*? On the other hand, she always kept close track of him. And on…and on…

Still, when the time came, there was no way around it.

FORTY-SIX

They presented their passports to the ticket agent and boarded the plane without incident. Paul's worry had been wasted energy. . .which didn't console him or calm him down.

"A layover in Miami, and then non-stop to Georgetown," Paul told Robert. "That's good. Sometimes you have to go through Trinidad and Tobago, and that's always a big—" He stopped.

Robert wasn't listening, anyway. He was studying a map in the airline magazine. "Here it is," he said. "Guyana. It's in the same time zone as Michigan."

The flight went smoothly, with Robert poring over a couple of auto racing magazines he bought at the airport. In Miami they had plenty of time to get something to eat, and for Paul to make some phone calls. Then, as soon as they were back in the air, Robert fell asleep. Paul was exhausted, too, but dozed fitfully, tormented by the voice in his head telling him it was foolish to go to Fair Hope Clinic, and reckless to bring Robert along.

†

It was close to nine a.m. when they broke through a high layer of clouds and touched down at Cheddi Jagan Airport, about an hour outside Georgetown. As they taxied along the runway, Paul and Robert stared together out the small window at what appeared to be a gray, chilly day. But Paul knew better, and stepping out of the plane proved it. It was like walking into a steamy shower room, but one that smelled like jet fuel. By the time they reached the bottom of the stairway and stepped onto the tarmac, Paul's shirt was wet and sticking to his back.

It was a fifty-yard walk through a strong hot wind to the terminal, a low brick building, painted white. It was cooler inside, but not by much. "Don't forget," Paul said, "don't eat any fruit and don't drink any water... unless it's bottled."

They had only carry-on luggage and, as they headed toward the customs counter, Paul's heart beat faster. This was another possible problem point. The agent, seeing that they were together, reached out with two hands to take both their passports. He was middle-aged, with jet-black hair as short as a marine recruit's, and a thin dark face that bore deep, disfiguring scars—maybe from smallpox. He seemed both bored and aggravated as he compared their appearances with their photos, and then set the passports down behind the counter, beyond their reach. He slid Paul's gym bag and Robert's backpack closer to him, opened them, poked into them with no apparent interest, and zipped them both closed again, all without a word.

He picked up one of the passports, opened it, looked at Robert, and then turned to Paul. "What is the purpose of your visit and how long will you be in Guyana?" he asked. His words were clipped and clear, and his accent reminded Paul of Harry Belafonte.

In his passport photo Paul wasn't wearing a Roman collar, but he said, "I'm a Catholic priest, from Chicago, and I've been to Guyana several times, to visit Fair Hope Clinic, a medical facility the Archdiocese of Chicago supports for indigenous people, near Mabaruma." He nodded toward Robert. "This time I brought Mr. Johnson with me. I know a boat leaves every Sunday, so if we can make it on time, we'll—"

"No need to hurry," the agent said. "No boat today. The waves are too high." He shrugged. "Maybe tomorrow. Or the next day."

"Then we'll have to stay overnight in a hotel. I hope the weather improves soon, though, because we were only planning on being here a week. We—"

"Thank you." The agent reached down for the passport still lying on the counter, and handed it to Paul. "Proceed, please," he said, and turned his attention to Robert. "What is the purpose of your visit and how long will you be in Guyana?"

"I told you," Paul said, "he's with *me*."

"Right," Robert added. "I'm. . .you know, just—"

"Wait." The agent turned toward Paul. "You may not stand here, sir. You must proceed." He pointed. "Beyond that white line on the floor."

Paul did as he was told. From where he stood he couldn't hear what the agent was asking Robert. He had him take the laptop from its case, lay it on the counter, and start it up. Beyond Robert a line was forming, led by three young women—college-age or a little older—dragging large, wheeled tourist bags.

Robert must finally have satisfied the man because he slid the laptop back into its case. He took his passport, and picked up the backpack. When he reached Paul, he said, "What an ass— I mean. . .idiot," he said. "It was like he didn't believe anything I said."

"Sorry," Paul said. "We should have discussed what to say, but I didn't think of it. They've always pretty much just waved me through. What did you tell him?"

"That I'm a student, a member of your church. I said I came along to check out the clinic and see if I wanted to volunteer there." He shook his head. "Jerking me around 'cause I'm young, y'know? I think the reason he finally let me go was because of those girls. Creep wants to poke around in their luggage and eyeball their—" He stopped. "Anyway. . .I don't like it here."

They passed through a turnstile and were immediately surrounded by a dozen boys and men, all in shabby t-shirts and shorts, waving their arms and shouting offers of transportation into the city. Each was desperate to point out that his was the fastest and cheapest ride. Paul waved them off and led Robert toward the exit doors, passing a booth fronted with bullet-proof windows of thick, clouded plastic. He usually stopped there for Guyanese dollars, but there was no time for that, and US dollars would have to do.

When they shoved their way through the doors they found themselves back in the heat—there was more of a difference than he'd thought—on a sidewalk where a dozen cabs, a few vans, and one black Cadillac limousine waited at the curb, as more men shouted and gestured.

"I usually take one of those mini-buses," Paul said. "But they never leave until they're over-stuffed with bags and people. A taxi will be quicker."

He picked a Ford sedan—bright green and probably ten years old—that said *Parrot Taxi* on the side. The driver, also in shorts and t-shirt, held the door for them. An older man, his wide smile revealed only five or six teeth, more yellow than white. "What hotel, boss?" Again the Caribbean accent, but thicker, more like Sammy Sosa.

"Mandela Field," Paul said.

The man looked surprised. "Very good, boss." He grinned again. "De cost is six t'ousand dollars."

"What does that—"

"Six *thousand*?" Robert interrupted.

"That's Guyanese dollars," Paul told him, and then asked the driver, "How much in US dollars?"

"T'irty dollars, boss. Cheap."

"How about twenty?"

"Twenty-five, boss. De wife, she beat me if I go for less."

Paul nodded and he and Robert climbed into the back seat with their bags. The driver slammed the door shut and hustled around and jumped behind the wheel, as though afraid they might change their minds. He switched on the ignition, and it was obvious the car badly needed a muffler. They lurched away from the curb and sped out into the exit lane, while Paul searched in vain for a seat belt.

†

They joined the flow of traffic—hardly enough to warrant the word "traffic" at all—headed for the city, but before long their driver swung them off the main highway onto a much smaller road. It was asphalt, but narrow and full of potholes, and proved that the taxi needed shock absorbers as badly as a muffler.

They rode through a flat landscape, most of it farmland, with occasional clusters of small homes. Unpainted wood shacks, really, weathered to gray, a few with battered, rusting cars squatting nearby. The clothes on the lines in many of the yards were stretched out horizontally by the relentless hot wind; and as the noisy taxi went by, chickens squawked and flapped their wings as though—like the taxi hawkers in the airport—desperate to get someone's attention. The few humans in sight—children as well as adults—merely watched in silence as the big green car bounced past.

As far as Paul could tell, no one seemed interested in them. No cars followed them.

Robert must have noticed him looking, because he asked, "How come you keep looking out the back window?"

"Just looking around."

"Uh-huh. So…what kinda hotels are way out here, anyway?"

"None. We're not going to a hotel."

"But you told that guy we'd stay in a hotel and take the boat to this Marumba place tomorrow."

"It's *Mabaruma.*" He leaned close to Robert and kept his voice low, although with the hot air rushing in the open windows, and the roar of the motor, he knew the driver couldn't hear. "And yes, I *did* say that, but…well…I lied."

"Lied? Why? And how come we have to take a boat, anyway? How far is it?"

"From Georgetown it's about a hundred-thirty miles. But, like a lot of Guyana, the area's filled with rivers and streams and swamps. It's wetlands and forests…or jungle. Hardly any roads. You can only get to Mabaruma by boat or by plane. The ocean boat's the cheapest, and I took it the first time I came down. But since then I've always flown. The boat's at least twenty-four hours on rough water along the coast—and that's if the weather's good. We don't have time for that. We're going back in a few days."

"But our return tickets are for a week from now."

"Because I thought someone might wonder about us if we paid cash and were staying only a few days. When we're ready to go back we'll have to change our tickets."

"*That'll* cost you, too. But you must have...like...a lot of money, right?"

"Wrong. Just the opposite."

"Oh." Robert looked out the window a minute, then turned back. "Anyway...I didn't know priests lied."

"Priests are people, and sometimes people... Well, forget *people*. Let's just stick with *me*. Sometimes I can't think of a better way to avoid trouble than to lie."

"Does that make it right?"

"No. It's wrong. Lying to try to keep things secret is a big part of what got me...us...into this mess."

"So why did you lie again this time...to that customs guy?"

"Robert, why don't you..." Paul stopped. "I lied because he seemed way more suspicious than they have the other times I've come here. I was afraid maybe he'd tell someone we were in Guyana. I wanted to make him—or anyone he might tell—think we wouldn't be getting to Fair Hope for several days."

"And you keep looking back to see if someone's following us, right? So...are we in *danger*?"

"I...I hope not." Paul shook his head. "But we *might* be. The thing is... well... this might really have been a terrible mistake. I'm sorry, Robert. I really am."

"Bullshit. I told you before, without you I'd be rotting to death in that fucking shithole jail. You got nothing to be sorry about, man. You're doing your best."

"I..." Paul didn't know what to say, so he said, "Thank you."

"No problem. And...maybe I should watch my language from now on, huh?"

"On our list of things to worry about, Robert, that's at the bottom."

Robert nodded. He seemed to be thinking for a few seconds, and then he said, "Thing is, if that customs guy *does* tell someone, whoever he tells will look to see what hotel we're in, and they'll find out we didn't check in anywhere."

Paul stared at him. "You're right."

†

What the sign announced as *NELSON MANDELA MEMORIAL AIRSTRIP* was a flat prairie with a couple of paved runways and a building about the size of a gas station, made of cement blocks painted white, with a green tin roof. Half a dozen small planes were lined up in a row, chained to the ground and wobbling in the wind. Painted on one side of the building in huge black letters was the word: *OFFICE*. Their taxi pulled up beside the only other vehicle in the parking area—an old Volkswagen bus.

"Stay here," Paul told Robert, and then leaned up toward the driver. "Wait for me. We may need to go somewhere else."

"Like you say, boss." The driver turned off the engine and it was suddenly much quieter, the only sound coming from a windsock flapping high above the roof of the office.

Paul got out and looked around. There were no cars in sight on the road in either direction. That was good. But the old Toyota pickup truck he'd expected—the one that said *GRANGER AIR* on the door—also wasn't in sight. That wasn't good.

FORTY-SEVEN

The girl at the counter was slim and pretty, and looked to be Robert's age, at most. Paul had seen her there before. Like so many Guyanese, she was of East Indian descent, with long black hair and brown skin that contrasted sharply with her sleeveless white blouse. The blouse looked surprisingly crisp, given the lack of air-conditioning in the office.

"May I help you, sir?" She had the diction and accent of a BBC announcer.

"I'm looking for Rudolph Granger. I spoke with him yesterday on the phone."

"Oh...yes, of course." Her eyes widened, as though suddenly understanding. "I didn't recognize you without your clothes." She smiled. "I mean...without your *priest* clothes." She pointed a remote at the TV she'd been watching, and the slick-haired preacher on the little screen went silent, although he kept pacing and waving his bible around. "You are the priest. Father Clark."

"That's right."

"Clark," she repeated, searching methodically through a stack of papers on the counter and finally coming up with a note. "Ah...that's *Paul* Clark, is it?"

"Yes. But look, I have someone waiting, and I really need to see Mr. Granger."

"Well, that's the problem. I'm afraid he won't be in today."

"But he's supposed to fly us somewhere. He said—"

"I came in this morning, hoping to get in some flight time for my license, and found no one here. Then Mr. Granger called. He said that if you came in I should tell you that he apologizes, but he is not feeling well. And besides, the wind is too strong."

"Well, *someone* has to take me. Get him on the phone, *now*, and—" He realized he was pushing too hard. "That is…excuse me, miss, but please call Mr. Granger. I'd like to talk to him. See if he's feeling better, or if he can get me another pilot."

"I will try." She reached under the counter for a cell phone and tapped out a number. While she waited she said, "On some Saturday nights my uncle…well…he parties. So…" She didn't finish her sentence, but held out the phone so Paul could hear the ringing. "There is no answer," she said. She put the phone away. "I'm sorry."

"Rudolph Granger is your uncle?"

"Yes, of course. My name is Magdalena."

"Look, Magdalena, can you think of someone else? I know there are other charter services that fly out of here, too. Can you try another pilot?"

"But…you see…still there is the weather problem. The wind is strong, and from the wrong direction. No one will take off from here until that changes."

"My friend and I have to be in Mabaruma tonight. It's quite urgent."

"I really don't—"

"Tell them I'll pay double the usual cost."

That seemed to impress her. "Well, the wind may change some by mid-afternoon. I will make some calls. Meanwhile, you can wait here if you like."

"Thanks, but we have an errand to run. You get a pilot and we'll be back in…say…two hours? Would that give us time to get to Mabaruma before dark?"

"Plenty of time. But only if there is a pilot, *and* if the wind dies down. I suggest you should say a prayer, Father."

"Uh…right," he said. It struck him that he hadn't given prayer a thought in… well…how long?

†

As they drove away Paul laid out the situation to Robert. "Even if she gets us a pilot, we won't be able to leave for an hour or two. Which is fine. We can use that time."

He went on to explain his plan to Robert, and then to a bewildered—but not displeased—taxi driver, and forty-five minutes later they were entering Georgetown.

It was an old city, dating from the late 1700s. With barely two hundred thousand residents, it was a place of poverty and street crime, but also of constant ocean breezes and sunshine not blocked out by tall buildings. They drove along broad, tree-shaded avenues lined with Victorian mansions, most of them in sad disrepair, with shutters hanging crookedly and paint faded and peeling. Some, though, were well-kept, including several mansions recently reborn as hotels, mostly for eco-tourists about to venture into the unspoiled Guyanese rain forest.

Their taxi took them to one of those hotels, the Herdmanston Lodge. A rambling two-story structure full of angles and verandas, it was in Queenstown, a mostly residential district, just a few minutes' walk from the ocean. Paul knew it to be clean and comfortable, and—at least by US standards—inexpensive.

Paul paid off the driver and he and Robert went inside with their bags. He'd made a reservation from Miami by phone, using his credit card, which wouldn't be charged—and thus, he assumed, couldn't be tracked—until they checked out. A room for one night—the "Deluxe," with an extra cot. He told the desk clerk they'd be taking the boat to Mabaruma in the morning. One more priestly false statement for Robert's disedification.

"We'll take our own bags up, thanks," he said, and he and Robert headed off in the direction of the elevator. When they reached it they walked right on past, down the hall and into the kitchen, and then out a service door.

In the alley, a green taxi with a faulty muffler was waiting.

†

They grabbed some fish and chips and bottled water from a take-out place the driver recommended, the White Castle Fish Shop, and ate as they rode back to Mandela Field. The fish was tasty, but came with a sort of Cajun sauce that was hot beyond anything he or Robert could tolerate.

As they approached the airstrip again, Paul's heart sank. The VW van still sat alone in the office lot. "You better wait this time, too," he told the driver.

The wind, which had been easterly before, was from the north now, off the ocean, and cooler. If it had eased up at all, the difference was slight, but there didn't seem to be the sudden gusts whipping up as there had been before.

Inside the office Magdalena stood behind the counter. "On such short notice, and on a Sunday, I could find no one."

He took a deep breath and let it out. Maybe it was God's will, but *why*? Always the unanswerable question. "With this wind," he finally said, "it's probably best."

"Except the wind is not so bad as before." She took a large leather bag from the counter and slipped the strap over her shoulder. "You said it was urgent that you get to Mabaruma today," she said, and came around the counter. "So, follow me."

"What do you mean? Oh. . .*you?* But you're too young. You don't even have a license. You said so yourself."

"I have a license to fly, but not yet to carry paying passengers. I have not logged enough hours for that. But I am twenty-four years old, and have been flying since I was eleven. I know the Mabaruma route well. My boyfriend is a teacher there. You will pay in cash? And double the usual cost?"

"Well. . ." He didn't want to fly over the ocean, or remote jungle terrain, with someone whose appearance belied her claim to be twenty-four. Still. . . "That will be fine."

"Of course no one must know I did this. You are returning sometime tomorrow?"

"Yes, that's the plan." And if it didn't work out, there'd be worse things than transportation to worry about.

"Good. I will stay with my friend, and fly you back. There will be no one at the Mabaruma airstrip on Sunday. Will someone meet you to take you where you are going?"

"I…there wasn't time to make those arrangements."

"My friend has a Jeep." She locked the door behind them, then turned and smiled. "So, you see? Because you are a priest, God makes everything work well for you."

FORTY-EIGHT

Paul still had his doubts, but Magdalena was confident in her flying ability and clearly excited about taking them. "I've already cleared us with air traffic control and I've got my uncle's Cessna Skylane ready for takeoff. It's older than I am, but it's very dependable. I'm sure you've flown in it before."

She left Paul to get Robert and their bags from the taxi and pay off the driver, while she ran ahead. When he and Robert caught up, she already had the engine fired up.

After she got them into life jackets—"We'll be over the ocean most of the time," she shouted—they climbed on board the small, single-engine aircraft and strapped themselves into the two seats behind the pilot's seat and the empty seat beside it. She engaged the propeller and they taxied onto the lone runway. They headed north, into the strong, steady wind, and were quickly airborne. As usual, Paul was surprised that the engine noise seemed less as they flew.

"Cool," Robert said. He looked around in every direction, then leaned forward. "Hey...Magdalena?"

"Yes?"

"Can I sit up there in the co-pilot's seat?"

"That's a passenger seat. And the answer's no."

That didn't seem to bother Robert, and nothing more was said for a while, as they passed over open farmland dotted with homes. In the distance to their right, they could see where the cleared land ended abruptly, and jungle began; to their left Georgetown sprawled out on both sides of a lazy river that fed into the ocean.

They flew past another airport, Ogle, on the edge of the city and much smaller than Cheddi Jagan. Ogle, still a work in progress, wasn't yet able to handle the larger jets, but did offer regularly scheduled flights to Mabaruma. Paul, though, had never taken one of those. On his first visit to Fair Hope he'd met a Seventh Day Adventist missionary, a dental technician who visited the tiny villages around Mabaruma in her own plane, bringing dental care and bible lessons—"both pretty rudimentary," she laughingly admitted. She had told him of Rudolph Granger's charter service, which was a little less comfortable, and a lot cheaper, than the scheduled flights.

On his flights with Granger at the controls Paul always sat up beside the man, who loved to describe life as a bush pilot in Guyana, including nighttime flights through the amazing darkness of areas which knew no electricity, and hair-raising landings at remote villages to transport sick or injured natives to the hospital in Georgetown.

Magdalena, though, was all business. No talk. Not that she showed any nervousness. To the contrary, she exuded confidence and seemed completely in control. There wasn't a cloud in sight, and he noticed she didn't bother to switch on the GPS system. He also noticed that when she spoke with air traffic control at Ogle, she didn't mention she was carrying passengers.

They quickly reached the ocean and Paul drew Robert's attention to the concrete wall that, for over a hundred years, had managed to keep the sea from pouring into the streets of Georgetown. "How much longer it will hold," he said, "no one knows."

Once they were well out over the water Robert leaned forward again. "Hey, Magdalena? Why don't *you* have a life jacket on?"

"Because I don't intend to go into the water."

"Then...can I take mine off?"

"No."

"Why not?"

"Because if something happens which I *don't* intend, I can put on my jacket. But you will be too panicked to think straight."

"Oh." Robert was silent again for a while, then said, "Uh... Magdalena? Can I ask you something else?"

"Only if it's really important. Otherwise," she said, sighing like an impatient parent, "please don't bother me."

Robert gave up and sat back, and Paul thought Magdalena might indeed be twenty-four. Also, she had a boyfriend and probably didn't want to encourage Robert, who was clearly taken with her. More importantly, she put to rest Paul's doubts about her. She'd been truthful about both her ability and her knowledge of the route. Mabaruma was near the coast, but far to the west, and Paul realized, from previous flights with her uncle, that she was taking them north over the ocean, and would eventually head in a generally southwest direction toward their destination. By doing this the north wind wouldn't be a direct crosswind, and they wouldn't be flying straight into the afternoon sun.

For about an hour they stayed out over open water, sometimes angling in toward the coastline and sometimes away from it, but never losing sight of it. Finally, with the sun sinking but still well above the horizon, they headed straight in toward land.

"Look," Paul said. "Down there." He tapped Robert's shoulder. "That's Shell Beach. About the only real tourist attraction in this part of the country."

Robert leaned to peer down. "Not much of a beach. Looks more like rocks than sand. Don't see any people."

"Those are shells...bits of seashells. And no, people don't swim there much. They come to look at the unusual turtles, who come every year to lay their eggs."

Soon they left the water behind and were passing over dense jungle, broken only by rivers, thin brown lines snaking aimlessly through the dark green cover. "Man," Robert said, "it goes on forever. It looks like a thousand square miles of...like...broccoli or something." He leaned up toward Magdalena. "Are we there yet?"

"Soon," she said. And a moment later she announced, "There. Ten o'clock."

Paul looked through the window and saw, ahead and to the left, what had by now become a familiar sight to him from the air. Mabaruma. With basically one main road, it reminded him of a ramshackle frontier town in a Western movie, but this one was cut into the jungle canopy and snuggled up to a river. As they got closer they could see occasional side streets leading away from the main road, and could pick out individual buildings. Nearly all were made of wood, and the majority, both the primitive huts most people lived in and the commercial buildings, stood up off the ground on stilts.

They flew past Mabaruma and, when they were a couple of miles south of it, Magdalena called, "Seat belts all tight?"

Before they could answer, she put the plane into a steep bank that took them on a one-hundred-eighty-degree turn, so that they were heading north again, into the wind and toward Mabaruma. Then they gained altitude for a moment and finally started into a downward slope, headed for a tiny strip of asphalt that ran down the center of a long, narrow clearing cut out of the jungle. They were about a mile southeast of town.

As usual, Paul felt as though the ground was coming up at them way too fast, but in fact Magdalena set them down right on the large numbers—23—painted on the asphalt at the start of the runway. After two hard bounces—"Sorry!" she called—they raced along the pavement until she hit the brakes hard and they slowed down. They taxied off the asphalt and onto hard-packed red earth toward the only structure in sight, a hangar of sorts, but just a roof with no walls.

FORTY-NINE

Magdalena positioned the Skylane under the shelter and, as soon as she cut the engine, Paul could hear a car approaching on the road from town. He and Robert clambered down with their bags, just as an open Jeep pulled into sight through a break in the trees. It sped toward them and came to a sliding stop on the hard-packed dirt.

The driver was a gangly, fair-skinned young man with shoulder length red hair, wearing blue jeans and a faded Hawaiian shirt. He ran over and greeted Magdalena with a very enthusiastic kiss. When they broke apart, he turned to Paul and Robert. "I teach at the secondary school in Mabaruma. Name's Curtis Strout." He shook Paul's hand and, before Paul could say anything, he added, "You're the priest who visits Fair Hope. I've seen you before." He paused.

"And this is Robert Johnson," Paul said. "He's about to graduate from high school, and he's...he's interested in seeing Fair Hope."

"Great. I was in the Peace Corps here. When my time was up I found I couldn't stay away." He draped his arm across Magdalena's shoulders. "I love it here."

Curtis helped Magdalena tie the plane down with nylon ropes fixed to steel stakes in the ground, to keep it from being tossed around if the wind—now down to a gentle breeze—rose again. Finally, with a heavy chain and a couple of huge padlocks, they secured it to an iron loop set in a block of concrete. Curtis explained that he taught science. "I'm an Iowa farm kid, though, and what I really enjoy is going around teaching basic farming techniques and livestock care." He looked at Robert. "So…you wanna work with the indigenous people down here?"

Robert, clearly surprised by the question, said, "I don't know. Maybe, I guess."

"You should try…" He paused, glanced up at the sky, and then down at his watch. "Jeez, it's getting late. We better get going."

They all climbed into the Jeep, Magdalena in the front passenger seat, and Paul and Robert in the rear. Paul wondered whether he'd have to explain why they were arriving on a Sunday, with no one to meet them, and leaving again the next day. But as they careened along on the rough gravel road—mostly ruts, with half of the gravel washed away—it was clear that Curtis was focused on Magdalena, and not interested in what Paul and Robert were up to.

The airstrip road ended at the main road, where there was a hand-painted sign with arrows indicating *Fair Hope Clinic* to the left, *Mabaruma* to the right. Curtis slowed down and called toward the back seat, "You'll be going into town now, right? And out to the clinic in the morning?"

"No," Paul called back. "We'd rather go right to the clinic, thanks."

"If you say so." Curtis turned left and they bounced onto a road that was slightly wider, but not at all smoother. "Are you sure Bogdan Adjar will be there to let you in? I mean, you know the clinic's not open on Sundays, right?"

"Right, I know," Paul said. "But Bogdan'll probably be there." Bogdan served as both custodian and quasi-security guard, and lived at the clinic, except when he took off to visit his mother. She lived in Port Kaituma, a town deeper into the rain forest and near the site of the Jonestown mass suicide.

"I don't know," Curtis said. "I haven't seen him around town for a few days."

"Yes, well, I have keys, anyway."

In a few minutes they came to a sign announcing the clinic, and then to the building itself, set in the middle of a clearing the size of half a football field. Except for the sign, it didn't look at all like a medical facility. It looked like what it had once been: a white, frame, two-story,

Victorian residence, with a multi-gabled, steeply peaked roof. It could have been the home of a wealthy merchant in nineteenth-century New England, except its windows were sheltered by the sort of louvered shutters common in the tropics, and it sat on stilts about five feet above the ground. Also, it needed a paint job.

Curtis skidded the Jeep to a stop on a patch of asphalt in front of the building. "I don't see Bogdan's truck," he said. "I know you always stay in town at night when you're here. How will you get there?"

"We'll be fine," Paul said, as he and Robert climbed out of the Jeep.

"Wait. We can't leave you." Magdalena's voice was full of concern. "It must be three or four kilometers to town, and you don't want to walk that road through the jungle after dark."

"We're not staying in town. I have time for just a brief visit, so we're spending the night out here. You and Curtis go ahead on."

"But you'll need some supper," Magdalena persisted. "You—"

"They always keep supplies here. Besides, we had a late lunch in Georgetown, and we stocked up on granola bars in Miami." He wished she and Curtis would just leave. He wanted to examine the building the CIA—or whoever—was using, before the sun went down. "My cell phone won't work here, but there's a phone inside. I'll call tomorrow and let you know when we're ready to fly back."

She wrote down Curtis's phone number down for him, and she and Curtis roared off.

†

"Granola bars?" Robert asked.

"I've got six of them in my bag," Paul said. He breathed in the warm, heavy air of the rain forest, so unlike the air back home, with the smells of exotic flowers mingling with the sweet odor of constantly decaying plants.

As the sound of the Jeep faded in the distance their surroundings got suddenly very quiet and he heard the calling of birds off in the trees, the rustling of the grass around them in the warm breeze, and some faint chirping of crickets. He knew that the crickets—or maybe they were frogs—were just warming up and that after dark the noise would be—not deafening, exactly—but loud enough to make quiet conversation difficult. And the bird calls, he knew, would switch to harsher cries from the night flyers, joined by monkey chatter, punctuated with occasional screams from rain forest cats.

He suddenly realized he was just standing there, looking around and listening, and then saw that Robert was doing the same. He thought Robert might be a little afraid out here, so he broke the silence. "What time do you have?"

"What? Oh." Robert checked his watch. "Almost four o'clock."

"You should change your watch. It's five here."

"I thought we were in the same time zone as Michigan."

"We are, but they don't have Daylight Savings Time here. Anyway, I'm not sure when the sun goes down and I want to look around before it gets too dark."

"Uh…yeah…dark." Robert slowly turned and looked in every direction. "You… uh…you been here a lot, right?"

"Sure." *If three times is a lot.*

"But at night don't you always stay in town? Do we really wanna be out here all night, in…like…the jungle?"

"You mean…will it be scary? Not really. I mean, the doors are solid and no animals could get in, even if they wanted to. And they don't. In fact, the doctors' house, where I usually stay, isn't in as big clearing as this, so the jungle's a lot closer."

"Hard to sleep, huh?"

"It'll be easier out here. There'll be jungle noises, but not all the music and yelling from the bars, like in town." He started toward the steep set of stairs leading up to the front door. "We'll drop our bags inside and put on long-sleeved shirts and insect repellant." He dug the keys out of his pocket. "Plus," he added, "there *is* indoor plumbing here."

FIFTY

"Doesn't look like a clinic," Robert said, following Paul up the steps. "Looks like someone's house."

"That's what it used to be. Two hundred years ago this land was part of a sugar plantation. When slavery was abolished the land owner couldn't make a profit and walked away, deeding the property to his ex-slaves. They gave it the name Fair Hope Plantation."

"Weird name," Robert said.

"Well, it's not 'fair,' like playing by the rules or something. It's 'fair' as in 'beautiful.'"

He used his key, not bothering to knock or to call out. If the rusty pickup truck wasn't there, Bogdan wasn't there. He might have been a big help, but at least now Paul wouldn't have to explain what he was up to.

The door was solid and strong, but it stuck—nothing down here worked smoothly—and he had to shove to get it open. Inside, he pushed it shut again, and led Robert down a short hallway.

"Sure *smells* like a hospital," Robert said. "So how'd this house ever get to be a clinic?"

"The ex-slaves couldn't make a go of it raising sugar and, for the next hundred and thirty years or so, people tried raising just about everything else—bananas, coconuts, coffee, cocoa, tobacco—but the soil's not so good and it's hard to get crops out to the coast. In the 1960s the land was donated to the Sisters of Mercy, whose headquarters is just outside Chicago, to run an orphanage. When there weren't enough nuns, they had to close it. They tore down most of the buildings—before they *fell* down—and left three sisters running a medical clinic out of their residence…this building. Ten years ago or so, the nuns asked the cardinal for help, and the archdiocese still supports it, as a sort of mission."

They dropped their bags at the foot of a wide staircase. "Do some of them still *live* way out here?" Robert asked, looking around in disbelief. "I mean…the nuns?"

"There are no nuns here anymore. It's staffed by doctors, who volunteer for a year or two, plus sometimes nurses and other people who stay shorter periods of time. They all usually live in town."

He showed Robert a waiting room, two examining rooms, and an operating room. In the rear were a kitchen, a bathroom, and Bogdan's sleeping room. They took their bags upstairs, past a room with two hospital beds for overnight patients—"which there almost never are," Paul explained—to two bedrooms in the front of the house. "These are for medical personnel if they ever *do* have to stay overnight. We can use them."

It struck Paul that Larry had stayed on-site, and must have used one of these rooms.

Robert went to a window and looked out. "Is it safe out here?" he asked. "I mean…from *people.* Like burglars or something."

"There's lots of alcohol abuse and small-time crime in Mabaruma, but no real problem out here. Bogdan's living here provides some security, but the thing is, whether he's here or not, there's nothing here small enough to carry away that's worth much."

"What about…you know…drugs and stuff?"

"No drugs are kept on-site. The staff brings those with them every morning."

†

On his previous visits it had seemed to Paul that dark clothes attracted fewer mosquitoes, so he lent one of his clergy shirts to Robert. They both sprayed on lots of repellant and Paul tucked his camera in his pocket. Ten minutes later they were headed back out the front door and down the steps.

"There used to be a thousand acres of open land here," Paul said. "Now what's left of the clearing has to be mowed constantly, to hold back the jungle." He pointed off to their right. "Look...down there. Can you see an opening in the trees?"

"Uh...not really." Robert stared. "But I see like a little white sign out there."

"Right. And just past the sign the cleared land bends around those trees and... well...it's like where a fairway on a golf course doglegs to the right or the left. This one's to the right. Hidden behind those trees... where the green would be...is what was once a tobacco barn. That's where we're headed."

While the road from town seemed to end at the patch of asphalt in front of the clinic, in fact, it kept on going—albeit as a set of tire tracks through tough, ankle-high grass. They set out along those tracks and, about a hundred yards out from the clinic, came to the white sign Robert had seen: *AURMINEX COMPANY. PRIVATE PROPERTY. KEEP OUT!*

They followed the tire tracks around the edge of the trees and were soon out of sight of the clinic. The ground sloped up at first, then gently downward along what Paul had described as the "dogleg" to the right, and another hundred yards or so to a large wooden building. It was rectangular, about two-and-a-half stories tall and, though its steeply pitched metal roof showed lots of rust, its sides had recently been given a fresh coat of white paint.

"That's it," Paul said, and stepped up his pace. "I've never seen the inside. It's been sitting there—full of junk and old farm equipment, I guess—for years. Until a few months ago. That's when I let the CIA start using it. At least I *thought* it was the CIA."

"Then what's Aurminex?" Robert asked.

"It's supposedly a mining company, but it's really a cover name Ann Swanson made up. It's *good* cover, too, because there's exploration going on all over Guyana, for copper, oil, gold, and other minerals you and I never heard of. Engineers and surveyors are always going in and out of the rain forest—using small planes, helicopters, river boats, Jeeps—and they all like to keep what they're doing secret from competitors."

"So...if it's the CIA...what are *they* doing here?"

"I don't know exactly, but we're not that far from the Venezuelan border. To the west." Paul pointed toward where the sun was sinking toward the trees. "Ann Swanson said they needed a base, to go back and forth across the border, gathering intelligence information about Venezuela."

"That would be...like...illegal, right? Spying?"

"Yes, but...most countries do that sort of thing." Paul took his camera from his pocket. "They cleared all the old junk out of that barn. They made some repairs, and enlarged the clearing around it." He took several shots of the building as he spoke.

As they got closer, Robert said, "I don't see any cars around. Probably no one's here." He glanced up at the sky. "It'll be dark pretty soon."

"Someone *could* be here. Could be parked inside." Paul gestured toward a metal roll-up door, obviously a recent installation, which was tall and wide enough to handle two semi-trailer trucks side by side. "It *does* look deserted, though." He hoped so.

The thick grass in front of the barn was worn down enough to show that vehicles were often parked there. To the right of the roll-up door was a service door with a small square window, about head high, and up near the peak under the eaves was a wide set of double doors that must have swung outward when the building was used as a barn, but now had wide planks nailed across them. A three-foot strip of fresh gravel had been laid at the base of the wall and doors along the front, and apparently continued all the way around the perimeter of the building.

Paul tried the service door. It was new, metal, and locked. He didn't have a key to this door, so he pounded on it with his fist. He got no response, and when he tried to look through the little window the view was blocked.

He and Larry had never discussed it in detail, but Larry had told him that, after noticing unusual late-night activities around the barn, he'd investigated. He'd seen trucks coming and going, and men unloading crates, and become convinced that weapons were being delivered, stored in the barn, and moved out again.

And now Paul was here to do his own investigation. *But how?*

"I'm taking a look around in back," Paul said. "You can wait here if you want."

"Uh...no. I'll come with."

The building faced east and he estimated it to be fifty feet wide across the front, and a hundred feet deep. There were windows spaced along the north side wall, but they were too high to reach without a ladder, and what little glass hadn't already been replaced with plywood was painted over.

They rounded the corner and, in the rear, found another service door—with no window. Nestled against the wall a few feet from the door were two upright propane gas tanks, side by side. There were no windows or other openings in the wall except for the tiny holes for the gas lines, and an exhaust fan vent above the tanks, maybe ten feet off the ground. The door was locked.

They continued on to the south wall, which, like its counterpart on the north, held windows too high to reach.

By the time they got back to the front, Paul had taken photos of both sides and the rear of the building. And just in time, too. The sun was already below the trees. It was definitely twilight. The sounds from the crickets or frogs—or who knew what?—grew steadily stronger, like an army of night creatures creeping closer through the grass, while the calls of the birds among the trees had quieted down. Mosquitoes hummed ominously, although so far the repellant was doing its job.

"We better go back, before it gets really dark," Robert said.

"You're right." Paul gave a last look at the building, then turned away. "There's nothing we can do here tonight."

But there *was* something, and he had to try it. Alone. He would not involve Robert any deeper.

FIFTY-ONE

"Man, my clothes are, like, soaked," Robert said, as Paul led the way up the steps to the clinic door. "Does it get any cooler at night?"

"Not much. No air conditioning, either." He unlocked the door, opened it with a push of his shoulder, and they went inside. "The electricity here comes from Mabaruma, and even when it's working it goes off at eleven o'clock every night."

"How does anyone *live* here?"

"They get used to it," Paul said. He closed the door behind him, but only so that it caught against the jamb, careful not to force it all the way closed. "They probably wonder how anyone can live in Minnesota, where it gets so cold."

"Yeah, well, we just turn on the heat and…hey…we oughta lock that thing, right?" Robert stepped past him and shoved the door completely closed, and turned the deadbolt. "I'm hungry. You said there'd be plenty of food, right?"

"That's what I told Magdalena, but with Bogdan not here, I don't know." On his previous visits to the clinic, he'd always had breakfast and supper at the house in Mabaruma with the volunteer doctors.

There was a microwave in the kitchen, and a refrigerator—unplugged and empty—and beside it several cases of bottled water. There was a propane gas range, too, with four burners, and an oven that was obviously never used, except to store pots and pans. In a cabinet they found a canister of what looked like dried peas, and another of rice. There was a tin bread box holding half a loaf of bread, which might have been edible once they cut off the moldy parts, but that didn't appeal to either of them. There were some dried peppers that Paul was certain were too hot to try, and a couple of large bottles of cooking oil.

"What's this?" Robert asked, reaching up to a shelf and taking down a ball about the size of a large grapefruit, but with green, pebbly skin.

"Breadfruit. They say it's pretty nutritious. I ate it once. It was sliced and fried in oil."

"How'd it taste?"

"Didn't have much taste at all. More like a vegetable than a fruit. Sort of starchy." Paul shrugged. "I only ate a little. I'm not good at eating foods I'm not familiar with."

"Me neither." Robert put the breadfruit back in the cabinet. "How long you think we can we live on those granola bars?"

"We're leaving tomorrow," Paul said. "Maybe we can get something in Mabaruma on our way back. There's a box of tea bags, though. I left the granola bars in my gym bag. Why don't you go up and get them, while I boil some water?"

He put bottled water in a pan on the stove, and Robert went upstairs and brought down the granola bars. They sat at the kitchen table and unwrapped one bar each, and ate them as slowly as they could, sipping tea between tiny bites.

"Hot tea on a hot night." Robert shook his head. "Makes you sweat worse."

"When I was a kid," Paul said, "my grandmother told me a hot drink was better for you on a hot day. 'The hotter the day, the hotter the coffee,' she said."

"So...were *you* raised by *your* gramma, too?"

"Oh, no. I hardly knew her." Paul's mind kept turning to what he had to do later, but Robert seemed ready to talk for once, and Paul didn't want to pass up this chance. "We visited her a few times, in the summer, in Texas. She had lots of little sayings like that. She was my father's mother. He died when I was little. I was raised by my mother."

"You were lucky. I just had grandparents."

"Both of them, though, right?" Paul asked.

"Until my grampa died. I was nine then. After that it was just me and my gramma."

"And how was she as...I mean...was she nice to you?"

"She loved me, I guess." Robert seemed to be studying how best to answer. "She was way older'n the other kids' parents, but she was...okay. She never, like, *hit* me or anything. When I got into high school she made me mad a lot, but now...I kinda miss her. More than I thought." He lowered his head and stared down at the table.

"Yes, well, sometimes it's when people die that we realize how important they were to us." Paul flattened the wrapper from his granola bar on the table top with his fingertips. "I'm very sorry, Robert, that your mother died when you were so young."

"Yeah...well..." Robert's hands were around his tea mug as though to warm them up...in the ninety degree heat.

"I knew her for just those few months, when we were in college. She was a nice person. Everyone liked her."

"Yeah?" Robert lifted his head and there were tears in his eyes, but then he looked down again, and sipped some tea. "Can I have another granola bar?"

"Sure. There's still three left. You can have all of them, if you want."

"You know," Robert said, "you don't have to..." His voice trailed off, and he seemed to be studying the label on the wrapper.

"I don't have to what?"

"You don't have to keep pretending, y'know?"

"Pretending? You mean about why we're down here? I *told* you why. I need proof that the CIA, or *somebody*, is here and—"

"Not that part. I mean you don't have to pretend about *you*. And me." Robert was looking right at him now, even leaned forward a little. "I know."

"You know *what*?" Paul's heart rate shot up.

"I know you're my father. I *thought* you might be, almost from the start. But you didn't say you were. And then, when I was helping Miss Kragan, I found out I was right."

"Miss Kragan? Who's—"

"The headmaster's secretary. When I was working in the office she left me alone once, and I found my records. You're my father."

"I'm sorry, Robert, but..." Paul stood up without thinking, and even turned away from the table, but quickly turned back again. He couldn't hide anymore, couldn't avoid this conversation. "I guess I don't know what to say."

"Yeah, well, it's not like I'm mad about it or anything. I mean about your getting my mother pregnant. I just wish...you know...that you hadn't run away."

"But I didn't just..." He'd known it would come to this, whether he was ready to talk about it or not. "We were both kids, not much older than you are now. When we broke up I didn't even know she was pregnant, I swear. I don't think she did, either. Just one day she said she wanted to keep her options open. That's the way she said it, 'keep my options open.' I felt really bad. I didn't know what to do. So I...I left school and went into the army. I never heard one word about a baby...about you...not until your grandmother showed up."

"Y'know...I never even asked my gramma about my father till I was like ten or something. She didn't say anything bad. She just said you...I mean, she didn't say *who*, but she probably knew all along it was you...she said the guy got scared, and ran off, and they didn't know where he went."

"That's not the way it was. Your mother—"

"I'm just saying what my gramma *said*, not that it's true. I mean, you don't seem like someone who'd just get scared and run away like that."

"I get scared sometimes, just like everybody."

"Yeah, well...anyway, it's just...it's kinda weird, meeting your own father after all these years." He finally took a bite from the granola bar. He chewed for a while and then said, "And finding out he's a *priest*, that's *really* weird. I didn't see that in the records. Does Mr. Grayson know that?"

"No, I didn't tell him that."

"I'm just thinking. I mean...you're a priest and all, and priests aren't supposed to have kids. I mean, they're not even supposed to have sex, right?"

"That's right."

"But I bet a lot of 'em do. And I don't mean the sickos who mess with kids."

"I...I suppose some do. Not too many."

"Well, *you* had sex, right? With my mother. I mean, you can't deny *that*."

"No, I can't." Paul couldn't believe how much he wanted this boy to like him, to *approve* of him. "It's true. Susan...your mother...and I, we were...we were intimate. But that was long before I was a priest. Since I've been a priest I haven't had sex with anyone." Although he'd lied—over and over—to save Robert, this was the truth, and he wanted the boy to believe him, to know that his life, his priesthood, wasn't a lie.

"You said you were in the army. Not even then?"

"I wasn't a priest then, either. But no, not even then. You see, your mother and I, we...well...for a while we thought we were in love. Maybe we were. I know I was. Anyway, when I went in the army, there were times when I could have had sex, sure. But I didn't. Partly because I guess I was scared of diseases, and partly because...well...when the situations came up, it was women I didn't even know." He'd been staring down at the table and he looked up to see Robert looking back at him.

"Yeah...well...there's something else." Robert lifted his mug, then put it down without drinking. "After that woman...Ann Swanson...after she brought me to Chicago, and I found out my gramma was dead, you said I shouldn't go back home to Minneapolis, not right away."

"I wanted you to go somewhere Ann Swanson didn't know about. I guess I already didn't trust her. I should have realized she could find—"

"I know, but what I mean is...you said you'd save everything from my gramma's and my house, right?"

"And I did."

"Does that mean all the pictures, too? I mean, there were some pictures my gramma had of my mother when she was young, and I was wondering..."

"I had everything put into storage. Every single thing. We can go to the storage place and get them whenever you want. The house is there, too. Empty and closed." Paul stood up. "Right now, though, we need to be up as soon as it gets light, and—"

"Wait. Just one more thing, okay?"

Paul sighed. "All right."

"It's just...well, you said, '*We* can go to the storage place.' Does that mean, after you get this all straightened out with the CIA and everyone... we could, like, be... *together*? I mean, yeah, it'd be complicated. You'd have to explain it to the people at your church and all, and I have to finish school. But, I mean, could we be like a father and a son? Maybe even, like, *live* together? And *do* stuff together? Is that possible?"

"I don't know how things will work out, Robert, but I'll tell you this, if that's what you want, we *will* stay close, and *will* get to know each other, and do stuff together. I'd like that, too. I'd like that a lot."

FIFTY-TWO

They each took one of the bedrooms on the second floor, and Paul had hardly closed his door when there was a knock. It was Robert, holding a white envelope. "I got something I want you to see," he said.

Paul took the envelope. It wasn't sealed and the wear around the edges showed it had been carried around for a while. "What's this?" he asked, even as he removed and unfolded what appeared to be a copy of a medical lab report, with Robert's name at the top. "Looks like a blood test. I guess I could study this for a while, but I still wouldn't understand most of it."

Robert took the paper back. "That guy that got killed," he said, "the one in the cell with me? One of the two men that came to get me killed him."

"Okay, but what—"

"Slit his throat. And the guy fell down and there was blood all over, and...and then they walked me out, like it was nothing. I was glad they did it, but I was scared, too, because they were so...so *cold* about it."

"Was he interfering? Trying to stop them from taking you? Is that why they killed him?"

"Not really. Not by that time. I mean, at first he told them they couldn't take me, that he was my 'protector.' But they had guns, and he couldn't do anything."

"So, why did they slit his throat?"

"I think because..." Robert shook his head. He turned away and walked across to the window. "It's kinda hard…" He turned back toward Paul, but looked past him, not meeting his eyes. "The thing is, the guy had…you know… messed with me."

"Messed with you? What, he beat you up? Or—"

"God *dammit*, he raped me."

Paul's chest tightened, and he felt lightheaded. "You mean—"

"I mean he bent me over a bench and *raped* me. The whole fucking thing, you know what I mean?"

"I understand," Paul said. He could hardly breathe. "The thing is… no one ever told me about that. I mean, when I first went to see you, I was afraid something bad like that *might* happen, if you stayed there. That's when I decided I'd…well, I'd do whatever I had to do, to get you out." In his heart he knew he'd do it all over again, too—the lies and all of it. "So you told them he raped you, and that's why they killed him?"

"Not exactly. They asked me was he really my 'protector,' and I said no, and then I told them he raped me. But I don't think they'd have killed him except… except he kept mouthing off about it. Saying how I tried to fight him off, and how he *liked* it when guys tried to fight back. He said, 'You two are professionals. You understand.' Like he really thought they'd think what he did was okay. He kept grinnin' and stuff, and I think the one guy, the black guy, just got sick of him and… and cut his throat."

Paul stared at him. "I…I don't know what to say, Robert. I'm sorry all that had to happen. What that man did to you…and then seeing them kill him. But what's that have to do with this blood—" Then he finally understood. "Oh my God. That's why you got a blood test?"

"Yeah. After those two guys took me out I kept shaking all the time. They asked, 'Why are you still so scared? You scared of us?' I told them no. I told them…the thing is…I asked them what if the guy they killed had AIDS. Then I'd have AIDS. They said it's not for sure, even if he did. Not from one incident. But it *could* be. So they took me for tests." He held up the paper. "And…you know…" His voice was shaking and there were tears in his eyes.

"It's okay, Robert. It's okay." Paul couldn't keep the tremble out of his own voice. "We'll get the best care. These days people live years and years when they're HIV pos—"

"No, no." Robert's eyes widened. "You think…I mean, *no.*" He held out the sheet. "Look." He pointed. "See right here? It says *'neg.'* That means *'negative.'* I don't have AIDS, or HIV or anything, but the thing is, I still keep crying every time I look at this paper." Tears were streaming down his cheeks now. "I was so scared."

Robert stepped forward and Paul wrapped his arms around him, and felt him trembling. Then Paul was crying, too. It had been a long, long time since he'd hugged—*really* hugged—another person. The last time it had been Susan. And later, when she needed him most, he'd been far away.

Not this time.

FIFTY-THREE

Paul was desperately tired, but couldn't afford to fall asleep. He sat upright on the edge of the bed, fully clothed, thinking. He knew from both Larry and Bogdan that the Aurminex "mining engineers" showed up once or twice a week, always after dark, usually around midnight, or later, and never paid any attention to the clinic itself. So the earlier he went, got in and got out, the better. Right now, though, two tall floodlights still lit up the clearing around the clinic. They went on when it got dark, and off when the electricity from town was shut down, at eleven. If Robert looked out his window and saw Paul leave, he'd insist on coming along.

On the other hand, if Paul waited for the electricity to shut down he'd increase his risk of still being at the barn if Ann's people picked this night to show up. He decided to wait until ten o'clock. The lights would still be on, but Robert would surely be asleep by then and not looking out the window.

He waited, and kept checking his watch.

When he looked for about the hundredth time, he was stunned. He was lying back on the bed and it was a few minutes past eleven. He must have dozed off sitting up, and then laid down in his sleep. He got to his feet, turned off the light, and went to the window. The ancient floorboards creaked under his weight as he walked, but otherwise he heard nothing. Robert had to be asleep.

The outside lights were still on, but he knew the power would be cut any minute. He wondered whether there were security lights around the barn, and if the barn was on the Mabaruma grid. He was quite certain there was no one there, since the noise would surely have woken him up if any trucks or helicopters had arrived.

Until now he hadn't actually felt afraid. He'd been tormented by whether it was a mistake to bring Robert with him, though always coming to the same decision. The boy had already been in danger at Bridgebriar and, if Ann Swanson's people didn't show up tonight, there'd be no special danger here. And even if they *did*, and if Paul could get in and out of the barn and back to the clinic before they arrived, there'd be no reason for them to know he and Robert were here.

But those were significant *ifs*, and he was scared. He stood at the window, trying to slow down and deepen his breaths, which kept coming in quick, shallow gasps. He realized then that he was praying. Praying for Robert, praying for himself. Surprising, really. He so seldom thought about prayer, or about God, these days. And now he—

Without a sound the floodlights went out, and he was staring out into the black night.

He waited, trying to adjust his eyes to the dark. The night sky was clear and it gradually became apparent that there was at least some starlight. But not much. He couldn't see where the clearing ended and the trees of the dense rain forest began.

It was time.

He turned from the window and stepped carefully, trying to minimize the creaking of the floorboards. In the near total darkness he sprayed fresh mosquito repellant around his ankles and hands, face and neck, and rubbed it in. He was dressed entirely in black, including a hooded sweatshirt, and he pulled the hood up over his head. The heat was stifling and his clothes would soon be soaked, but avoiding mosquito bites—and possible malaria, or dengue fever—was more important than comfort.

He went out the door and into the hall, and switched on his flashlight. Stopping at Robert's door he listened closely, and could hear Robert's steady breathing. He turned and moved as quickly as he dared along the hallway, and down the stairs.

There was a back door, but he had no key for that lock, and he wasn't about to leave Robert here alone behind an unlocked door. He'd have to risk opening the front door. He unlocked it again and pulled on the knob. As careful as he tried to be, the swollen door came open with a groan of wood on wood that seemed terribly loud in the otherwise silent building. He stood there, holding his breath, listening for any stirring from upstairs. There was nothing. He went out, pulled the door closed again as quietly as he could, and locked it.

With his flashlight off, he stood on the porch for a moment and stared out into the darkness. The night was alive with sound. Chirping and croaking from a million insects and frogs blended into unison, and rose and fell from the surrounding fields as though the ground itself was groaning as it breathed...in and out. He heard rustling and hissing and slithering noises, too, which might have come from the gentle breeze that stirred the grasses...or from unseen creatures he preferred not to think about. From the distant trees to his right, the general direction in which he was headed, came a series of long, mournful wails—like a high-pitched foghorn—each wail followed by three or four staccato hoots. Probably a type of owl. The air felt thick and heavy with moisture, and he'd have thought it was about to rain if the sky hadn't been so clear.

He hurried down the steps and found the tire tracks leading away through the thick grass and followed them, breaking into a trot, moving as fast as he dared, flashlight in hand. Although the stars seemed bright in the sky, without the flashlight on he couldn't see more than a few yards ahead. He thought he'd use it just in momentary bursts, to make sure he didn't stray off the primitive road—aware that what looked like solid ground held hidden pockets of swamp, thick mud, even quicksand—but he soon dropped the on-off idea and ran with the light on.

When he reached the Aurminex sign he stopped to catch his breath and, just as he did, the darkness was split by a series of blood-curdling screams. *Robert?* Panicked, he whirled, shining the light in all directions, but realized at once that the screams came from deep in the forest, and probably weren't human at all. They could have been the shrieks of a crab-eating jungle raccoon trapped in a jaguar's claws, or of a night monkey scrambling through the treetops after a mate. They stopped as abruptly as they began, and then he heard the wail of the owl again—if it was an owl—much closer now, almost scarier than the screams.

Sweat rolled down his back and sides, and insects buzzed around his head…so far not landing. He switched off the light and, looking back, thought he could just pick out the bulk of the clinic building a hundred yards away. Or did he just imagine he could?

He started out again, walking now, sweeping the flashlight beam back and forth before him. He made the dogleg turn around the trees, climbed the short rise and, from there, didn't need his light to see the big wooden barn. It sat at the bottom of the long gentle slope ahead of him, and either it had its own generator, or the lights shining down from under its eaves were battery-operated. They were a soft, bluish color, and lit up the ground for fifteen yards or so all around the building. The doors were still closed and it looked as deserted as it had when he and Robert had visited earlier.

He had to get inside and take some pictures. He'd gotten a strong impression from Ann Swanson that things were going on right now at Fair Hope, maybe even drawing to a head, so hopefully he could get real proof of the sorts of things Larry had seen. He'd have something, then, to take to the CIA, and police, something that would make it hard for them to brush his story aside as a fantastic lie from a desperate man.

Or maybe he'd find nothing.

The first step was to get inside. He'd been sure that Bogdan would have tools around but, on his tour of the clinic with Robert, he'd seen nothing but cleaning supplies. So, armed with only a couple of screwdrivers he'd found in one of the kitchen drawers and hidden in his pocket, he hurried down the slope.

FIFTY-FOUR

The doors of the barn were still locked, and the windows still too high to reach without a ladder. There was only one possible way in, short of smashing a hole through a wall—which would announce that someone had been inside, and which he didn't think he could do, anyway.

The vent for the exhaust fan looked new. It was set in a square metal frame, maybe two feet to a side, and had louvered slats that would raise when the fan was running and blowing air out of the building. Luckily, it wasn't running now. It was too high up in the wall to be reached from the ground, but Paul thought he might reach it by climbing up and standing with one foot on each of the two upright propane tanks.

Actually *doing* that proved more difficult than thinking about it, but he finally succeeded, and could reach just high enough to get at the screws along the top of the frame.

The angle was bad, though. He had to lean his body in against the side of the building to keep his balance on the tanks, and at the same time reach above his head, stretch his arms up and behind his head, a screwdriver's length away from the building, and try to fit the head into the slot of each screw.

Sweat kept dripping into his eyes, making them burn, and mosquitoes buzzed around his head. The first screwdriver he tried looked like it ought to fit, but he finally had to give up on it and admit the head was too big. He tried the other one, and it was a little too small. But if he was careful it would work.

There were twelve screws in all, evenly spaced around the square frame. They were too new to be rusted in place, but they were set tight, and not easily loosened. Each time he got one out he put it in his pocket, and had to lower his arms to give them a rest and keep his shoulders from cramping up.

He had just removed the fourth and last screw across the top when for the first time one of the buzzing mosquitoes actually landed on his cheek...*and bit him.*

His head jerked back and he lost his balance, dropped the screwdriver, and fell backwards off the tanks to the ground. He landed awkwardly on the outer edge of his right foot and it turned under and he felt a terrible tearing pain in his ankle. He stood for a moment, his weight on his left foot, and couldn't stop shaking. Jungle diseases were rampant in this area, and there'd been no time to get any inoculations before their departure.

The sweat running down his face must have washed away the repellant. He caught himself rubbing his cheek with his fingers...as though that would do any good. He dug the repellant out of his pocket and sprayed it again on his face and neck, his hands and wrists, and his ankles, rubbing it in with his fingers and then spraying more on. He heard a new rustling in the grass behind him and spun around, but saw nothing. Maybe the breeze had picked up a little. The cries and piercing calls of the night creatures in the trees, unseen, but easily thirty yards away, seemed much louder now, too. Maybe he'd been unconsciously shutting them out as he worked.

It was when he crouched down to search around in the grass for the screwdriver, though, that he realized he was hearing something else. A far-off whine, or drone, one not from any insect or animal. The sound of an engine. He waited a few seconds, and then didn't hear it any more. Whatever it was—a truck? an airplane?—he was sure he hadn't imagined it. It might have been someone racing an engine in Mabaruma.

He poked around and found the screwdriver, and climbed back up on the tanks. A more difficult climb this time. His back hurt, his shoulders ached, and he could barely stand to put any weight at all on his right ankle. He was tired and his hands were shaking. He didn't know if the drops running down his cheeks were sweat...or tears.

What was he *doing* here? Alone, at night, risking incurable disease and attack by animals he didn't even know the names of. And if Ann Swanson's people, whoever they were, caught him it was likely they'd kill him on the spot...and then kill Robert, too. They could create any story they wanted to. No one knew where they were. He should give up now, and take Robert back home. He'd be better off facing things there, with lawyers to help, and maybe Hank Manion.

But if he went home and kept quiet about Ann and her CIA mission, he might go to jail—or worse—which would leave Robert alone. If he fought the charges and told the police about Ann, without proof, no one would believe him. And Robert would be back in that Mexican jail...and die there.

He reached up again and forced himself to go on.

†

He'd removed the highest, most difficult, screws first. Next he did the sides of the frame, saving the easiest, the screws along the bottom, for last. He worked frantically. Not resting his arms between screws. Twisting the screwdriver and fighting to keep it from slipping out of the slot of each screw. Ignoring the pain in his back, his arms, his ankle. Paying no attention to the night sounds around him, and no attention to the soft, animal-like sounds that issued from his own lips as his hand and wrist cramped up.

How long it took he didn't know, but finally he removed the last screw and was able to pull out the external assembly of the fan, with the louvered slats. He leaned sideways and dropped it gently on the ground. The fan housing itself, though, with the blades and the motor, was still in place. He pulled on it, but with no luck. He had hoped he could get inside and take his pictures, leave the same way he entered, and then put the fan back in place—replacing at least enough screws to hold it for a time. But the fan simply would not come out through the opening.

The important thing now was to get inside. He'd have to worry about leaving a hole in the wall later. Pressing on the blades with the palms of his hands, he pushed inward and the fan gave a little, and he was convinced he could push it inside and out of the way.

First, though, he climbed down and picked up the external assembly, with the frame and louvered slats, and carried it away from the building. When he was several yards beyond where the light reached he hid it in the dark, knee-high grass. He might have to shove the fan itself back in place from inside, and leave by the front door. Even if he didn't have the time, or the strength, to reinstall this external part, it might be days before anyone noticed it was missing.

He went back and struggled back up onto the tanks again, ignoring the pains in his side and ankle. He pushed on the fan again, and it gave a little more. He expected it to fall backwards into the building. It didn't. It was stuck. He pushed again, harder. And again. "Move, damn you," he said. "Move!"

Hearing himself talking to a piece of machinery, as if it were deliberately resisting, finally made him stop. And think. And look. The fan was set back in shadow, not illuminated by the security light high up near the eaves. He dug the flashlight out of his back pocket.

Yes, of course. More screws.

There were four of them and he got them out and into his pocket, and tried again to push the fan inward. With its weight mostly in the motor behind the blades, once he'd managed to push it out of the tight space cut out for it, the fan toppled backward and down. Strangely, though, it didn't go crashing to the floor.

The opening left in the wall was a square, framed out with two-by-fours, barely the width of Paul's shoulders. The bottom sill was level with his chin and he rose up onto his toes and peered inside, shining the flashlight around and down. Directly below was a crude bathroom, a cubicle recently put together out of unpainted two-by-fours and plywood, with walls about eight feet tall and no ceiling other than the barn ceiling itself, high above. Inside the cubicle were a toilet, a sink, and a shower stall. What kept the fan from crashing all the way to the floor was that the metal conduit for its wiring held it close against the wall, and it had gotten hung up on the top edge of the shower stall.

He stood on the tanks and listened, but heard only the cries and rustlings of the rain forest at night. No engine noises. He checked his watch. Twenty minutes past midnight. He was exhausted, but there was no stopping now. Not to rest. Certainly not to think.

FIFTY-FIVE

Paul hoisted himself up and wormed his way headfirst through the opening in the barn wall. It was a tight fit, and he was grateful for the protection of his long pants and sweatshirt. When his upper body was through he was able to reach the top of the shower stall and hold on to that as he pulled his legs through. Somehow he managed to get inside and down to the floor without pulling the fan down with him, and without breaking his neck. But squeezing through was hard on his bruised ribs and dropping to the floor sent new pain shooting through his ankle.

He paused for a moment and listened, but again heard nothing except the night sounds from outside, and his own labored breathing. Given the commotion he'd made, he felt confident there was no one else in the building. Using the flashlight, he looked around the makeshift bathroom and up at the exhaust fan. Maybe he *would* be able to get that fan back in its place. But he wouldn't take the time now.

He limped to the door and swept the flashlight beam across the darkness of the barn's interior. The building wasn't as large as St. Hildegard's church, but with no rows of pews, no altars or pulpits and, most of all, because he couldn't see a thing beyond the narrow shaft of light from the flashlight, it seemed huge. And empty, and ominous.

The warm, damp air was heavy with the odors of gasoline and motor oil and animal droppings. Angling the light downward, he could see that, though clear of debris, the concrete floor was webbed with cracks running in every direction, and crumbling in places. He took a few steps forward, wincing with pain whenever he put weight on his right foot.

He raised the light higher. There was no loft or second level, though he was sure there once had been, because of the high double doors he'd seen from outside and because, in several places, there were ladders built flush against the wooden walls. Primitive ladders, just a series of two-by-fours nailed across two wall studs to form rungs. Now they led up to nowhere, ending several feet above crossbeams that ran across the width of the barn. Fluorescent light fixtures hung from these crossbeams. The beams themselves were supported by widely spaced four-by-four posts set in the concrete, and the loft floor would have been laid on them, maybe fifteen feet above where he stood. The barn walls continued some ten or fifteen feet higher than the beams, to where they met the roof.

He lowered the light and took another step, and when his shoe scraped across broken concrete he heard a sudden rush of fluttering, flapping, from high above. He swung the light up again, past the crossbeams to the rafters and the wooden roof. Huge, dirty cobwebs hung everywhere, obscuring his view. But then a tiny bird, as sudden as a thought, flickered through the beam of his light and was gone. Then another. And another. Dozens. But *not* birds, surely. Bats. Maybe vampire bats, which he'd been told were common here.

He moved farther into the darkness, lowering the light and sweeping it from side to side in front of him. Between where he stood and the front of the building, with the large metal roll-up door, was mostly open space. If there'd once been stalls for animals, or storage rooms for hay or crops of any kind, they were gone now.

But ahead and off to the right of the roll-up door was an area equipped with large machinery. He hurried closer, favoring his right ankle. There were two hydraulic lifts, like those in the shop where he took his car for service, and a large steel frame with a thick chain and hook hanging down, a hoist for lifting heavy objects, like motors. There were two gas-powered generators, and an apparatus with tanks and hoses that might have been welding equipment, and a large rolling tool chest...a multi-drawered metal cabinet on wheels.

Whatever else they did with this building, they repaired and serviced vehicles here, possibly including the helicopters Bogdan had told him came and went frequently. Along the side wall of the service area was a work table littered with tools, rags, and engine parts, and beyond that were several tall metal storage cabinets. Moving the light along that wall, he saw more empty space and then, in the corner far to the left of the bathroom, was another piece of machinery. It was an odd-looking, wheeled vehicle, and it took him a moment to recognize it as a forklift.

He swung the light across some wooden boxes and to the rear wall...and then swung it back again. And saw what had to be what he was looking for. A bunch of rectangular wooden crates, stacked on the floor near the forklift.

He walked over and found that there were probably thirty or forty crates, stacked two or three high. Each was the shape of a small pine coffin, maybe five feet long, two-and-a-half feet wide, eighteen inches deep. They were unmarked, unlabeled, and bound shut with wire.

As he moved along the row of stacked crates with his flashlight, he saw that the binding wires around one of them, the top one on a stack of two at the far end of the row, had been cut. It had probably been opened to inspect what was inside. Holding the flashlight in one hand, he tried to raise the wooden cover with the other. At first it wouldn't open, but he soon realized the cover was still wired to the crate along just one long side, so that it opened as though on hinges—again, like a coffin.

The contents were what he'd expected, although seeing them was still a shock. He'd never seen combat duty, and he didn't know what particular model these were, but the army had trained him in the use of similar automatic weapons.

He set the flashlight on the floor and pulled the camera from his pocket. He knelt on one knee, and his hands were trembling while he held the camera in the flashlight's beam. It was a digital camera and he'd read and reread the instructions, but he needed to check to be sure he knew where all the buttons were. He stood and backed up, and took a few flash photos of the whole collection of crates from several angles, and checked them on the little monitor.

He knew he had get out of there in a hurry, and he knew that, at the same time, it made no sense to have come this far and then not get the clearest evidence possible of the number and the type of weapons he'd found. He took one of the rifles out of the open crate—at maybe five or six pounds, it wasn't as heavy as he remembered from his army training—and laid it lengthwise on top of an unopened crate and photographed it from several angles. Turning back to the open crate, he rearranged the packing materials and propped a couple of weapons up at an angle so that they could more easily be seen in a photo.

Once he had everything properly positioned, he stepped back to get the right camera angle...and heard something that froze the blood in his veins.

A distant sound, but unmistakable. Engine noise. Rising and falling. A vehicle, probably a Jeep or a truck. Just one vehicle, he thought, and how far away he couldn't tell. Certainly farther away than the clinic.

But coming closer.

FIFTY-SIX

He took a couple of hurried shots and stuffed the camera back in his pocket. Working with one hand, holding the light in the other, he crammed the propped-up rifles and the packing material down into the open crate, trying hard to make them look like nothing had been disturbed. He closed the top and turned, and saw that in his nervousness he'd forgotten the weapon lying on top of the other crates. He swung the cover open again and shoved the last rifle in. But now the cover wouldn't close. Not even close.

In a state of near-panic now he took out the rifle and closed the crate. The engine noise seemed louder. He swung the flashlight around, desperately looking for a hiding place, but there was really no time to hide it carefully, and wherever he left it, it might quickly be noticed.

Flashlight in one hand and rifle in the other, moving as fast as his ankle would let him, he headed for the front service door. He wasn't sure he could make it to the bathroom, climb up ten feet, squeeze back through the fan opening, and drop to the ground in one piece. He'd have to use the front door and get beyond the reach of the security lights before whoever was coming got here. If he got to the trees he might make it back to the clinic—and to Robert. He was sure the door would have a dead bolt which he couldn't lock behind him, so they'd find it unlocked. But they'd find the hole in the wall where the fan had been, anyway, and know someone had broken in.

Still, even if they knew he was down here—and, despite his attempts at secrecy, Ann Swanson might already know—they'd have no reason to suspect him as the intruder. It could have been thieves...who got scared off and ran away.

When he got close he saw he was right and the door did have a deadbolt, but it also had a spring lock in the knob which would engage when he pulled it closed from outside. Maybe they'd find it locked and wouldn't notice the deadbolt wasn't thrown. All of that ran through his mind as he reached for the door...but stopped, suddenly aware of how loud the engine noise was. He switched off his flashlight and lifted a corner of the black curtain over the small window, and looked out.

He was too late.

The vehicle—by its widely spaced headlights, a truck, not a Jeep—was already headed down the long slope, bouncing wildly on the uneven terrain. Its lights lit up the front of the barn and the whole area in between. They couldn't possibly miss seeing him if he opened the door. He dropped the curtain and spun around.

He heard the truck pull to a stop just outside. If they came in now and turned on the lights he wouldn't even get to the bathroom. He edged the curtain aside and pressed his eye against just the tiniest crack between it and the window frame. The vehicle's engine and headlights were turned off and he could see it now under the bluish security lights, a dirty, banged-up old truck, bigger than a pickup, with crude, homemade wooden sides lining the bed behind the cab. His mind raced. If there were only one or two of them, maybe he could fool them with the empty gun and take the truck.

His heart sank as five or six long-haired, wild-looking young men jumped to the ground from the back of the truck. They didn't approach the door, though, and didn't even look his way. They were too busy laughing and joking, obviously taunting each other, stretching their arms and legs and twisting their necks this way and that, as if the ride had been a rough one.

They wore work boots and wide-legged, light-colored pants that were rumpled and stained. Some were in long-sleeved shirts and some in baggy t-shirts, but all had large pistols in holsters at their waists. At least two carried rifles as well, weapons much like the one he carried.

But unlike his, theirs would be loaded. The fact that they spoke Spanish meant they were almost certainly not Guyanese.

He'd had four years of Spanish in school, and had considered himself pretty fluent, but these men spoke far too fast for him to catch more than an occasional *si*, or *aqui*. There were six of them, and he was certain they were Venezuelan, and connected with Ann Swanson's operation. Although they were joking, and clearly glad to be off that bouncing truck, these were no happy peasants. They looked more like the sort of sullen, cruel men who'd accosted him in front of St. Hildegard's. They terrified him.

The driver's door of the truck opened and a seventh man climbed down. He was dressed like the others, but seemed a little older, and his clothes looked cleaner. He was also the only one wearing a cap. It was a billed cap, and Paul couldn't tell for sure in the poor light, but he thought it was olive drab. The driver yelled something at the others in Spanish and when they quieted a little he turned with a scowl toward the door.

Paul let go of the curtain and pressed himself against the wall. He raised the weapon above his head and, realizing he'd never be able to overcome seven armed men, he stood in the dark and waited.

The driver's feet crunched on the gravel. He tried the door, and when he found it locked he didn't tug on it, didn't knock on it...and didn't unlock it. He walked away.

Paul forced himself back to the window to look out. The driver was talking to the others. They shrugged or nodded in response, and he climbed back into the cab. They were waiting for someone to arrive, someone with a key. The men settled in, lighting cigarettes, talking, arguing, laughing. Some crouched on their haunches, some half-lay on the ground. One man remained standing. He said something and started to unbutton his fly. One of the others said something back to him and they all laughed. He turned away and went to the rear of the truck and stood with his back to the others, urinating.

If Paul had any chance to escape, it was now, while the men were relaxed and waiting. He turned from the window, but had barely taken a step toward the rear of the barn when he heard an excited yell from outside. He turned back and looked out again. The man near the back of the truck was the one shouting. He was pointing off into the darkness. It was clear he'd seen or heard something, possibly some animal.

The men were all on their feet now, and all talking at once, but the driver jumped down from the truck and yelled an order, and they shut up. They all listened, and Paul listened with them. He didn't hear anything, and obviously they didn't either. The driver reached back into the truck's cab and came out with three flashlights. He distributed them among the men and they paired up and went off into the darkness, some with guns drawn. At first Paul could see their lights bobbing and weaving through the darkness as they moved away, but they split apart and soon they were all out of his line of sight.

The driver returned to the cab and reached in again, and came out this time with an automatic rifle. He went to the rear of the truck and stood looking out into the darkness, the weapon cradled in his arms.

Paul could hear the men calling back and forth to each other, but he couldn't tell just where each pair's search was taking them. All he knew was that they were headed away from him, and the driver's attention was with them. If he could open and close the door quietly, he might get away. He hesitated, then decided it was better to try, and *maybe* get away, than to wait, and *certainly* be caught when someone with a key arrived.

He peeked out the window again and saw the driver himself step away into the darkness. Paul could disappear in the other direction, and it wouldn't be too hard to get back to the clinic and lie low. Ann's people had never bothered the clinic before, and they had no reason now to think anyone was there.

He unlocked the door and inched it open, and just as he did, more excited yelling rose up in the distance, from several different men. They must have caught sight of something. Their shouts were all in one or two syllables now, and he was able to make out certain words—like *"Alla!"* and *"Aqui!"*—and was sure they were calling: "Over there!" and "This way!"

He leaned out the open door. He could see two distant flashlight beams, and then a third, sweeping this way and that, the closest maybe fifty yards away, as the three pairs of men made their way through the deep grass. They were headed generally back up the slope they'd just driven down, but they angled off to the left and frequently lifted their lights to shine them along the line of trees at the edge of that side of the clearing. Paul couldn't see whatever it was they'd spotted, but the pairs were merging together as they headed toward the trees.

The driver called out to the men. He was still hidden in darkness, but hadn't ventured very far away. Paul stepped out the door, and as he did, a gunshot rang out, and more yelling, and another shot. The driver called out a question, and one of the men called back, and no more shots were fired. Then, just as Paul was about to pull the door closed behind him and make his run, all the searchers began yelling at once, and among the jumble of words were a few he heard quite clearly.

"Hombre!" they called. *"Gringo!"* They had their prey, and their voices rose with whoops of victory...mixed with what he knew were cruel taunts, and mocking laughter. Then, worst of all, *"Muchacho!"* and *"Chico bobo!"*

FIFTY-SEVEN

Paul's heart pounded in his chest. There was still time to slip away into the darkness and make it to the trees, but all thoughts of running away were gone now. He stepped back into the barn, locked the door, and peeked out.

"Gringo! Gringo! Chico bobo!" the men were chanting.

What "gringo"...what "stupid boy"...could it be? Only one.

It must finally have occurred to the driver to use his best source of light, and he was climbing back into his truck. He started it up and turned it around, angling it until his headlights landed on the men coming back.

They were shouting and waving and pumping their fists in the air like victorious athletes, at the same time squinting and shielding their eyes from the light. All six were in a tight group now, with the two in the middle half-dragging, half-carrying their captive. Even at that distance, and with one side of his face dark with what had to be blood, Paul could tell it was Robert. He must have heard the truck and, finding Paul not in his room, gone to see what was going on.

Paul stood with one eye to the window, breathing hard. Robert tried to pull away several times, but that won him only a vicious elbow in the ribs, or a hard slap on the back of his head. Paul felt he should *do* something. He couldn't fight the men off, but he could challenge them, announcing that he and Robert were United States citizens. Except they already knew Robert was a *gringo*...which maybe made catching him sweeter. Besides, they wouldn't do anything until whoever they were waiting for arrived. It was best to wait and watch.

They dragged Robert into the area lit by the security lights. The driver spoke up and they let go of him. He swayed a little, but managed to stay on his feet while the driver searched him, running his hands over Robert's torso, arms, and legs. He seemed to be talking the whole time, or asking questions, and Paul had the impression that, in addition to searching, he was checking for wounds or injuries. Robert remained silent, with a sullen look on his face...a look Paul himself had gotten pretty familiar with.

The blood on his face had come from a cut over his left eye and, while the bleeding seemed to have stopped, the eye itself was swollen half-shut. His face was full of scrapes and scratches. His shirt—the black shirt Paul had lent him—was hanging open, and his t-shirt was spotted with blood. He didn't seem to have any broken bones, though, and apparently hadn't been shot.

The driver completed his search, coming up with nothing but a plastic container of insect repellant which he transferred from the boy's pants pocket to his own. Again he seemed to be questioning Robert, but Robert said nothing.

Finally, the driver spoke to his men and two of them grabbed Robert and made him climb up into the back of the truck. They climbed up after him, where they tied his hands behind his back and made him sit or lie down—Paul couldn't really see—in the truck bed. The men jumped back down and the driver, making a point of looking at his watch, said something and climbed up into the cab behind the wheel.

Still staring out, Paul moved one hand to the turn knob of the lock, ready to unlock the door and run out if the driver started the engine. Maybe he could make it to the truck, pull the driver out, and drive away with Robert. More likely he'd be shot, or pulled down and beaten. At any rate, he wouldn't let them take Robert away...not unless they took him, too.

But the engine didn't start up and the men settled back down on the ground, to wait for whoever was on their way.

Paul knew what would happen then. Larry Landrew was right, and without wanting to admit it even to himself, Paul had known that. He'd known it since the day Ann Swanson told him what she wanted. Whoever came would have a key, and they'd come inside and raise the overhead door, and the truck would be backed into the barn and loaded with the crates full of weapons. And whether Ann was actually with the CIA, or with some other clandestine group—private or governmental—those weapons were headed for Venezuela, to be used to overthrow the government.

Larry hadn't been willing to keep his mouth shut about it, so he'd been removed from the scene. Celia couldn't be trusted to remain silent either, so she had to go, too. Despite the heat that was sticking his shirt to his back, Paul felt a cold shudder go through his body.

He let go of the curtain and made sure it completely covered all the edges of the little square window. Then he switched on his flashlight and swept it around the interior of the barn again, stopping it on the tall metal storage cabinets beside the workbench. He took one step toward them and almost screamed when his right foot hit the floor. He'd forgotten his sprained ankle, and now it felt swollen, and hurt even worse than before.

He managed, though, to make it to the first of the cabinets and open the door. The shelves inside were stacked with boxes of parts for engines: oil and air filters, fan belts, hoses, batteries, and electrical components whose names he didn't even recognize. He moved to the second cabinet. This one had no shelves, and was nearly full, from floor to ceiling, with cases of quarts of motor oil stacked on top of each other. He removed one stack of cases and set them neatly against the wall. This left room for him to stand up inside the cabinet—if he stooped over—and hold the door closed from inside.

He left the empty gun in the cabinet and limped back to the window. The men were either dozing or talking quietly. Time dragged heavily. He tried to pray, but his mind was too full of fear and guilt and hopelessness. He tried to plan what to do if Ann Swanson came...or if someone else came...or if no one came and the men decided to leave. A plan, though, seemed as far away as a prayer. He knew only that he had to stay out of sight as long as he could and, in the end, he had to stay close to Robert. He'd brought his son here, and he would keep him safe...or die with him.

†

It seemed like hours later, but by his watch it was 1:45 when the voices outside grew louder. He peeked out and they were all on their feet, and then he heard what they must have heard. Engine noise, but more than one vehicle this time, he was sure.

The sound grew steadily louder and finally headlights popped into view at the top of the rise and started down. Two vehicles, one following the other. Both, he thought, smaller than the truck. The first stopped just outside the edge of the illuminated area and sat there, while the other—Paul couldn't see either vehicle well, but was sure they were both Jeeps—pulled up and stopped. Both drivers got out and, after a few seconds, first Ann Swanson stepped forward into the light. And then CIA Special Agent Orlando Melendez.

FIFTY-EIGHT

The truck driver moved to greet Ann and Melendez, while the other men stood watching. Ann was obviously much more fluent in Spanish than Paul was, and she and the driver had a brief conversation before the driver turned to his men and said something. One of them clambered up into the truck. He got Robert to his feet, untied him, and made him climb down to the ground.

By his speech and gestures, it was clear the driver was explaining how they'd found Robert. Ann asked something and he answered, nodding and spreading his arms out to indicate the clearing around the barn, seeming to say, *Yes, this whole area was searched,* then shaking his head, *No, there was no one else.*

Melendez spoke up then, and Paul thought he heard the word *clínica.*

The driver looked startled. "*No, señor.*"

Ann turned to Robert. "Where is Father Clark?"

"Huh?"

"You heard me. Where is he?"

"How do I know? I don't—"

She leaned toward him. "Don't lie to me." Her voice was calm, but far from friendly. "You'll only regret it."

"I told you," he said. "I don't *know* where he is."

"Is he out *here* somewhere?" Spreading her arms out. "Or back at the clinic?"

"All I know," Robert said, "is I heard this…like…loud truck." He spoke slowly, as though explaining something to a child. "I got up and came out to see who it was. I don't know *where* my...I don't know where the guy is. Maybe he's out there in the woods, watching us. Or maybe he's on his way to...Marumba or whatever."

Melendez took a step toward Robert. "Keep lying, you dope-dealing piece of shit, and you'll buy yourself a ticket back to *El Convento*."

Robert stared back at him. "Go fuck yourself."

Paul was stunned. Robert couldn't know who Melendez was, but he could tell the man was teamed up with Ann, and he certainly knew what Ann could do. Maybe what people said about the aggression prisoners developed to survive in jail was true.

Melendez looked at Ann and she nodded, and the two of them turned and headed for her Jeep. She called something back to the truck driver, who looked surprised and angry, but said nothing, and she and Melendez drove off.

Paul was sure they were headed for the clinic, and as the men waited they seemed apprehensive. They couldn't have known who Robert was, or that his being here meant Paul would be nearby, but the driver, at least, must have known he should have more thoroughly searched the area, including the clinic, for other intruders.

Finally, after a terribly long fifteen minutes, the two Americans returned in the Jeep. Paul turned at once and started for his hiding spot, knowing they'd soon be coming inside.

But that didn't happen. Instead, all hell broke loose.

†

Maybe he'd been preoccupied, not paying attention, but the first thing Paul heard was a frightening *WHOP...WHOP...WHOP...* high up in the sky and to the rear of the barn, growing louder and louder, and freezing him in his tracks. He stood in the dark and, before he could wrap his mind around what was happening, the pounding grew to deafening proportion, and was joined by a similar *WHOP...WHOP...WHOP...*this time from high and to his left. And then a third.

The monstrous drumming from above seemed to make the earth itself pulsate. Paul could feel the ground beating through the concrete floor, and was afraid for a moment the old barn might come down around him. By then, though, he'd realized what was happening. Unable to resist, he moved the curtain aside and peeked out.

As he'd hoped, Ann and Melendez hadn't come any closer. In fact, they had their backs to the barn and along with everyone else—the truck driver, his crew, and Robert—they stood looking out across the clearing, to Paul's right. Paul couldn't see what they were looking at, but he knew what the noise was. Helicopters, at least three of them, hovering now above the ground. The widening beams from their downlights—very bright, with a blue tint—swept this way and that across the clearing, where the tall grass waved wildly in some places, and in others lay flat under the force of the downdraft.

When the first aircraft touched ground and the fierce pounding of its engine ceased, Paul could see just the tips of the blades of its main rotor, swinging into, and then out of, view and then slowing to a stop. He counted two more landings, and then a fourth helicopter swung into view, hovered a moment, and settled to earth out past the truck, beyond the reach of the barn's lights. It was the last one and when its engine stopped the world became suddenly silent.

Both Ann and Melendez took plugs from their ears and, looking out toward the final helicopter, waited. Three more men joined them, probably the pilots of the other aircraft. They looked Hispanic to Paul, and wore khaki pants and shirts. They were bareheaded, all with headsets hanging around their necks, all with guns at their hips.

Dim light shone from the final helicopter, and the truck mostly blocked Paul's view, but he heard a metallic bang as though a door were thrown open. Then there was movement and he saw someone—several people, in fact—stepping down to the ground. Soon two large men walked into the light, both in black pants and dark, long-sleeved shirts. They stepped aside in obvious deference to the person behind them.

Melendez stepped forward to greet the newcomer, blocking Paul's view, while Ann simply stayed where she was, as though not interested in any exchange of greetings.

It wasn't until Melendez turned, and the other man stepped beside him and spoke to Ann, that Paul got a look at him. But what he saw wasn't possible. It was Hank Manion.

FIFTY-NINE

Manion was clearly in charge. He spoke to Ann and she pointed, and he turned and looked at Robert. He didn't approach the boy, but said something to the truck driver. The driver grabbed Robert by the arm and everyone started toward the barn.

Paul limped as fast as he could to his hiding place and managed to pull the metal cabinet door closed just as he heard the door to the barn open. Someone flicked a switch and thin slivers of light appeared around the edges of the cabinet door. At once he heard the whirring of an electric motor and a scraping sound, announcing that the overhead door was being raised.

As he'd expected, the truck was backed into the barn. Its motor was turned off and men went to work loading the crates into it. They didn't use the forklift, but passed back and forth just a few feet from him, breathing hard and complaining in Spanish. He held his breath, and hoped that more than just one of the men had answered nature's call outside, because if someone went back to the bathroom they'd see the hole in the wall where the fan had been and, as a result, they'd surely search the whole barn.

Meanwhile, there was a hushed conversation going on a little farther away. Paul could pick out Ann's voice, and Hank's, but couldn't tell what they were saying. There were other participants, too, and at least one of them spoke in Spanish.

Suddenly they were interrupted. "Dammit, let *go* of me." It was Robert, and Paul could tell he was struggling with someone.

"For God's sake," Manion said, "where's Otoe and that other guy of yours?"

"In Mabaruma, looking for whores," Ann said. "I didn't need them out here. The less they know, the better."

"Well...someone get that son of a bitch tied up." There was more scuffling, and Hank said, "No...no tape. I want to talk to him." Another pause, and then, "Listen to me, dammit. Answer my questions." The group had moved deeper into the barn, across from where Paul was hiding. "What are you and Father Clark doing down here?"

"Nothing," Robert said, and that was followed by a loud *slap*. Robert moaned, and then said, "He...he had to visit the clinic, and said I could come if I wanted. The truck woke me up and I—"

"Where is he now?" Hank asked.

"I dunno. Back at the clinic, I guess."

"Not true." It was Ann this time. "We looked there. Searched every—"

"We're wasting time," Melendez said. "The priest and the kid...they're *your* problem, Mr. Manion, not mine." He paused, then added, "You've had problems through this whole operation. I wonder if we're dealing with someone who—"

"*You* aren't dealing with *anyone*." Hank's voice was low, but hard and cold. "You have a limited function here: to watch a bunch of so-called freedom fighters pick up their merchandise, and then hand over payment. It's not your job to *wonder*. Remember that, and you'll be better off."

"Hey, Jesus, just pullin' your chain." Melendez sounded like a kid who knew he'd stepped out of line. "So anyway," he said, "these crates here... there's gotta be more than this, right?"

"The bulk of the weapons—and all the ammo—are already aboard the Huey," Manion said, "which is rebuilt and combat-certified, as are both Apaches. What's here is the remainder. Assault rifles, primarily. XM8s. Brand new, and—"

"And rocket launchers?"

"A dozen M72 LAWs. The shipment's complete. Your guy...Alfredo, is it? Let him check it out if you like. But that's where any 'wasting time' will occur."

"Yeah, well...company orders, y'know? When he says it's all here, you get your diamonds."

"Our *what*?" Ann's voice was loud, almost shrill. "What the hell are—"

The slam of the truck door, and the roar of its engine coming to life, drowned out all talk, except for some yelling back and forth in Spanish. The men must have finished loading the crates.

Paul's neck ached from standing stooped over so long. He tried to assimilate what he'd heard. Freedom fighters. Ammunition, automatic rifles—"XM8s," Hank said—and rocket launchers. Three helicopters. How many millions was Hank making on this deal? And who, exactly, was he dealing with? The United States Gov—

With a terrible grinding of gears the truck moved slowly out of the barn, and then the overhead door was lowered. It hit the floor with a metallic clank, and only then could Paul hear Melendez talking. "...matter of minutes," he was saying, his voice sounding more distant. "After that I'm outta here and the two of you can argue all you like."

"Jesus Christ," Ann said, and the service door slammed shut.

From the sound of it, they'd all left the barn. Did they take Robert, too? Somehow it hadn't sounded like it. Did they leave someone to watch him? Light still leaked in around the edges of the cabinet door and Paul waited, hearing only the truck as it drove farther away. And then he heard something else, a rustling sound. From inside the barn. And someone breathing hard, as though from exertion.

Silently, Paul pushed open the cabinet door.

Robert was sitting on the floor, with his back to the wall on the opposite side of the barn, twisting and pulling, straining to free his hands. They were behind him and obviously tied to a low rung of one of the primitive ladders nailed to the wall. He didn't see Paul at first and, when he did, his eyes widened and his mouth dropped open. He tried to say something, but didn't get it out. Instead, he began sobbing uncontrollably.

Unsure what help it could be, Paul took the empty XM8 with him and hobbled painfully across the barn. He laid a shaking hand on Robert's shoulder. "It's okay," he said. "Calm down. I'm here. I'm proud of how strong you've been."

Robert managed to stop crying. "I…but…how did—"

"Shhh, they might hear us," Paul whispered. "We're going to be just fine."

He laid the gun on the floor and attacked the knots, but Robert's struggle had only made them tighter and he knew there wasn't time to work them loose. Warning Robert to stay quiet, he hurried to the wheeled tool chest and opened drawer after drawer until he found a pair of heavy-duty tin snips. Returning, he cut the boy loose and pulled him to his feet. "Stay here," he said, laying the tin snips on the floor by the gun. "If you hear someone coming, sit down. Pretend you're still tied up."

"But…but where are *you* going?"

"Just to look out the window in that door. If I don't see anyone watching, we'll go out that way and run for the trees. They'll have no idea where to look, and they'll be in a hurry to leave." He tried to sound confident, wondering if Robert thought that was as unpromising a plan as he did: the two of them, crouching in the dark, while men with vehicles, bright lights, and automatic weapons—*loaded* weapons—came after them. Still, he couldn't think of anything else. "We'll hide until daylight."

"Why not use this," Robert said, reaching down for the gun. "This AK-47 or whatever. You can hide behind the door, and when they come in you—"

"The door opens out, and the gun's not loaded." He turned and limped toward the door. "We have to run for it."

"You can hardly *walk*," Robert said, this time much too loud. "How—"

"Quiet," Paul whispered back. "We don't know how close anyone is."

On his way to the door he could still hear the truck's motor running, off in the clearing where the first three helicopters had landed. He recalled that Hank had mentioned loading the crates of weapons into one of the helicopters, the Huey. From his time in the army Paul knew that Apaches were two-man attack helicopters, while a Huey was much larger and could carry significant cargo, or fifteen or twenty fully armed troops.

At the door he drew the flashlight from his back pocket and showed it to Robert, then turned out the overhead lights. He drew the curtain slightly aside and peered out.

Out beyond the reach of the security lights, with the truck no longer blocking his view, he made out the dark outline of the helicopter Hank had arrived in. He couldn't see the truck, but could still hear it...and then heard nothing at all but the roar of a helicopter starting up, and the *WHOP, WHOP, WHOP* as it lifted off the ground. It was followed at once by a second aircraft, the noise of the two of them filling the air, then fading surprisingly quickly as they sped off to the west.

Shouting came from the area they'd lifted off from, and then what sounded like the doors of a truck or a car—or a helicopter?—slamming shut. At once an even louder engine started up. That had to be the Huey. And then the *WHOP, WHOP, WHOP* again.

It was possible that Hank Manion and the others were over there watching, but equally possible that someone was up close to the front of the barn and out of Paul's view. He had to take a chance. He opened the door just a crack and looked out. There was no one in sight. Slim as it was, this was the chance they had.

He pulled the door closed and shone the flashlight on the floor between himself and Robert. "Let's go," he called, gesturing with his arm, not sure if Robert could hear him. The Huey was getting louder and louder, as it prepared to lift off. "Hurry!"

At once Robert was beside him, the gun in his hand. "You want this?"

"Yes," Paul shouted above the noise. "You carry it." He pushed the curtain aside and looked out again. "They'll be watching the helicopter. Don't look back. Just run to—" He stopped. "No, wait!"

The Huey wasn't off the ground yet, he was sure, but two figures, Hank Manion and Ann Swanson, stepped into view and were headed straight for the door.

SIXTY

"Go back! Pretend to be tied up." Paul dropped the curtain. "Hurry!"

He shone the light so Robert could make it back to where he'd been sitting, and took a step toward his own hiding place. But the cabinet was all the way across the barn, and with his ankle he'd never make it. They'd switch on the lights and he'd be caught like a roach in a morning kitchen.

By now the Huey was in the air and moving away, and he could hear Hank and Ann talking outside, their voices raised. Arguing, he thought, and coming closer. Then Melendez called out from some distance away, in Spanish. The truck drove close to the barn, and kept on going and up the slope. Melendez called out again, and there was a shouted response. The truck was leaving.

"Hey," Robert said, "what are we gonna—"

"Quiet! Pretend you're tied up...and hide the rifle behind you." He had nothing else to suggest.

With the helicopter gone and the noise from the truck fading, he could hear Hank and Ann again, but they no longer seemed to be coming closer. He took a chance and peeked out. They were standing maybe ten yards away, obviously still arguing, and at the same time looking off toward where the Jeeps were parked. Then Melendez came into view. He walked up and handed something—a slim, soft-sided attaché case—to Hank. After a brief exchange of words, Melendez turned and walked away, toward his Jeep. Ann, clearly angry about something, was talking to Hank again, but Hank turned his back on her and came toward the barn.

Paul suddenly realized he could have made it to his hiding place after all, if he'd known they'd be stopping to wait for Melendez and the attaché case. But there was no chance of that now.

He swung the flashlight beam into the corner, a few feet to his left. There was another ladder there and, like all the others, this one's two-by-four rungs went up to just beyond the crossbeams—which were maybe twice as high as the top of the doorway. The lights hung down from those crossbeams, so that getting to the beams—or above them—would put him, if not in total darkness, at least in shadows.

He shoved the flashlight in his pocket and started up.

A straight vertical climb is hard enough under any circumstances, but with his right ankle screaming in pain when he put any weight on it at all, he had to stand on his left foot, grab a high rung and pull himself up by his arms, then lift that foot to the next rung.

By the third rung his shoulders were already aching. But he kept on, dragging himself up by the arms, fighting the impulse to use his right foot. His head was above the lights, and he was pulling his left foot to the next rung, when the door opened.

"...diamonds, goddammit," Hank was saying. "Not cash, not these days, and certainly not dollars. So it'll take some time to get you your share."

"That's bullshit," Ann answered. "The deal was I'd be paid at once and you—"

"Damn, who turned the lights off in here?"

"I might have," she said. "I don't know. Or Melendez."

Paul stood on the ladder six or eight feet above the doorway—not moving, scarcely breathing—looking nearly straight down on the two of them. In the dim light from outside he saw Hank fumble around for the switch. "I was the last one out," Hank said, "and I don't recall turning them off." He flicked the switch and the entire floor area was lit up and Paul, though above the lights and in shadow, was surely visible if someone looked right up at him.

"So Alfredo or one of his men must have come back for something," Ann said. "Anyway, no one's here but the kid." Robert was sitting on the floor against the wall, his hands behind his back and his head hanging down. "The priest must have been with him," she added, "but Alfredo and his idiots let him get away. By now he probably really *is* on his way into town." She took a step in Robert's direction. "Maybe I can—"

She was interrupted by two people coming through the door. They were the men who'd arrived with Hank in his helicopter. They didn't say anything, but the distraction of their arrival allowed Paul to climb another rung up and deeper into shadow.

"I'm not concerned about the priest," Hank said. "He'll turn up. And anyway, he and the boy aren't your problem."

"Oh?" Ann had started toward Robert again, but she stopped and looked back at Hank. "Actually, they *are* my problem. You need me to—"

"*Need* you? When did I ever *need* you? You and your delusions are becoming problematic. You should have stayed with the agency, y'know? With your beloved *'company.'* You get out on your own, hiring your own people…it makes you think you're bigger than you are. Demanding a percentage, from *me*, as though we were partners. Well, my dear, I don't *have* partners. So, Franco, let's address that problem."

One of Hank's men stepped forward. He was a tall, husky, light-skinned black man, and he held an automatic rifle trained on Ann.

Paul stared down. His shoulders were cramping up, but even the slightest movement might draw attention, so he stood absolutely still, all his weight on one foot, his upper body twisted so he could see the scene playing out below. He didn't want to see. He wanted to squeeze his eyes shut, but for some reason he couldn't do that. He could only stand up here and watch Ann Swanson die.

She clearly thought so, too, because her eyes widened and, for just an instant, she looked around as though searching for some way out, though there was none.

But no shots were fired. "Not here," Hank said, his voice very matter-of-fact. "I'd rather not have to tidy up this place…unless, of course, you make it necessary. I wonder, are you a good swimmer?"

She didn't answer, but to Paul she seemed to relax...more than he would have thought possible. "You claim it's my attitude," she said, "but it's not that. It's the money. You don't want to split it."

"Well," he said, "there *is* that."

"And instead of wondering how well I can swim, you should be thinking about what a stupid mistake you're making." She shook her head like a disappointed parent. "There are people who know I'm here."

"What, that second-rate artist girl friend of yours? I doubt she has any—"

"You pretentious, fucking prick."

"Not to worry, though," Hank said. "I'll see she gets a tearful good-bye card... from a lover who found she couldn't take being tied to an invalid."

"You know I'm not talking about her." Ann had recovered her control.

"Oh? Well, your two mercenaries certainly won't waste any tears over you. Men like that aren't loyal to anything but excitement...and money. They'll move on. And Melendez? He *is* loyal, to a fault. He's like our friend Father Clark. Both of them minor players in powerful organizations. Both believing what they're told to believe, both doing what they're told to do. If the CIA claims it's not doing business in Guyana, Melendez will swear to it."

Paul shuddered—at Hank's contempt for him and his priesthood, yes, but also because the man so clearly enjoyed the thought of Ann's helplessness.

"...the priest," Ann was saying. "With no reason to keep quiet, he's a problem."

"Oh, I think not. He's out there right now, running for his life. Let him make it to Mabaruma if he can. He'll never get out of the— But enough." He turned. "Palka, let's get on with it."

Ann stayed calm as the partner of the man called Franco stepped up and made her raise her arms high over her head. He took a small pistol from her jacket pocket and handed it back to Hank, then removed her jacket. She wore what looked like a silk turtleneck, and he ran his hands over every inch of her torso—front, sides, back—from her neck down. When he reached her waist, he squatted, felt around her ankles... then yanked her pants down to the floor. He made her pivot before him.

"That's fine, Palka," Hank said. "Franco and I will take it from here. You go get the chopper ready. Oh...and dig out those plastic restraints."

Palka left and Ann pulled up her trousers. Throughout all this Robert still hadn't raised his head, and Paul wondered if the boy thought he could suddenly jump up when someone came near him, and overpower them. He hoped not, because no way would that work. Not that he himself had a better plan.

"The boy's faking," Hank said, as though picking up on Paul's thoughts. "He's not unconscious, and he's certainly not asleep. Untie him, Ann, and get him to his feet. And if he tries anything...or if *you* do...Franco will shoot you both on the spot."

Ann walked across and stood over Robert. "Did you hear what he said? The man has an automatic weapon, and he couldn't miss if he tried. So look up at me."

Robert looked up. Paul could tell he was frightened, and trying not to show it, but he kept his hands behind him as though he were still tied up.

Ann leaned over him to untie him, and though she must have seen at once that his hands were free, she didn't skip a beat, and made a show of having difficulty loosening the knots. And then it struck Paul that—even though from where he was he couldn't see it—by now Ann must have spotted the weapon hidden behind Robert.

Don't! Paul wanted to shout. *It's not loaded!*

But Ann's head was close to Robert's and maybe Robert whispered something, or maybe she knew that if she reached for the gun she'd be cut down before she could swing it around. At any rate she merely continued her show of untying Robert.

By then Paul was confident that if he didn't move they wouldn't see him. And if Robert didn't give him away, no one—not even Ann, who had to assume it was he who had cut the boy free—would know where he was hiding. They would leave the barn. And then what?

"That's it," Ann said, feigning success in finally getting Robert untied. "On your feet, dammit." She pulled up on his arm.

Paul watched in silence and knew that Hank and Franco would take Ann and Robert out to the helicopter, where Palka waited with "plastic restraints." They'd head for the coast, and then out a few miles over the water. And what could he do about it?

He could wait until they were out of the barn, then climb down, grab the gun, and follow them. And challenge them, and maybe they wouldn't discover it was an empty weapon, and maybe…

Maybe nothing. Only the certainty that Hank would then have *three* people to drop into the ocean.

What made sense was to save the only life he *could* save, stay where he was until they were in the helicopter and gone. He had no doubt he could make it to Mabaruma, and from there out of Guyana. He'd found a way to avoid the police in the US and get down here, and he would find a way to get back home. And, whatever happened to him after that, he knew he would survive long enough to shout out everything he'd seen.

And for what? A bold exposé of an arms delivery to Venezuelan rebels, financed by the CIA? Screaming headlines about private mercenaries and government agencies, regime change and the murder of an innocent parish priest? All of that, yes.

And none of it would bring his son back to him.

SIXTY-ONE

The man called Franco stood below Paul, a few feet out from the wall, his back to the half-open door, as Ann Swanson helped a very unsteady Robert to his feet.

"Let's go," Hank said. "The clock's ticking."

Robert was bent over, clutching his stomach. "Alfredo's guys beat him up pretty bad," Ann said. "He's all cramped up." Robert groaned and she struggled to get him upright, stretching one of his arms across her shoulders. They started toward the door, their movements agonizingly slow.

"Christ," Hank said, "where the hell's Palka with those restraints?"

"You said he should prepare the aircraft, sir." Franco had a deep, calm voice that seemed somehow familiar to Paul. Keeping his weapon trained on Ann and Robert, the man reached back with his left hand and pushed the door open further behind him. "We'll use the restraints when we put them on board. These two won't be any problem, sir." He waved the weapon just slightly and said, "Am I right, ma'am?"

"Fuck you," Ann said.

Paul stood on just his left foot, both hands clinging to a rung above his head…and made up his mind. Not for Ann's sake—she was in this by choice—and not with any real hope of saving Robert. Mostly for himself, maybe. To save himself from a life spent remembering how he'd shrunk back into a dark corner, while they took away the son he was just beginning to know.

Ann and Robert had taken a few stumbling steps, but were still maybe ten yards away. Paul lowered his hands—first one, then the other—to the rung even with his shoulders. He'd have to crouch to give himself leverage to push away from the ladder and reach Franco when he jumped. Very slowly, he bent his left leg...and heard a little *crack* from inside his knee.

Franco must have heard it, too. He turned his head left, then right. And then up toward Paul. "What—"

Franco's head jerked back and a dark streak appeared high on his right cheek, and splinters flew from the wall below Paul's feet, all at the same time as the sound of a shot from outside. Franco screamed and spun toward the doorway...and was hit again, this time in the chest. His knees buckled, but he didn't go down. He managed to stumble out the door, firing his own weapon. Three, four, five bursts, in rapid succession. Firing even after—from the sound of it—he was down on his knees on the gravel outside the door.

As Franco fired wildly, Hank stepped into the doorway and Paul thought he was going to run for it. But he didn't. He yanked the metal door closed, even as several bullets slammed into it, but didn't penetrate.

The shooting stopped, then, as abruptly as it started. Franco was dead. Paul was certain of that. And he knew that, with the right weapon, whoever had killed Franco could send rows of bullets ripping through the wood of the barn wall. But that didn't happen. The shooter couldn't know whether he'd hit Hank, or Ann, or Robert.

Meanwhile, Hank locked the door and stood with his back to it. Clearly unaware of Paul up on the ladder in the dark, he was focused on Ann and Robert. Paul turned his head and saw Robert down on his hands and knees, and Ann getting to her feet. They'd either both hit the floor intentionally when the shooting started, or—as Paul thought more likely—Ann fell as she tried to disengage herself from Robert and charge Hank. He was sure she'd have made short work of him, hand-to-hand.

Her problem, though, was that Hank held what was probably her own pistol, aimed straight at her.

She backed up a couple of steps and raised her hands, palms outward, clearly confident in Hank's ability to use the gun. "Franco's dead," she said. "And you can be sure Palka is, too. You could kill me, of course, but then Otoe and Tree will kill you. They *are* loyal, in their own way... not to mention they'd never let you fly off with the proceeds from your sale." She smiled. "Sort of a stand-off, wouldn't you say?"

"What I'd say is you won't get out of here alive unless you do as I tell you."

"Which is?"

"Which is that you announce to your thugs that I have a gun. And that you and I are coming out. They stand in the open where I can see them. We leave together in your Jeep. And if they follow us...I shoot you."

"And after you kill me, they kill you. We're back where we started from." As she spoke, she slowly lowered her hands to her sides.

Hank apparently didn't care...or maybe he was too busy thinking. "You say you trust their loyalty," he said. "Well, we're about to test that out. If they interfere it means they don't care if we *both* die; they just want the diamon—"

"Ann!" It was a man, calling from outside, and Paul recognized him as the "homeless" man who'd pushed a grocery cart outside St. Hildegard's. "You okay?"

"I'm okay," she called back. "We're...uh...we're working things out. Hold your fire."

"Roger that."

"That's the one called Otoe, right?" Manion asked and, when she nodded, he said, "The *other* man, make him answer, too."

She shrugged, then called, *"Tree?* You read me?"

"Loud and clear," came the answer. A black man, Paul was sure, but a voice he didn't recognize. "Just give us the word."

"Tell them," Hank said.

"Listen up!" she called. "Manion's got a gun. I don't. He's going to walk me and the boy out. Hold your fire. We'll be taking the chopper. We—"

"Shut up!" Hank said. "I told you the Jeep. And I didn't say the boy."

"Right," she said, lowering her voice. "The Jeep's what you'd like.

And once we're far enough away from here I'm dead and you drive on. But the chopper? I can fly it, and I know you can't." She spread her arms wide. "And the boy comes along. Take it or leave it."

Seconds went by. It was the first time Paul had ever seen Hank in a situation where he didn't seem entirely in control. And as Hank tried to think things through, Paul's attention went to Robert, who'd scooted farther back toward where he'd been tied. His hands were behind him. Was he feeling around for the weapon? The empty XM8?

No, Robert! Don't do it.

"Make up your mind, Manion," Ann said. "The clock *is*, as you say, ticking."

"Okay," Hank said, "the chopper." He took a step toward Ann, keeping the gun trained on her. "And get the kid to his feet. You two go out the door first, and—"

Paul pushed off and jumped feet first...just as Hank took another step. He missed Hank, landing hard on the floor behind him. He was off-balance and landed square on his right foot on the concrete, and screamed when his ankle took his weight and then gave way. He grabbed wildly at Hank's shoulders to hold himself upright, while Hank, howling in surprise and rage, tried to shake him off. Paul couldn't get a solid grip and if Hank could have turned around he could have shot Paul. But Hank couldn't turn. He had to back Ann off with the gun.

Paul tried to wrap both arms around Hank's chest, but Hank jabbed his elbow back, deep into Paul's belly, driving the wind out of him. He fell back, his right hand managing to grab hold of the back of Hank's collar. He couldn't breathe, couldn't think, only knew he must not let go, must not let himself fall to the floor.

He tried to get his left arm around Hank's neck, but Hank lowered his chin and Paul's fingernails raked across his face. Three of his fingers slipped into Hank's mouth and he forced them deeper in and held tight. Hank, still bellowing, swung his arms and head to free himself from Paul's grip. Then the gun hand went off. Whether intentionally or not Paul didn't know. Three shots, maybe four. Paul lost track, because of the screams and cries that filled the air, and because of the pounding that started on the locked door.

Paul might have cried out, too, but he couldn't catch his breath. He was in a panic, his fingers still jammed into Hank's mouth, fighting with his right hand to keep Hank from twisting around and turning the gun back toward him. Hank tried to bite down on his fingers and Paul yanked the man's head back. He pulled as hard as he could, surprised he didn't tear Hank's skin away from his cheekbone. The two men stumbled backwards together and Paul's back hit the wall beside the door. He pushed off and his elbow hit the switch…and the lights went out, plunging them all into darkness.

Finding his left hand free, no longer in Hank's mouth, Paul wrapped his arm around Hank's neck, and squeezed tight. Hank seemed to panic then, and threw himself backwards, slamming Paul back against the wall a second time. This time, though, Paul's head snapped back and hit the wall, too. Stunned, he lost his grip on Hank, and found he had no strength left at all.

He sagged back against the wall, helpless, yet feeling strangely grateful that the struggle was over. Head hanging down, he heard, or felt, Hank turn to face him. He looked up, could just see Hank's arm reaching toward him. Could see the gun…

And then heard a terrible thud…the crunch of breaking bone…and a great groaning sigh, as Hank toppled forward and fell against him. The two of them crashed together to the floor, Hank on top.

The men outside were shouting, banging on the door, trying to pull it open, but the cries inside had died to low moans and sobs. Paul struggled to push the limp, leaden weight of Hank's body off him. He heard Ann moaning. And…was that Robert, too? Was Robert—

A burst of gunshots blotted out everything. Dry wood ripped and splintered just above him and to his right, and the lock was gone and the door was open.

SIXTY-TWO

Paul lay flat on his back in the helicopter—the one Hank had arrived in, and wouldn't be needing anymore. His arms were down along his sides, and something was poking him in the spine. He shifted around as much as he could and discovered that, whatever it was, it was moveable. He couldn't ease the pain throbbing through his ankle, or the aches in his other muscles and joints, but by squirming he managed to nudge the lump to the side a little, so it didn't press right into his backbone.

Ann lay beside him on the floor, both of them under thin blankets—"shock blankets," according to the man called Tree. And both on collapsible stretchers—"evacuation litters," he said. There was a big difference, though. Ann wasn't strapped down to hers.

She'd suffered gunshot wounds to the left upper arm and the right thigh. "Arm's not much, just a graze," Tree said. "Thigh's a through-and-through. Hurts like fucking hell, I know, but no bone or major vessel involvement." Both he and his partner, Otoe, seemed to be experienced in treating such injuries. They said the bullet was small caliber and she'd done a good job stopping the blood flow. They set up an IV, from a pack labeled *COMBAT TRAUMA KIT*, to keep her hydrated, and added an antibiotic. Nothing for pain, though. She refused it.

Robert hadn't been shot, but seemed to be suffering from some sort of psychological shutdown. When the men blasted their way into the barn and switched on the lights, he'd been sitting on the floor, cradling the rifle he'd smashed against Hank's skull. "Damn, kid," Tree said, "you musta hit a sweet spot. Split that melon right open." Robert didn't even look up.

Paul had seen all that, but as though through a fog. He was hardly aware he'd been put on a stretcher until he felt the straps being tightened around him. He'd moaned in pain and Robert must have thought he was worse off than he was, because when Tree and Otoe moved over to help Ann he jumped up and threw himself on top of Paul. "Dad! No!" he cried, wrapping his arms around him, hugging him...as well as a person strapped to a stretcher can be hugged.

There were only two stretchers, or they'd have strapped Robert onto one, too. As it was, the men pulled him off Paul and made him drag Paul's stretcher along the ground ahead of them, while they carried Ann. It was a painful, bone-jarring trip for Paul...and that odd-shaped lump poking him in the back didn't help. In the helicopter they sat Robert on a fold-down bench seat and secured his hands behind him, using the same sort of yellow plastic straps that held Paul to his stretcher, attaching them to a metal ring in the wall.

Now the two men were leaving, to go back to the barn. Tree leaned over Ann. "You gave us a scare, but you're stabilized. We got a little time now, and we need to clean up. Not just the bodies. Everything—blood, casings, whatever. And see about that fucking door. But not to worry. Won't be long 'fore we're headed for Georgetown."

"Right," Otoe said, "and we'll deep-six the cargo on the way. *All* the cargo." Ann lifted her head as though to respond, but he raised his hand. "I know," he said, "but you got a better idea?"

She didn't answer, and Tree said, "A shame, really, but nobody *asked* 'em to stick their noses in."

†

When the men were gone, there was a long moment of silence, and then Ann said, "None of us knew you were up there. You...you could have..." She stopped, as though out of breath, then said, "You must have a death wish."

"Death wish?" Paul saw how pale she looked in the dim green glow of the cabin lights. "What other choice was there, when you insisted on taking Robert along?"

"Yes...I thought you must be nearby, hoped you'd interfere...if we were taking him." She seemed very weak, but also anxious to talk, maybe to keep her mind off her pain. "And even if you didn't...it meant more for Manion to worry about. But...my men...you knew they were there. You didn't think they could handle Manion?"

"What difference did it make who handled who?" Paul asked. "Robert was a problem to whoever won. I knew I'd never see him again." He glanced at Robert, who sat motionless, head down.

"And you really thought you had a hope in hell you could save him?"

"I thought..." He paused, listening to Robert breathe, wondering if they'd drugged him. "Anyway, I did what I did."

"Right, but *why* you did it...that interests me. I mean, a few months ago someone shows up..." She squeezed her eyes shut, opened them again. "Shows up," she went on, "talking about a son you've never seen. You meet him...talk to him a few times...you don't even *know* the kid. Not really, not yet. You could've saved yourself. And then..." She paused again, this time her breath hissing through clenched teeth. "And then said a prayer that he'd survive somehow."

"Prayers don't seem to work that way," Paul said. He wanted to keep her talking. He hoped she'd find it harder to drown someone she'd just had a meaningful conversation with. "You're right," he said. "I *did* know there was no hope. But still...I had to try. Or at least be *with* him. I mean, I'd already done so many things I thought I'd never do." He shook his head. "It's hard to explain, even to myself. Do you...do you have a child?"

"No," Ann said. "But I...I understand."

"Yes...well...it's one thing to understand something. It's another to *feel* it." Tears flooded his eyes, and he wished he could wipe them away. He'd never talked this openly, not to anyone. Yet here he was, opening up to this woman who was about to drop him in the ocean. Talking now not so much because it might change her mind, but because he *wanted* to talk, to share what he was feeling. "All those years," he said, "people calling me 'Father.' And me without a clue what a 'father' might *feel* like."

She didn't answer. Her eyes were closed, and he wondered if she'd passed out. He shifted his back from side to side. What *was* that hard, flat, movable thing that kept poking him? And suddenly…*The tin snips! My God! Robert must have—*

"I have someone, too," Ann said, and he turned and saw her looking at him. "Her name's Jessie. Not my child, but…she needs me. And I…I've done things, too."

"Things. Right." Under the shock blanket he twisted his arm, forcing his hand between his back and the rigid stretcher. *Distract her. Keep a conversation going.* "Things like having Larry killed."

"That was…I told Manion…it didn't have to go down that way…told him I could keep the priest quiet."

"No," Paul said, "you *couldn't* have kept Larry quiet." Sliding his hand farther under his back…stretching.

"Still…you'd bought us time. We could've left the clinic, gone somewhere else. The company…they know the drill. Deny everything. Accuse the accuser. Let time pass. The public…they just wanna be safe. Nobody cares *how*."

"I guess Hank Manion didn't agree." Paul strained to reach the tin snips.

"He…he thought his deal would fall apart. He couldn't wait. So…first the priest…then the woman…" She shook her head. "It all got out of—" She closed her eyes, gritted her teeth. *"Shit!"*

"You should've let them give you something." Stretching out his fingers.

"No. It's pain, that's all. And…when my men get back…I have things to decide."

"Right. Like which one will push us out the door." His fingertips touched metal. "But you don't have to do that. I proved I could keep quiet. We both did." He worked his fingers through the loops of the handle. "Besides, you told Hank…even if Larry talked…things would blow over."

"Yes, because he was known as misguided, a radical priest... attacking his country... ranting on about some far-off conspiracy. But now...with both him and his sister dead, and the accusations coming from *you*, someone who...well...you're not Father Landrew."

"No, I'm not." He tugged on the tin snips. He wasn't Larry at all. He didn't cry out for justice, didn't live side-by-side with the poor, didn't risk everything for the truth.

"And there's Tree and Otoe to think of," she said. "They're good men, and—"

"*Good?* I was *there* when Tree shot..." He stopped, suddenly recalling the voice he'd heard in the barn. "That man," he said. "Franco. *He* shot Larry."

"Yes."

"Still, you were part of it. You, the CIA, Melendez. You're *all* responsible for Larry's death. And Celia's." By then he had the tin snips out from under his back, by his side. "And all those innocent people who'll be killed, by all those weapons."

"Yes, I was...I *am*...part of it," she said. "And you are, too. When Manion got crazy I could have...walked away, even blown the whistle. I didn't. You didn't, either."

"Me? How *could* I?" Still under the blanket, he maneuvered the snips, slid them past his hip, down alongside his leg. "You said you'd send Robert back."

"Right. So, for you, it was Robert. For me, Jessie. She... Anyway, for Manion it was profit. For Melendez and the agency, it's...their mission... their country. We all have our reasons."

"Yes," he said. Just then, a pounding, like someone hammering nails, came from the barn. He used the distraction to shift around and get one of the tool's blades under the strap across his thighs, above his knees. "Everyone has reasons," he said.

"These stones..." He saw her look at the briefcase on the floor beside her. "Way more than I dreamed. But no good if..." She lay back, teeth clenched against the pain. "Gotta stay strong." Talking more to herself than to him.

"You think you might not make it," he said, and coughed loudly as he squeezed the handles, and felt the strap across his thighs snap loose. "You're scared."

"Damn right." She rose up, glared at him. "But not for *myself.* Jesus, *you* should understand. You were safe...gave yourself up for Robert." She lay back.

"Right." Twisting his hand in a way his wrist didn't want to go, he managed to get the blades of the tin snips around the strap that ran across his belly. "And look what good it did." Another cough, another squeeze, and that strap, too, gave way, setting both of his arms free from the elbows down.

"I'm all Jessie has. Gotta make it. Can't..." Gasping, as though from a newer, sharper pain. "Can't leave it to them." She seemed to sink deeper onto her stretcher.

Shifting around to cover his movement, he angled his hand up under the blanket, coughed twice this time, and cut the strap across his chest. Almost free. He lay back, closed his eyes. He couldn't hide now...just had to be quick. He'd throw off the blanket, cut the strap across his ankles—the last one—and then free Robert. Ann was breathing hard. Was she strong enough to yell for help? Could she—

"I wasn't sure," Ann said, "but I know now what you're doing."

He opened his eyes and turned his head. She was in a half-sitting position, supporting herself on her left elbow, the arm with the IV running into it. Breathing hard, gasping really, and he couldn't read anything in her eyes but her own pain.

Still, the gun in her right hand showed no sign of wavering.

SIXTY-THREE

Staring back at Ann, Paul found himself sliding again into that same strange mix of despair and relief he'd felt back in the barn, when he saw Hank about to shoot him. It was over now, no need to push himself any—

"I didn't mean to kill the guy." Robert's voice, barely more than a whisper, struck Paul like the snap of a whip. "I just wanted to...to stop him."

"I know," Paul said. "It's okay."

"It's *not* okay. My gramma, too...she was sick and I coulda stayed and helped, but I went to Mexico. And *she* died. And now you. Everything's my fault."

"No, Robert. That's not true." Paul knew exactly whose fault this was, but he also knew now that, like Robert's grandmother, he would not give in to despair, would not let even a death sentence stop him. He would die fighting to save Robert.

Without taking his eyes off Ann and the gun, he pushed the thin blanket aside. Against both pain and overwhelming fatigue, he forced himself up to a sitting position.

Ann said nothing. Her face was drawn and terribly pale and her breath came in short, sharp gasps. He knew she longed only to lie back down, the same as he did. But, instead, she angled the gun a little higher, training it on his chest.

He thought he should say a prayer, and what came to his mind were Jake Kincannon's words, from what seemed like a thousand years ago: *I don't know if I'm ready, Lord, but I sure as hell hope you are.*

He leaned forward, reached down near his ankles, and cut the last plastic strap. His legs were free, but then he saw for the first time how swollen his ankle was, and a wave of nausea swept through him. He swallowed hard and, without seeing it, he sensed a slight movement from Ann's direction. He stiffened, not turning to look.

I don't know if I'm ready, Lord.

"Time," Ann said, "it's…running out." Her voice was tight and thin. "Maybe for both of us."

He turned and saw the pain and the fear in her eyes, and he thanked God—and Robert's grandmother—for not letting him give up. "Listen to me, Ann," he said. "I can help you."

†

It took mere seconds to discuss, not much more than the time it took to get to his feet and cut the plastic strips that held Robert to the ring on the wall.

"And you'll do this?" she asked.

"Yes."

"Even if I…if I don't make it?"

"I give you my word," Paul said. "Both of us do. If *we* make it."

"Okay," she said. "Let's do it."

"But what about Tree and Otoe?" Robert asked. "Won't they come after us?"

"At first they'll want to," Ann said. "But their training…their code… 'Leave no one behind.' They won't spend the time on you. They need to get me to a hospital."

"What about after that?" Paul asked.

"I'll do what I can…*if* I can. You keep your word," she said, breathing hard again, "and they'll get what they agreed to, and…and much more." She lay back, stared up at the cabin ceiling. "They aren't the sort who need things…wrapped up in neat packages."

She wouldn't give them the gun, and Paul didn't waste time arguing.

He wasn't even sure he *could* shoot a person. Although...to save Robert...

Anyway, Ann said she was keeping the gun. She had Tree and Otoe to deal with. They'd see the tin snips and have to admit it was their fault that he'd gotten ahold of them. She'd tell them she'd blacked out, and they'd know that no one could've taken the gun from her, not without waking her up.

"I'll watch," she said. "When they start this way, I'll call out for help."

"Okay." Paul wondered whether she had the strength to sit up, let alone call out. He hoped so. "This side," he said, indicating the cabin door on the side away from the barn. Robert slid it open and jumped down, then helped Paul to the ground.

"I'll be...like...your crutch," Robert whispered.

Paul stretched his arm across Robert's shoulders and together they struggled through the tall, stiff grass...away from the helicopter and into the darkness.

†

The Jeep was beyond the reach of the barn lights, but Paul had a good idea where it was and they moved toward it in a wide arc. A straight line would take them too close to the barn, which was now some fifty yards to their right. The glow of light around the old building seemed dimmer—maybe the batteries were running low—but he could see a man down on one knee by the service door, and another man dragging a large bundle along the ground. A body, he thought.

If they could make it to the Jeep before Tree and Otoe knew they were gone, and if the key was in the ignition—where Ann said she'd left it—they had a chance. There was no other land vehicle around, and he didn't think the men would try to hunt them down in the helicopter. Not if Ann could stay conscious a little longer...and strong... and in charge.

He believed she could. Or maybe he just hoped. Because he'd made another agreement with her. Another promise, another—

"Otoe! Tree!" Ann called out. *"Goddammit, hurry!"* Just that. Not saying what happened, not saying where to hurry to. *"Otoe! Tree!"*

The men yelled back. They were running for the helicopter.

"Shit," Robert said, "we'll never—"

"Quiet," Paul whispered. "There it is. Straight ahead. See?"

Ann and the two men were still yelling back and forth, but Paul and Robert had reached the Jeep. The key was in the ignition.

"I can't drive with this foot," Paul said. "Can you drive a stick shift?"

"Shit, I think so." Robert helped him into the passenger seat, then got behind the wheel and started the engine. He found first gear, revved up the engine with a great whine, and let out the clutch. The Jeep lurched forward, snapping Paul's head back…and stopped. The engine was dead.

Robert started it up, tried again, and they lurched forward. This time they kept moving. He stayed in first gear, swung into a wide turn, and started up the incline, the engine roaring and whining until Paul thought it would burn out. Then, finally, with a great crunching of gears, Robert made it into second. Throughout all of this there was shouting behind them, then shots were fired, and something clanged against the metal of the Jeep. Robert kept going. Third gear came more easily, as they bounced wildly up the long rise. Finally they were over the top and out of sight of the barn.

Robert switched on just the parking lights, as they drove around the edge of the trees, and continued on, past the clinic. They found the opening to the road to Mabaruma and turned onto it, the canopy of trees arching over them.

Minutes later they heard that frightening *whop, whop, whop* overhead, coming on fast from behind. "Cut the lights!" Paul yelled. They had to slow down, almost to a stop, because they couldn't see anything. The helicopter, though, passed over them and kept on going.

As the sound died away in the distance, Robert turned the headlights back on and accelerated, but Paul said, "Wait! Stop! Turn around."

Robert hit the brakes. "What?"

"Go back to the clinic. We'll get our bags. It'll be dawn soon. We'll find Magdalena…get her to fly us back right away. Maybe she can even land us at the Cheddi Jagan Airport."

Robert managed to get turned around on the narrow road, and as they started back he said, "You think they might wait for us? In town?"

"No. Right now they need to get rid of those bodies and get Ann Swanson to a real hospital. The closest one's in Georgetown."

"Jeez, she looked like she might *die*, y'know? I mean...shot in two places?"

"Yes, but those men know what they're doing. She trusted them to tell her the truth, to rush her right away if it was that urgent. And I think she was right. They weren't lying. But the weakness and the pain...it got to her. Worried she might be worse than they thought. Afraid she might die, and that Tree and Otoe wouldn't feel any obligation to this 'Jessie' person...if they even *know* about her."

"So then, they'd take all the diamonds themselves."

"Right, and leave Jessie out."

"Can't do that now, though, huh?" Robert glanced over at him. "They're gonna be pretty pissed off, y'know?"

"Oh, I don't think so. Only Hank Manion knew how much he was getting paid tonight. And only he knew it'd be in diamonds. So how would Tree and Otoe, or even Ann, know how many diamonds there were? Or what they were worth?" He patted his jacket pocket. "And she gave me only half of them to take with us."

SIXTY-FOUR

Four months later. Early February, mid-afternoon. The bone-chilling rain had ended without turning to snow, but the ache in Paul's ankle throbbed on. It would do this in cold, damp weather, he supposed, for the rest of his life. He said good-bye to his mother, and moved a few steps to his right.

"It's me, Jake," he said, looking down. "I thought I should come and tell you in person. I'm not going to fight those proceedings. Sorry."

There was a bronze plaque set into Jake Kincannon's stone, bearing an inscription which Jake's brother—the one Jake had called "a pain in the butt"—hadn't been pleased with. But Paul had paid for the marker, so Paul won the argument. The inscription said:

I Don't Know If I'm Ready, Lord, But I Sure As Hell Hope You Are.

Paul stared down at the marker, and thought of how Jake's passing had seemed to affect no one but himself—and Max, the dog.

Hank Manion's mysterious disappearance, of course, had caused more of a stir. According to the media, the police were able to trace Hank as far as Houston's George Bush Intercontinental Airport. After that… nothing. It wasn't long, though, before interest in Hank died away, too. Even the staff at the Office of Pastoral Care, people Hank had wined and dined so lavishly, never talked about him. Paul had learned that from a phone conversation. He hadn't set foot in the office since returning from Guyana. He had no reason to think he ever would.

He'd talked again to Grayson, the headmaster, and Robert was back at Bridgebriar. It meant Paul was putting a lot of miles on the Corolla, visiting him nearly every week, but at least he didn't have to keep that a secret any more. The police had found out about Robert, and about Bridgebriar, and had leaked the news to the press...which resulted in Paul getting another "invitation" to lunch at the cardinal's mansion.

Paul never denied to the cardinal, or to anyone else, that he had a child, didn't even deny the accusation that he'd "hidden" that fact for years from church authorities. In fact, he neither denied nor admitted anything, but consistently refused to answer any questions at all along those lines, from anyone. Because of this "obstinacy," and because the possibility of him having been involved in a murder had made him something of a public figure, the cardinal obviously felt that some action should be taken. In November Paul received notice that "laicization proceedings" had been initiated, which could result in his being stripped of "all priestly powers and authority." He knew such proceedings could take months, even years, and might even just quietly die away, especially if the subject stayed out of the public eye. Meanwhile, though, he remained on a leave of absence.

On a more positive note, not long ago, word had come out that the investigation into Larry Landrew's murder had stalled, the police "having exhausted all leads and having no suspects." When a reporter brought up the fact that detectives had once been looking quite seriously for Paul, in order to question him further about the case, a police spokesperson said, "Father Clark has cooperated fully with our investigation. There is no evidence supporting any charges against him, or any other individual, at this time."

Paul stayed on at St. Hildegard's, still saying mass only in private. Jake brought up the laicization thing constantly, even during those final weeks when Paul and the hospice workers were caring for him at the rectory. "Two things, kid, that's all I want," Jake said, two days before he died. "Fight for your priesthood, and take good care of Max." Then he winked, and added, "But not necessarily in that order."

As it turned out, Max died, apparently of a broken heart, the day after Jake did. Paul had the dog interred with Jake—which was not entirely legal, and thus cost way more than it should have.

Paul had missed Larry's funeral, and he'd skipped Celia's too, to avoid publicity. Nor did he visit their graves. He did, however, keep up his visits to his mother. And, since he'd given Jake the one remaining family burial site, he was able to visit Jake at the same time.

"Sorry, Jake," he said again. He kept his voice very low, although there was no one around to catch him talking to the dead. "I don't know if they'll actually take my priesthood away, but I'm not going to fight it." He couldn't help feeling that Jake was actually listening to him. He knew better, but he went along with the illusion.

Why the hell not? he imagined Jake asking.

"Because I can't give testimony. Not about any of it. I never..." He pulled his wallet from his pocket. "There's a lot I never told you." He slid out a newspaper clipping and carefully unfolded it. It was from the *Miami Herald*, which he'd picked up in the airport on the evening he and Robert arrived back from Guyana.

He didn't read the article out loud to Jake. That would have been a bit much. But he read it to himself...for the thousandth time.

> Secretary of State Christopher Hanaford today denied United States involvement in what Venezuelan government officials described as "a failed US-backed military coup." Observers on the scene report that well-armed rebels, equipped with helicopters and rocket launchers, attempted to seize government buildings in Caracas, but were driven back by government forces.
>
> "We regret the numerous civilian casualties reported," Hanaford asserted, "including the injuries said to have been incurred by the Venezuelan president." He denied charges that the CIA had supplied equipment and weapons to the rebels, and stated that Venezuelan leaders need not look beyond their borders for opposition to their socialist policies. "Where there is tyranny and oppression," he said, "those who love freedom will always rise up."

Paul returned the clipping to his wallet. "It says 'numerous civilian casualties,' Jake," he half-whispered. "I can't help—"

"Praying for the dead, are you?"

He froze. Ann Swanson. "Talking to myself," he said, and turned to face her. "You seem to be fully recovered." She didn't reply, and he said, "Those...those diamonds. I did what you said. I take it you got them."

She smiled...or as close to a smile as he'd ever seen on her face. "You'd have heard long before now if I hadn't."

"And...Jessie? Is she...okay?"

Ann nodded, but obviously wasn't going to go there. "I understand," she said, "that your problem with the police has gone away."

"I assume someone spoke to them," he said. "But you're not with the CIA any more, right? You *used* to be, that's what Hank Manion said. So how did—"

"Do you really think I'd answer you?"

"Well, then, let's get to the point," he said. "I suppose you're here to threaten me? Me and Robert? Warn us to keep on being quiet?"

"I don't think I even have to bring that up."

"Then *what*?"

She handed him an envelope.

She clearly expected him to open it, and he did. He pulled out a sheet of paper and looked at it. "I see my name," he said, "and Robert's. But the rest...is it Japanese? Some kind of bank statement?" He felt his eyes open wide. "Is that amount what I think it is?"

"It's Chinese. A statement of a trust account. Your share of the sale proceeds."

He looked up at her. "It's blood money. I don't want a share."

"You're just the trustee. Robert's the beneficiary. He's young. He needs... an education...among other things."

He looked down at the paper. "With this much he could go to...I don't know... *Harvard*...maybe ten times."

"Probably not *ten* times. Anyway, there's also some allotted to you from time to time. A trustee's fee. Take it or not. When he's thirty it's all his, free and clear. There's a phone number there. They'll explain it all...in English.

As a gift, it won't be reported anywhere, and there are no tax consequences. You could burn this paper and the money will sit there, earning interest. But Robert *did* save both our lives. And…he *is* your son."

He put the paper back in the envelope and handed it back to her.

She took it. "I like Robert. He's a tough kid. Did he tell you what happened in that Mexican jail?"

"Not much, but…well…I guess he told me…the worst thing."

"The rape?"

"Yes."

"He tell you he tried to fight the guy off?"

"We didn't get into much detail."

"Well, he did," she said, "and he managed to land a pretty solid shot to the eye. But the guy was way too big, so…it happened. When my guys took Robert out he was in terrible condition. I sent him for a medical evaluation."

"I know he had blood tests. He showed me a page of the results, that night at Fair Hope. He was carrying it around with him. He'd been so scared…about HIV."

"Yeah, that's what really panicked him. But I ordered everything. The sort of evaluation they do for released hostages." She still had the envelope in her hand, and ran her fingers along one edge of it. "They look for disease, physical trauma. And emotional trauma as well."

He stared at her, not liking where this was going. "Are you saying they *found* something?"

"Physically, nothing serious." She waved her hand, dismissing the idea. "Just malnutrition, a few scrapes and bruises, head lice, the usual."

"And…" He paused, not sure he wanted an answer. "And emotionally?"

"Stripped of all the psycho-jargon, he's a pretty healthy kid. But they had recommendations." She was tapping the edge of the envelope on the palm of her hand. "He went through a lot. The arrest, the unspeakable conditions in that jail, the daily fear of sudden violence. Then…the rape itself. Which was very real, by the way. They found the signs. Anyway, it was a lot."

"Including watching one man slit another man's throat."

"That, too."

"So what are you saying?"

"I suppose you know what PTSD is?"

"In general, yes. Combat veterans, maybe more of them than—"

"Right, right. Anyway, the docs say Robert's basically healthy. Whether he'll ever show any severe reaction, they can't predict. But it's possible, and the sooner you address any underlying anxiety, the less severe things will be."

"You're saying Robert should get professional help."

"He should have it starting yesterday." She moved close to him and before he could step back she'd stuffed the envelope into his coat pocket. "And it's expensive."

His hand moved instinctively and he withdrew the envelope and stared down at it. *Blood money.* He looked up. "I don't—" He stopped, because she had her back to him and was already ten feet away.

He watched her walk out of the cemetery. When she was gone he slipped the envelope back into his pocket and looked down at the grave in front of him.

"You catch all that, Jake?" he said, finding himself speaking out loud to a dead man again. "She's probably right, y'know? But the thing is, Robert really *likes* Bridgebriar now. He'll be upset, mad at me, if I take him out and bring him back here to get the help he needs. Although, maybe after he thinks about it, he'll understand. I don't know." He paused. He was standing there with a ton of money in his pocket, and it still wasn't easy to know what to do. "Damn, Jake, how in God's name will I ever figure out what's best for the boy?"

He knew Jake wasn't going to answer.

Then, for no reason at all, Paul suddenly pictured that day in the sacristy when the police were looking for him and he'd asked Jake not to tell anyone where he was. Jake had realized right away how overwhelmed Paul was feeling. And what Jake did was lean down and pat Max on the head, and say: *Keep the faith, big guy. It'll all work out.*

"You think so, Jake?" Paul paused a moment, then nodded. "Well, then, I guess I do, too."

THE END

ALSO PUBLISHED BY ALLIUM PRESS OF CHICAGO

Visit our website for more information
www.alliumpress.com

ଔ

A Bitter Veil
Libby Fischer Hellmann

It all began with a line of Persian poetry . . . Anna and Nouri, both studying in Chicago, fall in love despite their very different backgrounds. Anna, who has never been close to her parents, is more than happy to return with Nouri to his native Iran, to be embraced by his wealthy family. Beginning their married life together in 1978, their world is abruptly turned upside down by the overthrow of the Shah, and the rise of the Islamic Republic. Under the Ayatollah Khomeini and the Republican Guard, life becomes increasingly restricted and Anna must learn to exist in a transformed world, where none of the familiar Western rules apply. Random arrests and torture become the norm, women are required to wear hijab, and Anna discovers that she is no longer free to leave the country. As events reach a fevered pitch, Anna realizes that nothing is as she thought, and no one can be trusted...not even her husband.

ଔ

Set the Night on Fire
Libby Fischer Hellmann

Someone is trying to kill Lila Hilliard. During the Christmas holidays she returns from running errands to find her family home in flames, her father and brother trapped inside. Later, she is attacked by a mysterious man on a motorcycle. . . and the threats don't end there. As Lila desperately tries to piece together who is after her and why, she uncovers information about her father's past in Chicago during the volatile days of the late 1960s . . . information he never shared with her, but now threatens to destroy her. Part thriller, part historical novel, and part love story, *Set the Night on Fire* paints an unforgettable portrait of Chicago during a turbulent time: the riots at the Democratic Convention . . . the struggle for power between the Black Panthers and SDS . . . and a group of young idealists who tried to change the world.

Beautiful Dreamer

Joan Naper

Chicago in 1900 is bursting with opportunity, and Kitty Coakley is determined to make the most of it. The youngest of seven children born to Irish immigrants, she has little interest in becoming simply a housewife. Inspired by her entrepreneurial Aunt Mabel, who runs a millinery boutique at Marshall Field's, Kitty aspires to become an independent, modern woman. After her music teacher dashes her hopes of becoming a professional singer, she refuses to give up her dreams of a career. But when she is courted by not one, but two young men, her resolve is tested. Irish-Catholic Brian is familiar and has the approval of her traditional, working-class family. But wealthy, Protestant Henry, who is a young architect in Daniel Burnham's office, provides an entrée for Kitty into another, more exciting world. Will she sacrifice her ambitions and choose a life with one of these men?

THE EMILY CABOT MYSTERIES

Frances McNamara

Death at the Fair

The 1893 World's Columbian Exposition provides a vibrant backdrop for the first book in the series. Emily Cabot, one of the first women graduate students at the University of Chicago, is eager to prove herself in the emerging field of sociology. While she is busy exploring the Exposition with her family and friends, her colleague, Dr. Stephen Chapman, is accused of murder. Emily sets out to search for the truth behind the crime, but is thwarted by the gamblers, thieves, and corrupt politicians who are ever-present in Chicago. A lynching that occurred in the dead man's past leads Emily to seek the assistance of the black activist Ida B. Wells.

Death at Hull House

After Emily Cabot is expelled from the University of Chicago, she finds work at Hull House, the famous settlement established by Jane Addams. There she quickly becomes involved in the political and social problems of the immigrant community. But when a man who works for a sweatshop owner is murdered in the Hull House parlor, Emily must determine whether one of her colleagues is responsible, or whether the real reason for the murder is revenge for a past tragedy in her own family. As a smallpox epidemic spreads through the impoverished west side of Chicago, the very existence of the settlement is threatened and Emily finds herself in jeopardy from both the deadly disease and a killer.

☙

Death at Pullman

A model town at war with itself . . . George Pullman created an ideal community for his railroad car workers, complete with every amenity they could want or need. But when hard economic times hit in 1894, lay-offs follow and the workers can no longer pay their rent or buy food at the company store. Starving and desperate, they turn against their once benevolent employer. Emily Cabot and her friend Dr. Stephen Chapman bring much needed food and medical supplies to the town, hoping they can meet the immediate needs of the workers and keep them from resorting to violence. But when one young worker—suspected of being a spy—is murdered, and a bomb plot comes to light, Emily must race to discover the truth behind a tangled web of family and company alliances.

☙

Death at Woods Hole

Exhausted after the tumult of the Pullman Strike of 1894, Emily Cabot is looking forward to a restful summer visit to Cape Cod. She has plans to collect "beasties" for the Marine Biological Laboratory, alongside other visiting scientists from the University of Chicago. She also hopes to enjoy romantic clambakes with Dr. Stephen Chapman, although they must keep an important secret from their friends. But her summer takes a dramatic turn when she finds a dead man floating in a fish tank. In order to solve his murder she must first deal with dueling scientists, a testy local sheriff, the theft of a fortune, and uncooperative weather.

CPSIA information can be obtained at www.ICGtesting.com
Printed in the USA
LVOW061304140912
298777LV00003B/10/P